Dan, ashen-face, seen it all, Genera

Ben had sent Sc ground corridor, to see what lay around the next bend. Dan waved a few of the Scouts forward and pointed to naked bodies on meat hooks. "Take them topside and bury them properly," Ben said.

Ben walked out of the corridor, into the tunnel, crawled out of the hole and up to ground level, stepping out into the cold night air. He had uncovered the plans of the Night People. Now what? He would not send his people into a death trap, but he knew one thing for certain: the areas that had been cleared would have to be checked again. Every damn building and basement!

"What are we going to do, Ben?" Cecil asked.

"I'm going to push on down to the bridge, secure it, and make damn sure it stays open," Ben said. "If we're going to be trapped in the Big Apple, I want us to be well-supplied. Block every street, every avenue, every alley, every hole. And look for the sons of bitches to hit you from Brooklyn; they'll be coming across at night, in boats. It's desperation time, people."

Ben broke off.

Cecil glanced over at Ike, sighed. "First we're soldiers," he said. "Now we're combat engineers and tunnel rats."

Ben and his troops were facing their greatest challenge. If the gods of fate and chance and war did not smile upon them, the invasion of New York would destroy the Rebel army. The Night People would slowly spread and finally devour the nation—literally.

The hideousness had to be stopped . . . NOW.

VALOR
IN THE
ASHES

WILLIAM W.
JOHNSTONE

PINNACLE BOOKS
KENSINGTON BOOKS
www.kensingtonbooks.com

PINNACLE BOOKS are published by

Kensington Publishing Corp.
850 Third Avenue
New York, NY 10022

All Kensington Titles, Imprints, and Distributed Lines are available at special quantity discounts for bulk purchases for sales promotions, premiums, fund-raising, and educational or institutional use. Special book excerpts or customized printings can also be created to fit specific needs. For details, write or phone the office of the Kensington special sales manager: Kensington Publishing Corp., 850 Third Avenue, New York, NY 10022, attn: Special Sales Department, Phone: 1-800-221-2647.

Pinnacle and the P logo Reg. U.S. Pat. & TM Off.

ISBN-13: 978-0-7860-1965-6
ISBN-10: 0-7860-1965-4

First Pinnacle Books Printing: July 1998

10 9 8 7 6 5

Printed in the United States of America

Dedicated to: Paul Copher

BOOK ONE

"Here's looking at you, kid."
—From *Casablanca*

Chapter 1

"Seven major bridges, six rivers, five boroughs, four stadiums, three airports, two states, and what was once a very exciting and beautiful city."

Then Ben had to explain to the younger members of his contingent of Rebels exactly what a borough was. And it wasn't something that groundhogs did.

Some of them had to go back to school, Ben concluded. They were going to have to be pulled off the line and given the chance to gain more knowledge. And like it or not, they would do it, if Ben ordered it.

Maybe after New York City.

The sheer magnitude of what lay ahead of them, the awesomeness of the job, was mind-boggling . . . at least to Ben and some of the older Rebels, who had visited New York City before the great war a decade past, and who understood that the cleaning out of the mutant, cannibalistic Night People, headquartered in the Big Apple, was not going to be a short-term operation.

It would certainly take all of the fall and all of the

winter, and could well extend into spring or even summer . . . or longer.

But it was something that had to be.

The Judges were here, somewhere within the concrete-and-steel canyons of the city: those men and women who ruled the Night People, who dictated the terrible deeds that they did.

They had to be destroyed.

And there was only one army on the face of the earth—that Ben was aware of—that had the capability to tackle and ultimately accomplish that task: Ben Raines and his Rebels.

Ben stood in the cool fall air and looked over the watery distance that separated St. George, on Staten Island, from lower Manhattan.

When the Rebels had first arrived on Staten Island, they had—Ben included—mistakenly believed the place was deserted.

Came the first night, and they were proved wrong. Bloody wrong. The Night People crawled out of the basements and tunnels and dark musty places to attack in stinking, foul, human waves. The fighting had been fierce, but with the Rebels always, slowly, pushing the Night People back. Sometime during the third night, the Night People had decided to retreat back into the city, leaving silently, their dead behind them.

"Handle the bodies with extreme caution," Ben had ordered. "Gowned, gloved, and masked. Stack them up and burn them."

The bodies had been loaded and transported out to the edge of the Atlantic Ocean and burned. Staten Island was secure.

But still Ben hesitated to send his people into New

York City. Doubts assailed the man: Was it worth it? Would whatever they would find there compensate for the Rebel lives lost in securing that great city?

Ben sighed. He just didn't know.

His daughter, Tina, commander of a contingent of Gray's Scouts, came to his side. "What's the matter, Dad?"

"Second thoughts, girl. Second thoughts a hundred times over."

"The treasures in that city, Dad: the recordings, the paintings, the knowledge . . . all the things you told us about. Those alone would be worth it."

Would they? Or had vandals destroyed it all? Ben inwardly shuddered and was sickened at the thought of some two-bit street punk slashing a Renoir, simply because he or she was too damned ignorant— voluntarily and eagerly so—to care what was ruined. He thought of the hundreds of master tapes and CDs stored in the vaults. Great treasures of music. The millions of books, some of which would be lost forever if not salvaged now. The medical knowledge contained within that seemingly silent and dead city.

Ben looked at the World Trade Center, jutting up a quarter of a mile into the sky. He had been on the observation deck there several times, and remembered that on a clear day a person could see for nearly sixty miles. And the elevators would take your breath away: from the 107th floor to ground level took less than a minute.

And if, or when, his people went into the city, they would have to climb every damned step of the way up in every building. And then back down.

"What's the word from your brother, Tina?"

"He's recovering fast. He'll be up here in a couple of weeks, on limited duty."

Ben's son had been badly wounded by a pack of rednecks while attempting to secure a piece of land down in Louisiana and bring some education to the ignorant.

Ben had killed them all.

Ben Raines had absolutely no patience or tolerance for people who are ignorant, know they are ignorant, are proud of being ignorant, and intend to remain ignorant until the day someone does the world a favor and shovels dirt in their face.

Ben turned to face his daughter, a slight smile playing around his lips. "You feel like taking a ride, girl?"

She cocked her head to one side and mentally braced herself. Her father, if he made up his mind to do it, would charge Hell armed only with a glass of water. "Ah . . . what do you have in mind, Dad?"

"You game, or not?"

She sighed. "OK. Now tell me where we're going?"

Ben was amused. Half the camp had gone into hysterics when he walked into his CP and announced that he and Tina were going to take a little drive into the city.

"The Scouts haven't even gone into the damn city, Ben!" Ike had yelled at him.

"Perfectly ridiculous idea, Ben!" Cecil snapped at him. "I won't hear of it."

"I say, General," Dan Gray—the ex-British SAS officer—put his two cents' worth in, "I find that suggestion to be quite unreasonable and not fully thought through."

Doctor Chase muttered obscenities under his breath and glared at Ben.

Little Jersey, about four feet ten inches tall and a Rebel to the core, summed it all up. "You might go into the city, General; we don't have the right to stop you. But you damn sure ain't goin' in alone!" She turned to face him, the top of her bereted head hitting him just about chest high.

Ben laughed at her. "All right, Jersey. What'd you have in mind?"

Now he was rolling along, stuck in a damned greasy old APC, with tanks in front of and behind him.

"It would seem," Ben said sourly, "that since I am the commander of this army, I might have some say in my method of transportation. I cannot see one lousy thing!"

They were rolling along over the just-cleared Bayonne Bridge. What they were going to encounter once the bridge was past them was anybody's guess. Gray's Scouts had only advanced as far as one block past the bridge, and were waiting there for the convoy.

"It's for your own good, General," Jersey told him.

"That's what my father used to say, just before he beat my butt with a belt."

Little Jersey laughed at the expression on his face, thinking: Yeah, and you probably deserved it, too!

"As far as we go, General," the driver called. "Scouts are signaling for us to halt."

"Good," Ben muttered. He banged his head on the way out and was muttering curses as he walked up to the Scouts, already in a confab with Dan Gray.

"J. F. Kennedy Boulevard is a real mess," Ben was

told. "A squad just came back from checking it out. Not worth the effort, at this time, to clear it."

Ben looked at an old map. "Five-oh-one?"

"Scouts are only a block up now, General," Dan told him. "It's slow work."

"Any sign of life?"

"No, sir. Nothing. But lots of skeletons that have been picked clean. Scouts report the bones appear to be old."

Ben nodded and spread his map on the hood of a Jeep. "All right, people. We'll have to do this by the numbers. I want all the bridges cleared and passable. And heavily guarded at both ends around the clock. Round up portable generators, especially near the waterline. I want the bridges lighted at night. Ike, see if you can find some Navy or Coast Guard vessels and get them running. And block off the subways. They've had years of neglect and no telling what shape they're in. I also don't want these Night Crawlers to come at us from them."

Ike nodded.

Ben turned to Dan. "Tell your Scouts to return. We don't move until our pilots have done extensive flybys of the entire city." To Cecil: "Contact Joe at Base Camp One and have him fly up some heat-seekers. Let's just see what we're up against."

"Maggie Thatcher's girdle!" Dan blurted, looking at the pictures from the flybys. The heat-seekers showed almost entirely red on any grid they chose to look at. "There must be several hundred thousand people left in the city."

"But which ones are friendlies and which ones are bogies?" Cecil asked.

"And how do they survive?" Doctor Chase asked.

"Probably with human farms," Ben told them all. "Their outriders bring back prisoners and they force-feed them until they're nice and fat. Then the Night People eat them." He glanced at Chase. "Don't look so startled, Lamar. You were briefed on the dietary habits of the Night People."

Doctor Chase drew on nearly seventy years of living—although he neither looked nor behaved like a man that age—to sum up his opinion of the Night People. Not one word of it was in the least complimentary.

"You through?" Ben asked him.

"Perverted, savage, Godless, despicable bas-tards!" Chase finished it.

"Thank you, Doctor, for that highly professional summation of our immediate enemy." Dan smiled at him.

"Up yours, too!" Chase stalked away, Ben's cur-rent ladylove, Doctor Holly Allardt, walking fast to keep up with him.

The Rebel commanders once more bent over the pictures taken from spotter planes; but this time they were looking at blown-up black-and-white photos.

Ike pointed a finger. "Look there. Hand me that magnifying glass, Jersey." He grinned at her. "You ap-point yourself General Raines's personal bodyguard, half-pint?"

"He hasn't complained yet," she fired back.

Grinning, Ike studied the picture. He compared the picture to a detailed map of the city. "On top of the Solow Building, Ben. That's a man and a woman, both of them neatly dressed and both of them armed. Take a look."

Ben bent over the picture, using the glass for magnification. But he only briefly studied the man and woman. He moved the magnifying glass upward, north, into Central Park, past the Pond, carefully studying the area. "Gardens. Gardens all over the place, and damn well tended. Look how clean it is, people. From Fifty-second at . . . ah . . ." He checked the city map. ". . . Madison, all the way over and including Columbus Avenue. Then north all the way up to . . . ah . . . Seventy-second Street. Nearly spotless. What the hell is going on here?"

"Who do you suppose they are, Gene?" the woman asked the man.

"Hopefully, Ben Raines and his Rebels. But I can't be sure. It might well be some invading army. Maybe the Russian. Could be the Libyan. Might be that mercenary bunch from up in Canada. Monte what's-his-name. I just don't know."

"Whoever they are," another man said, "they're very carefully doing an air rec of the city. They haven't tried to come in."

"Do we try to contact them, Gene?"

"Not yet. Let's be sure just who they are and what their intentions might be before we attempt some lines of communication."

"General Ben Raines," the woman said with a sigh. "God, please let it be so."

* * *

"Do you want me to lead a team in, General?" Dan Gray asked softly.

"*Hell*, no, Dan! But I wish we could get our hands on some choppers."

"I'm working on that, Ben," Cecil told him. "I've got people working around the clock trying to piece some old birds together." He shrugged his muscular shoulders. "A week at least before I'll know anything for sure."

Ben nodded and glanced at Jersey. "Half-pint, notify the commo people and tell them to try and make contact with those inside the city."

She nodded and walked out of the room just as a young Rebel was entering.

"General Raines?"

Ben turned. Noted that the young woman's face was pale and she appeared to be shaken.

"What's wrong, Sandy?" Dan asked the woman, one of his Scouts.

"I got a prelim report on one of the subways our people entered, sir. It seemed . . . well, not plausible, so I personally checked it out."

"And?" Dan prompted.

"It seems the Night People have been using the subways—at least this particular subway—as a repository, sir."

"A repository for what, Sandy?" Ben asked.

"Bones, sir. Must be a couple of miles of bones in the one I looked at. Scattered all over the place. Human bones."

Chapter 2

The collapse of civilization, the downfall of governments, and a rapid return to barbarism and savagery had begun a decade past when some of the major powers in the world decided that years of talking had produced nothing except talk. It was time to fight.

The world exploded in war, with many European cities—and a few American cities—taking nuclear strikes. But America and Canada had taken more germ and chemical hits than anything else.

It made no difference, America, as a united country, was finished.

The role of leader had been forced on a man named Ben Raines. He had not wanted it. Resisted it for many months. Ran from it.

Ben Raines reluctantly stepped into the job of leading a shattered nation back to civility. But he did not attempt to lead the entire nation; only those who felt they could live under a form of government that had never before—in the history of the recorded word—been attempted.

The experiment in living was called Tri-States.

With the help of an ex-Navy SEAL named Ike McGowan, a retired Navy doctor named Lamar Chase, an ex-college professor named Cecil Jefferys, and so many, many more good, decent people—most of them now dead, killed while fighting to make their dream into reality—Tri-States did, for a time, become reality. And it worked.

Meanwhile, outside of the Tri-States, the nation of America was trying to pick up the pieces and start anew, under the direction of a man who was slightly deranged: Hilton Logan, self-proclaimed president of the United States.

And Hilton was a man who hated Ben Raines.

Ben's Tri-States had full employment, virtually no crime, no hunger, the finest schools in the world, and everything that Hilton Logan's hard-pressed America did not have.

Hilton declared war on the Tri-States, vowing to smash it and kill Ben Raines.

Hilton succeeded in smashing Tri-States and killing a lot of people. But Ben Raines was still among the living, and Hilton Logan and those senators and representatives who had voted to smash the Tri-States would not be among the living much longer.

After months of guerrilla fighting, with most of the legitimate military staying out of it, and the new president having to rely on mercenaries to combat Ben Raines, the military put the man out of office and installed Ben Raines as president of the United States.

Then the plague came scurrying into the homes and lives of the survivors of one holocaust, bringing yet another maelstrom upon the heads of people who were still trying to dig out of the ashes of global war: a ratborne killer disease spread by fleas.

The United States of America was no more.

Ben Raines pulled his people back together and headed for safety.

Over the long bloody years, Ben Raines and his Rebels had fought ignorance and barbarism, the Russian Striganov, the mercenary Hartline, war lords and roaming gangs, and the Libyan terrorist, Khamsin—who now controlled nearly all of what had once been known as South Carolina.

Now Ben and his people were to face the Night People, on their home turf: New York City. And Ben knew full well that the Canadian mercenary, Monte, with an army that outnumbered his own Rebels, had aligned himself with the Night People, and might be coming at Ben's Rebels at any moment.

But Ben and his Rebels had had their backs up against that well-known wall many times before. They were used to it. This time would be no different, for the Rebels all knew—to a person—they could make no real effort toward setting up any really effective, workable, caring form of government until all the crud had been removed from their path. Human and otherwise.

And the people who leaned toward mindless violent acts against others, who robbed and raped and killed and tortured and ran rampant over others simply because they were strong enough to do so . . . they knew all about Ben Raines and his Rebels. They knew what had happened to others like them when Ben caught up: a bullet or a rope. Justice came down swift with the Rebels.

Ben looked at the outline of the great gray city in the gloomy twilight of late fall. "There are survivors in there," he muttered. "Good decent people who for decades before the Great War had to contend with gangs of street punks, robbers, rapists, murderers, thugs, and crapheads." He was unaware that Holly and several other Rebels had moved to within hearing distance of him. "And now for a decade after that war, a few of those same people have had to live under the shadow of a pack of cannibalistic sub-beings, so vile, so savage, it would be a slur against the animal kingdom to refer to them as animals." He lifted his eyes to the graying outline of the city vanishing swiftly as night began enveloping it. He wondered how the people in that city managed to control their fear as night slipped around them. And with the night, the creatures would prowl. "Hang on, people. Hang on. We'll get you out. And that's a promise."

The woman came close to the man. They stood on the observation deck of the building and both shared a smile as their eyes filtered the darkness.

They could see some of the fires from the Rebel camp.

"Is it really them, Gene?" she asked.

"The tunnel people say it is. They say it's really General Ben Raines and his Rebel army. God! Let it be so."

"Shall we have a small celebration with that thought in mind?" an older man asked from behind them.

Gene turned. Smiled. "Yes, Dad. I think that would

be in order." His smile faded. "And of course we shall have to have a larger celebration when the general and his people link up with us. Correct?"

"Unfortunately, yes. But perhaps General Raines will take pity on an old man and let bygones be bygones."

"I'm sure he will, Father. That was a long time ago."

The older man shook his head. "A man like Raines, son, has a long memory. Remember, he was a mercenary for a few years before our . . . incident."

"Ben Raines always said he was a soldier of fortune, not a mercenary. He always fought on the side of freedom and democracy and against tyrants and dictators and communists."

"I came close to destroying him, son. He'll remember. I shall gather the wine and cheese and bread and call a few of our friends for the party." The older man walked away from the couple.

"I have always been told that General Raines was a compassionate man." The woman turned to face him.

"Strong law and order man, Kay. Compassionate . . . yes, to a degree. To the very young and the elderly and the handicapped. I can't see him harming my father. But . . ." He shrugged his shoulders. "With a man like Ben Raines, you just never know. All we can do is hope."

"I wonder if the Night People know he's here?"

"They know, Kay. They know. God damn their evil hearts to Hell! They know."

"Have you heard when he plans to enter the city?" The question was pushed harshly from the throat of a hooded woman, one of a dozen robed and hooded men and women who sat in the semi-gloom of the big room. Two shielded torches were the only light.

The Judges were in session.

Dozens of lesser officials of the Night People remained standing.

"No word yet, Judge. We know only that the Hated One has arrived."

"And there is no doubt; it is Ben Raines?"

"It is Ben Raines. Some of the survivors from Staten Island caught a glimpse of him through binoculars. It is the hated one."

Another Judge spoke. "Now we have people not only below us in the tunnels who fight us, and above us in the skyscrapers and apartment houses and in the Park; but now we also have Ben Raines."

"Still we outnumber them all," he was reminded by another Judge.

"But we will be fighting on three fronts," yet another Judge spoke, the hood concealing his horribly burned face. "We must get word to Monte."

"But how? Ben Raines's people scan every known frequency. To use the radio would be giving our plans away."

The woman settled it. "We must send runners. They can exit through the tunnels that we control. Do it now. We have Ben Raines close; we know he is going to enter the city. This time, he dies!"

A week passed, and still Ben and his people made no attempt to enter New York City. The Rebels blocked off the subways and secured the bridges. A dozen harbor patrol boats and tugboats were found and patched up. Ike was once more back in the navy.

The remainder of the Rebels were rested and ready to go. Their weapons had been field-stripped and oiled and checked. Clips had been filled and clip pouches were full. Rations and other gear had been drawn from the supply depot. Maps of the area had been found and duplicated and passed out to squad leaders, who in turn went over and over them with their people.

Now the Rebels were enduring one of the hardest parts of impending combat: the waiting.

Ben had gathered his people around him in his CP. Everybody from Ike and Cecil and Dan Gray and the mercenary Colonel West, to company commanders.

"We go in at dawn," Ben told them. "Colonel West, you and your people will go into New Jersey and secure Newark Airport so our bigger birds can get in."

"Yes, sir," the mercenary quickly responded.

"Ike, you and your people will cross over into Bayonne and clear everything up to the George Washington Bridge. There, you will leave a detachment and cross over into Manhattan, eventually linking up with me."

"Gotcha, Ben," the ex-SEAL acknowledged.

"Cecil, you and your people will cross over into Brooklyn and clear two-seventy-eight for at least six miles. I want it cleared all the way up to and including the Brooklyn Bridge. There, leave a team and come over and join me."

"Right, Ben."

"Dan, split your Scouts among the three objectives."

"Four objectives, sir," the Englishman replied. "And I shall accompany you into Manhattan."

Ben smiled. "Very well. As you wish. Questions, anyone?"

No one spoke.

"Then I'll see you all at dawn, tomorrow. We'll see what's left of the Big Apple."

Outside the CP, a young CO turned to a buddy. "What the hell's the Big Apple?"

"Beats me," his buddy replied. Both of them had not yet been ten years of age when the Great War erupted. "Maybe they used to grow apples in there." He jerked his thumb toward the dark outline of the city.

His friend gave him a very dubious look. He cut his eyes as Ben's daughter, Tina, a member of Gray's Scouts, approached. He waved her over and posed the question to her.

She thought for a moment, then shook her head. "I don't know, guys. I just know this . . ."

The young men waited.

". . . We're gonna take a hell of a big bite out of it!"

Chapter 3

As was almost always the case, with the exception of the cooks and the guards already on duty, Ben was the first one up in the morning. He had always been a restless man, and age had not tempered that. He dressed in tiger-stripe BDU's, slipped into harness, and picked up his old Thompson SMG. Ben stepped out of the building and walked to one of the several mess tents.

This would be the last hot meal for several days—perhaps even weeks. The last meal of any kind for some of his Rebels.

His tray filled with fried potatoes and beef and gravy and fresh-baked bread, his mug sending up savory steam from what currently passed for coffee—with a lot of chicory in it—Ben sat down at a table and began his breakfast, watching as the mess tent began filling up with yawning troops, all dressed for war. He hid a smile as Little Jersey came rushing into the tent, looking around for him, her eyes finding him, a frown on her face at his slipping away without her noticing. But Ben had been doing that with his bodyguards for years. Ben's self-appointed guardian filled her tray and sat down at a table a few yards away from her general.

Rank held no privileges in the Rebel army when it came to eating: colonels stood in line with privates and waited their turn to be served. And this close to the upcoming battle zone, the ranking officers each ate at different mess tents, to lessen the chances of a rocket attack taking them all out together.

Doctor Holly Allardt walked in, waited to be served, then joined Ben. Although it was common knowledge that Ben was seeing Holly, since arriving on Staten Island, the two had been busy, with little time for social contact. And no time for sexual contact.

"Doctor Chase told me to go in with your people, Ben. Set up aid stations." She took a bite of food. "How are we going in? And where?"

"Boat. We'll put ashore at Battery Park. The park is about twenty acres, as I recall, and I'm hoping to use it as a staging area."

"A place for us to work?"

Ben shrugged. "We'll have to play that by ear, Holly. We won't know until we get there. That's why Chase is sending along a full MASH."

"Ben, do you have *any* intelligence about these people? What to expect?"

He shook his head. "Practically nothing, Holly. We've been trying to raise those survivors inside the city in hopes they'd have some up-to-date intel for us. Nothing . . ."

Dan Gray walked in and up to Ben's table. "Pardon, sir," the Englishman said. He was dressed in full battle gear. "We're shoving off now. We'll establish a CP for you inside the ferry terminal . . . hopefully," he added.

"Very good, Dan. Tina going in first wave?"

"Yes, sir. Her team will be going ashore at the South Ferry and entering the park."

"I'll see you all in a couple of hours, Dan."

"Yes, sir." The ex-SAS man did a smart turnabout and walked out of the mess tent, hollering for his people to gather.

"Finish your breakfast, Holly," Ben said, mopping up the last of his gravy with a piece of bread. "We're shoving off shortly. Dan and his people are sure to take some casualties. We want to be there to treat them."

"Aren't you afraid just a little bit, Ben?" Her eyes searched his face.

"No." The question seemed to take him by surprise. "And neither is Cecil or Dan or Ike or a great many of the other Rebels. Probably more are not than are, would be my guess."

"That is not a natural reaction, Ben."

He met her steady gaze. "I've been at war for years, Holly. Most of us have. We had a few peaceful years in the Tri-States; but even there, we were at a constant state of war-readiness. It comes down, Holly, to this is what we do. I'm sorry to have to say this—deeply sorry—but we have made war our careers. And we will continue to fight until the scum and the warlords and the human filth and those who prey on the weak are gone from the face of this land that we still call America."

"And then, Ben?"

"And then I will lead my people—or if I'm dead, someone else will lead them; Buddy, probably, if he's ready—back to Base Camp One and live in peace. I would do it today, Holly."

"Ben Raines dead?" she questioned, with more than a modicum of bitchiness in her tone. "Oh, Ben Raines can't die. Ben Raines is a god! Oh, I know all about those people in the woods and underground in the forests who worship Ben Raines, who have built shrines and altars to his exalted name. All hail King Raines."

"What's got your panties in a wad, Holly?" Ben fired back.

"My *panties in a wad!* What a disgusting thing to say!"

"Well, par-don me!"

She jumped up and stood glowering at him. "I'll see you on the ship, *General!*"

"It's not a ship. It's a boat!" Ben had raised his voice.

"Whatever!" she shouted, then stalked out of the mess tent.

Everybody in the mess tent was very careful to keep their eyes on their food.

Except one.

Ben cut his eyes to look at Little Jersey, looking at him. "You ever heard of Sigmund Freud, Jersey?"

"No, sir."

"He was a psychiatrist."

"Yes, sir."

"I recall a line from one of his articles. I must have been doing some research on a book at the time. Freud wrote . . . 'The great question, which I have not been able to answer, despite my thirty years of research into the feminine souls, is: What does a woman want?'"

Little Jersey, in all seriousness, replied, "Maybe she's just horny, sir."

Ben was still laughing and hoo-hawing and wiping his eyes with a handkerchief as he walked out of the tent.

Ben looked at the boat with a great deal of trepidation in the glance. "Is this tub seaworthy?" He stepped on board.

"We're not going to sea, General," he was told. "It's only about five miles over there."

Ben looked at him. Under all the grease he recognized one of the men from the motor pool. "Grissom? Is that you?"

"Yes, sir."

"Hell, Grissom, you were born in Iowa! What the hell do you know about boats?"

"Nothing. But I can get an engine running. Stafford's the pilot on this thing."

"Then I assume we're ready to shove off?"

Grissom looked at him. "Yes, sir. Just as soon as I get my butt off this thing! I can't swim."

Shaking his head and grinning amid all the laughter from his heavily equipment-laden Rebels sprawled on the deck, Ben walked forward and climbed up to the bridge just as the lines were cast off.

Faint colors were beginning to pale the eastern sky, faintly highlighting the skyline of New York City.

Ben glanced at the man behind the wheel of the big tug. "Just get us there, Stafford."

"No sweat, General." He patted the wheel. "She's in pretty good shape considering all the neglect. She'll get you there."

Ben sat down in a tall chair beside Stafford and stared through the empty space where glass should have been. A .50-caliber machine gun had been set up forward, its crew ready. He cut his eyes. Two more big tugs were rumbling on the left, two others on the right. Port and starboard, he mentally corrected.

Holly was right, he reflected. His lack of fear was not a natural thing. He felt excitement, not fear. He was returning to New York City. How long had it been? He counted back. About fourteen years. That was the time his publishing company had put on the party for him . . . well, not just for him. There were several other writers involved. Fourteen years. For sure, he would have to visit the offices, see if anything was left.

That brought him out of his reverie. What could be left? Rat-chewed manuscripts? Tattered contracts that didn't go into the last mailing?

The last mailing. Before fear and panic and horror struck.

Why did Hilton Logan and the military do it? Why did they keep the fact that New York City still stood a secret? What was their reasoning?

Unanswered questions. Questions that would forever be unanswered.

Hilton Logan had been a madman, sure. But that wasn't enough. There had to be more.

But Ben felt he would never know.

When he again lifted his eyes to the open window, New York was on top of him.

"You were daydreaming, General," Stafford said. "I didn't want to bust in. The city hold some fond memories, sir?" He had throttled back the engines; docking was only moments away.

"Yeah, it does. I used to go with a lady from New York. Back in the seventies."

"A looker, General?"

"Oh, yes." Esther. Hated that name. Never realized that Ben knew about it. Had her name changed to Rebecca. Esther Hellerstein. Her parents had hated Ben . . . Hate was too strong a word. Disliked him intently. Wanted their daughter to marry a nice Jewish fellow. She probably had.

Ben wondered if she had made it through the initial germ onslaught.

Stafford had cut all the inside lights. Ben sat in the darkness and waited until his eyes adjusted to the dimness. He watched as one tug pulled ahead of the others; that would be Dan Gray's teams. The Scouts almost always went in first. Another tug, a smaller one that Ben had not noticed at first, chugged out of the darkness and was docking off to Ben's left. Tina and her team would be entering the park. No gunfire yet.

"Let's go, Stafford," Ben said quietly.

"Sir?" Stafford started to protest.

"Dock this boat, Stafford." Ben's order was quietly given and offered no room for argument.

"Yes, sir. Stand by with lines," he called, inching the tug closer.

No gunfire.

Ben moved from the wheelhouse to the deck, making his way to the side, Rebels stepping out of his way. Ben jacked a round into the chamber of the old Thompson and clicked the weapon on safety. Over the sounds of the rumbling engine, his people were loading and locking. Ben looked down at Little Jersey, standing close beside him.

"You ready, Jersey?"

"Let's do it, General."

Ben stepped off the tug and onto the pier just as hard bursts of gunfire from left and right cut the gray gloom. Ben grabbed Jersey by the seat of her field pants and jerked her behind a jumble of crates, kneeling down beside her as lead hummed and whined its deadly song, ricocheting around them.

Ben's eyes were pinpointing the muzzle flashes from the windows and low rooftops. He lifted his walkie-talkie, lips to the cup. "Rocket launchers forward and knock out those riflemen. Troops and medical personnel off the tugs. Stay low. Tugs back off. Cast off and go!"

A vengeful whooshing sound hammered the deceptive air, that time between dark and light when everything is gray and shadow-filled. Explosions rocked the semi-gloom as the rockets hit their marks and shredded living flesh into bloody chunks.

Ben's eyes picked up a bump on a low rooftop that did not seem natural. "Jersey, your M-16's got the range I don't have. See that bump a couple of points left of our position? Rooftop high?"

Jersey's younger and sharper eyes quickly found it. "Yes, sir."

"That's a head, I'm thinking. Put one between its eyes."

Jersey lifted her M-16, sighted in the target, and

gently squeezed off a round. A rifle clattered to the street below, falling from the rooftop. The head disappeared.

"One less," Ben muttered. He wondered how Tina was doing. He lifted his walkie-talkie.

Tina and her team were pinned down on the Promenade, between the Verrazano statue and the memorial to those who lost their lives in the Western Atlantic during World War II.

Ham lay beside her. "Place is crawling with creepies," he said, raising his voice to be heard above the rattling of gunfire.

Tina's walkie-talkie crackled. "How you doing, girl?"

"Not worth a damn, Dad. We're pinned down. Place is spooky as hell."

"Hold your position," Ben ordered. "All teams— hold what you've got and make no advances. We'll sit it out until full light. These people supposedly can't take the light. We'll see. Just keep your heads and butts down."

"General?" Dan's voice came out of his walkie-talkie.

"Go, Dan."

"The ferry terminal is a snake pit. All windows and openings have been blocked off to prevent light from coming through. It's dark as a grave in here."

"Get out of there, Dan. We'll pump the place full of chemicals at full light. That'll flush them."

"Right, sir."

Ben paused, then gave the orders. "All troops

near the ferry terminal into gas masks. Knock out those boarded-up windows and prepare to lob in tear gas canisters at full light. Get in position to knock them down when they run."

Rockets slammed into boarded-up windows, clearing a path.

Gray light began changing into silver and gold as the sun fought its way, bubbling and boiling, out of the horizon. Tear gas canisters were fitted onto rifles and shotguns; tear gas guns were readied.

Hard bursts of gunfire banged to Ben from Tina's position. His daughter's voice came out of Ben's walkie-talkie. "They're packing it in, Dad. We're dropping them but not pursuing."

"Ten-four Tina. We'll start mop-up just after full light."

"Ten-four. Holding."

"Fill the terminal with gas," Ben ordered, then slipped on his mask. He had tested the wind: blowing from out of the south. That was to their advantage: the wind would keep the gas contained—for the most part—inside the ferry terminal.

Dan had placed some of his best shots directly behind the ferry terminal. They waited with heavy rifles.

The early morning coolness was sharp with the odor of drifting gas. Robed and hooded Night People began rushing from the terminal, trying to escape the choking gas that burned their lungs and teared their eyes.

The Rebels shot them while others continued to lob tear gas canisters into the huge terminal, driving more and more of the Night People from their cavernous hiding places and into the dreaded light.

Some of the Night People chose to chance New York Bay, leaping like lemmings from the terminal into the water, panicked and frantic in their efforts to escape the blinding gas.

But Ben had anticipated that move and had ordered Rebels out onto the long piers on either side of the terminal building. The Rebels shot the Night People as they thrashed about in the water. The bodies bobbed in the dirty bay for a moment and then slowly sank toward the bottom, the current moving them out toward the Narrows and eventually into the Atlantic.

"Cease firing," Ben ordered.

All was quiet over near Battery Park. Tina's people had held. Ben lifted his walkie-talkie. "Mop up," he ordered. "Troops out."

The sun had burst forth over the city, bathing the Big Apple in golden light.

Ben slipped off his gas mask and smiled a warrior's smile. All in all, he thought, it was going to be a beautiful day.

Chapter 4

Far to the north and west, Monte, the Canadian warlord who had a pact with the Night People, had met an American mercenary who hated Ben Raines nearly as much as the Night People. Monte's army numbered almost a thousand more than Ben's Rebels, but they were not nearly so professional; what they did amount to were killers, thugs, thieves, rapists, perverts and just about any other low-class, no good creature one might wish to name. But they did have the best of equipment, and what they lacked in professionalism they made up for in sheer numbers.

"Your name?" Monte asked the man who had requested a meeting with him.

"Colonel."

"Colonel . . . what?"

"Colonel will do quite nicely. And you are General Monte?"

"I never met a man named Colonel before," Monte bitched.

"You are General Monte?"

"Yeah, yeah! I hear you got yourself an army?"

"Approximately battalion-size, yes."

"And you intend to do what with this army?"

"I intend to eventually kill Ben Raines," Colonel said calmly. "But whether that is possible without help is the question."

"And you want my help?"

"Shall we say a mutual need?"

"What's that mean?"

"Do you know what Ben Raines looks like? How he operates? Who his top commanders are? Anything at all about the man?"

"I know he ain't no god like some people claim him to be."

"That is correct. But you did not answer my questions."

"We've been tracking you and your people for several days, Colonel."

"I have made no effort to hide our advancement."

"For a fact. No, Colonel, I don't know much about General Raines. But I do know this: the man is rapidly turning into a large pain in the ass as far as I'm concerned."

"Because he has moved into New York City and just might succeed in wiping out the Night People, thereby ending a very lucrative operation between you and those dreadful beings?"

Monte leaned back in his chair. Not exactly his chair; he had liberated the home from a man and his wife just the day before. He had shot the man and then raped the woman. His troops were now passing the lady around. When they tired of her, they would either kill her or stable her with other men and women being held for eventual transportation to various enclaves of Night People.

"You're a very knowledgeable man, Colonel."

"I try to keep abreast of matters that might some-day be of use to me, thank you."

"Why do you hate Ben Raines, Colonel?"

"Purely a personal matter, General."

"What do you know about the Night People?"

"A very odious gathering of allies, General."

"For a fact," Monte agreed. He had never liked those spooky suckers, for sure. Didn't even care to get around them. The idea of eating human flesh made his stomach do flip-flops.

Monte stared at the Colonel. "I've heard your voice before, Colonel. When we intercepted various radio transmissions. And Colonel wasn't what you were called then."

The man shrugged his shoulders. "All in good time, General. The truth will out. Let us just say that for the past several months, it was my misfortune to be associated with Khamsin. The Hot Wind. You are familiar with that fellow, aren't you?"

"Ah!" Monte smiled. "Now I think I know who you are. But I can't recall your name."

"Shall we keep that between us, General?"

Monte nodded his head. "Suits me, Colonel."

The Colonel laid several pieces of paper before the warlord. "All of the General's frequencies. The second sheet tells you how to decode the scramble channels. The third sheet shows you all of the out-posts he and his Rebels have set up in the lower forty-eight. The fourth sheet is a description of the man himself and his likes and dislikes."

Monte picked up the sheets of paper. "All right . . . Colonel. We'll talk more later. Right now, we're all going to be busting our butts getting to New York City. I got word late last night that Raines is beginning his push into the city. I'll be honest with you: I am not familiar with New York City."

"Oh, I am reasonably knowledgeable of the city, General."

The Colonel paled under his deep tan at Monte's next remark. "Good, Colonel. Then you and your people can act as our point. You'll be the first to enter the Big Apple."

It was going to be much slower and much bloodier and ever so much more awful than even Ben had realized.

Tina and her teams had cleared the park and moved across State Street. They had entered the Custom House and spent most of the morning clearing just that one building.

Dan and his people had cleared the terminal and then began working up the pier, with the tall buildings of New York Plaza across from them, waiting to be entered and cleaned out.

Ben and his people had pushed on up Whitehall, clearing and cleaning up anything found at ground level. He had linked up with Tina and they were eating rations while sitting on a bench facing Greenwich Street.

"Hell of a way to run a war, Dad," Tina observed. She looked nervously around her. "And isn't this a bit dangerous? We are rather exposed, you know?"

Ben chewed for a moment. Cut his eyes across the way. "That's clear over there. You don't think Jersey would let me sit out here if it wasn't, do you? She'd be bitching and hollering and jumping up and down. Besides, you do have your body armor on, don't you?" He looked at her. "You damn well better have—we went to a lot of trouble to find those stockpiles."

She smiled and nodded her head. "Yes, Dad." They all agreed that the body armor was hot and uncomfortable, but working the way they would be for the next several months—at least—the vests were lifesavers. "How many buildings in this city, Dad?"

"Oh, Jesus, kid. Hundreds. That's just in Manhattan. Thousands if you take it all in." He glanced at his watch. "Leave a small contingent to guard what we've cleared so far, Tina. We'll join up with Dan and start working on the buildings in the Plaza."

"I am not looking forward to this," she admitted.

"Nor am I," Ben confessed.

Dan was just finishing his tea when father and daughter strolled up.

"Frightfully ugly and distasteful business, isn't it, General?"

"The fighting?" Tina asked.

"No." Dan crumpled up what was left of his meal. "The horrible food!"

That broke up the slight tension and flung it about as laughter rang out from the Rebels just finishing their noon meal. Holly and several medics walked up, handing out fresh surgical masks and rubber gloves. The medical people carefully inspected each Rebel for minor cuts that under normal conditions would require nothing more than a dab of antiseptic. But no one knew what diseases the Night People carried, and no one wanted to take a chance of getting infected through an open wound, no matter how small the cut.

Ben noticed several things: one, that his people were all blood-splattered from the close-in killing; and two, that Holly was deliberately avoiding him. Neither came as any surprise to him.

He did not believe that the slight quarrel they'd had earlier that day was an accident. Ben felt that she had deliberately provoked it, for he had sensed that the pressure she'd been enduring as the girlfriend of Ben Raines was getting to her. She wanted out, the relationship over, and he did not blame her for that.

Ben turned his back to her and walked up to a medic, getting a fresh mask and gloves. Both Tina and Dan had watched the man, and both knew what the problem was.

They exchanged glances, Dan saying, "What price fame, eh, Tina?"

"Poor Dad. He's had more than his share of troubles with the ladies, hasn't he?"

The Englishman smiled. "Your father, Tina, loves the ladies. He wants everyone to think he is like a bee, blissfully flitting from flower to flower, sampling first this one, then that one. But there is a reason for it. You know, of course, that he's never gotten over Jerre?"

"Jerre? But I've heard him curse her name!"

"Yes." Dan's reply was soft. "And I've gotten more than slightly wobble-legged with him on more than one occasion and watched him turn maudlin discussing the lady. He loved the girl very deeply, and loves the woman just as deeply. But from afar." Dan smiled sadly. "'Such a one do I remember, whom to look at was to love.'"

"That's Tennyson."

"Good, Tina. Yes, you're right. Always return to the classics, for they never go out of style." He sighed. "I fear the good general will go to his grave loving Jerre."

"Does she know how he feels?"

"I don't think so. She might know that his feelings are very strong for her; but how deeply he still loves her? No. And there is something else he doesn't know . . ."

She cut her eyes to the Englishman.

"She rejoined the main Rebel contingent at Base Camp One, just after Ben pulled out for Michigan."

"Oh, God, Dan! Don't tell me she's here!"

"Yes, I'm afraid so."

"God *damn* her!" There was considerable heat in the daughter's voice. Tina looked at Dan and mentally braced herself.

"Elaine the fair, Elaine the loveable, Elaine, the lily maid of Astolat."

"You're mocking my father, Dan."

"No, girl. No. I, too, know his pain. I went dippers over a lady much younger than I, just before the Great War. A Scottish lassie. I had just returned from antiterrorism duty in Northern Ireland; took some time off. I met her on the moors just as the mist rolled in, lightly sparkling her hair and blooming her cheeks, freshening her lips. She was so lovely. That first picture of her has never faded from my mind. And she knew not my true feelings. Not in all the days we spent together did I ever tell her."

"Why, Dan?"

"Oh . . . the difference in our ages, I kept telling myself. I don't know, Tina. I wish I had told her."

"Is she still alive?"

"I don't know that either. That's what makes it so difficult at times. The grave is the great healer, Tina. For both sides of an unrequited love. If a bit on the final side for one," he added dryly.

Ben had walked away, slowly circling one of the buildings that made up New York Plaza. But he was not alone: Jersey was a few steps behind him, and several more Rebels flanked him. He stopped suddenly, catching a glimpse of tousled honey-blond hair under a black beret. Something in the walk . . . something about the way the person carried herself . . . something . . .

She turned.

It was not her.

Of course not! Ben coldly calmed his mind and loosened the velvet ties that invisibly clutched at his heart. The last he had heard of her she had dumped the guy she'd married and was homesteading alone out in the northwest, writing poetry or some fucking thing.

Never did have a lick of sense.

No, he corrected that. She had plenty of sense. Just free-spirited and sort of vain. Beautiful.

Ben brushed the bird droppings off a bench and sat down. He hadn't thought of Jerre for some time. Not consciously, that is. Liar! he berated himself.

For a time, he had believed her dead. That news proved untrue.

The rattle of gunfire momentarily interrupted his thoughts and turned his head. His people had resumed their search and destroy of the Night People. He saw Tina and Dan looking at him. They quickly averted their eyes.

What the hell was going on?

Something sure was funky, that much Ben knew for sure. Dan had been acting strangely for several days, and so had Ike and Cecil and Chase.

Amazing, Ben thought, so many windows in the buildings were still intact. He guessed those people so inclined to wantonly destroy and loot just hadn't had the time to do so. The Great War had accomplished one good thing, anyway: it had gotten rid of a lot of human crud.

And a lot of good, decent people, too, Ben amended that thought.

And then *she* slipped into his head. Coming to him gently, quietly, bringing a myriad of emotions with her, all scented with softness.

Ben sighed, shifted on the bench.

"Get away from me," he muttered, the words too low to be overheard by his guards. "Leave me alone, Jerre."

She!

The words to an old song entered his head. Charles Aznavour was one who'd recorded it. She. Ben had once had a copy of it. He'd smashed it several years back. Thinking of Jerre, of course.

No, Ben Raines was no god. Ben was just as human as any other mortal being. He occasionally cut himself shaving. Stubbed his toe now and then. Sometimes drank too much. Every once in a while allowed himself the luxury of sinking into a morass of self-pity.

With Jerre on his mind.

Naturally.

Jerre.

With the muted rattle of gunfire drifting to him from the buildings, the stink of death wafting through the late fall air, she entered his mind. He could almost hear her say, "Hi, Ben."

Chapter 5

He'd first seen her a few miles north of Charlottesville, a dejected-looking figure trudging along the side of the road. At first Ben had thought it a boy; his life would have been a hell of a lot less complicated had that been the case.

At the sound of his truck, she had tried jumping over the ditch, heading for the woods, but the jump was short and she fell hard, twisting her ankle. When Ben reached her, he found a very lovely young lady, holding a small semiautomatic pistol. Pointing at him. Lots of honey-blond hair, dark blue eyes.

"I don't mean you any harm, miss."

"Yeah? That's what the last bunch of guys said, while they were trying to tear my clothes off me."

"How'd you get away?"

"Kicked one in the nuts and split!"

"You want me to take a look at that ankle?"

"Not particularly. Why don't you just take off?"

"I don't mean you any harm, miss. What is your name?"

"None of your damned business!"

"OK, None-of-Your-Damned-Business. My name is Ben Raines."

"Big deal. Who cares? Ben Raines. That sounds sort of familiar."

"I'm a writer. What are you, 'bout seventeen?"

"I'm nineteen, if that's any of your business—which it isn't." She fixed her blues on him. "OK, you can look at my ankle if it means so much to you . . ." One of her typical smart-mouthed statements that Ben would come to hate to love as the years rolled by. Without her. ". . . But I'm gonna keep this gun on you all the time. One funny move and I'll shoot you."

"That's a deal." Ben didn't have the heart to tell her that with the weapon she was holding, one first had to cock it before it would fire. It was not cocked.

Ben inspected the ankle and concluded it was sprained. "OK, None-of-Your-Damned-Business. We've got to find a creek and have you soak that ankle for an hour or so."

"My name is Jerre. J-e-r-r-e. Jerre Hunter." She looked at her swollen ankle. "It looks gross."

"Yes, it does. Come on, Jerre, put your arm around my shoulders and keep your weight off that ankle."

She gazed at him for a moment. "Oh, what the hell? You might rape me, but that's not gonna hurt as bad as my ankle hurts."

Ben laughed at her. "You have a hang-up about people lusting about your body, kid. You can put that pistol away, too, Jerre. It's not going to fire unless you cock it."

She grinned at him. "I don't think it has any bullets in it anyway. I don't know how to load the stupid thing." She tossed the pistol into the ditch.

It bounced off a rock and fired, blowing a chunk of wood out of a tree.

Ben looked at her and slowly shook his head.

That was the beginning . . . and in some ways, it went downhill from there.

While she soaked her ankle in a cold little creek, they talked, with her alternately bitching about the temperature of the water and how she would probably catch pneumonia, or how her foot would surely rot off from radiation.

She had just started her second year of college, up in Maryland, when the bombs came and everybody got sick. She had gotten sick and survived while most of the others died around her.

The whole experience was gross. The absolute pits, man.

They touched on the subject of music. Briefly. When Ben had told her his opinion of certain types of rock and roll music, she had cocked her head to one side, blond hair falling over one eye, and stared at him for a time. "I think, Ben, that if we're going to be friends, we'd better not discuss our tastes in music."

"Or until you grow up."

"Whatever."

"Why were you walking and not driving? Millions of cars and trucks around with the keys in them."

"I felt like walking, that's why."

The logic of Jerre.

"How come, Ben, we're not all falling over dead

from radiation sickness? I mean, I thought great clouds of that stuff would be floating around."

"Clean bombs, Jerre."

She cut her eyes. *"Clean bombs?* What kind of silliness is that?"

"I guess it is silly, after a fashion."

Then she admitted she had heard of him other than being a writer. She had heard he was commander of a great Rebel army.

Ben got a kick out of that. "That's what people keep telling me. I have been avoiding them, I suppose."

"Why?"

"Do I look like a general to you, Jerre?"

She had to admit, he did not. Just kind of big and tough-looking and sort of old.

"Thanks, Jerre."

"Forty, I'd guess."

"Thereabout," Ben said dryly.

Her eyes shone with mischief. "But I like a little gray in a man's hair."

"Uh-huh."

"I think you'll hook up with the Rebels, Ben Raines. I think you're a decent man who will almost always do the right thing. I think you've got the right stuff, Ben Raines."

"Thanks for the latter. No way to the former."

"Yeah, I think you will, Ben. You'll walk around it for a time, but you'll join them, and probably, eventually, lead them. I've read some of your books. You're a dreamer and a romanticist and you'd like to go back to the laws of a hundred years ago.

Maybe that's what the country needs. No harm in trying, is there?" she winked at him. "Hey, General?"

"You're a nut." He smiled at her.

"But a pretty nut." She laughed. A Carly Simon tune came to Ben's mind.

"Yeah," he said softly. "You are a pretty nut."

"Gonna be dark soon, Ben."

"Yes." He looked at her ankle. Some of the swelling was gone. "We'll find a place. You'll be safe with me."

"I believe that. But the dark . . . scares me. It didn't used to. Until . . ." She let that trail off.

She told him about finding her parents. The man who lived next door had survived. He tried to rape her. She'd hit him with a fireplace poker. "Something popped when I hit him, Ben. I think I killed him. He wasn't breathing and I wasn't about to stick around and do any nursing. I just took off."

She was silent for a time. Finally, Ben took her hand and helped her up. "We'll find us a place to spend the night, Jerre. Fix us some dinner."

She studied him for a moment. And right then and there, by that little creek, Ben fell in love. That one-time-only sort of love. That kind of love that a person knows, if given a chance, was so strong that only death could part them . . . providing, he was to reluctantly admit as the years marched past, both parties felt the same way. "All right, Ben," she said quietly.

He lay in his bed that night and had to smile at all that Jerre had said that afternoon and evening. She was a character, a true one-of-a-kind.

And Ben was falling more deeply in love with

every word from her mouth, every moment that slipped by.

She came to his bed; Ben could smell the clean, fresh soap smell of her.

"You're not like any man I have ever met, General-author Ben Raines. I think you're a tough man, but a sensitive one, and that you try to hide that sensitive side."

"Perhaps."

She limped to the bed and sat down.

They talked for a time and when she came to him, all soft and warm and full of fire and excitement and youth. She softly yelled as the first climax shook her, and then they settled into the ageless rhythm of the game with only victors to signify the coming of Omega.

And while the world tumbled in chaos about them . . . two were not alone.

Jersey touched him on the shoulder. "General." He looked up at her. "Gettin' hot, sir. You're making the others nervous. Afraid you'll get hit by a stray."

"You're right, Jersey. Sorry." Ben rose to his boots. Looked at his watch. Only a few minutes had gone by while he had allowed himself to be lost in dreams. He glanced at the twenty-two-story red brick building of Number Four New York Plaza. "Come on, Jersey. Let's see a little action. I'm in a dandy mood to work off some mad."

"Whatever you say, sir," the half-pint with the M-16 replied. As they walked toward the doors of the buildings, Jersey asked, "One of us do something to get you angry, sir?"

"No, Jersey. I did it to myself. You ever had an itch you couldn't quite reach to scratch?"

"Yes, sir."

"I've had one for years."

Ben pushed open the doors and the stench assailed his nostrils. No doubt about it: the enemy was present. Hiding in the gloom. But Ben was sure they'd be too smart to stay at ground level. He looked back; a squad of Rebels had joined them.

"Everybody in gloves and masks," he ordered. "And everybody damn well better be in body armor. Split your team. Check below. You people take the second floor. I'll take Jersey and start on the third floor. Move."

Bones on the steps leading up. Human bones. Somewhere in the city, the Night People had to have a breeding farm, breeding human beings for food.

But where?

Ben tried the fire door on the third floor. Locked. He motioned Jersey back and pulled the pin on a grenade, wedging it between bar and door, then stepped back to join Jersey behind a stone wall at the first angle of steps.

The explosion was nearly deafening in the closed space. The door blew off its hinges and was knocked inward as shrapnel bounced around in a deadly rain. Ben keyed his mike. "We're all right. Just blowing a door." He motioned Jersey to follow him and to stay behind him. She didn't like it, but obeyed.

Ben advanced slowly up the smoke and dust-filled stairway, the Thompson off safety, set on full auto. He stepped onto the third floor, and a foul-smelling, dark-robed creature came howling at him from across the dusty, musty corridor.

Ben gave him some .45 rounds for lunch, and the nasty stopped abruptly in the hallway, then was propelled backward as if hit by a giant fist. The being—Ben couldn't tell if it was male or female— sat down in the hall and died.

Ben walked over to it and jerked back the hood. The face was horribly burned—by fire or radiation Ben could not be sure.

He dropped the hood back over the abomination and motioned Jersey to follow him.

The stench here was much worse than on the ground floor. Ben fought back an urge to gag. Cutting his eyes, he could tell that Jersey was struggling to hang onto her lunch.

"I guess we'll get used to it." He spoke through his mask.

"They must have a terrific sex life." Jersey rolled her eyes. "Can you just imagine?"

"Please, Jersey. The mere thought is enough to make one join the monkhood."

She laughed. "But not for very long."

"True."

A very slight puff of dust at the corridor's end brought Ben up short, his arm outstretched to halt Jersey. He whispered, "Some nasties around that corner. Roll a grenade in with me."

She nodded and pulled the pin, holding the spoon down, waiting for Ben. Just at the last second, to prevent the grenades from being tossed back at them, they lobbed them around the corner and pressed up against a wall.

The fragmentation grenades blew bits and chunks of nasties all over the dirty corridor. One rolled to its feet and Jersey's M-16 barked.

They waited. Only the sounds of someone, or something, moaning could be heard.

"Drag your funky butt out of there!" Jersey shouted.

The wounded unfriendly cursed them.

Ben began inching his way toward the sound, staying close to the wall. Jersey slipped to the other side, staying even with Ben.

With a maddened scream, the subhuman charged around the corner, a shotgun in its dirty and bloody hands. Jersey and Ben fired as one, .223 and .45 slugs stopping the nasty dead in its tracks.

Crouching down, the two Rebels waited. The sounds of gunfire had ceased on the floors below them. Footsteps were heard coming up behind them. Ben cut his eyes. Rebels. They crouched down beside Ben in the now blood-splattered hallway.

"Everything is clear below us, General."

Ben nodded. "I think we're clear here, too." He stood up and started walking toward the corridor opening. The Rebel blocked his way with a seemingly unintentional movement; Ben knew it was anything but that.

Members of the team moved ahead, checked out the body-littered hallway, and waved the rest forward just as Ben's walkie-talkie spewed its message.

"We're filling up in the park, Dad," Tina's voice reached him. "Need you down here."

Ben had a suspicion that he was deliberately being called out of combat for no good reason—other than to get him clear.

He acknowledged the message and turned to leave, Jersey following him. "Handle the bodies carefully and stack them in the designated burn areas, people. Secure the building."

He stepped out of the building, into the fall sun, and looked around him. Nearly all the Rebels assigned to his personal command had made the trip to Lower Manhattan; Jeeps and trucks and light tanks and APC's were now being towed over.

Ben suddenly realized he was neatly surrounded by Rebels, all of them staying a discreet distance away. And they were not Rebels from his personal battalion.

Seeing the irritation on his face, Jersey said, "Those are from General Ike's group, sir. They're just obeying orders. If you fuss at them, you'll just be putting them between a rock and a hard place."

His slight anger vanished as Ben smiled. Ike had done it to him again, covering him like a blanket. "You're right, Jersey. Come on, let's get this circus on the road. I want this place completely cleared by nightfall."

"Water is going to be at a premium," Ben told his commanders. "At least for a while. One-minute showers. Pass the word." He had just received casualty reports. One dead, five wounded, one seriously. The dead Rebel had not been wearing his body armor. Ben did not have to lecture any of his commanders. He knew the next person found without body armor was going to get his or her butt kicked.

The sky was darkening as twilight settled in. Guards had been mounted around the perimeters of the tiny part of Manhattan the Rebels had cleared. Ben had nixed the burning of bodies. Gasoline was too precious to waste burning these damned ugly cannibals. The bodies would be taken out and tossed onto a barge, anchored in the river, and would be towed out to sea once a day and dumped. Let the sharks dine.

Colonel West and his mercenaries had fought their way to just south of Newark Airport. They would try to take the field tomorrow.

Ike and his people had hammered their way into Bayonne; his plan was eventually to clear J.F.K. Boulevard all the way to the Holland Tunnel and clear that over to Manhattan. The George Washington Bridge plan had been junked as too time-consuming. It would have to wait.

Cecil and his Rebels had crossed over into Brooklyn and were attempting to clear everything within the loop from Bay Ridge over to the Shore Parkway. The fighting, according to radio communiqués, had been fierce, but Rebel losses very light.

Ben and Jersey rode over to the park.

There, he inspected the aid station and, unable to locate Holly, who was supposed to be in charge, spoke briefly with Doctor Chase.

"I reassigned her to Cecil's battalion, Ben. They're taking more heat over there."

If Ben had a comment, he kept it to himself. Chase ran the medical teams with a free hand.

"Had dinner?" Ben asked.

"No. I was about to ask you to join me for a bite of our delicious cuisine. Alone. I've got to tell you something, Ben."

"I sensed something was up. All of you have been behaving oddly. So you got elected to buck the tiger, eh, Lamar?"

"I elected myself because I'm too goddamned old to be afraid of you or anybody else! Come on."

The two friends sat on a bench in a secure area and unwrapped what currently passed for field rations. The food wasn't very good, but it was nutritious. The best part was when it was over. Chase maintained it was good. He wouldn't admit it was awful.

"New York City had about fifteen thousand restaurants before the war," Chase bitched. "You'd think someone would have the good graces to reopen one." He said that with a smile.

His smile faded at Ben's reply. "Considering just who makes up the majority in the city now, I'd hate to see the menu."

Chase looked at his packet of food and grimaced. "That was uncalled for, Raines. Jesus!"

Ben chuckled.

He stopped chuckling when Chase said, "Jerre just reported in at the replacement depot on Staten Island."

Chapter 6

Monte looked at the report just handed him. The last thing in the world the warlord wanted to do was mix it up with Ben Raines and his Rebels. Even though he had Raines outmanned by several battalions, his people did not have, and never would have, the professionalism of the Rebels. And he knew why: Monte's people were not fighting for a cause. The warlord knew that his troops stayed together for the basest of reasons: greed, women, power, a chance to exercise their cruelty and perversion, and for some degree of safety.

But the Night People had been good to Monte over the years. Good, to Monte's way of thinking. And it was really getting better as their breeding farms grew in number. Monte and his men always had their choice of young girls and the best-looking women—sometimes young boys, for those under his command who leaned in that direction. Since many of the Night People claimed to be unable to sire or bear children—he didn't know whether he believed that or not—it was up to Monte and his men to impregnate the captured women . . . a job they all looked forward to.

No, Monte thought, as he crumpled the paper and tossed it aside, this confrontation had to be. If he could get Ben Raines out of the way, the entire United States would be open to him, and his perversions could go unchecked for the remainder of his worthless life.

But, he thought, as a sour taste lay on his tongue, that damned Russian, Striganov, had given his troops the go-ahead to pursue Monte to New York; two battalions of Russian troops and one battalion of Canadians were hot on his tail, rushing to help Ben Raines, Colonel Rebet commanding the Russians and Major Danjou commanding the Canadians.

God*damn* them!

Monte smiled as a plan slipped like a poisonous snake into his brain. Yes—it might work.

After all, Manhattan was an island—at least on three sides. He would send a runner to the Judges.

"They are spread dangerously thin," one of the Judges spoke. "But they are aware that most of us can tolerate light for a time."

"What is that supposed to mean?" another Judge asked querulously.

"It means they are ready to fight all the time. It means we cannot use our aversion to light to surprise or trick them into an ambush."

"They are slowly, slowly advancing," the woman Judge who sat in the center of the council circle said. "But advancing is the key word."

"Where is Monte?"

"Coming, but with trouble on his heels. A Canadian and Russian combat force is pursuing them. They will surely link up with the Hated One."

"We could slip out, get away," it was suggested.

"Even if that were possible, which I doubt, they would just find us again. No," she spoke with a sigh, "this must be a battle to the finish. But we must change our tactics." She leaned forward. "I have a plan . . ."

"Who in the goddamn hell OK'd her transfer up here?" Ben spoke through clenched teeth.

"Ben," Lamar tried to calm his friend, "whatever you and Jerre had—and according to you, it was damn little and all one-sided—happened years ago. Her name would be meaningless to some young man or woman in records."

"Guess this pretty well blows away the rumors that she died."

"Would you prefer her dead, Ben?"

Ben did not reply.

"How long has it been since you've seen her, Ben?"

"Long time, Lamar. Just a quick glance then."

"And you still love her?"

"Oh, yes. Loved her all the time I was lying to Salina. Loved her all the times I was lying to all the others."

"What is it about her, Ben?"

Ben shook his head. "I don't know. It's . . . ah . . . just one of those loves that only come around one time in a person's life. And you never forget them.

Never. Her face has been just behind my eyes all these years. Jesus! No fool like an old fool sure tags me right."

"How old is she now, Ben?"

"Let's see . . . she'd be . . . thirty, I suppose."

"Hell, Ben, the difference in your ages is not that great, man!"

"I'm not sure that age had anything to do with it, Lamar. I still have the letter she wrote me; left it on my pillow early one morning. Wanna hear it?"

"You memorized it!"

"Sure."

"God, Ben! The love bug didn't just hit you—it ran clear over you!"

Ben chuckled, his usual good mood returning. "Damn sure did, Lamar. She wrote: 'Dear Ben, I'll make this short 'cause if I try to write too much I'll just tear it up and stay with you, and I think that would be bad for both of us—at this time. Maybe what I'm doing is foolish. I don't know. But I feel it's something I have to do. The world is in such a mess, I have to try to do something to help fix it. Maybe the young can. I don't know. In my heart I kind of doubt it, but we have to try—right?

"'I don't know what my feelings are toward you, Ben. I like you a whole lot and I think I probably love you a little bit. That's a joke—I think I probably love you a whole lot. That's one of the reasons I have to split. There are other reasons, of course, but my feelings toward you are right up there at the top.

"'You've got places to go and things to see before you find yourself—your goal, preset, I believe—and start to do great things. And you will, Ben. You will.

"'I hope I see you again, General.'"

Ben's voice was breaking as he finished it. "'Love, Jerre.'"

Lamar let a few moments pass before he asked, "When was the next time you saw her?"

"I drifted for a time. That's when I found Juno— you remember the husky. Shortly after that I ran into Ike and that funky radio station he'd built down in Florida." Ben laughed aloud, a hearty laugh that felt good to both men. "Radio station KUNT. I married Ike and Megan right round Christmas. Shortly after that, the group split up, and I started wandering again. Drove up to North Carolina, looking for Jerre. Lost her trail. Met some more people who thought like me. Pal and Valerie . . ." He sighed. Both of them dead now. "I ran into a group of young people in Oklahoma who told me that Jerre had put together a bunch of young people and headed west. So I knew she was still alive. Shortly after that, I met you."

"I remember."

"I learned later that Jerre was deliberately avoiding me. I never learned why. By then I'd returned to Louisiana and gotten involved with Salina. I don't regret that. I regret that I lied to her. Anyway, months rolled by, and we were all settled into the Tri-States when Jerre walked up to me. More beautiful than I remembered. Said she wasn't staying in the Tri-States. She had some beefy young man with her. I think she married him and later dumped him. I tried to keep track of her as best I could over the years. I helped her from time to time—without her ever knowing it, of course—but I haven't seen her in a long time." Ben fell silent.

"You know, old friend, we're supposed to be manly and tough and all that happy horse-shit. Men don't cry and all that. So I'll confess something to you. Way back, years ago, before I met my first wife—God rest her soul and God damn Hilton Logan to the pits of Hell for killing her—I was a young doctor on a tin can. Got some shore leave in Spain. Her name was Maria. I still remember her. Love? God! Walking into walls type of love. No point in going into all the tearful details. But do I still love her? Oh, yes, Raines. I still do. I think the last thing that will pass my eyes before death takes me will be the face of Maria." He patted Ben's knee. "You hang in, old friend. You and your Jerre just might make it yet."

He rose, cussed as his bad knee popped, and walked away.

Leaving Ben alone.

As usual.

A condition he should be accustomed to by now.

But somehow never quite got the hang of it.

Jersey shook Ben awake at three in the morning.

"Guards at post three are gone, General."

"Gone!" Ben sat up in his blankets and looked at Jersey. She had obviously just been awakened.

"Yes, sir. And I mean gone without a trace. I personally checked before waking you."

Ben pulled on his boots and grabbed his Thompson, then followed Jersey to post three. Tina and Dan were already there.

"What happened, people?"

"We don't know, Dad," his daughter told him.

"They failed to report in and when this post was checked, they were gone."

Ben got down on his hands and knees and sniffed the pavement like a hound dog.

"What in the world are you doing, Dad?"

"No Night People came close to this post. Their odor lingers for hours." He looked at Dan.

The Englishman took it. "So they were lured away. But these were seasoned combat veterans, General. Both of them in their thirties. They've been with us for years. What on earth could have pulled them away?"

"You know," a Rebel spoke, "I could have sworn I heard a baby crying about an hour ago. But we had a little breeze blowing at the time and that's what I chalked it up to."

Dan and Ben exchanged glances, Dan saying, "You probably did hear a baby crying. And so did these men here." He stabbed a finger at the deserted guard post.

"A captive baby," Tina's words were soft. "Kidnapped or from one of the breeding farms."

"Pass the word, people," Ben told the small gathering. "No matter what you might see out there," his finger stabbed the dangerous night, "or think you see, no one leaves their post."

The screaming of the captured Rebels began bouncing and echoing around the brick-and-concrete streets. The hideous wailing would continue until dawn.

At first light, teams began the second day of their search-and-destroy missions. Beginning at Bridge

Street, Ben's teams began working slowly up the center of Manhattan, while Dan and Tina began working inward from West Street and South Street. After securing Beaver Street over to Broad, working toward Dan's sector, Ben called a rest for his people.

"It's going to take us five years at this pace," Ben bitched to Doctor Chase, who had just joined him. "There has got to be a better way."

"Bring the older buildings down with explosives," Chase suggested.

"I thought of that. It would work for perhaps one day; then the creepies would move in captives under the cover of darkness, and we'd be right back to square one." He shook his head in disgust.

"Are you having second thoughts about this objective, Ben?"

"No." Ben's reply was quick. "It's just that we've got to get as much done as quickly as possible. We know that the Canadian warlord, Monte, is moving toward us, with Rebet and Danjou right on his heels. But Monte has perhaps five times the number of men of those pursuing him. Rebet and Danjou can't afford the luxury of a head-to-head confrontation; they're going to have to wage hit-and-run warfare.

"We can't cordon off the city and starve the nasties out—troop strength being just one of the reasons. And I'm going to have to assign a full platoon to go outside the city in search of fuel. Wood-cutting and kerosene. In about three weeks, winter is going to be full on us. And I don't have to tell you that since the war, the winters have been getting rougher and longer. Fighting as we'll be doing, the people are going to have to be fed very substantial meals; cold will sap a person's strength faster than anything."

Ben sighed. "And at the rate we're progressing we're weeks away from breaking through to where we *think* the survivors might be located." Ben opened his map case and again studied the problem. "We've got to have a place to land our birds and store equipment. That's imperative."

"No smaller airports?"

"None that would do us any good. They're all way to hell and gone from the city. J.F.K. might as well be on the moon. We'd have to fight our way through Brooklyn and Queens to get to it. Westchester is out of the question, as is Fairfield. Teterboro would be ideal. But getting to it is another matter. Linden is too far south. I guess I'm going to have to chance some patrols—volunteers only—and check out Teterboro Airport. I've already ordered a low-level flyby of it. But the pilots have to land down here," Ben punched at New Jersey, "and then make their way back up here—the last leg by boat. Jesus! It's a damned logistical nightmare, Lamar. The Indians got the last laugh after all."

Dan strolled up to the men. "General, we found what is left of Peters and Dickerson. They died awfully hard."

Ben and Chase both turned, the doctor saying, "I want to see them."

"Brace yourselves," the Englishman warned them both. "It is anything but pleasant."

That was putting it mildly, Ben thought, standing over the tortured remains of the two dead Rebels.

Chase and one of his medics had knelt down, inspecting the bodies. The doctor rose slowly, his face a hard mask of fury.

"They were tortured by experts, Ben. Probably kept conscious the entire time."

"Pull the people in a few at a time," Ben ordered. "I want them all to see what manner of subhuman filth we are confronting. Pass the word: no quarter, no pity, no mercy, and no prisoners."

Chapter 7

"Tina has volunteered to take the patrol up to Teterboro Airport," Dan informed him.

Ben did not hesitate. To do so would have been showing favoritism, and Tina would have been highly irritated. "All right, have her start pulling equipment. Dan, how in the hell is she going to get across?"

Dan traced the route with his finger, as he leaned over the hood of Ben's Jeep. "I have suggested this: she backtracks through Staten Island and picks up this Two-eighty-seven loop, following it all the way to Interstate Eighty; then she'll cut back east. This way will also give us some intel as to how far out this despicable bunch extends."

Ben agreed. "Same route I would choose. I want her on the road this afternoon."

The two men stared at one other across the hood of the Jeep. "Something, Dan?"

"I feel it is my duty to inform you of something, General."

Typical British always-do-the-right-thing attitude. Ben kept a straight face and let Dan plow on. Even though he knew damn well what the man was going to say. "All right, Dan."

But Ben was only half right.

"As you know, General, I've lost some Scouts and am hesitant to pull any regulars out of the city to send with Tina."

Ben leaned against the fender, puzzled. It was not what he had anticipated hearing. "You take the people you need, Dan. How many do you want? It can't be many."

"No, sir, not many. Tina is two short of her usual complement of twenty-five. Of the new replacements just arrived, only two have completed Scout training and they have requested immediate assignments. It is my belief that out there," he jerked his thumb away from the city, "would be a better place to test them than here in the city."

"I agree, Dan. OK. What's the rub?"

Dan looked awfully uncomfortable. He sighed and exhaled slowly. "I am loath to approve their requests, General."

"Why, Dan?"

"Because one of them is Jerre and the sissy-looking one with her is her boyfriend."

"Holy shit!" one of West's mercenaries breathed, looking through binoculars.

"What's wrong, Curly?" the mercenary leader asked him.

He was called Curly because he was totally bald.

"It's worse than what we seen over at the Linden

Airport, Colonel. Those spooky creepies have destroyed the runways."

West lifted his field glasses and studied the wreckage. Great holes had been blown into the concrete; entire sections had been torn loose, rendering the airport useless. West motioned for his radio man to come forward. He lifted the handset from the backpack and started to report in, then hesitated.

"What's wrong, Colonel?" Curly asked.

West shook his head and replaced the phone. "Funny feeling. I can't shake the feeling that we're being monitored." He waved for his XO. "Take over here. I'm going over to talk with Ike." He turned to another merc. "Get a platoon together. Two light tanks. We're going straight up Ninety-five then cut east across the bridge. Ford, no critical chatter on the air. Keep it all crap. I've got a bad feeling."

Dan had walked away, leaving Ben alone with his thoughts. And they were not pleasant ones.

It would be like her, Ben acknowledged. To wave some son of a bitch in his face like a matador's cape to a bull and then smile that smart-aleck grin and see what took place next.

Ben had told Dan not to worry about it. If Jerre and her latest heartthrob wanted to join the Scouts, so be it. They needed every breathing soul they could muster.

Dan was dubious, but merely shrugged and said he would take care of it.

Ben smiled grimly. He hoped Jerre didn't get up in Tina's face. Tina was a few years younger, but she was tough as a paratrooper's boot and knew more of that Oriental kung-fu stuff than just about anyone else Ben could name. Except for Dan, who had been Tina's teacher.

And Jerre wouldn't have told her current sweetie about Ben. During their time together, she had told him she liked to do that to boys.

Ben had been forced to admit, some years back, that Jerre was a purebred bitch!

Didn't make any difference, though. It hadn't changed his feelings; he still loved her.

"Shit!" Ben shouted, turning a dozen heads. He kicked at a can, missed and hit his toe on the curb. He sat down, grabbed his foot, and then proceeded to turn the air coarse with profanity.

It seemed that everybody suddenly found some urgent task that just could not wait.

All except for Jersey. She stood a few yards away, holding her M-16, watching the antics of her general . . . and trying very hard to keep a straight face.

West chanced a short coded message to Ike. Ike radioed back that come hell or high water—or nasties—he'd meet him on the bridge.

"Have any trouble, Ike?" West asked, getting out of his Jeep and walking to the man. They shook hands, two warriors who understood the hard business of war.

"No. And after yesterday, that surprises the hell out of me. You?"

West shook his head. "Not once we got up to the airport. We haven't seen one ugly. And by the way, the airport is ruined." He gave him a short report about the runways, then said, "I guess the lack of un-friendlies got me to thinking, Ike. I think we're being monitored. I think these uglies know every move we're going to make."

Ike stuck a lollipop in his mouth—he always had a pocketful of the homemade suckers for the kids—and offered one to West. The mercenary smiled and shook his head.

"That may be what's been causin' that uneasy feelin' of mine, West. We're gonna have to turn this problem over to Katzman. What he and his bunch don't know about communications and electronics ain't been thought of yet."

"I've instructed my people to put nothing vital on the air."

"I'll do the same. Let's ease over and take a boat ride. Break this gut hunch to Ben and lay it all in Katzman's lap."

The mercenary turned his head, staring in the direction of Manhattan. "It's been a long time since I've been to the Big Apple. That used to be my fa-vorite city to have a good time. See the shows, the ballet, the opera. I hope we can discover some master tapes of the great singers."

You never knew, Ike thought. Here was a man of violence, of war, of blood, who loved the classics. You just never knew about people.

"We've got our hands full," Ben told the men. "Seems like we're running into more nasties today than yesterday. Every time we turn around we're hitting pockets of them. So if they are monitoring our frequencies . . . what are they doing with the information? How is it affecting the operation?"

"Look out!" a frantic yell cut through the cool afternoon.

The men turned in time to see half a dozen concrete blocks come hurtling down from a rooftop. One block smashed into a head, ending a Rebel's life. Another shattered the shoulder of a woman.

Gunfire ripped from the ground level, and several dark-robed figures soaked up the lead. No more objects were thrown from that rooftop.

Returning fire knocked a Rebel spinning and sent the rest of the ground troops diving for cover. Machine guns began spitting and chugging from the ground, pocking the facade of the building, shattering glass, and momentarily stilling the sniper fire.

A rocket launcher howled, the missile slamming through a window of the building and exploding, showering the street below with debris.

The area fell silent.

"So much for all of the Night People having to avoid the light," West said, disgust in his voice. He stood up, brushing dirt and dust from his BDU's.

"I never really believed it was necessary on their part anyway," Ben replied. "I think it's more a way of life."

"Yeah," Ike said dryly. "Like not takin' a bath. I think they bathe once a year, whether they need it or not."

* * *

The two women looked at each other. Both their backs were stiff. Tina stepped up and extended her hand. The blonde took it.

"Miss Hunter."

"Just Jerre." She looked at the collars of Tina's battle dress. "I don't know what to call you. I was told you were a captain."

"We don't stand on much formality, Jerre. Tina will be just fine." *The lady who has my father tied up in knots. I wonder if he's seen her?*

"This is Ian." Jerre indicated a young man standing just to her left.

"You're in Sergeant Wilson's squad," Ian was informed. "You come with me, Jerre."

"I had assumed that we would be together," Ian said.

Tina turned slowly to face the man. Her Uncle Ike had told her once that Jerre seemed to have the ability to twist men around her finger, rendering them down to the level of small boys. "You may assume this, Ian: you take orders from me, and you obey them without question. If you feel incapable of doing that, then carry your ass!"

Ian blinked in surprise; then his hard Scout training took over. He nodded his head. "Yes, Miss Raines. Of course." He looked at Sergeant Wilson, squatting down, staring at him. Wilson waggled a finger and Ian obeyed the signal, walking away from Tina and Jerre.

"If he ever again questions an order of mine," Tina told Jerre, "he'll be out of this unit in five minutes. Or hurt or dead, if he wants to get physical about it," she added, a flat tone to the statement.

Jerre shrugged. "We're friends, Tina. Nothing more. You don't like me very much, do you?"

"I don't know you. I don't have to like you. As long as you do your job, we'll get along fine."

Tina turned and Jerre followed her. "How is the general?"

"The general is fine. A few more gray hairs on his head. A few more bullet scars. Other than that, he's in as good a physical shape as any man years younger."

She waited for Jerre to say she'd like to see him. The woman made no such request.

Blond-headed bitch! Tina thought, then softened that by reminding herself that she didn't know much about what had gone on between her father and this woman. Just bits and pieces and rumors. And, she was forced to admit, she was more than a bit prejudiced. They came to Tina's Jeep and stopped. Tina introduced Jerre to her driver, Sharon.

"She can ride with Pam," Sharon said, looking at Jerre. "That's point. You uneasy about that?"

"Not a bit."

"Fine." Tina took it. "You all geared up?"

"Yes. Equipment is back at the truck with the others."

Tina hesitated, then stuck out her hand. "Welcome to the team, Jerre."

Jerre smiled and took the hand.

"Oh, look," Sharon said. "There's General Raines. I'll introduce you."

Tina was watching the woman's face. Only a very slight narrowing of the eyes gave any indication as to her inner feelings. This should be interesting, she thought, watching as her father walked up, with Ike and West and Dan Gray with him.

Ben didn't wait for any introductions, not wanting to prolong the meeting. "You're looking well, Jerre."

"Thank you, General. You haven't changed a bit."

Neither have you, Ben thought. You're still so damned lovely. "Thank you." He looked at Tina. "Where's the other replacement?"

"With Wilson."

Ben picked up on the flatness of her tone. "Some conflict?"

"Nothing I can't handle."

Ben cut his eyes to Jerre. "These are small teams, Jerre. Each person must depend on the other. If there is something I need to know, say it."

"Ian was surprised that we were being separated. He opened his mouth before he thought. He . . . well, has read more into . . . ah, our relationship than is really there."

I certainly know that feeling, Ben thought. His gaze went to Tina. "Are you going to be able to get off this afternoon?"

"No, sir. We've had some equipment malfunction. Tomorrow morning at the earliest."

Damn! Ben silently cursed.

"May I speak with the general in private?" Jerre asked.

West stood silently by. He knew there was something going on here that he didn't really understand. But he would make it a point to ask Ike. Something between Ben Raines and this woman, he felt sure. He would tell his men that Jerre was strictly off-limits.

It wouldn't do for one of his men to try to cozy up to a lady that Raines had his eyes on. Or did he? West could feel the tension in the air.

The muffled sounds of gunfire drifted to the small group standing in Battery Park.

Jersey stood to one side. She had heard some of the scuttlebutt about the general and this woman. Well, that was the general's business. Her job was to protect him, not mother him.

"Of course, Miss Hunter." Ben pointed to a bench some yards away. "Over there."

Ike started whistling music from South Pacific: "Some Enchanted Evening."

West looked at the man, a smile playing around his lips. Ike had more brass on his ass than a ship's bell.

Ben gave Ike a look that would wilt a plastic flower. It bounced off the ex-SEAL.

Jerre stood quietly, with Dan wondering if the lady was familiar with that song.

Ike continued whistling.

"Don't you have something to do?" Ben asked him. "Like fight a war, for instance?"

Ike stopped whistling. "I'm taking a break. The pressure was getting to me." He resumed his whistling. An old Dolly Parton hit: "I Will Always Love You."

Ben muttered under his breath and walked toward the park bench, Jerre following.

"The man just doesn't appreciate talent when he hears it," Ike said.

That was too good an opening for Dan to let slide by, since the two men were constantly putting the needle to one another. "Are you all through calling hogs, now?"

Ike said some very uncomplimentary things about Dan while Tina and the mercenary stood laughing at the pained expression on Ike's face and the smug look on Dan's face.

Chapter 8

"It's been a long time, Ben."

"Just about a decade, Jerre."

They were sitting on the bench, a respectable distance between them.

"That sounds like forever."

Ben offered no reply.

"I've thought about you, Ben. Many times."

"I can truthfully say the same about you." He wondered what her game plan was this time? He knew she had something up her sleeve. None of this was pure accident. He'd bet his boots on that.

"You're being very cautious, Ben."

"Let's just say that I prefer not to unlock doors that have been closed for years."

"Can't we at least be friends?"

Ben had to laugh aloud. Same words, same music, same jukebox, different time.

"What is your game this time, Jerre?"

"That's a pretty crappy thing to say, Ben. You were a grown man and I was in college . . . or had been. We had some good times. I didn't exactly have to rape you, if you'll recall."

True.

"I never lied to you, Ben. And I never made any promises, either. Maybe things would have been different if you hadn't showed up in the Tri-States with that woman . . ."

Salina.

". . . The karma just wasn't right for us earlier."

"Jerre . . . you wanna get off the East Indian mysticism crap?"

"I seem to recall we talked along those lines."

"We talked about a lot of things . . . and side-stepped a lot more. Just about like what we're doing here."

"You want to end this conversation, Ben?"

"We might as well. It's taking us nowhere, as usual."

"Tina is your adopted daughter, right?"

"That's right. Her brother was killed in the fighting out in the Tri-States. As was Salina."

She was silent for a time, then asked, "Did you love her, Ben?"

"No. But we were comfortable together."

"Did you ever cheat on her?"

"No."

"You're a strange man, Ben Raines."

Ben stood up. Looked down at her. Beautiful. Still looked about nineteen. "I have a war to fight, Jerre. Correction—*we* have a war to fight. I wish I could say that I'm glad to see you. I'm not. I am glad that you're alive—I think," he added honestly. "Maybe I'll see you around. Did you ever learn to cook?"

She looked at him, blinked her blues, then laughed. "Oh, yes, Ben. I did that."

Ben nodded and walked away, waving for Jersey to follow. "I'll see you later on, Tina."

Tina walked over to where Jerre was sitting on the bench. She looked like she might cloud up and rain at any moment. "Doesn't appear to me that it was a very cheerful reunion, Jerre."

"Oh, just like old times, Tina." Jerre wiped her eyes.

"What do you mean?"

"One or the other turning their back and walking away."

Katzman leaned back, rubbed his eyes, and sighed. He pushed the stack of blowups of the city away from him and looked up at Ben. "I think you're probably right, General. We probably are being monitored by these creeps. But which tower among half a thousand is picking up our signals? As far as that goes, General, they might be utilizing scanners; there might be one right across the damn street, for that matter. The building has only been cleared about halfway up."

Katzman leaned back in his chair and smiled.

"What are you grinning about?" Ben asked.

"Let them keep on monitoring, General. They won't understand what's going on."

"All right, Leo. End the suspense. Why won't they know what's going on?"

His grin broadened. "Because I'll bet you not a damn one of them speak or understand Yiddish."

When Ben stopped laughing, Leo pointed a finger at a young woman. "You. Beth. You're the general's personal radio operator. You stay with him and interpret for him." He looked up at Ben. "That OK with you, General?"

Ben shrugged. "Sure. I'm going to need someone. I damn sure don't speak Yiddish!" He looked at Beth. Very, very nice. This was not going to be hard to take at all.

Then Jerre entered his conscious mind and screwed it all up.

The dark-haired, dark-eyed young woman picked up a backpack radio and buckled in, then picked up her CAR and waited for Ben.

"I'll find some more nice Jewish girls and boys and send them to your CP, General." Katzman said with a grin. "Then we'll have some fun with the night crawlers."

Ben motioned her on out and followed her, his eyes on her derriere. Nope, this was not going to be hard to take at all.

Jerre's blue eyes and smart-aleck smile bullied their way into his mind.

"Leave me alone, damn it!" Ben muttered.

Beth looked around. "Beg pardon, sir?"

"Nothing, Beth. Just muttering to myself. Watch me, though. If I start answering myself, we're in trouble."

She laughed her reply and walked on.

Ben checked in with his CP—located in the park—and found that West and Ike had wandered off somewhere. He did not spot Jerre and was thankful for that. Then he realized that he had heard no gunfire in half an hour or more, and that piqued his curiosity. Stepping out of his CP, he waved a Rebel over and asked him.

"They seemed to have pulled back, General. The last several buildings we've entered show signs of a very hasty bug-out on their part."

"Curious. I wonder what they're up to now?" He cut his eyes as a rusted old limousine turned the corner and stopped at the CP. Ben laughed and looked at the driver. "Where the hell did you find this old thing?"

The driver laughed. "At a funeral home." He indicated the half-dozen people inside the limo. "Katzman told me to bring these folks over. I'm rounding up another bunch later on. Ian and Cecil have several people with them who speak Yiddish. We're going to have to transport some over to West."

"That won't be necessary," Ben told him. "I'm pulling West around to South Street; his men will start working up and inward. Just bring the others here, please."

"Right, General." He dropped the old limo in gear and went chugging and smoking off.

Before the Rebels were through, every vehicle in the city would be torn down and every usable part tagged, catalogued and sent to a stockpile somewhere. The Rebels would leave nothing usable behind, from pins and needles to tractor trailer rigs. If it couldn't be fixed on the spot, they towed it off to where it could be fixed. Name it, and the Rebels had it.

At Base Camp One, and at other outposts Ben was setting up across America, factories and research labs were working around the clock, producing everything from clothing and medicines to better cows and hogs and seed grain.

Ben had munitions factories and tire-recapping plants, producing oil and gasoline refineries, he had labs that worked on weapons of war and labs that worked to better what was left of humanity. His schools did what schools were supposed to do: they taught young minds. Rebel children had a book placed in their hands practically at the moment of birth. There was no illiteracy in any area controlled by the Rebels. Ben would not tolerate it. And Ben was keeping languages alive; it was not uncommon to see small children walking along chatting in French or German or Spanish or whatever.

Ben had reopened several radio stations in outposts and at Base Camp One. He had ordered all TV equipment disassembled and stored. Those who knew Ben doubted the man would ever request that television be reintroduced to what remained of the population. If he did, those close to him knew that the format would be on the order of the old PBS. But that was years down the road—if ever.

But for now, Ben and his troops were facing their greatest challenge, and no one was more aware of the risks involved in that gauntlet-throwing-down than Ben. If the gods of fate and chance and war did not smile upon them, the invasion of New York City might well destroy the Rebel army. But if the Rebels did not take that chance—and they were all aware of it—the Night People would slowly spread and finally devour the nation, literally.

The hideousness had to be stopped. And there

was no one around to do that except for Ben Raines and his Rebels.

No one else.

As Ben watched the translators being assigned to companies, he was reminded of Tennyson's "Charge of the Light Brigade." His Rebels were facing no telling how many thousands of Night People within the city, but also a larger army than theirs bearing down on them from Canada.

Ben Raines was a much-loved and respected man, but he was also a much-despised and feared man among the survivors who had banded together in hordes of outlaw gangs, roaming the country and the cities, raping and murdering and enslaving.

If those gangs ever came together, under one leader? . . . Ben did not like to even consider that thought.

And why had the Night People suddenly and silently pulled back?

Another as yet unanswered question to worry and nibble at him.

He turned his head as Beth began speaking very fast into her handset. Ben couldn't understand a word of it. She ended the conversation and looked at him.

"Katzman. Checking equipment"

Ben nodded, smiled. A germ of an idea had jumped into his head. "Tell him that I'm sending a five-person patrol up Broadway, all the way up to Trinity Church. But before you do that, let me get some spotters in position and we'll see if the creeps understand Yiddish."

She grinned her understanding.

Ben called a Rebel over and told her to get people in position as close to the hot areas as possible and what to look for. She took off at a run.

When Ben had his spotters in place, he told Beth to get in touch with Katzman and to make sure he broadcast the message on several of their most-used frequencies.

Ben and Beth, with the ever-present Jersey and the squad of Rebels Ike had saddled him with, began moving to a vantage point close to the hot area. His bodyguards didn't like it, but Jersey told them they'd better get used to the idea if they were going to follow the general around.

Ben had to smile at that. He heard running bootsteps behind and someone yell to hold up. He turned. Ike and Dan and West.

"I just got wind of your plan, Ben," Ike told him, sliding to a halt. "Thought we'd tag along." He was puffing from his run.

Ben poked him in the belly with a fingertip. "You better start laying off the corn bread and black-eyed peas, Ike. You're getting fat."

"Home cookin', Ben," he grinned. "You ought to try it."

Ben's answer was a very thin smile. Ike realized that he'd hit a sore point and decided to very quickly change the subject. He fished in a pocket of his field jacket and pulled out a tattered book, turning it to a marked page. "Anybody an Episcopal?" he asked, as the group made their way up the trash-filled sidewalk, walking toward Trinity Church. "That's what this church is." When nobody replied, he said, "Me, I was raised up a Southern Baptist. That means I can't cuss or dance or take a drink or make love standing up."

Beth cut her eyes and stifled a laugh. "General Ike, that's dumb! Why can't you make love standing up—if you want to?" she added.

"'Cause someone's liable to see us and think we're dancin'!" Ike laughed.

Ben laughed and held up a hand. "This is as close as we'd better get, people." They were at the corner of Broadway and Exchange. A bob truck had been driven up on the sidewalk, plowing into the building. The Rebels used that for concealment, some kneeling down, some crawling under the rusted old truck.

Ben turned to Beth. "Have Katzman acknowledge that the advance team is now in position inside the church and explosives have been planted in buildings directly across the street."

Inside the gloomy and odious main HQ's of the Night People, located in the old Columbia University complex, far north of the Rebels' current position, radio operators were frantically trying to figure out what language was being aired.

No one knew.

"Get a Judge in here," the request was shouted. "The Hated Ones are speaking in Russian or something."

"It isn't Russian," a Judge informed them, after listening to the radio chatter. "It's the language of those damnable Jews. It's Yiddish."

"Can you understand it?"

"Nobody can understand that gutter garbage. God damn Ben Raines!"

"Alexander Hamilton is buried over yonder," Ike

said, reading from his book. "I'll be damned. Think about that, will you."

"Over where?" he was asked, the question coming from a Rebel under the bob truck.

"Over there in the cemetery of Trinity Church. And Robert Fulton, too. You reckon that's the same fellow who invented the steamboat, Ben?"

"Probably. I seem to recall that he died in New York City. Anybody see any uglies?"

No one had spotted any night crawlers.

"Beth, ask Katzman if he's monitored any chatter from the unfriendlies?"

She spoke briefly, listened, and then smiled. "They can't understand the transmissions, General. They're trying to find someone among them who speaks Yiddish. So far, they have not, and I rather doubt they will. I'd be very surprised to find a Jew joining something that hideous."

"But they might force a Jewish prisoner to translate for them." Ben spoke quietly. "In return for his or her life. Everybody has their breaking point, and no one should condemn anyone else for breaking under torture."

"Yes, sir. There is that," Beth acknowledged.

Ben nodded. "We'll use this method for a time. Ike? How many Native Indians do we have scattered among our troops?"

Ike grinned. "Got a whole passel of Sac and Fox, Ben. I see what you mean. I'll send for them. We'll really confuse these creepies."

He left, Colonel West going with him. Ben's bodyguards were getting antsy about their position, but Ben showed no interest in going back behind safe lines. He had Ike's tourist guide and was reading it when he suddenly smiled broadly.

"What have you found, General?" Dan asked.

"Something we're going to need if we ever go back to a money standard."

"I beg your pardon, sir?"

"Providing, that is, the loot is still there," Ben mused.

"Money standard, sir?" Jersey asked.

"I'm looking ahead, years in the future, Jersey." He turned to Dan. "Ever rob a bank, Dan?"

"Good heavens, no!"

"First time for everything," Ben said dryly.

Chapter 9

Cecil Jefferys and his Rebels had battled their way up 278, after first sealing off the Brooklyn Battery Tunnel. They then proceeded to clear an area two blocks in and all the way up to the Brooklyn Bridge. They now had a mainline into Manhattan.

Cecil turned to his translator. "Get Ben. Ask him if he'd like to buy a bridge."

The radio operator grinned. "Yes, sir!"

Dan had convinced Ben to return to safe lines when the call came in. Dan groaned and rolled his eyes. "We don't have it clear on our side, General," he tried to convince Ben, knowing full well what was coming next from Ben's mouth.

That bounced off Ben. "Get some people, Dan. Let's go see Cecil."

Everything was clear from the plaza to Maiden Lane, but from there it got iffy all the way over to the bridge. And even though it was late afternoon, Ben was adamant.

Dan stomped away, cussing. Most of his Scouts were now attached to other units scattered around various boroughs—all but one. With a sigh, he told his radio person to get in touch with Tina and get her team over to Water and Maiden Lane. On the double.

The distance was short and Tina and her team were at Dan's side in less than two minutes. Dan saw Jerre and silently cursed the gods of Fate.

"What's up, Dan?"

"Your father. Bull-headed person. Cecil has cleared the Brooklyn Bridge. The general wants to go over and meet him. Tell your point people to move out. Take Water all the way over to the bridge. Your team directly behind point. I'll have two staggered squads coming up on either side of the street behind you. Now . . ."

A runner panted up to them. "Sir, the general's taken off, heading for the bridge. Hell, I couldn't stop him!"

"Go Tina. Pass him up and slow him down."

Tina turned to her point people, Pam and Jerre. "You heard it. Move!"

Ben was not surprised when the Jeep roared past him. He had known Dan would send someone to slow him down. What did surprise him was who was in the Jeep.

The Scout Jeep slowed and forced Ben's driver to stop at an intersection. Pam jumped out of the Jeep and walked back to Ben. Jerre crouched down beside the Scout Jeep, her M-16 at the ready.

"Colonel Gray's compliments, General. He asks that you wait for him here."

Ben smiled. "As you wish, Pam."

"Would the general please get out of the Jeep so he will not be so exposed."

Ben looked down at his fly. Jersey and the driver laughed and Pam rolled her eyes.

"Please, sir?"

"Oh, all right." Ben got out and knelt down in the littered street. Beth and Jersey and the driver all vacated the Jeep and knelt down around Ben. It was obvious to Ben that this was something they had worked out in private. They had him completely protected: the Jeep to his left side, Jersey to his right, his driver, Cooper, behind him, and Beth in front of him.

"Has that Plaza over there been cleared?" Ben asked, pointing across the street.

"It's had a quick run-through," Jerre called back to him. "I just came out of briefing."

"Why do you ask, General?" Pam asked. She hoped he didn't have it in his mind to go sight-seeing.

"Because I want to see it, that's why."

Before anyone could make a move to stop him, Ben slipped through the bodyguards and was running across the street.

Speaking before she thought, Jerre called, "Ben! Damn it, Ben, will you stop?"

"Ben?" Cooper asked, looking at Pam and Beth.

The women shrugged.

Jerre left her position and ran after Ben, as he was just disappearing into the plaza at 88 Pine Street. Bullets began ricocheting off the street, just inches behind her boots. Ben reappeared in the entranceway, found the sniper's position and uncorked a full clip from the Thompson. Jerre slipped past him and leaned against the inner wall, catching her breath.

Beth was speaking into her handset, advising that they had come under fire and the general and Jerre were pinned down.

The windows across the way had filled with black-robed creeps, all heavily armed.

"Now we know why they pulled back." Ben said. "It was a sucker play."

"Hell of a way to find out," Jerre replied.

"I thought you liked excitement in your life?"

"I'm older now, Ben."

"Still look nineteen."

"Thank you." She looked around her. "What is this place? It looks weird."

"Something I always wanted to see but never got around to it." Ben spoke over the rattle of gunfire. In the distance, he could hear the roaring of vehicles coming up fast. "That's a two-part sculpture over there. Step through that opening, and unless somebody swiped it, there's a big reflective disc."

"You wanted to come in here and admire your handsome face, maybe?"

"No, I wanted to comb my hair!" Ben popped back at her.

A bullet almost did part his hair, knocking bits of stone out of the entranceway and showering them both with dust.

"Get some damn fifties up here!" Ben shouted across the street.

"Coming, sir!" Pam yelled. "Are you all right?"

"Just ducky!"

"Behind us, Ben!" Jerre shouted, dropping to one knee and leveling her M-16.

Ben turned and added his Thompson's heavy growling to the bark of the .223. "Try not to hit the sculpture!" Ben said, fighting the upward climb of the SMG.

If Jerre said anything in reply it was lost in the gunfire. Two night crawlers made the distance and leaped at Ben and Jerre. Jerre's M-16 chose that time to pump its clip empty. She judged where the creeper's balls might be, under the dark robe, and gave him a shot with the stock of the rifle. The blow doubled him over and put him on the ground, squalling in pain.

The other one landed on Ben, both of them falling to the dirty, littered floor of the entranceway, Ben losing his grip on the Thompson. The night crawler had a hatchet in his hand. Ben grabbed the stinking man's right hand in his left hand, and jerked out his long bladed Bowie, driving it into the man's side. The luck was with him again, the blade sliding between ribs. Ben twisted the blade and again rammed it in to the hilt. The stinking robed figure stiffened as the blade nicked the heart, and then slumped as darkness took him.

Ben pushed him off and jumped to his feet. Jerre was standing over the moaning man with the sore balls. "Kill him!" he ordered.

Jerre looked at him.

"I said kill the son of a bitch, Jerre!"

The entranceway was filled with Rebels, Dan and Tina at the front of the pack.

Still Jerre would not kill the man.

Ben reached down and cut the man's throat with his Bowie knife.

Ben glanced once at Jerre, then stepped out onto the sidewalk.

"Miss Hunter," Dan said, "report back to the depot. I will see that you are reassigned to a noncombative position."

"It was worth all the fighting getting here just to see your ugly face, Cecil." Ben said with a grin, extending his hand.

The men stood on the Brooklyn Bridge. They were both ringed by Rebels.

"You old goat!" Cecil replied, taking the hand. His own smile faded. "I heard you were pinned down. With Jerre."

"We got out," Ben said simply.

"How'd Jerre do?"

"She did all right until it came time to kill an unarmed unfriendly. Then she balked." He shrugged. "It isn't something that everyone can do, Cecil." Damn you, Raines! he cursed his mind. Always defending her, aren't you? "Dan reassigned her."

"There won't be any stigma attached, Ben. A lot of people join the Scouts and don't pan out, then do well in another unit."

Ben nodded absently. He had a hunch that Jerre would not be with the Rebels long. She had never been the type to take public humiliation. "Anyway, I got to see Yu Yu Yang's sculpture in the plaza. But by then it had sort of lost some of its appeal."

"Let's talk while we've still got some light, Ben.

I'll level with you: clearing Brooklyn and Queens is going to be a bitch."

"Yeah? Well, at least you won't have so damned many skyscrapers to climb." He shook his head. "I know it's rough, Cec. Manhattan is not that big, areawise—about twenty-three square miles—and we haven't even begun to make a dent in it. Brooklyn and Queens make up about a hundred and seventy-five square miles. Are there Night People in every building, Cec?"

"Just about. We've learned that they tend to be loners during the day. Seldom more than two or three bunched up together when they sleep. It's at night when they congregate. And they don't eat every day, Ben. Maybe two or three times a week. We learned that much from some rather frantic writing on a wall in a walk-up. The person who wrote it added that he was going to try to make a break for it before they caught him."

"I wonder if he made it?"

"God only knows, Ben. It's sickening and hideous and disgusting and . . ." He spat on the concrete to clear his mouth of the bad taste.

"I know, Cec. I just had one of the stinking uglies on top of me."

"Yes, I can tell," his friend forced a smile with the words. "The odor still lingers."

"I haven't told any of my people—other than the ones who brought him to me—but I've already had one man go down, mentally, under the strain. He's going to be all right. He'll be back on limited duty in a week or so; however, he won't be the last one to take a mental beating."

Cec agreed. "How is your mental state, Ben?"

"I'm fine, Cec. You, me, Ike, Dan, West—most of us older people—we've been through enough of this to be able to steel ourselves."

"I wasn't talking about the combat, Ben."

Ben knew what he was talking about, and chose to ignore it.

"All right, Ben. I'm here if you ever need to talk."

"I appreciate it, Cec. Have you thought about fuel to heat and cook with this winter?" Ben not too tactfully changed the subject.

"Yes. I propose utilizing coal and wood and heating oil. There should be storage tanks full of heating oil close in."

"How many people can you spare to go looking?"

Cec grunted. "Not many. Two squads?" he asked hopefully.

"I'll match that and so will Ike. West is operating short as it is. But holding his own. I'm sending Tina out on a scouting expedition—over to Teterboro Airport. If it's operable, we'll land our birds there. Have you sent anyone over to J.F.K.?"

Cec sighed. "Yeah. Sorry. It slipped my mind. They just got back last night. I sent them in black-faced . . ." He grinned, and the good humor usually within the man touched his eyes for the first time.

Ben laughed at his friend. "You should have sent some of your brothers in, Cec, save all that grease."

"Screw you, Raines! Anyway, they reported back that the place is literally swarming with creepies. The airport seems to be their headquarters for that area."

"Wonderful." Ben's word was bitterly spoken. "Strength estimate?"

Cecil grimaced. "Five hundred or better."

"That might be where some of the breeding or feeding farms are located."

"I hadn't thought of that, Ben. You're right. Shit!" The profanity was very nearly like an anguished scream for strength and courage.

"Cec." Ben put a hand on his old friend's shoulder. "If it's getting to you, man, tell me. Take a break; get some rest. Hell, come over and we'll get drunk if you think that will help."

Cecil met his friend's gaze. "You wanna get slopped with me, Ben?"

"Yeah," Ben said without hesitation. "I do."

"Sounds good to me."

Ben turned to Beth. "Tell Katzman to radio to Cecil's CP. Tell his XO to take command for this evening. General Jefferys will be in my quarters, ah, going over logistical charts."

"Yes, sir!" Beth laughed.

The voices raised in song, the words drifted out to the Rebels within a one-block area of Ben's CP.

"THERE ONCE WAS A QUEER FROM KHARTOUM

"TOOK A LESBIAN UP TO HIS ROOM

"THEY ARGUED ALL NIGHT, AS TO WHO HAD THE RIGHT,

"TO DO WHAT, AND TO WHICH, AND TO WHOM!"

Beth, Jersey, and Tina were sitting on the curb outside the CP. The women shook their heads as the words got rougher.

"What would happen," Beth asked, "if they both get drunker and we come under attack?"

"Don't kid yourself," Tina told her. "I've seen them do this many times. They're not nearly as drunk as they let on. This is just a smaller version of what is called male bonding.

"I've read about that. I hope to be a doctor someday, and in my free time, I'm reading everything I can get my hands on. I just finished a study on men's clubs, both formal and casual. Men felt a much greater need to bond than most women, according to the report."

"Sure. I'll accept that . . . for the most part. From what I've been able to read about it."

Dan Chase came wandering up and passed the women, Chase muttering, "Big ox throws a party and doesn't invite us. By God, we'll just crash it."

"Why are they really doing it, Tina?" Jersey asked.

"Uncle Cec, because he's sickened by what we have to do in dealing with the Night People. This is just a blow-out valve for him. Dad, because probably the only woman he ever truly loved just wandered back into his life."

"Tina," Jersey looked at her. "I froze the first time I was supposed to shoot an unarmed enemy."

"I did, too. But then what happened to us?"

"I got jerked out of combat."

"So did I. Jerre's all right. She held her own in that plaza. Look, it's no crime to wash out of the Scouts.

And I hope she doesn't feel that way. I think Dan was just looking for some excuse to reassign her."

"Colonel Gray should keep his nose out of it," Jersey said, quite uncharacteristically. "Your dad is a grown man."

Beth, being a comparative newcomer this close to the Inner Circle, kept her mouth closed on the subject. But she agreed with Jersey.

Then Tina shocked them both by saying, "I agree. At first I thought Jerre had a lot of gall to show up here. Maybe she still does. But she and Dad have to work this thing out by themselves."

The voices rang out anew:

> "JACK AND JILL WENT UP THE HILL
> "EACH WITH A DOLLAR AND A QUARTER,
> "JILL CAME DOWN WITH TWO AND A HALF,
> "YOU THINK THEY WENT UP FOR WATER?"

Jersey shook her head. "Pitiful."

Chase broke into song about a woman stranded on an island with no men. Only banana trees. That grew large bananas.

"I think it's gonna get rough, girls," Tina said.

"*Get* rough?" Jersey looked at her.

"Oh, you haven't heard anything yet. Wait 'til they start singing about 'Humping in the kitchen and screwing in the hall.'"

Beth cut her eyes. "That's a new one on me. I'm wondering if I really want to hear it."

Tina laughed. "Lie to yourself, baby, if you want

to. But don't try lying to me and Jersey. Hell, yes, you want to hear it."

Beth laughed and shook her head.

"I think we ought to charge admission for this performance," Jersey suggested.

"That's a good thought," Tina agreed. "However, it has one drawback."

"Oh?"

"Yeah. What do we use for money?"

Chapter 10

Ben was up hours before dawn, as usual, with only a slight hangover. He took several aspirin and began to feel human as he worked on his second cup of coffee. Walking into his office—a large room next to what he used as his bedroom—he looked over at Beth, still sleeping on a cot. Being as quiet as he could, he picked up a clipboard and scanned the night's reports. Very little had happened, only a few widely scattered and very brief firefights within the area the Rebels now occupied.

He stepped outside and stood in the very cool early morning air. Winter was very close now. Ben paused, thinking, Has Thanksgiving come and gone? He couldn't remember. Didn't think so. Surely somebody would have remembered it.

No, Ben concluded, Thanksgiving was next week. Have to tell the cooks to have some dressing and pumpkin pie along with whatever type of meat they might serve. A lot of dressing. There were a lot of people up here. And Ben wished he had a couple of thousand more personnel.

He was going to get about five hundred additional people, soon, but not the type that he had in mind.

Tina walked up to him, her form taking shape from out of the darkness. "We're just about ready to pull out, Dad."

"I've added two squads to your contingent, Tina. One from Cecil and one from Ike. That'll give you fifty people. I want you to take mortars and heavy machine guns. I ordered them loaded on trucks last night; also additional Claymores."

"All right. With the additional troops we'll have adequate strength to cope with just about anything we might run up on. Dad, I think Dan was wrong in ordering Jerre to stand down."

"I don't interfere with his handling of his people, Tina. Jerre is going to have to learn that when the orders are given that no prisoners are to be taken, that is exactly what I mean."

"Ian deserted last night, Dad."

Ben sighed. "That means, probably, that Jerre won't be far behind him. I won't try to stop her. You know as well as I do that this is an entirely volunteer army."

Tina looked up at him. "You wouldn't try to stop her, Dad?"

"No. I wouldn't try to stop anybody who wanted to leave this army."

She reached up and kissed his cheek. "Gotta go. See you, Pops."

"Take care, kid."

Tina melted into the darkness. And Ben Raines was once more alone.

* * *

"Friends," Emil Hite spoke to his flock in the darkness of predawn Louisiana. "I have reached a decision. While Ben Raines is not exactly our friend, neither is he our enemy. He has allowed us to live in peace and under the cloak of his protection. He has gone to fight those nasty buggers up in New York City, while we sit here and twiddle our thumbs. That ain't right."

His flock, a strange collection of humanity if ever one had gathered anywhere, all nodded their heads.

"I have spoken with the people remaining at Base Camp One," Emil continued. "They have agreed to look after and school our children. And you have all agreed to that."

Again, his flock murmured low and nodded their heads. Most of that murmuring low was due to the dreadful hour of the day. None of Emil's flock, all followers of the Great God Blomm—another of Emil's scams—ever got out of bed before eight in the morning. And this morning . . . Hell, it wasn't even *dawn* yet.

Emil looked at one of his so-called deacons. "Are we packed and ready to go, Brother Carl?"

"Yes, Father Emil."

"I still think this move is shit-stupid," Brother Matthew muttered. Matthew was one of those followers of Emil who knew the whole thing with Emil was nothing but a great big con. But life was pretty good around Father Emil, so Matthew stayed on.

"Quiet," Emil shushed him.

"I agree with you, Matt," Brother Roger whispered. "But if Emil says we go to New York City to help Ben Raines . . . most of the others will follow."

"I know," Matthew said, disgust in his voice. "But after he pulled off that scam and ran Francis Freneau out of here . . . even Francis proclaimed the little sucker the spiritual leader of all the earth. Look how many new people we've pulled in."

"Well, I guess we're going to New York City."

Emil took a deep breath. "My children, prepare yourselves for a visitation to the pits of Hell. Gird your loins and all that other stuff. And pack up all the damn ammo and bombs that we got in camp."

"A victory dance, Emil!" Sister Susie shouted, then fell into a coughing spell from a tad too much hemp smoking the night before.

"Yes, Emil," Sister Martha cried. "A dance to lift our spirits before we go to the aid of General Raines and face the dreaded Night People."

Emil thought about that. And thought about that. Just as the first fingers of silver began opening up the night, Emil made up his mind. He had been studying a book on ballet and had memorized most of the positions. He hadn't tried any of them yet, but they hadn't looked all that tough.

"Very well, my brave warriors and warrioresses. I shall call this dance the Big Apple."

"Ohh, what an original title!" Young Sister Susie gushed.

Emil lifted one foot slowly and did something that loosely resembled an *en l'air*. Then he executed an attitude and would have looked pretty good had not his robe been so tight. He had to catch himself before he fell on his face. All this drew much applause.

Then he did a *jete* and almost went over the side

of the bed of the bob truck where he was speaking. He hauled up his robes and attempted a fundamental fourth position, complete with *port de bras*. He slowly pirouetted, the hem of his robe puffing up dust. Then with a victory cry, he did a leaping *entrechat*, came down wrong, and did a wild, arm-waving header off the bed of the truck, knocking several of his followers sprawling.

Loud applause echoed around the marshes as Emil picked himself up and bowed several times. Several of his followers picked up the small man and hoisted him to their shoulders.

Emil thrust one arm out, luckily in the right direction, and shouted, "To New York City, brave men and women. We may be few in number but we are strong at heart. Onward, to save Ben Raines!"

"Would you ask Katzman to please repeat that transmission from Base Camp One and be sure he got it right?" Ben asked Beth.

The transmission was repeated. Ben had heard correctly.

"Emil and his flock are on their way up here! To assist *me?* Assist me in doing *what?*"

Beth shrugged. "Don't know, sir. But didn't they hold their own pretty well against those rednecks outside of Base Camp One?"

"These uglies aren't rednecks, Beth. These people can think. But you're right: Emil and his flock did hold their own. Well, if they make it up here, I'll damn sure put them to doing something."

He looked at Beth. "And Joe said they left, the whole bunch of them, before dawn?"

"Yes, sir."

"Well . . . stranger things have happened," Ben muttered. "But offhand I can't think of any." Then something that he'd been told on his way up to the city entered his mind. Then he remembered some bits and pieces. He'd been speaking to a Rebel sergeant at the Chippewa Airport, in Michigan, where they'd been sent on that wild goose hunt. But what had the sergeant said?

Then he recalled the words. "Rumor has it that Monte has one hell of a big detachment somewhere around the New York City area."

He turned to Beth. "Beth, tell our people to hold what they've got. Don't take another step farther. Hold their position. When you've done that, advise Ike and Cecil and West to do the same. I'll see them all today, personally."

"Yes, sir."

He checked his watch and silently cursed. Tina and her bunch had been gone for more than an hour. And they might be driving straight into an ambush.

When Beth had finished, Ben said, "You can't reach Tina with that backpack, Beth, so tell Katzman to reach her—*whatever it takes*—and have her cease advance immediately. Tell her to stand by for orders from me."

"Yes, sir."

"I must be getting senile," Ben muttered, walking to the intersection. But he knew he wasn't; he knew that other things—one other blond-headed thing—

had been very nearly uppermost on his mind. And that was something he was going to have to correct.

He stood on the corner of Wall and Broad, momentarily alone, free of his bodyguards. Everything behind him had been cleared. The air stank from the remnants of the tear gas they'd been using to flush out the creepies, and it was mixed with the eye-smarting smell of gunpowder and the hideous smell of Night People.

Ben stepped out and stood on a manhole cover (to the best of his knowledge, no one had ever gotten around to renaming them person-holes). Impatiently, he stamped his boot on the metal.

He heard as well as felt the returning knock from underground.

"What the hell . . . ?" He muttered. He looked around him. No Rebels in sight.

Ben knelt down and put his ear to the metal. Aside from nearly freezing his ear, the move produced nothing. He did not notice as his bodyguards found him and began moving toward his position, Beth and Jersey with disgusted and aggravated looks on their faces.

"General!" Jersey said. "What in the hell . . . ?"

"Be quiet, Jersey," Ben told her, then smiled at her, softening his order. He pointed toward the manhole. "Somebody is down there."

Ben, using the handle of his knife, began tapping out morse code. . __ __ .... __ __ __ __ · __ · __ · · __ __ __ __ __ · · __?

"Who are you?" Beth whispered to Jersey, who had a confused look on her face.

"Thanks. I never learned that stuff."

The reply came back. . . __ . . __ . . . . __ . __ . .
Friend.

Ben tapped out: Can we meet and talk?

No.

Why not?

Don't trust you.

"Crap!" Ben muttered. He tapped: How long have you lived under the city?

Since many years before the Great War.

Ben looked at Beth, who was looking at him. "You remember a TV program, Beth?"

"Yes, sir. I was just a little girl, but I remember it."

"I remember that program!" a Rebel officer blurted. "That was one of me and my wife's favorites. Are you suggesting . . . ?" He let that trail off.

Ben shrugged. "I've learned that anything is possible."

He tapped: Is there any other way we can talk?

Go to 54.4.

Ben looked at Beth. She shook her head. "Can't do it, General. I'm one hundred to one-fifty-eight."

Ben tapped out: Will be a while. Listen for us.

OK.

He stood up. "It smells like a trap. But it just may be for real, too."

"What now, General?" Jersey asked.

"One of you people get me a radio that can be tuned to 54.4." He looked at his watch. "And get me a sandwich while you're at it. I forgot to eat breakfast."

Ben watched with some amusement as Beth stepped back a few yards and spoke to someone. Within minutes, half a dozen Jeeps and trucks had pulled up, placing a shield around Ben. Rebels had quietly moved into position all around him, on all four corners.

Ben looked at Beth. "Your concern is heartwarming."

The sarcasm bounced off her and she smiled sweetly. "Thank you, sir."

"Nannies." Ben muttered. "I'm surrounded by nannies."

Jersey smiled just as sweetly as had Beth. But still stuck by her general's side.

"All units are holding, sir," Beth informed him. "Generals Ike and Jefferys have been notified and acknowledge transmission."

"What about Tina?"

"Nothing yet, sir."

"By nothing, do you mean she has not responded to Katzman's radio messages?"

"Yes, sir."

"That means she's hit trouble. Radio probably took a round."

Ben stood silent for a moment, uncertain what his next move should be. His brow furrowed in thought. "Beth, tell Katzman to keep trying to reach her. She's on Two-eighty-seven and probably not far inside New Jersey. I got a hunch that unit of Monte's has finally made their move. After you do that, get hold of Dan, tell him to ready a team and stand by."

"Yes, sir. Sir?"

Ben looked at her.

"How large a team?"

"Fifty. And have a couple of Abrams warming up on Staten."

"Yes, sir. And Colonel Gray will be leading this patrol?"

Ben smiled at her. "No, Beth. Colonel Gray will not be leading this patrol."

Jersey stirred and then braced herself for what she knew was coming.

Ben shifted his Thompson from left hand to right. "I shall be leading this patrol."

Chapter 11

Dan argued, but to no avail.

Ben listened, smiled, and continued gathering his gear. "You'll be in charge of this sector, Dan. Make no further advances until you hear from me. I don't know whether Monte's people are inside Manhattan, waiting to spring a trap, or over in New Jersey and have Tina and her bunch pinned down. You'll be the first to know if the latter is the case."

"Yes, sir," the Englishman said, resignation in his tone. He knew to argue further would be pointless. "Of course I shall notify Ike and Cecil."

"You will whether I want you to or not."

"Quite."

"My team ready?"

"Already over on Staten Island, waiting for you."

Ben crossed the Brooklyn Bridge and picked up 278. Ike was standing by the side of the road, at the intersection of 278 and Prospect Expressway, waving frantically for Ben to stop.

Ben returned the wave, smiled, and barreled on past him. He laughed as he watched Ike jerk off his beret and throw it to the ground. The stocky ex-SEAL began jumping up and down in frustration. But he didn't try to make radio contact with Ben. He had left his translator behind him in his dash to intercept Ben.

Dan had prevailed in one area: he had convinced Ben to leave his Jeep and take a Chevy Blazer. Ben had to admit it was more comfortable and secure.

Ben had already told his people to split at the loop; Ben would take Shore Parkway, and they'd rejoin at the bridge.

There was no sign of Tina. The Rebels guarding the Verrazano-Narrows Bridge told him that Tina's plan had been to cut off at Richmond Avenue and take the expressway down to 440. From there she'd pick up 287.

Ben thanked her and drove on, his speed now cut back due to the Abrams tanks that had joined the column from the main depot on the island.

As they crossed over into New Jersey, Ben broke radio silence for the first time. "Heads up, people. Moving into bogie country." He told Cooper to reduce speed and then rolled down his window, trying to catch the sounds of gunfire. He could hear nothing. Again, he lifted the mike. "Point report."

"Nothing, sir."

"Close to five hundred meters and maintain distance, Point."

"Yes, sir."

He looked around to the rear seat. Beth was listening to a walkie-talkie, the short antenna stuck out the window. "Got them, sir!" she shouted. "Eagle to Scout, Eagle to Scout, come in."

Tina cut her eyes to Ham and grinned. "Dad's on his way. You owe me a million dollars."

"Pay you the first bank we come to," Ham said, grinning.

Tina turned her head, meeting the eyes of Jerre. "You know of course, that both our butts are gonna be in a sling when Dad gets here?"

"I told you it was foolish taking me along."

Tina lifted her walkie-talkie. "Scout to Eagle. We're pinned down off the interstate. Interstate blocked at Ten. Take highway Twenty-two. We're pinned down south side of highway. Large force. Maybe four to five hundred, we guesstimate."

Beth relayed that information to Ben. "Ask them how secure is their position?"

"They're fighting inside an old farm complex, General," Beth said. "Stone fences. They're secure unless the enemy has mortars or tries a mass attack."

Ben lifted his mike. "You monitoring all this, Point?"

"Ten-four, General."

"We're pulling over and holding. Check it out."

"Yes, sir."

Only a few moments passed before the point team radioed back. "Scout team is completely surrounded, General. A few ridges, then flat ground where they're trapped. The fire is heavy so I doubt the bogies will hear our tanks coming in. You're still about five miles from battle site."

"Ten-four. Hold what you have and prepare coordinates for shelling." Ben walked back to the tanks. "Move them up to here," he pointed to a map. "And get ready for sustained shelling."

The tank commanders nodded and clanked

their Abrams forward. The 105mm M-68 guns were effective up to about 3300 meters.

"Eagle to Scout," Ben radioed.

"Come in, Eagle," Tina told him.

"Moving Abrams up. We'll fire short and then you call them in, kid."

"Ten-four, Pops."

Ben again lifted the mike. "We're moving out, people. Doing it slow and going in cold. Bear this in mind: these bogies are aligned with the Night People. They're the ones kidnapping human beings for the feeding and breeding farms. That should tell you all you need to know about them. No quarter, no pity, no prisoners. Move out."

A few minutes edged by as the short column inched their way up the road. They could all now clearly hear the sounds of battle. By now the tanks would be in position.

Ben ordered his column halted behind the positioned tanks and dismounted his people. He ran up a slight ridge, Beth and Jersey and Cooper with him, and knelt down.

Ben pointed out various spots in the terrain. "Cooper, I want machine guns in those three places. The rest of the personnel spread out between. So advise the squad leaders. Move!"

Cooper ran down the ridge. Ben lifted his field glasses and studied his daughter's situation. "Not too bad," he commented. "Could be a hell of a lot worse."

"Tank commanders report they are ready to fire for range, sir," Beth relayed.

Ben looked at the machine gunners, rushing to get

in place. "Tell the tanks one minute then fire for range. Tina will act as FO."

"Yes, sir."

"And, Beth?"

"Sir?"

"Tell them not to blow up my kid, will you?"

"Yes, sir!" she grinned.

The seconds ticked past. Ben knew his gunners well; had watched them train many times, and knew the almost pinpoint accuracy of them. Their 'fire for range' shots would probably land extremely close to the line of bogies.

The 105's roared and both shells landed just behind the line of dug-in troops. Tina called in corrections and the 105's began pounding. The warlord's troops tried to use mortars. But the light mortars they had did not have the range to reach the tanks or the machine gunners.

"Why hadn't they used those mortars before?" Beth questioned.

"They were trying to take my people prisoner," Ben growled. "To give to the damn night creepies. Now I'm gettin' mad!" To Beth: "Tell Tina to keep her head down. We're coming in. And cancel my orders about prisoners. I want to talk to some of those outlaws."

Ben lifted his own walkie-talkie. "Get that Big Thumper humping, damn it!"

The Big Thumper was a 40mm grenade-launching machine gun, a heavy sucker weighing almost a hundred pounds when ground-employed with tripod. But its kill radius was almost one hundred percent in a ten-yard area, and its rate of fire was awesome.

"Big Thumper in position on the west side of Tina's location, sir!" Ben was informed.

"Get it humping, son."

"Yes, sir!"

The 40mm began adding its noise to the crash of the 105's and the heavy chugging of the .50's.

"Some of them trying to run, General!" Jersey called.

"Order the snipers to try for leg shots, Beth," Ben told her. "Tell the Abrams to cease firing 105's. All troops up on the line and let's see if the outlaws want to slug it out."

They didn't.

Most of them, dazed and disoriented from the heavy pounding, seemed too confused to really understand what had happened to them. Most had never been under attack from any heavily armed and disciplined force of troops; they were accustomed to attacking small settlements of people who, strangely enough—but not to Ben's mind— still operated against an enemy with some degree of civility and compassion.

Ben Raines was not burdened with any such illusions. Never had been.

"Thumper cease firing. Fifties cease firing." Ben lifted his walkie-talkie. "Over the walls, Tina. We're coming in from both sides and down the middle. Go, people, go!"

Ben squatted on the ridge, looking through field glasses, watching the short and very deadly battle unfold before him. Tina's Scouts, already extremely irritated at being ambushed and pinned down like a bunch of amateurs, came over the stone walls growling, eager to mix it up hand to hand.

To the east of the farm complex, Ben could see that several of his people had already rounded up about a dozen of the bogies and had them lying facedown on the ground. He turned to Beth.

"Radio Katzman, in Yiddish, to have a psychological interrogation team readied."

"Yes, sir."

"Ah, sir?" Jersey said.

Ben picked up on a strange note in her voice. "Yes, Jersey?"

"Miss Hunter's down there."

Ben leaned against a stone fence, smoking a hand-rolled cigarette—he allowed himself about four or five a day—and listening to his daughter's report.

"The way I see it, Dad, they must have intercepted some radio communications, and that gave them the time to get in place and dig in so effectively."

"Why is Jerre here?"

"After considering that possibility, I don't feel so badly about getting hit. I do feel bad about losing two people and having several more out with wounds."

"Why is Jerre here?"

"Did you bring equipment to resupply us or will we have to return to the depot?"

"Why is Jerre here, Tina?"

"Do you have replacements for us with you, Dad?"

"Tina, why is Jerre here?"

"If we could take off now, we could easily get way to hell and gone up the road, Dad."

"Damn it, girl, will you kindly answer my question!"

Tina shifted from one boot to another.

"Do you have to go to the bathroom, Tina?"

"No, I don't have to go to the bathroom!" she fired back. "Jerre is here because she isn't a coward like Dan would have you think."

"Dan never said she was a coward, Tina. And I don't think she is, either. But you know as well as I that we have many people within the Rebel ranks who could not and would not shoot an unarmed person. But they are not front-line combat troops." He frowned. "I don't like her," *I just love her,* "but I don't think Jerre is a coward."

Tina blinked. "Now, what the hell does that mean, Dad? You're in *love* with her!"

"I may be. But that doesn't mean I have to like her. Which I don't. She's a con artist."

Tina's mouth dropped open as she stared at her father. "And you're not?"

"I beg your pardon, girl!"

"You have four thousand people fighting and willing to die for you, Dad. You've got no telling how many thousands of people out there," she waved her hand toward the war-torn vastness of America, "who *worship* you! Many of them think you're a god! Granted, Dad, you use people for, or toward, a much more noble cause, or objective, than she. But that's just semantics."

Ben grunted. "Are you quite through lecturing me, Tina?"

"No, I'm not."

"I was afraid of that."

The other Rebels were staying far away from the father and daughter by the fence.

Tina stuck a finger in Ben's face. Ben drew back, startled at the move. "And let me tell you something else, *General:* you've got your butt up in the air because you've been carrying a torch around for years, and the only reason you're angry is because she doesn't share your feelings!"

"Bullshit!"

"Well, then . . . what is it?"

"It's, ah . . . none of your business. That's what it is."

"Personally, Dad, I like Jerre."

"That is your prerogative."

"And I'll call for a review board if I have to; but she stays in my team."

Ben stared hard at her, then slowly nodded his head. "Tina, putting my feelings aside, listen to me: OK, you can keep her in your team. But don't lean too heavily on her. There are people in this world who *wish*, and there are people who *do*—you talk with her and then make up your own mind as to which category Jerre falls into."

"But you'd take her even though you think she's a quitter, wouldn't you, Dad?"

Ben walked away from the fence, toward his Blazer. He passed Jerre. He stopped and walked back to her. "Tina believes in you, Jerre. But I know you. You get my daughter killed, and I'll track you through Hell to personally cut your throat. Believe it, kid."

* * *

"Any word from the interrogation teams?" Ben asked.

"Too soon, General," he was told. "Be a few more hours at best."

"Keep me informed." Ben walked to his Blazer and told Cooper to take him to the new lines. Since they now knew that Monte's detachment was not in the city (most of them were dead, stiffening and bloating in New Jersey), Ben, on the way back from the rescue mission, had ordered the search-and-destroy operations to resume.

The Rebels, on the south end, had now cleared everything up to Liberty Street. Colonel West's people had pushed in from the shoreline, and the Colonel was now looking at and contemplating the enormity of clearing the Chase Manhattan Bank Building: sixty-five stories aboveground and five stories belowground. It was the belowground area that he knew was going to be grim. They were going to have to pump it full of tear gas and shoot the bastards as they made a run for it.

All in all, West mentally summed it up, it was not going to be a pleasant operation.

And he and his men sighed with relief when Ben told them it could damn well wait until tomorrow.

"Stand down," Ben told his people, just a few moments before the first lines of darkness began streaking the city, signaling the approach of night. He returned to his CP, now moved up several blocks on Broadway, and sat down behind his desk.

So far, their push up Manhattan had not been terribly spectacular. They had advanced about 1500 meters.

Only about 25,000 meters to go, and that was just counting one way: north. The island broadened out the farther up they went, until reaching its widest point, about 5,000 meters, just a few blocks from where the Rebels now clung precariously to their tiny few blocks.

Five thousand meters didn't sound like much to anyone who had never stood in the middle of Manhattan. To those who had, the immenseness of it was awesome.

Sighing, he poured a cup of coffee and then remembered that he'd forgotten to ask Jerre about Ian. The simpleminded jerk. There was no way he could get clear of Manhattan. All the escape routes were carefully guarded. Of course, Ben mused, he might find a boat and row across the Hudson or the East River; but Ben doubted that.

He picked up the files on Ian and Jerre and scanned them quickly. Ian had just made it through Scout training. Very marginal. Jerre, on the other hand, had done quite well. That really didn't surprise Ben, for he knew she could do just about anything she set her mind to. Sticking to it was another matter.

He tossed the files to his desk. Jerre was Tina's problem now. Ian could go to hell.

Ian would pop up again, scared and hungry. If he didn't, then it would have to be assumed the Night People had grabbed him.

Jersey and Beth entered his office, with three mess trays of hot food. Jersey plopped one down on Ben's desk. Ben looked at it. He could recognize potatoes and green beans and a piece of pie. He did not know what the meat might be. He asked Jersey.

"I don't know, General. It's some sort of processed stuff the lab came up with."

"It's not too bad if you put lots of hot sauce on it," Beth said. "Kills the taste."

Ben picked up his fork and looked at the gravy-covered inert slab of whatever on his tray. "Pass the hot sauce, please."

Chapter 12

Ben's eyes popped open. He felt rested, wide awake, and ready to go. He looked at his watch on the nightstand before buckling it around his wrist. Three-thirty. He dressed quietly and then slipped into his boots, blousing his field pants. Buckling into his battle harness, he picked up his Thompson, knew from the feel of it the drum was full, and stepped out into his office.

Beth and Jersey were sleeping soundly on their cots, air mattresses softening the canvas of the cots. Very pretty ladies, Ben observed. And should be very desirable. But the sleeping beauties produced no feelings of sexual arousal within him. Jerre had a habit of doing that to him, he recalled. Just her memory could produce the same effect as a cold shower in December.

When he held some other woman up to her, that is. And it wasn't that Jerre was so beautiful. She wasn't, not in the classical sense. She was just . . . It was just . . . love.

"Screw it!" Ben muttered, jerked open the door and stepped outside.

He almost scared the sentry out of his boots.

"Easy, son." Ben told him. "Settle down."

The young man grinned, embarrassed. "Sorry, sir. It's kind of a jumpy night."

"And cold, too," Ben added. "You want some coffee, son?"

"That sure would be nice."

"I'll stand your post. You go to the mess and bring us back some."

"Sir!"

"Go on. I'll stand your watch. Put a little sugar in my coffee. No cream. And I'd like to have a garlic bagel, too."

The young man stared at him.

"Just kidding, son. Did you have to stand outside my door all damn night?"

"I came on at midnight, sir. My relief will be here at four."

"What's your name?"

"Carson, sir."

"I assume there is no password?"

"No, sir. But there's a bunch of creepies out there. Problem is, you can't get a clear shot at any of the jerks."

"Take off. Stretch your legs and get back here."

"Yes, sir."

Ben stepped back into the darkness of the stoop. Neither time nor age nor circumstances had dulled his enjoyment of the early predawn hours. It was, to Ben, the best time of the day, although certainly not everyone shared that opinion. Ben enjoyed watching the world come alive after a period of rest. But, he cautioned himself, in this city, while one segment rested, another much more deadly species came out of their dank and stinking hovels.

A quick flash of dark movement caught his attention. He knelt down, the Thompson coming up, Ben easing the SMG off safety. There it was again. But what was it? He looked left, then right. Carson had rounded the corner, heading for the mess. Ben could see no other Rebels, although he knew he was not the only sentry on duty.

He remained motionless, squatting in the darkness. His vision was still excellent at a distance, although he had, of late, been forced to wear glasses when doing extended close-up work. Whatever it was skulking across the street was laying low. Waiting. But for what?

The click of metal against stone faintly reached Ben's ears.

A gust of wind came whipping and spinning coldly down the stone and steel and rubble-littered trails of the city, picking up bits of trash and winding them up like a top before hurling the debris in all directions as the wind devil lost power.

But the slight noise of the wind was enough for the hidden person across the street to make his move. Their move, Ben corrected, as three shapes darted from the darkness, their robes flapping, heading for his position.

They never made it. Ben leveled his Thompson, and the SMG began chugging out .45-caliber justice, the big slugs knocking the creepies sprawling. But one had been carrying something, Ben was sure.

That one got to his feet. Ben could see the suit-case-like object.

Rebels began running toward the sounds of action.

"Get down!" Ben shouted. "Get your butts down! Satchel charge!"

He pulled the trigger back and held it back. The entire street seemed to mushroom into blazing balls of light and fury. Ben was knocked back against the door, hard into the door, and then through the door, rolling and tumbling into his outer office.

The tinkle of falling glass and the thudding of larger objects torn loose, slung into the air, and re-turning back, smoking and ruined, came to him faintly. His hearing had been momentarily dulled by the tremendous explosion and his vision im-paired by the sudden flash.

He got to his knees, still holding onto the Thomp-son, and looked around him. The hastily boarded-up windows to his office—done the day before by Rebels—had been shattered, blown completely out. His office was a wreck. Jersey was on the floor, the cot on top of her, with her turning the air pink with cussing, so Ben assumed she was fine. He looked around for Beth. Found her standing up in a corner, clad only in very skimpy bra and panties. Ben grinned at her.

"Now that is a very nice way to greet the morn-ing, Beth." His voice sounded as though it was coming from the bottom of a water bucket. "Thank you?"

She finally realized what he was talking about,

yelped, and grabbed up a blanket. Jersey flung back the cot and sat up, wild-eyed.

"What the hell happened, General?"

"Satchel charge, Jersey. You ladies get some clothes on. Lovely as you both are, if we start romancing now we're going to draw a crowd."

He got up and stepped outside. What a mess. Windows blown out all over the place. His boots crunching tiny shards of glass littering the ground, he walked to the knot of Rebels gathering in the middle of the street.

"You all right, General?"

"Oh, yeah. There were three or four of them. I'm not sure. Jesus. There must have been fifty or sixty pounds of C-four or five to make this big a bang."

"Lemme through, damn it!" a voice shouted, a man shoving his way through the crowd. Carson. He looked at Ben. "Are you OK, General?"

"Sure." Ben smiled. "But you forgot the coffee."

There was not even a greasy spot left of the man who had carried the satchel charge. And of the others, they had been spattered all over the place.

Ben had looked up at the sky. No stars. And the air was wet as well as cold. "It's going to rain anyway. No point in us wasting our time scraping them off the buildings. Let Mother Nature do it. Let's go get some breakfast."

In the building that was serving as a mess hall, Ben ran into one of Chase's doctors and waved him over. "What's the word on those prisoners we brought in yesterday?"

"No help at all, sir. It appears that only Monte and maybe a couple of his closest people know anything at all about the Night People." He hesitated. "What do you want us to do with them?"

"Turn them over to Dan Gray." The doctor seemed relieved to hear that. His jaw dropped when Ben added, "We'll try them for crimes against humanity and then shoot them."

Ben buttered a piece of bread and resumed eating, leaving the doctor sitting, staring at him from across the table. Ben looked up. "Pass the salt and pepper, would you, Doc?"

The rain was coming down in cold silver slashes when Ben stepped out of the mess hall. He was glad he had returned to his shattered office and rummaged around until he could find his poncho. He looked at Beth, standing beside him, the radio a covered hump on her back. He grinned at her.

She knew what he was grinning about and blushed.

"Come on. I want to see Trinity Church since it's been cleared."

"Do we drive or walk?" Jersey asked.

"Walk."

"That figures," she muttered, dutifully trudging along beside Ben.

Ben laughed at her. "You'd have made a greater character to add to Willie and Joe, Jersey."

"Yes, sir. Whatever you say, sir." Mentally adding, Whoever in the hell they are.

They slogged along toward Broadway, with Ben stopping at every little shop and store, peering in, the expression on his face that of a little kid looking into a toy shop.

"How come," Jersey asked, "we haven't really seen much signs of looting, General?"

They walked on. "I don't know, Jersey. It's puzzling to me, too."

"Nothing down here to loot, you ask me," Beth said. "What was this place, General?"

"The financial hub of the world, ladies. From Whitehall over to Wall and up to Cortland. Billions and billions of dollars, in currency and stock representing all nations, were traded and bought and exchanged here in this area every day. Monday through Friday," he added.

"I don't remember much about anything before the war," Jersey admitted. "Just bits and pieces. Maybe I just don't want to remember."

"Hell of a lot of things I'd like to forget myself," Ben told them.

They ran across the street and into Trinity Church, Ben, Beth, Jersey, and Ben's ever-present squad of bodyguards.

Ben glanced at Beth. "This OK with you?"

"Doesn't make any difference to me, General. My mother and father were not practicing Jews."

They stepped inside and Jersey cried out in dismay, automatically crossing herself.

"I didn't know you were of the faith, Jersey." Ben cut his eyes at her.

"I was raised a Catholic. Doesn't make any difference. Just *look* at this mess. And I bet it was once so beautiful."

The interior had been vandalized and slashed and ruined. Profanity had been spray-painted all over the walls. The place stank of the odor of Night People.

"Anybody who would do this to a church ought to be hung up by their balls!" Jersey said, considerable heat in the statement.

Several of the Rebels sat down in pews and bowed their heads, praying softly.

Ben walked up the aisle. "Well, Jersey, some people blamed God for what happened to the world. The Great War. They did, and are doing, some pretty terrible things."

"You think God had anything to do with the war, General?"

"I don't know. I'll ask Him if I ever see Him. But personally, I doubt if He did. I think He just let humankind screw it all up on their own." He shrugged, drops of water dribbling from his poncho onto the dirty floor. "But that's just one man's opinion."

"I don't wanna go into no more churches, General," Jersey said, tears in her eyes and running down her face. "Let somebody else do it."

"All right, Jersey." Ben patted her shoulder. "If you don't want to, you don't have to. Let's get out of here."

By ten o'clock that morning, the temperature had turned around, dropping, and the steady rain was mixed with bits of sleet. West and his people were battling up the Chase Manhattan Building, and it was slow going, as well as gruesome. Bits and pieces of human bodies littered each floor. West guessed that some of the bones were a year or two old, while others had been stripped of flesh only days before.

By midmorning they had battled their way up to the eighteenth floor. Then Ben gave the welcome orders. "Seal it off, Colonel. Weld the doors shut wherever possible and build barricades for any others. Let's concentrate on the basement floors."

The lower floors had been saved for last, all knowing that they would be the worst.

Ben had not forgotten the people under the streets of Manhattan. He simply had not had time to try and contact them.

Construction Rebels went to work sealing off the eighteenth floor. "Let the bastards eat each other," Ben was heard to mutter.

There had been no sign of Ian. Tina had reported in, saying the roads were getting terrible and she was still some miles from the Teterboro Airport. Ben told her to pack it in and wait until tomorrow. It was still early in the season for this kind of weather to last long.

The day was wet and cold and gloomy.

"Look at them, looking at us," Jersey said, her face uplifted to the center of the bank building.

Ben looked up. He could see a few black-robed figures staring down at them from what was going to be their tomb.

"Order gas masks on, Beth. Everybody get into position. Are the hoses in place?"

"Yes, sir."

"Start the trucks."

Ben had hooked into the building's ventilation system, running hoses from the exhaust of the trucks and Jeeps and Hummers. Once the carbon monoxide started filling up the bottom floors, it would not be long.

The rain and the cold dulled the gunfire and the senses, for it was an awful job, even for the most hardened of Rebels. The Night People began trickling out, coughing and screaming their hatred until gunfire silenced them forever.

Doctor Chase had come to stand beside Ben across the street from the carnage, protected somewhat from the rain by an awning.

"Why," Chase asked, his voice just audible over the driving drops of rain and sleet and the cracking of gunfire.

"Why . . . what, Lamar?" Even though Ben knew perfectly well what his old friend was talking about.

"What turned them into this manner of . . . creature? What did it to them? I've got to have some alive, Ben. For the sake of history a hundred years from now—and you above all should understand that—I've got to talk with at least some of them."

Ben sighed. "All right, Lamar. But answer me this: What are you going to do with them when you've finished your . . . conversations?"

Lamar picked up on the sarcasm in Ben's tone. "You let me worry about that, Raines!"

"No. We'll worry about that *now*, Chase."

"You want an honest answer or a lie?"

"I would prefer an honest answer."

"I don't know."

"I was afraid you'd say that. You have a yearning to play Doctor Schweitzer in your advancing years, Lamar?"

"Screw you, Raines!"

Ben looked at Dan and West. "What do you people have to say about it?"

West shrugged his total indifference and Dan said, "If you want some alive, General, we'll take some."

Ben instructed Beth to radio the orders to take some of the night crawlies alive for observation and study.

"Anything else, Doctor Chase?" Ben asked.

"One of my doctors came to me this morning. He was very upset about the fate of the prisoners you brought in for interrogation."

"I'm sure he was." Ben's return was a complete opposite of the weather.

They stood in silence for a moment, rain shrouding the dreary gray of the captive city.

"Well?" Chase demanded.

"Well . . . what?" Ben looked at him.

"The prisoners, Raines. The damn prisoners. You know perfectly well what I'm talking about. What about the prisoners?"

"Hell, I don't know. That's not my department. I called for a military tribunal to convene. That's all I know about it."

Chase wore a disgusted look on his face. "Then who do I ask?"

"Try Dan."

"Well, Gray?" The doctor glared at the Englishman. "What about it?"

"I was the presiding judge," Dan admitted.

"When?"

"This morning."

"It must have been a damn short trial."

"It didn't take long."

"And the verdict?" Chase's words were bitter. He'd already reached a conclusion about that.

"Guilty of numerous heinous crimes against humanity. They admitted it."

"And their punishment?"

Dan Gray looked at the doctor and put an end to the conversation. "They were hanged several hours ago."

Chapter 13

Another block had been cleared; another building—at least up to the eighteenth floor—had been secured for the future generations.

There was only one way for those trapped to escape: they could try to climb down, using ropes, and be shot by Rebels assigned to the area for just that purpose, or they could jump.

It didn't make a damn bit of difference to Ben.

After the carnage at the bank building, Ben called a halt to the day's search and destroy and told his people to knock off.

Then he couldn't find where his office had been relocated.

He opened his mouth to start cussing. Jersey touched him on the arm. "Follow me, General. It's been moved one street over."

After a very quick bath, in cold water, Ben shaved, dressed in clean, warm clothing, and ate a meager supper. Like most in his command, his appetite had been dulled by the hideousness of the day's work.

His office had been moved to the second floor of

a building for security. It had no windows—which irritated Ben—and was located in the center of the second floor.

He opened his mouth to bitch about it, then closed his trap, knowing it was not the fault of Jersey or Beth. Ike had trapped him again. Probably with the help of Cecil and Dan and West.

He looked around him. The office had, at one time, been quite a nice setup. Some upper-management hotshot, Ben figured. He picked up the phone and muttered, "Think I'll buy a million shares of AT and T."

He jerked in surprise when a man said, "Can I help you, General?"

"Who the hell is this?"

The man chuckled. "Shepherd, sir. We got the phones working to a few areas late this afternoon. We can now patch you through direct to the other CP's."

"Are they secure?"

"Yes, sir. Scrambled at both ends."

"Good work. Get me Ike, will you?"

"Right away, sir. You want General Jefferys on the line as well?"

"Can you do that?"

"No problem. Hang on, sir."

Within a few seconds, Ike came on the horn. "Ben? How's it lookin' over your way?"

"Grim. But slow and steady. Cec?"

"About the same, Ben. But I'm thinking the main body of these creepies is going to be found in your sector. We've discovered that there are different tribes of them. I was going to send a runner over to you with that information. Then I was informed about twenty minutes ago that some lines were open. I was just about to call you."

"Tribes?" Ike asked, before Ben could.

"Right. I've extended my sector over to Brooklyn College—or what's left of it. Part of it has been used as a CP and a force-feeding farm." He sighed deeply and audibly.

"What's wrong, Cec?" Ben asked.

"We found some survivors here, Ben. But they're broken people. Mentally mostly. God knows, you can't blame them for breaking under the strain. I've been sitting here for over an hour trying to write out a report for you to read. It's, well, mind-boggling."

"Cec, get some rest. I'll be over with Chase in the morning. Give me a secure route."

"It's best if I have a contingent meet you at the bridge, Ben. They'll escort you in."

"I'll meet your people at the bridge at eight in the morning, Cec."

"Good enough, Ben. I'll see you then."

Both Ben and Ike heard him click off.

"Must be bad over there, Ben."

"Yeah. How's it with you?"

"Not bad. We hit pockets of them, but like Cec, I agree that you and yours have the funkiest job."

Ben told him about those people living under the streets of New York City.

Ike grunted. "That doesn't surprise me, Ben. I learned a long time ago not to be surprised about anything taking place in New York City. What do you intend doing about it?"

"Try to talk with them. If they're friendly, we need all the help we can get."

"Ben . . . I can't speak for you or Cec, but for me and mine, it's too easy. We're just coasting over here. I've taken no casualties. None. One guy fell out of a truck and broke his ankle. But that's it. I got a real bad feeling about this."

"How so?"

"Well . . . it's kinda like you go into a bar and all of a sudden the best-looking woman in the place starts coming on to you. If you look like me, you'll start to figure that you're being set up for something. You know what I mean?"

"Yeah. I sure do. But what are we being set up for?"

"I don't know, Ben. But me and Cec talked about this thing. He feels the same way."

"And you think we should do . . . what?"

"I don't know. Think about it and be careful, I reckon."

"All right, Ike. Talk to you later. Hang in." He broke the connection.

Ben turned to look out the window, then realized, again, that he didn't have a damn window. He got up and slipped into his field jacket and picked up his poncho.

"You won't need that, sir," Jersey told him, standing in the door to his office. "It's stopped raining."

Ben tossed the poncho to a chair.

"While you were on the phone, Katzman radioed. He's picked up signals from Monte and his main group. They're definitely heading for this city."

She paused.

"And . . . ?" Ben prompted.

"The warlord has picked up more people. Some guy who calls himself the Colonel."

"Colonel what?"

"Just the Colonel, sir."

"What else is going to happen on this operation?" Ben asked, not really expecting Jersey to reply. He glanced at his watch. "Get some sleep, Jersey. We meet with Cecil tomorrow at oh-eight-hundred. And what we're going to view is not going to be pleasant. Contact Doctor Chase and advise him to be ready to leave with us. Colonel Gray will be in charge during my absence."

"Yes, sir. What we're going to see tomorrow—is it going to be any worse than what we saw today?"

"Probably."

That was putting it mildly.

Even the usually much self-controlled Ben Raines was shocked at the sight.

The people that Cecil had rescued—and he said that most had been naked, or at best, dressed in rags—huddled together in a far corner of the gym where Cecil had transported them. They looked like zombies, and didn't behave much better.

Chase and his medical team moved to them immediately, while Ben stood with Cecil and talked.

"What's the matter with them, Cecil?"

His friend hesitated.

"Come on, Cec."

"Most of the men have been castrated. Those that will talk at all say it wasn't done immediately upon arrival. But done much later—after their, ah, entertainment value had waned, or whatever. And done because they were, for some reason we have not yet been able to fathom, unsuitable for breeding purposes. All of the women and many of the men have been sexually molested by Monte and his people. The Night People have also had their way with many of them, forcing them to perform . . . rather perverted acts for the enjoyment of these so-called Judges and others. Then the men were castrated and put in here to fatten for food."

When Ben found his voice, he said, "I have to agree with Lamar on at least one thing, Cec: the *why* of it all?"

"I can give you a theory."

"All right."

"The hard core of the Night People were perverted before the war. But their, ah, unusual sexual appetites were, for the most part, kept in check by the law. After the war, a few got together, those few each knew a few more, and so forth. They have a fine communications network, Ben, and this thing is nationwide. We had already guessed that. But I think the hard core live here in the city."

"And if we wipe them out . . . ?"

"We might be able to break their backs." But he sounded very dubious. Ben didn't immediately pursue it.

"So all this crap about disfigurement from the bombings and radiation poisoning and so forth is just garbage."

"Yeah. Just like the crap that Hilton Logan put out about the entire Northeast Corridor being off-limits due to direct nuclear strikes. Ben, you want to hear another theory?"

"Might as well."

"I think it's global."

Ben narrowed his eyes and stared long at his friend. "You think *what* is global, Cec?"

Cecil met Ben's eyes. "The Night People. That's why we have never—*never*—in all the years we've been monitoring radio traffic, been able to pick up chatter outside the forty-eight contiguous states and Canada."

Ben digested that bit of theory. Looked again at Cecil. "Go on."

"Now granted, some nukes did fall. But as many as we were led to believe? I don't think so, Ben. I don't think Hawaii got hit. I think Hawaii is anything but a paradise now. Think back, Ben. Those papers we got off of that dead courier from Khamsin's bunch. We misread those papers, Ben. When Khamsin's bunch landed in South America, Khamsin himself, a butcher if there ever was one, said the area had reverted to barbarism. And they left. What in God's name could be too barbaric for a creature like Khamsin?"

"And they found willing recruits in all the places they landed," Ben spoke the words quietly. "Sure. Hell, I'd join Khamsin to get clear of these creepies!"

"So would any even semi-normal person."

Chase rejoined them. The man was trembling with rage. "Disgusting, Ben. Perverted and hideous and . . ." His anger choked off the rest.

"Lamar, I want a psychological team to start work immediately on those prisoners Dan got for you yesterday. I want their brains picked clean. And I don't give a damn what conditions they're in afterward."

Lamar nodded. "What shall we do with those

poor . . . wretches?" He cut his eyes to the huddled survivors.

"Get them out of here and over to Staten Island. From there, we'll ship them back to Base Camp One and try to do something with them. Lamar, is there anything that can be done with them?"

The man sighed heavily. "Yeah. Probably. Their spirits have been broken, Ben. They've been beaten down to nothing mentally. Living in a state of sheer, utter, mind-numbing fright for months and with some, even years. Tortured, sexually molested . . . and other things so vile it makes me want to puke!"

"Did all of these people come from outside the city?" Ben asked.

"No," Lamar said. "As a matter of fact, about half of them claim to be native New Yorkers."

"So there are pockets of survivors within the city. Just like we guessed."

"There have to be," Lamar replied.

Ben could see that the man's mind was not on the conversation, but rather on the people he had just spoken with, still huddled together at the far end of the room.

"Go on, Lamar," Ben urged the man of medicine. "Take them back to a safe locale and see what you can do with them until I can arrange transport."

Ben and Cecil watched as Lamar and his team gently herded the badly frightened men and women out of the room and into waiting vehicles which Cecil had arranged for.

"Pitiful," Jersey summed it all up.

* * *

Ben sat on the edge of his desk and looked at his commanders: Cecil, Ike, Dan, West, Chase, and a few more of his upper-level personnel, including Katzman. "That's it, people. That's Cecil's theory, and I agree with him. We have no proof at all to back us up."

The mercenary was the first to speak. "If what you say is true, General, then we're in a hell of a mess."

"The thought of ending up as a meal for one of these nasties is really quite repugnant to me," Dan Gray added.

Ike caught Ben's eye. "I guess I'm gonna have to be the one to say it, so I'll get it said. Then y'all can boo and hiss or agree with me. Whatever. There is another way to deal with these nasties, and we've touched on it before. Now I know we've got innocents in this city. I understand that. But they won't communicate with us. They won't respond to our signals. We might be forced into some rethinking. Like, we lay it on the line to the survivors. We tell them flat-out: We're going to destroy this city. Now you tell us where you are, and we'll come in and get you out. There isn't going to be any second chances. If they respond, fine. We go in and get them. If they don't . . . ?" He shrugged his muscular shoulders in a go-to-hell gesture.

Chase arched one eyebrow and asked, "And then what, Ike?"

"Chemicals or napalm."

Dan looked over at him. "That's a bit extreme, isn't it, old boy?"

"I'm opposed to torching the city," West said. "We've all seen that looting has, miraculously, been minimal. To my way of thinking, that means the city still contains hundreds, thousands, of irreplaceable treasures. We'd be doing a great disservice to future generations if we were to destroy them."

"I agree with West," Chase said.

So did the others.

Ben stayed out of it, reserving comment. "What kind of chemicals, Ike? And how would we deliver them?"

"We've got stockpiles of the deadliest chemicals mankind ever invented. How to deliver them? Planes, rockets." Ike stood up. "People, I'm not saying I agree with it. I'm not saying I want to do it. All I'm doing is laying options in front of you to kick around."

"Let's talk about the other options," West said. "Cordoning off the area—or areas—is impossible. We don't have the personnel. We couldn't starve the bastards out in a lifetime. Hell, we don't know how many of these breeding farms they have. Worst came to worst, they'd eat each other. And there is this: There are probably a thousand survivors, fighting the Night People—that's those aboveground—located between Columbus and Madison, all the way up to God knows where. But for some reason they're afraid to make contact with us. More effort has got to be made to get in touch with them. I suggest four tanks and a half a dozen APC's make a push to their position and see what the hell happens then."

"And what about these people living below the city?" Katzman asked. "My God, there might be a thousand or more of them down there. They'd be some powerful allies if we could contact them."

"Somebody had to say it," Ike said. "I said it. So torching the city is out. OK. I'm glad. How about chemicals?"

That was out as well. Unanimously.

"So we slug it out?" Ike continued. "OK. That's fine with me. But we'd better brace ourselves for a damn long campaign." He looked at Ben. "Have you given any further thought to what we discussed yesterday?"

"Yes. To those of you I have not spoken with, this is what we're talking about. Both Ike and Cecil have a gut hunch that we're being set up for something. By whom? We don't know. What and how? We don't know that either. Give it some thought and keep your eyes open. Leo, you and your people record every outside conversation you monitor. If we get a clue, it'll probably come from a radio transmission slipup on somebody's part. I talked with Tina just before this meeting. She's hitting pockets of resistance, but nothing that she can't handle. And she has found no survivors in her area. To me, that means the night crawlers have been active around here for a long, long time, and there are a hell of a lot of them. Now then, if Tina finds the Teterboro Airport functional, that means we're going to have to clear the expressway all the way up to the George Washington Bridge. Supplies will be coming in that way. Anything else anybody wants to talk about?"

No one did. Ike and Cecil stayed after the others had filed out, as Ben suspected they would.

"Tina better get to that damn airport pronto, Ben," Ike told him. "This is going to be a sustained campaign, and we're going to have to be resupplied every week. And a full company is going to have to be quartered there at the airport to make certain it doesn't get overrun by nasties. And I got this suggestion: I'd like to split my people and move half of them over here to help you. Cecil feels the same way. How about it?"

"Suits me. I can damn sure use the help."

"All right. I'll leave Broadhurst in command and take charge of clearing the expressway up to the bridge. OK?"

Ben nodded.

"I'll leave my XO in command and come on over in the morning, Ben," Cecil said. "We can work out the placement of my people over breakfast."

"Good enough."

"Ben," Ike gripped his arm, "I'm glad my suggestions were nixed. But I felt that I had to voice them."

"Ike, it may well come to germing the city. I hope not, but I just don't know. We just may have—for the first time—bitten off more than we can chew. I will confess that at times, I have my doubts as to whether we can pull this thing off."

"Oh, it's going to be a real bitch," Cecil admitted. "And we're going to be here until midsummer, at least. But I think if we hang tough, we can pull it off." He shook his head.

Ben caught the head movement. "What's the matter?"

"I just can't shake the feeling that we're being conned."

Ben thought of Jerre. "Yeah. I know that feeling very well."

Chapter 14

"They keep calling for us to make contact with them." Gene told his father. "And we know now that it is really Ben Raines. And they have switched to Yiddish in any important communications. And sometimes in some sort of language that is totally a mystery to any of us."

The elder Savie smiled. "Smart. The second language is probably some Indian dialect. I read where troops in the Pacific, during the Second Great War, used Indian language to confuse the Japanese. You are asking me if now is the time to reply to General Raines?"

"Yes, Father."

"You are in command here, Gene. Not I."

"But you have more to lose coming face-to-face with Ben Raines."

"I'm an old man, son. If by making contact with Ben Raines would guarantee the rest of you freedom from those damnable Night People . . . I would gladly give my life for that."

The son made up his mind. "We'll wait a few days longer."

"What in the hell are they waiting on?" Ben asked. "What do they want—some sort of engraved invitation?"

"Beats me." Ike spoke around a mouthful of fried potatoes. "You've told them who we are and what we're doing in every language known to mankind . . . except Swahili."

"What about Colonel West's suggestion that he take a patrol up to where we think their control begins?" Cecil asked.

"Not yet. First we wait and try to determine if they're friendly."

"What's on the agenda for today?"

"About a week's worth of work."

That got everybody's attention.

Ben smiled grimly. "The World Trade Center, gentlemen."

Ike groaned. "Two of those monsters over there are a hundred and ten stories each!"

"Relax, Ike. You're too fat to climb all those stairs. Dan is taking tower two, I'm taking tower one." Before anyone could protest, Ben said, "Ike, you and your people take building four. Cecil, you take building five. We've got time. The flybys of Teterboro Airport show it pretty well junked-up. And it's going to take Tina most of today just to get to it. Once there, I figure two days to get it clear of crap. Then, Ike, you can start clearing out the expressway up to old George's bridge. Finish your coffee, boys. Then let's go to work."

"Too fat," Ike bitched. "I'm not fat. I'm just . . . pleasantly plump, that's all!"

"What you are is a lard-butt!" Dan finished it.

Ben stood in the plaza of the World Trade Center and looked up. "Windows on the World, here I come," Ben muttered.

"Sir?" Jersey questioned.

"That's a restaurant, Jersey. I had lunch there a couple of times, years back, of course. Be interesting to see it again."

Jersey looked up and almost fell over backward staring at the skyscraper. "You *ate* . . . up *there?*"

Ben grinned at the expression on her face. "It's really a spectacular view, Jersey."

She looked at him. "I would take your word for it, General, but I think I'm gonna see it for myself, right?"

"That's right, Jersey."

She shook her head and looked at Beth, who was looking up. "I can't even see the damn top for the clouds!"

"Clouds are low today, ladies. Come on, let's go."

There was no denying the unmistakable odor once inside the lobby. The creepies were here. Or had been very recently. The concourse level was a shambles. Ben looked down, grimaced, and kicked a human bone away with his boot. It went bouncing and clicking across the floor. The flitting shape of a huge rat skittered along a wall and vanished.

"I *hate* rats!" Beth said with a shudder.

"I'm not too fond of them myself." Ben looked back at his detail. "Everybody all checked out with three days' rations and water?"

They nodded their heads.

"Ammo detail?" Ben shifted his gaze. "You loaded down, gang?"

They were.

"Scouts down to the lower level. Easy does it, people. I don't want any dead heroes. Move out."

Outside, the day was cold and dreary, with occasional bursts of drizzle. But no sleet fell with it—yet.

Ben waited with his people in the lobby, Beth wearing earphones, monitoring any signals from the Rebels entering the lower level.

"They say it's a real mess, General," she relayed the first message to Ben. "But they've encountered no creepies."

Ben nodded his head. Odd, he thought. And once more that feeling of being conned entered his head.

The Rebels waited for sounds of combat from beneath them. None came.

"Beth, ask Dan how he's doing, please."

She relayed the message. "Nothing happening, sir. They have encountered no unfriendlies."

"Try Ike and Cecil."

"Nothing, sir. All commanders report signs of recent occupation, but no sign of bogies."

A Rebel emerged from the lower level and walked up to Ben. "Nothing, sir. What the hell is going on?"

"I don't know. Let's go, people. First team out. We've got a quarter of a mile to go—straight up."

* * *

The Rebels secured the first three floors in quick time. They encountered no resistance of any kind. They found human bones and human waste—leading one Rebel to comment that the Night People just had to be the filthiest bunch of people on the face of the earth—but no creepies could be found.

It was baffling to Ben's mind. The enemy had put up stiff resistance for a time, then just seemed to give up and pull out. He couldn't make any sense of it, knowing that the Night People far outnumbered his own forces.

And Ike, Cecil, and Dan were reporting the same thing: nothing.

"Keep at it," he told his people. "I'm going back to ground level." To Beth: "Tell Ike and Cecil and Dan to meet me in the plaza."

"Something's rotten here," Ben told them. "And I don't mean the smell, either. What the hell's going on?"

"I don't know," Ike said. "But I'm sure gettin' a funky feelin' about this lash-up."

"Not too eloquently phrased," Dan said with a smile. "But I agree with the thought contained within the statement."

"I hate to harp on it, Ben," Cecil told him, "but I'm getting that old gut feeling again."

Ben agreed, adding, "But it doesn't make any sense. They keep pulling back, pulling back . . . but to where? And why?"

The sudden roar of gunfire put an end to the debate and sent the man racing toward the street.

"Coming under heavy attack all up and down Church and West Broadway, General," Beth told them, listening to frantic radio transmissions crackling into her ears.

"So much for our gut hunches," Ike said. "Chalk it up to indigestion, I reckon. I'll get my people out and throw up a line of defense wherever I'm needed. See you boys."

The commanders split up, yelling for their radio people to get the troops out of the WTC buildings and into the streets. None of the men were aware of the hard, hate-filled eyes that watched them from the top two floors of the two nine-story buildings that flanked the main entrance at Church Street. The Rebels could not see the cruel smiles that sneered from under the hoods.

Ben felt eyes on him and moved back against the building that at one time housed a number of financial and international trade firms, Beth and Jersey and Cooper moving with him.

"What's wrong, sir?" Cooper asked.

Ben shook his head. "Paranoia, I suppose. Come on. Let's find out what's going on."

A Rebel CO had called for tanks, and several rumbled past Ben's position at the corner of Church and Vesey. The gunfire was much heavier now, the lead whining and singing deadly songs as it bounced off the bricks and concrete of downtown Manhattan.

"It would be such an easy shot," the man spoke from the top floor of the nine-story building. He looked down at Ben. "Now that we have him spotted."

"Don't be a fool!" another robed man told him.

"We must not give away our positions. With patience, we will be able to destroy the entire Rebel army. Not just Ben Raines."

"But I have always been told his empire would collapse without him."

"Perhaps. But I doubt it. He has a strong son to step into his boots. Now get away from the window. Come eat. We have fresh meat, taken from that strong young Rebel we captured the other night."

Ben studied the top floor of the building through strong binoculars—studied it for several minutes, then lowered the long lenses.

"See anything, General?" Jersey asked.

"Not a thing. I just had a creepy feeling wander around my spine, that's all. Mouse ran over my gravesite, I guess."

"Sir!"

"That's an old expression, Jersey. Let's go see some action." Ben was off and running before any of his bodyguards could get in front of him.

"Damn it, General!" Jersey cussed, then took off running, hard pressed to keep up with Ben's long legs.

"General!" Cooper hollered. "Wait for us."

"Come on, kids!" Ben shouted, zigging and zagging across the street. "Surely you can keep up with an old man like me."

"Old man, my butt!" Jersey puffed.

Beth, Jersey and Cooper slid to a halt behind an abandoned car. The squad of bodyguards had been forced to dive for cover, still across the street. A hard burst of gunfire slammed into the car, the slugs penetrating one side and almost punching through the other.

Ben pointed out the pockmarks to Beth. "Seven point six two at least." he said calmly. "Probably AK's."

"Yes, sir," she said glumly. She didn't seem a bit thrilled with the news.

Ben slipped to the front of the vehicle. A dark alleyway loomed in front of him. "Beats the hell outta where we are," he muttered, waved to the others. "Come on, gang. Let's go head-hunting."

"I have heard about his exploits all my life," Beth said to Jersey. "I never thought I'd be a part of the damn things."

"I was there when he fought Sam Hartline," Jersey told her. "First with fists and then with knives. That was a fight, honey."

"Now!" Ben called, and disappeared into the gloom of the alley, Beth and Jersey and Cooper right behind him, slugs hammering the concrete all around them.

Ben halted them just inside the alley. "At least we're out of the wind in here," he grinned at them.

Movement behind him turned his head and dropped him to one knee, the Thompson coming up. Ben caught the flash of pale faces under dark hoods and pulled the trigger, holding it back, fighting to keep the powerful SMG on target and not climbing.

The .45-caliber slugs sent the night crawlers jerking and spinning in a macabre dance, their blood splattering the brick walls of the alley.

Not waiting to see if all were dead, Ben turned

the muzzle of the Thompson to a door and blew the doorknob off. The door lurched open, exposing the darkness within. Ben went in fast and low. The others had no choice but to follow him.

"Easy," Ben called to them. "Take a good whiff of that wonderful odor."

They all wrinkled their noses at the almost overpowering smell of the Night People. With the stench that strong, they all knew the creepies were very close. Maybe on the floor above them. Maybe behind any of the closed doors on the ground floor. Maybe all around them.

Ben, smiling, put a finger to his lips and motioned the others to back up and get down. He took a Fire-Frag grenade from his harness and pulled the pin, holding the spoon down. Then he started moaning. "Oh, my legs are broken. Oh, Jesus, Jesus, help me, please!"

A door opened just to Ben's left, the creaking of rusty hinges giving it away. A powerful stench assailed his nostrils. He rolled the grenade into the room and lifted his Thompson.

The Fire-Frag, probably the most lethal grenade ever manufactured, made a great big mess inside the room. One creepie was flung out into the hall, his face hanging out, all mixed up with brains and other assorted ick.

Jersey shot him just to make sure.

Cooper swung his M-16 around at the sound of footsteps racing down the stairs. The entranceway filled with night crawlers. Four automatic weapons yammered, filling the narrow hallway with brass and noise and gunsmoke. Ben jumped over the piled-up bodies and ran up the stairs, Jersey right behind him and Beth and Cooper bringing up the rear.

Ben paused at an open door, then rolled in; Jersey stepped into the open doorway, covering him with a practiced movement.

The room was void of Night People.

But by an open window was an M-60 machine gun, with several cases of ammo by its side.

Ben turned to Beth. "Radio Ike, Dan, Cecil, somebody, and tell then where we are."

Beth gave him a disgusted look. "Well, hell, General! Where are we?"

Ben laughed and took the handset from Beth. "This is the Eagle. You listening, Shark?"

A few seconds passed. Ike came on. "Roger, Eagle."

"What's your twenty?"

"In a church. St. Peter's, I think it is."

"All right, Shark. That's gonna be right across the street, catty-cornered, sort of. I'm on the second floor with a captured M-60. I'm gonna start letting the lead fly. Pass the word that I'm friendly."

"Now, damn it, Ben! I . . ."

Ben hooked the phone and grinned at Beth. "Now let's have some fun!"

Chapter 15

Ben grabbed up the M-60. "Get that ammo, Cooper, and follow me."

He ran from the room, the others grabbing up cases of ammo and running to catch up with him.

Ben ran to the other end of the building and kicked in a door. He bipodded the M-60 by a window and then smashed the glass with the butt of his Thompson. Lead started coming at him from the building across the street. Ben sat down behind the M-60 and let it rock and roll. "Help me feed, Jersey. Keep it coming."

Ben knocked down a few creepies and put the rest of them on the floor as he raked the second floor of the building with machine-gun fire.

One bogie lifted his head at the other end of the firestorm of lead, and Cooper drilled him between the eyes. Beth had tucked her radio in a closet and was doing a more than respectable job of dusting black-robed figures on the ground-level floor of a building across the street.

The sounds of many boots on the steps turned

them all around, their heads kept down below windowsill level. Dan rolled into the room and wriggled on his belly to Ben's position.

"Come to join the party, Dan?"

Dan gazed at him, a reproachful look in the man's eyes. "You're a naughty boy, General. You had us worried for a time."

A hard burst of gunfire from across the street tore into the wall behind the Rebels, knocking loose hunks of paneling and sending debris flying all over the room.

With a low curse, Ben again positioned himself behind the M-60 and let it bang.

"Two windows over from your left, General!" Jersey called. "That's the machine gun."

Dan twisted on the floor. "Oh, Jimmy! Be a good lad and run up to the roof with your rocket launcher and kindly direct a few rounds into that building across the street. It would be ever so much appreciated. Thanks."

"Right, Boss!" the Scout called.

The black-robed spooks from across the street were really letting the lead fly in the Rebels' position, forcing Ben and his people on the second floor to keep their heads down.

"So much for thinking they were giving up," Ben muttered, facedown on the dirty floor.

"Quite," Dan replied.

The Rebels were content to lie belly-down in safety until Jimmy and his people got into position. Several moments passed before the front of the creepie-held building erupted in a shower of stone and broken glass and shattered bodies. Several more rockets were hurled into the building. The unfriendly firing ceased.

"Out," Ben ordered, crawling backward, pulling the M-60 with him. "Cooper, don't forget that ammo. We might need it before this day is over."

In the hall, Dan commented, "The Night People are certainly well armed, General. And seem to be well trained, too."

"I noticed. Listen." He held up his hand.

"Fighting has all but stopped nearby," Dan observed. He motioned his Scouts ahead of him. "Secure the alleyway."

Ben led the way down the dark and rat-dropping littered hall. His Thompson was slung; he carried the M-60, bipod swinging loose.

"Alley secure," a scout called.

"Let's check out the block, Dan. I want the federal building secured from top to basement. I have a pretty good idea where the night crawlers got a large part of their electronic gear."

"Oh?"

"Yeah. I forgot what floor it's on, but that was one of the Bureau's command centers. I did some research on it one time. It was filled with sophisticated computers and radio gear. Get a team, Dan. We're going in."

"We're going to be pushing ahead of the others, General, ranging out pretty far."

If Ben heard Dan's remark, he did not acknowledge it. "Send your Scouts on ahead, Dan. Clear us a route. Go behind City Hall Park. We'll come out behind the federal building."

The Rebels darted across the street over to Barclay

and came out behind the Woolworth Building. "Got to get in there and clear that," Ben noted. "It used to be a beautiful place. We'll take it next, Dan."

"Yes, sir." The park was making him nervous. "Spookies in the park, you suppose?"

"Probably, Dan. Even though I don't think they like open spaces very much. We'll go in heads-up."

The Rebels walked along the promenade, Ben pointing out, "City Hall. That'll have to be cleared, as well."

"Right, sir."

Beth called, "Sir? Ike and Cecil want to know your twenty?"

"Tell them we're taking a rather enjoyable stroll along the promenade, coming up on Park Row."

"Yes, sir."

"Very pleasant along here, isn't it, Dan?" Ben asked, still toting the M-60 with a long belt of cartridges slung over one shoulder.

"Oh, just lovely, sir!" The sarcasm in the Englishman's voice did not escape Ben. "Especially when one takes into consideration that none of this area has been cleared."

"Sir?" Beth called. "I'm not about to repeat what both generals Ike and Cecil just told me to tell you."

"Clean it up and tell me."

"They said to get your butt outta here!"

"Tell them to relax. Jesus Christ! I got fifty people surrounding me."

Just as they were leaving Park Row, making the dogleg to Foley Square and Centre, the two point Scouts hit the sidewalk and rolled behind cover. The others quickly followed suit just as automatic-weapon fire raked the air.

Ben, Jersey, Beth, and Cooper went into the small park and down into a ditch. Ben bipodded the M-60 as Jersey lay beside him, ready to feed. Cooper and Beth had grabbed a couple of fallen branches to reinforce their position.

"Behind us, I guess," Ben said, studying a tourist's guide to New York City. "I can't make heads or tails out of this damn thing. Dumbest maps I have ever seen."

"What's behind us?" Cooper asked, while Beth thought it was a damn strange time to be reading a tourist guide. Jersey was used to it.

"Pace University. I'm thinking that would be a good place to set up an HQ."

The gunfire had ceased. Somewhere in the park, a bird was singing. The lilting sound made everything seem almost normal. Almost, if one stretched one's imagination just a bit.

Ben put the little book in his pocket as a faint rustling came to their ears.

"Just to the left of that old bicycle or motorbike," Jersey told him. "Something dark moving through all that brush."

"Beth, find out if we have any units at all in this park," Ben whispered. "No! Scrap that order. Some of our people may be out head hunting. We'll just have to wait and see."

Then the breeze changed, and with that wind shift, the Rebels no longer had to worry about wasting any of their own people.

"Phew!" Jersey screwed up her face.

Ben put the M-60 stock to his shoulder and lined up the sights. The movement in the brush had stopped, but Ben had caught a glimpse of non-color that didn't seem to fit with the terrain. He gave the slash of black a good squirt from the M-60. The black robe became dotted with crimson as it was turned around and flung backward, the 7.62 rounds taking the creepie directly in the belly. The cannibal lay on the cold ground in the bushes, kicking and squalling and howling its miserable life away.

A half-dozen night crawlers, with more guts than sense, charged Ben's position. The air became ripped with .223's and 7.62's. None of them even got close to Ben's position. The slugs stopped them and brought a few up on their toes, dancing in that peculiar manner of the standing-up dying with bellies and chests filled with bone-smashing and organ-ripping lead.

Hard bursts of gunfire erupted from behind Ben's field of fire, forcing them to change positions. Ben and Jersey faced the park, Beth and Cooper spread out, facing the Municipal Building . . . which appeared to be filled with Night People.

Dan's bunch was holding their own, containing at least the front of the building. Ben pulled a sandwich out of his jacket pocket and unwrapped it. "Want to share, Jersey?"

"Thanks." She took her half of the sandwich and they chewed, washing the food down with sips of water from their canteens.

The firing intensified until it was clear to Ben that his people were badly outnumbered and outgunned. He washed down the last bite of sandwich. "Beth?

Call in and tell them we need some Abrams or Bradleys up here pronto. Tell them to come straight up Broadway and cut off at Park Row. They'll see us."

"Yes, sir."

"Then tell Dan to be on the lookout for them and to keep his people on this side of the street."

"Yes, sir."

It wasn't long before three big 55-ton Abrams, each pushed by a 1500-horsepower Avco Lycoming turbine, came roaring around the dogleg, their gunners already adjusting for fire. The Abrams is equipped with one 105mm rifled gun, one 12.7mm anti-aircraft, and two 7.62 machine guns. The tanks roared up to the building, slid into position, and then proceeded to blow the place into burning chunks of rock and brick and shattered bodies.

Two smaller tanks, M-42 Dusters, had swung around to the back. The Dusters were armed with 40mm cannons and .50-caliber machine guns. The Municipal Building would never quite be the same after this onslaught, but then, neither would those crawlers trapped inside.

Ben gave the orders to cease fire. The area fell silent—eerily quiet after the booming and rattle and screaming of battle.

Ben walked out of the park and surveyed the devastation his people had wrought. Rebels had entered the building to mop up and to put out the small fires caused by the shelling. Some of his people had been working on half a dozen fire engines found within the area they now controlled, but any raging out-of-control fire was something they all feared until they could get fire-fighting equipment running and ready for on-the-line use.

"Find out how West is doing, Beth."

She relayed the request and waited for the translators to get to work; then she turned to Ben. "West is steadily clearing his sector, General. The South Street Seaport area is cleared, and he's pushing in toward us."

"Very good. My compliments to him . . ."

Ike and Cecil came roaring around the dogleg in a Hummer, both of them with angry looks on their faces. Ben put an end to any comments from them before they had a chance to open their mouths.

"Ike, take your people over to Independence Plaza and get to work. Start pushing in toward us. Cecil, spread your people out with mine and take over here. Start clearing east and west toward Ike and West. I want everything clean from this area south."

He turned to Jersey before either man could comment. "Come on, Jersey, let's go take a look at our new CP."

"And where in the hell might that be?" Cecil asked, exasperation on his face.

"Tweed Courthouse."

"But the damn thing hasn't been cleared!" Ike exploded, jumping up and down and waving his arms.

"I know," Ben replied calmly. "I'm going to do that little thing—right now."

Ben and his team walked through the park. They passed the dead creepies.

"Get them out of here," Ben said, and Beth relayed

the orders. "I want this park nice and clean. Have this crud stacked with the others for dumping at sea."

He had given his M-60 to a startled Ike and now carried his Thompson with a full drum.

"What the hell do you want me to do with this heavy bastard?" Ike had yelled.

"Use it," Ben had smiled. "It served me very well." He walked away, leaving Ike sputtering.

"Dan," Ben called. "I don't think we're going to meet any resistance up here. I think the bogies have had it for this day. But if it'll make you feel better, send some of your people in to check out the courthouse."

"Already done, General," Dan replied blandly.

"I figured as much."

The courthouse loomed in front of them. "We'll stop here," Dan said quietly. "We've heard no gunfire, so I think your assumption was correct, General." He lifted his walkie-talkie and spoke quietly, then listened. He turned back to Ben. "My people are sweeping the place for booby traps. Give us an hour and it'll be ready for you."

Ben nodded. "Good enough. Beth, get out of that backbreaker radio and take a rest. Rest of you people take a break." He walked off a short distance and stood staring toward the direction of New Jersey. He wondered how Tina was getting along.

And Jerre.

Chapter 16

Paterson was a barren shell, seemingly a ghost town. Tina and her Scouts had cautiously entered the city—once with a population of a hundred and fifty thousand—only to find no sign of life, and with the wind echoing hollowly through the broken windows and moaning up the empty streets, it made each member of the team resist an urge to look over his or her shoulder.

"We've been in a lot of towns, Ham," Tina said, her voice low, "but this takes the cake. If you know what I mean."

"Boy, do I," her XO agreed. "This place is giving me the jumping willies."

"Bones over here!" Jerre called. "Several skeletons. I make it out to be a family. Male, female, and small child."

The Rebels gathered around and peered inside at what at one time had been a sporting goods store. It had been looted.

All wore grim expressions on their faces at the

sight of the bones. All three skulls had been caved in by a club or a rifle butt.

"Jesus," Sharon summed it up. "That kid couldn't have been more than three or four years old."

"Yeah," Pam said grimly. She had lost a child a couple of years back. She turned away from the sight and walked back to her vehicle.

Doctor Ling entered the building and knelt down beside the bones for a moment. When he stepped outside, he said, "Not too old. I'd guess they were killed a year, maybe eighteen months ago. No flesh left on the bones. What wasn't eaten by the Night People, the rats probably got."

"Let's get out of here," Tina ordered. She spread a map out on the hood of her Jeep. "We'll take the Interstate out of here and pick up Forty-six there." She punched the map. "That'll take us right to the airport. Let's get the hell gone from this town."

No one needed to be told twice. The short column moved out, driving around abandoned cars and trucks, twisting and turning in the littered streets. They saw no one and nothing that even came close to life. Not a dog. Not a cat. Nothing.

All breathed a little easier when they hit the Interstate and rolled on.

Sharon, Tina's driver, broke the silence. "The creepies have been here a long time, Tina. They've been raiding the surrounding towns and eating these people."

"That's the way I see it," Tina said with a sigh. "And I have this hunch, Sharon, that Dad is going to order us to stay at the airport and clean it up and then guard it once that's done."

Sharon grinned. "That's what you get for getting up in your dad's face, girl."

Tina grinned at the memory. "Yeah. But it was worth it just for the expression on his face."

"Well, anyway we got some APC's and two Dusters out of the deal."

"That does make me feel some better."

It was a short run to the airport, and the Scouts hit no resistance along the way. The advance Scouts radioed in.

"Airport under visual and no signs of life. It looks pretty good except for the mess."

"We'll be with you in five."

"Christ, what a mess!" was Tina's first reaction after viewing the airport through binoculars.

They had linked up with the advance team and stood on the north end of the field. Tina lowered her binoculars. "Load 'em up, gang. Let's go in and see what we can scare up."

For once, Ike, Cecil, and Dan were all pleased and satisfied with Ben's choice of a CP.

"Easily defensible," Cecil smiled.

"A place befitting a man of your importance," Dan beamed.

"Place is just right," Ike said.

"I don't like it," Ben bitched.

Three faces mirrored disbelief. Ike was the first to speak. "What the hell's wrong with it?"

"Too damn pompous. I just remembered that I never did like courthouses."

Cecil threw his hands up in the air and began walking around the office. Ike started cussing. Dan was the first to put it together.

"Relax, boys," the Englishman said, a smile playing around his mouth. "The general is having a bit of fun at our expense. Right, General?"

"You guys are too serious," Ben told his friends. "Lighten up, boys. The office is just fine. Katzman's people are installing radio equipment now. He's going to move part of his operation over here. I'll use this as the main CP until we get to Central Park South. Then I'll have to move."

"And pushing up that far, General, might take all winter," Dan warned.

"I know. All right, boys, pull up a chair and let's get down to business. Where's West?"

"Here, sir." The mercenary stepped into the big office. "Sorry I'm late. I ran into a pocket of bogies on the way over. Took two alive and turned them over to Chase's people for interrogation."

"Pull up a chair, West. Speaking of the night crawlers and Chase . . . I haven't seen the old goat. Did he tell you how the interrogation is going?"

"Yes. Slowly. Seems the ones we initially took are hard-core, and they're going to be tough to break."

Ben nodded his head. That was Chase's baby. He'd let them know when there was a breakthrough. If ever. "Katzman just handed me the latest on this Monte person. He's closing, but still a long way off. Rebet and Danjou are nipping at his heels and slowing him down. They're badly outnumbered and can't close with him. They're helping us in the only way they can."

"They're going to try to enter the city, Ben?" Cecil asked. "Rebet and Danjou, I mean."

"Yes. But they don't know when, of course, or even where. Since no one knows what route Monte is going to take when he gets close." Ben stood up and moved to a huge wall map just hung in place. "Monte didn't cross at Toronto." He thumped the map. "And he is approximately here." He pointed to a spot. "So my guess is that he'll turn south on Eighty-one. Rebet sent a company across at Toronto to try to intercept Monte's columns somewhere between Binghamton and the border. They won't be able to stop Monte, but they can sure aggravate the hell out of him. Rebet and Danjou are just trying to buy us some time."

"Our weather people say we've got some snow on the way," Ike informed the group. "They're saying it's building up to be a hard winter."

"That's all we need. OK. Let's get some fuel-hunting teams out and start rounding up some stoves."

Ben looked out the window. He had made damn sure his new office had at least one window. Dark in the city, and when there is no man-made light in a city, it seems to be more than dark. "I spoke with Tina. The runways at Teterboro are intact, but it's going to take them several days to clear it." A smile touched his lips. "And then they're going to guard it."

"How about additional personnel over there?" Ike asked. "That airport is going to be vital, Ben."

"I'm sending one platoon over. That's all Tina requested. That will beef them up to a hundred. I'm sending them mortar crews, a couple of Big

Thumpers, two Abrams, and some Fifties. That's in addition to the new platoon. When we know for sure what route Monte is taking, we'll make our decision about how many more troops to send over. We've made our choice of airports, and now we've got to hold it, and we damn sure have to keep the George Washington Bridge open." He hit the wall with the palm of his hand. "Damn, but I hate to destroy bridges."

They all knew what he was saying: the bridge linking America with Canada on Interstate 81. But they also knew they had to buy some more time and one way to do that was to force Monte to change his route, putting him far away from the Teterboro Airport.

Dan took it. "I can have Sappers up and dropped by daylight, General."

"That will also be a dead giveaway to Monte," Ben reminded them all. But he knew with a sickening feeling in his gut that the bridge had to go.

"Perhaps," West said. "And perhaps he'll just think we're trying to slow his advance toward the city. We have to assume the Night People know of Tina's move to the airport. But we can't be sure."

Ben nodded. "All right. Blow it, Dan. But knock enough of it out so a Bailey can't be stretched across. That's going to mean some fast and dirty work for your people. Support columns are going to have to come down."

The Englishman nodded and stood up. "I'll get them outfitted and on the way. You want them to then link up with the Canadians or Russians?"

"Yes."

Dan nodded and left the room.

Ben turned to Beth. "Have Katzman send a coded message to Rebet, advising him of this action and to be aware that some of my people will be linking up with the company he's sent across the border."

Beth walked across the room and picked up an in-house phone.

"Another vital link destroyed," Ben mused aloud. "And one that will never be rebuilt in our lifetime. Just like the bridges along the South Carolina border."

"What I wouldn't give for an air force," Cecil added some musings of his own.

"In a sense," West said, "we have reverted back to the caveman type of warfare. All our once-fabulous technology and million-dollar-plus aircraft lies rusting and useless. Our guns and tanks can be equated to the caveman's clubs and stone axes. I suppose it's true that what goes around, comes around."

West never talked about his past. But it was obvious to all that he was a highly educated man. And refined in a strange way. Ben also knew that Tina and West saw each other. But their involvement was kept on a discreet basis . . . as discreet as is possible in any army camp.

And Ben never interfered in his daughter's social life.

Once again, Jerre entered his mind.

"Brother Emil." Sister Martha approached him. "Where are we?"

"We're in Virginia, Sister," Emil told her. "And we appear to be surrounded by some sort of cretinous savages."

"Perhaps you could call on Blomm to come to our aid?" it was suggested to Emil.

Since Big Louie's rocket had changed course and exploded over Louisiana, Emil had suffered through many second thoughts about whether Blomm was real or not. He concluded that Blomm was not real . . . but then, it never paid to screw around with gods. Just on the off chance that Blomm really did exist.

"Those people are coming closer," Brother Carl said.

Emil looked around him in the near-darkness, the gloom broken only by the flickering lights of the camp's fires. Looked to him like there was about a hundred of . . . whatever the hell they were. Human, he hoped.

"Away with you!" Emil shouted. "Be gone. Out, out, damn spot! Before I call down the wrath of Blomm."

The figures came closer.

"OK, you turkeys," Emil muttered. "You asked for it."

He began some slow shoulder movements. "Oh, Blomm! I am asking that you look into the hearts of those who have invaded the sanctity of our camp and send us friends, and not enemies." He began doing some footwork, looking for the most part like a drunken Egyptian paying homage to Ra.

"That old boy is doing the Moonwalk!" a strange female voice came to Emil.

"Relax, man," another voice came to Emil. "Everything's cool. We just wanted to see who you folks were, that's all."

Emil threw his arms wide. "Thank you, Blomm." Then he took a closer look at the men and women who had stepped into the light of the campfires. "Great scott! It's a whole gaggle of *hippies!*"

"I can't tell you how good it is to hear that word again," the long-haired man with a bandana around his head said, stepping closer to Emil. The man took a closer look at Emil. "Ah . . . exactly what *are* you, man?"

Emil drew himself up just as tall as he would ever be. Which was short. "I am known as Father Emil, divine spiritual leader of the earth, disciple of the Great God Blomm."

"No kidding!" the woman by the man's side said. "Wow, that's awesome. Who the hell is Blomm?"

Emil opened his mouth to tell the woman not to blaspheme. Before he could speak, the man stuck out his hand and said, "I'm Thermopolis."

Emil shook it. Noted that both the man and the woman and everybody else with them were well armed.

"This is Rosebud." The man indicated the woman next to him. "Where are you bound, friend?" As Emil had done, Thermopolis noted that Emil and his group were all very well armed.

"We are on a mission of love and respect, Thermy."

"Oh?"

"Yes. We have put aside our personal interests—not to mention our safety—to travel into a land of savages, going to the aid of our good and great friend, the Supreme Commander of Allied Forces in America, General Ben Raines."

"Ummm!" Thermopolis said.

Rosebud said, "Is Ben Raines in trouble?"

"He is fighting the Night People in New York City."

"I never did like that authoritative bastard's method of government," Thermopolis grumbled.

"Well, hell!" Emil blustered. "You think I do? But it sure beats the crap out of being eaten by *cannibals!*"

"Yeah," another voice was added. "That ain't cool at all, man."

Emil peered at him. "Wenceslaus," he was told. "This is my old lady, Zelotes."

"Pleased, I'm sure," Emil muttered.

Yet another voice spoke. "He does have a point. That adds up to what we've been hearing. I'm Adder. This is my brother, Udder." He jerked a thumb toward a man standing beside him. "Them's our old ladies, Ima and Ura."

Emil was beginning to wonder if he had accidentally camped close to a still-operational nuthouse.

Thermopolis sighed. "I guess I'd rather live under Ben Raines's rule than run from Night People for the rest of my life."

"He's left you alone, hasn't he?" Emil questioned.

"He doesn't know where we live," a woman said.

"Swallow," Rosebud introduced them.

"Don't be foolish," Emil told the group. "Of course Ben Raines knows where you live. He knows about the hippie communes in Arkansas and California and Washington and Oregon and in Missouri . . . and a hundred other places. If you're more than a hundred strong, with some form of government, and you raise gardens and have schools . . . he knows about you. He has patrols out working the entire country.

Mapping and logging communities. But I have been told by more than one Rebel that people like you pose no threat. You have laws, you have rules . . . you must, or you couldn't exist. The point is, you obviously don't break any of the few laws the Rebels live under. And you don't interfere with Ben Raines and the outposts he and his Rebels are setting up all over the nation. If you want to get right down to it, there isn't that much difference in your group from my group, or our groups from Ben Raines's Rebels."

"You're a funny little man, but you can make sense," another voice spoke.

"Zipper," Rosebud said. "That's his old lady, Fly."

Emil couldn't help it. He had to smile. Then he laughed, and the laughter was infectious. Emil's people laughed and the hippies were quick to join in. Soon they were all hugging and shaking hands and talking.

There is a myriad of differences between true hippies and straights—especially if those straights are rural and so-called religious. Hippies can laugh at themselves. Laugh at a redneck and see how violent matters become.

"We'll come with you," Thermopolis said.

"Thermy," Emil replied. "You all dress funny, but you're my kind of people!"

Chapter 17

Snowing, and Ham was bitching.

"Months of hard-assed training to join Dan Gray's Scouts. And what are we doing? Stringin' fence!" he said disgustedly.

Jerre laughed at him as she and Pam struggled to work the homemade come-along that pulled the wire tight. "You can blame it on me, Ham. I don't mind."

"It isn't your fault," Tina said, hooking the wire on the post. "It's my fault for getting up in Dad's face. I should have known better. But Dad has his faults too. I'm his kid. I know. Dad can be awfully ruthless and vindictive."

"That's a trait that all world leaders and great military people have," Doctor Ling told them. The doctor was working right along with them. "And back when the world was whole, nearly all self-made men and women, millionaires and billionaires and heads of great corporations. They have to be. That's the way the world is." He caught his finger in some wire and cussed. In several languages.

"Why?" Sergeant Wilson asked, when the doctor had exhausted his vocabulary of cusswords.

"Because they are dealing with, controlling, getting along with, and asking all types of personalities to follow them. They've got to be tough, sometimes hard, sometimes ruthless, sometimes charismatic, sometimes cruel—they've got to run the entire spectrum. Very few people have that many qualities they can fall back on. Ben Raines does."

"My people are on the ground and planting charges, General," Dan told Ben.

"Everybody down all right?"

"They lost one man. His chute malfunctioned."

"I'm sorry, Dan."

"They know the risks involved in becoming a part of my Scouts."

Ben said no more. Dan would grieve for this Scout in his own way. Stoically and wooden-faced. But grieve nevertheless. He was a hard man, in the midst of men and women just as hard—in a hard time.

Ben ordered coffee sent in and added a healthy slug of booze to each coffee. He lifted his mug. "To the SAS and Her Majesty."

"Thank you, sir." He sipped and lifted his mug. "To General Ben Raines and what he stands for," the Englishman proposed.

"You're putting me in awfully lofty company, Dan. But I appreciate it."

"The Queen would have liked you, General. And so would have Maggie. They both might have had to set you down from time to time and give you a good talking-to, but they would have liked you."

Ben leaned back in his chair and laughed. "Yeah? I wish I could have met them."

"You had contact with Tina?"

"Oh, yeah, just a few minutes ago. She and her team are busy stretching fence wire."

Dan allowed himself a slight smile. "I'm sure they're all thrilled with that task."

"Oh, they seemed overjoyed at it."

Coffee finished, Ben shrugged into battle harness and picked up his Thompson. "You ready to go to work?"

The Rebels pushed on, fighting through the snow and the slush and the cold of that day. West and his people bulled their way toward the center of Lower Manhattan and by late afternoon had linked up with Ben and his teams in Confucius Plaza. Ike and Cecil and their troops were still some blocks away, battling all up and down Lafayette.

"You check out the Manhattan Savings Bank, West?" Ben asked.

"Yes. Very interesting architecture. It's been looted, of course."

The Manhattan Savings Bank, a branch of it, located in Chinatown, had been built in the shape of a Chinese temple.

"Find anything else interesting?"

The mercenary and the Rebel locked gazes. West knew what Ben was leading up to; he had been noting the same thing all day. "With few exceptions,

General, the looting was done sanely and selectively. Someone with a good eye picked over the jade, the ivory, the silks and brocades. And I get the feeling it was not done for profit."

"That's the feeling I got, too. That someone did it with an eye on the future."

"But who?"

Ben shrugged. "Good question. I've tried several times today to reestablish contact with those living under the city. No luck. Katzman just told me he's tried a dozen times to contact those living around Central Park. They refuse to answer."

"Has he picked up any chatter from them— among themselves?"

"Just a bit. They're operating with CB's. And they speak in code. A very simple code. Intelligence broke it very quickly."

Dan walked up, to stand listening.

Ben brought him up to date, ending with, "It seems that the primary reason they are reluctant to make contact is that someone among them is afraid I'm going to kill him."

"Then you are assuming they are unfriendlies?" the mercenary asked.

Ben shook his head. "No. I don't see how they could be since they speak of killing Night People."

"I wonder how they're heating their apartments?"

"I think I figured that out, too," Ben replied. "What's the one thing that stands out as missing in almost every building—the thing we've had to bring in from outside the city?"

"Furniture," Dan pegged it. "That is to say, anything wooden."

"Precisely. For a time they did that. Then I got to wondering why, when our people did their flybys, the city was so free of smoke. The Night People, filthy beings that they are, seem to huddle together for a sharing of warmth. Their main CP, let's call it, as the heat-seekers have shown us, is probably the old Columbia University complex. They're packed in there like rotten sardines. I studied the pictures of the flybys. Some smoke is coming from there. But the people around Central Park—that's a different story. I went back to the blow-ups." He held out his hand and Jersey gave him a map case. Ben pulled out a dozen blow-ups and laid them on the hood of a truck. "Look here. On top of these buildings."

"Well, I'll just be damned!" West exclaimed. "They're not dummies, General. They've built solar equipment to trap the sun as a source of energy, converting that into heat."

Dan studied the blow-ups. "Yes. Obviously they have some means of storing whatever they pull in, probably by heating water. Although I will admit that I don't understand all that I know about solar power."

"An observation, General?" West asked.

"Of course."

The mercenary tapped the blow-ups. "Professional people live here. For the most part. People with education—although that learning might not be in the form of earned degrees, I'd wager that many of them are college graduates."

"I tend to agree with you," Ben said. "But if that is the case, why would they think I would want to do them harm?"

The sky had increased the intensity of falling

snow, and the Rebels shifted locations, moving under an awning. Jersey was studying the blow-ups. Ben watched her for a moment.

"What have you found, Jersey?"

She looked up at him. "Solar power is not the only thing those people over by the park are using, General. Look here. You got to look hard to see them, because they're painted the same color as the rooftops."

"What?" Dan leaned closer.

"A whole bunch of little-bitty windmills."

Ben had removed his boots and socks—his feet had been soaked for hours—and was rubbing some warmth back into his feet, sitting on a couch in his office. "Rubber boots," he told Beth. "Make a memo for Katzman to send to Base Camp One. We need rubber boots. Insulated types. Get them up here pronto."

"Yes, sir."

"Solar energy and windmills," Ben mused. "Educated people, and yet they're afraid of me. Why?"

"A lot of educated people are scared of you, General," Jersey bluntly informed him.

Ben stared at her, amazement etching his features. No one had ever told him that before. "What do you mean, Jersey? I don't burn books and destroy institutions of higher learning. We reopen schools wherever we go. Why would an educated person be afraid of me? And where did you hear that?"

She sat down on the edge of his desk. "Hell, General, everybody has heard that. How many ex-college professors and hotshot writers and TV people and those types are in the Rebel ranks?"

Ben didn't have the vaguest idea. There were several thousand Rebels in New York City alone, another thousand spread out all over the nation, patrolling and setting up outposts and recruiting and what-have-you. Joe Williams was commanding a full battalion back at Base Camp One. Juan Solis and Alvaro had set up a tiny version of Tri-States in the Southwest. Ben couldn't be expected to know the names and previous occupations of everybody in his army.

"I don't know, Jersey. How many?"

"Maybe five or six. Ask General Jefferys. He'll tell you the same thing. They just don't like our form of government."

That didn't come as any surprise to Ben; but he had never given it much thought.

"Too repressive, huh, Jersey?"

She shrugged. "Not for me. But for them? . . . I guess so. You remember how much hell the professor-types raised when the military put you in the White House."

Ben had forgotten all about the fury raised from academia-ville during his short stay as President. He had been trying to put the country back together and those yoyos were resorting to 1960's tactics, trying to burn it down again.

He caught the folded-up socks she tossed him. "Screw 'em." Ben muttered. He put on dry boots and stood up, slipping into battle harness. "Let's go get something to eat. Damn, I'm hungry."

* * *

Ben put the puzzle of why the midtown survivors were so afraid of him out of his mind and stepped out onto the street at four-thirty the next morning. This time he did not have to worry about startling any guards, for his new office building had shifts working all night long: in communications, intelligence, supply, evacuation, transportation, service and personnel.

They were skeleton crews, to be sure, but each department was staffed on a twenty-four-hour basis.

Dan's call turned him around. He stood with West and Ike and Cecil and Chase. "We've been waiting for you, General," the Englishman said. "We'll walk to breakfast with you. Tell you about a few new tricks we ran up on during the night."

Over a breakfast of beef and gravy over biscuits—better known universally as Shit on Shingle—Dan dropped it on him.

"The creepies are smartening up, General. It's really going to be slow going from here on in."

Ben looked at him, waiting.

"It appears as the creepies pull back, they're booby trapping everything they can."

"Damn!" Ben said.

Chase took it. "We lost two last night. Three more were hurt so badly they're out of it for the duration."

"What kinds of booby traps?"

Ike shrugged. "All kinds, Ben. Trip wire, swing stakes, signal-breaker types. Some of them are crude, some are very, very fancy"

Ben chewed for a moment and took a sip of coffee. Jersey and Beth and Cooper sat at the next table. They were all three privy to everything that might be said. Traitors in the Rebel army were a rare thing, and when they were caught the punishment was always the same: they were put up against a wall and shot.

"Well, people," Ben said, "let's go back to the military classrooms; we've all been there. The class is called Estimate of the Situation."

Ike groaned.

Ben smiled. "You take the pointer, Ike."

"Thanks a bunch, Ben!" the ex-SEAL said. "OK. Number one: mission. Number two: situation and courses of action. Number three: analysis of opposing courses of action. Number four: comparison of our own courses of action. And number five: the decision—who, what, when, where, how, and why."

"We know the mission," West took it.

"Our situation," Dan said, "while not grim, could certainly be better. Our course of action is going to have to be much slower, with much more caution. We're going to have to accept the fact that our use of explosives will be much greater. That's for our own safety. Many of the buildings we'll encounter are ready for the wrecking ball anyway. And while we're at it, let's talk about chemicals."

"I thought we rejected that idea," Chase spoke up.

"We rejected the use of lethal chemicals," Ben told him. "Not incapacitating ones such as a hydrolytic form of H-series. Which we have plenty of, by the way." Ben did not wait for any further discussion on that matter. His was the final say, and he was not going to risk the lives of his people unnecessarily. "Beth. Tell Katzman to honk at Base Camp One. Tell Joe to start shipping up the H-series. Mustard and Blister. We can mix it here. And tell him we wanted it yesterday." Ben stood up. "Stay put. I'll be back in twenty minutes." He walked away, Jersey and the squad of bodyguards trooping behind him.

"Now what do you suppose he's up to now?" Chase tossed the question out.

Ben went to the same manhole cover and pounded on it with a wrench. "You better talk to me, people. All Hell is about to break loose." Silence. "Now, goddamn it, I've tried to contact you on the frequency you gave me. You won't reply. I'm trying to save your lives. Now, by God, talk to me."

"All right, General Raines." The voice was muffled but understandable, and coming from directly under Ben's feet. "You are who you say you are. Forgive our suspicions. We each have news; I will share mine first. The survivors around Central Park are very anxious to link up with you and your Rebels. Their leader is named Gene Savie. He is fearful of you killing his father should you meet."

Ben looked up at Jersey. "You ever heard of anybody called Savie?"

She shook her head. "No, sir."

"Those people have nothing to fear from me," Ben called.

"Nevertheless, this is their reason for not answering your calls. Now what is your news?"

"A question first?"

"Of course."

"Do you people ever come out into the light?"

"Only during the day. But not in a long time and not since you and your army have arrived in the city. We used to come out to kill Night People while they slept. Then they became too many for us to cope with."

"How do you live?"

"We grow foods organically in hothouses. We are entirely vegetarians and really eat quite well. There is no cause for you to worry about us in that respect."

"You speak like an educated man."

"I have my doctorate in Philosophy."

"How far away can you get from this area? The area being from here up to West Fifty-seventh Street."

"None of us live in this area. We only came this far down because you were here."

"Then clear out. We're being forced to use something I had hoped we could avoid."

"Is it lethal?"

"No. But a prolonged concentrated exposure to it might be."

"I thank you, General Raines. We'll talk again when you reach the survivors around the Park."

Ben put his ear to the cold metal and could hear the sounds of footsteps vanishing, probably down a steel ladder. Ben stood up.

"How do you know you can trust him, General?" Jersey asked.

"I don't. But sometimes, Jersey, you just have to play your hunches."

Chapter 18

The old prop-job cargo planes began landing at Teterboro Airport at noon the next day, most of them carrying a very deadly cargo, a couple of them carrying winter boots for the Rebels.

The cargo was off-loaded onto trucks and transported to an old chemical plant some miles away, to the south, where the process of dilution would be carried out.

On the morning Ben was informed the Night People were booby-trapping buildings, he had told most of his people to take a rest. It was time for the explosives crews to go to work.

Ben stood on the south side of Canal, facing SoHo and Little Italy. "We don't blow the art galleries or the museums in SoHo, people. I'm just hoping to God that something is left to salvage."

"SoHo is a funny name for a community, General," Jersey said.

"It's a shortened version for South of Houston Street, Jersey."

"How can you keep all those facts in your head, General?" a young Rebel asked him.

Ben laughed and showed him a tourist guide of NYC. "I just read it in here, son." He pointed to an uncleared building across the street. "Toss a couple of concussion grenades in that one, people. Let's see what happens."

What happened was the entire ground-level floor erupted in a wall of roaring debris that would have knocked Ben and his party flat on their butts had not Ben ordered them all in an alley and down on their bellies.

"Are you people all right?" Ben yelled to the two Rebels who had chunked the grenades. He had seen them dash to the front of the buildings next to the one being tested.

"We're OK!" came the shout. "Looks like everything was directed forward."

"The nasty buggers also know what they're doing when it comes to explosives," Dan observed, getting to his boots.

"Unfortunately for us," Ben agreed. "But unless we're awfully lucky, concussion grenades are not going to break a beam, and since the crawlers seem to know what they're doing, they'll have the explosives rigged so that a simple concussion won't set them off. Back to square one."

Ben squatted in the alley, staring at the devastated building across the snowy and debris-littered street. He studied a map intently for a moment, then abruptly stood up and turned to Beth. "Bump Katzman. Tell him I said to order all APC's and tanks to immediately begin grouping at the intersections of

Canal and Bowery and Canal and the Avenue of the Americas. We're jumping ahead, bypassing everything that lies between Canal and Washington Square. That also includes everything east and west, from the East River to the Hudson. With any kind of luck, that should move us past the booby-trap zone. Let's go! Strike hard and fast. Move!"

Ben was off and running to his Blazer before anyone else could move.

As soon as Beth had finished relaying the order, she and Jersey were right behind Ben. Cooper was already behind the wheel.

Dan lifted his walkie-talkie, hesitated, then keyed the handy-talker. "The Eagle is preparing to lead the newly ordered push. Cover him as best you can." He switched to his Scout frequency. "All Scouts. Supplies and ammo for a week and gather around me at the main CP. I want it done fifteen minutes ago. Move!"

Dan was off and running, slipping and sliding in the snow and uttering some decidedly ungentlemanly oaths, most of which were directed toward the Night People.

A few were directed at the audacity of one Ben Raines. The Blazer, unless it took a direct rocket hit, was practically a rolling fort—Dan had seen to that. The doors and roof were steel-reinforced and the glass was bulletproof. It was just that generals did not lead wild charges into enemy territory. It just . . . well, wasn't done!

With the exception of Ben Raines.

He was always doing something that was totally unexpected and thoroughly irritating to those who cared about the man's safety. Which was, without exception, every member of the Rebel army.

When he got to the main CP, Ben was throwing gear into the back of the Blazer.

Dan lifted his walkie-talkie. "Lead tanks out. Good luck, gang."

Ben turned. "I didn't OK the sending of tanks yet, Dan."

"No, you didn't. I did." Dan stood his ground. "Somebody has to take the initiative in protecting the general's ass—begging the general's pardon, of course."

Ben laughed at him and closed the rear of the Blazer. "Are you going to sit back here and sip tea, Dan? I'm gone."

Ben got into the Blazer and pointed his finger. "Go!" He gave the order to Cooper.

The Blazer moved out, leaving Dan shouting orders for his people to get the lead out of their butts and get moving.

As Cooper turned north off Canal, onto Bowery, two Abrams cut in front of him, two APC's pulling in behind him. The tank commander spoke into his headset, Ben watching his lips move.

"Got you now!" Ike's voice came through the speaker in the Blazer.

It had come as no surprise to Ben. He lifted the mike. "What's your twenty, Shark?"

"Sittin' on ready at Canal and Avenue of the Americas."

"Cec?"

"He lost the toss. He's rear guard."

"You're in command, Cec," Ben radioed. "Hang

tough and watch for a possible swing-around from the creepies."

"Ten-four, Eagle. Good luck."

Ben lifted his eyes. The tank commander had twisted and was looking at him. Ben pointed a finger up Bowery. The Abrams lurched forward, the tank commanders closing the hatches and buttoning up.

"Go!" Ben issued the orders and the columns, widely separated by a dozen city blocks, moved into unknown territory.

"I joined the Rebels because I didn't want to get married and raise cows," Beth said. "What the hell do I know about cows? Except that you're always stepping in the mess they leave behind. Katzman promised me a nice safe job in communications. Now here I am riding into bogie country with a good chance of getting my butt shot. You can't trust anybody nowadays."

Ben turned and grinned at her. "Where is your sense of adventure, Beth?"

"Back with Lev and those damned cows!"

"Where is back there?" Jersey asked.

"Illinois."

The 105's on the Abrams began pounding, putting an end to conversation. Hatches popped open and gunners began working the 7.62 machine guns. The 12.7mm gun on each tank joined in. It took about one minute to clear both sides of the block; but it left the area smoking and ruined, with bits and pieces of night crawlers all over the place.

The column moved on, slowly. A black-robed figure ran into the littered street, his clothing on fire. Maddened by the pain, the creepie leveled his

AK at an Abrams. The 55-ton tank ran over him, the huge tread grinding him into the street.

A grenade sailed down from a rooftop. It bounced off a tank and exploded harmlessly in the street. The gunners in the APC's behind the Blazer opened up with machine-gun fire as the column moved out of that block and crossed Grand Street.

The street change had put them right on the edge of Little Italy, but those were not friendly Italians waving pizzas at them from the windows and the rooftops and the alleyways.

Ben's move had caught the creepies completely by surprise; whatever they had been expecting, this certainly was not it.

Ben grabbed up his mike. "Button everything down and ram on through!"

Ike heard the order. "It's hell over here, partner!" he radioed. "The bastards are crawling and slithering out of the woodwork."

"Ram on through, Ike. This proves that they didn't get far with their booby-trapping. I think we're clear of it now. West? You monitoring this?"

"Ten-four, General."

"What's your twenty?"

"Coming right down the middle of Houston. We'll intersect in a couple of minutes if you don't get stuck in traffic."

"Ten-four, West. Ike, what's your twenty?"

"I'm parallel to you, Ben. Coming up to Broome Street."

Ben heard a thump coming through the speaker. "Did you take a hit, Ike?"

"Naw," Ike drawled. "We ran over one of the

creepies. He's hangin' on the hood, squallin' at me. Jesus, he's ugly. Wait a minute."

Ike didn't even take his thumb off the mike key. Ben heard the sound of a shot. Ike came back on.

"He's off now. We gonna set up north or south of Washington Square Park?"

"Just north of it. We'll clear out the NYU complex first thing."

"Ten-four. Shark clear."

The Night People began hurling grenades from the rooftops. The tanks were impervious to the grenades, but Ben's Blazer was rocked with each explosion from the minibombs. The sounds of shrapnel slamming into the sides of the four-wheel drive was nerve-racking, if not terribly life-threatening.

It was not a particularly enjoyable few moments for anybody. Ben noticed Jersey had crossed herself and her lips were moving in silent prayer. Beth had her eyes closed. He looked at Cooper to see if his eyes were open. They were.

Then they were free of the deadly hail. They had crossed Kenmare and were picking up speed, roaring up Bowery.

"Colonel West and his bunch just up ahead, General," one of the tank commanders radioed back.

"Is he tank-reinforced?"

"Ten four, sir. Dusters."

"West? This is Eagle. Take the point and clear it out for us."

"My pleasure, sir," West's calm voice came over the speaker.

The 40-mm twin guns of the old Dusters were time-proven; the only problem was carrying enough ammo, for at a max of 240 rounds per minute, with both barrels going, the Dusters could spit out a lot of grief.

And heading up Bowery, toward the split where Bowery ends and branches off into Third Avenue, the 40mm cannons dealt some misery to the creepies.

The Dusters were running in a Wolf pack, three abreast, the middle tank slightly ahead of the flankers. A lot of modification had been done to these old tanks, first introduced as the M-19. Fifty-caliber machine guns had been mounted on some, with cannibalized gunshields from other models. Some Dusters had twin-mounted M-60's—whatever the crews were happiest with.

The column, now grown in size, angled off onto Fourth Avenue. Ben picked up the mike.

"West, take your people on north and cut over on East Eighth. Start working south from there. I'll cut over on Broadway now and come up under you on West Third. Good hunting."

"Thank you, General. Take care of yourself."

"Ike? You cut east at Waverly Place. That'll put you and your people right on top of Washington Square Park. See you shortly."

"Ten-four," Ike drawled.

"Dan? Where are you?"

"Right behind you, sir."

"Dan, when I cut off on Third, you continue on to Washington Place and start securing that area."

"Yes, sir."

"Let's do it, gang."

As the Rebels' objectives became known to the Night People through their monitoring of the transmissions, the creepies tried to move into place, to get into better defensive positions. But Ben and his people were moving too fast, their advance too sudden, and the crawlers were caught with their pants down—or their robes up. Whatever.

The Abrams swung onto Third, with Ben right behind them. Ben had been busy hooking grenades onto his battle harness. He looked up as a library came into view. "Right here, Cooper," he ordered. Ben bailed out of the Blazer before it even stopped moving, Beth and Jersey scrambling out and running to catch him, as Ben's squad of bodyguards were hard pressed to keep up.

Creepies met the Rebels on the steps. Ben cleared the first row of them with one sustained burst from his Thompson. The big .45-caliber slugs slammed through dirty robes and tore into filthy human flesh, knocking the crawlers backward and to either side. The steps became slippery from the blood of the creepies. One stared up at Beth through hate-filled eyes and tried to grab her ankle. She shot him between the eyes, ending, among other things, the hate.

"Cows have nicer eyes," she muttered, then followed Ben and Jersey inside the library.

The place was a wreck. Rat-chewed books and magazines littered the floor, ankle-deep. And black-robed spookies were all over the place, stinking it up, profaning the knowledge and entertainment between the covers of the thousands of books.

Ben ducked behind a counter just as one bogie leveled his AK and sent half a clip in Ben's direction. The slugs tore holes in the counter and blew dusty rat-shitted papers flying.

Jersey stopped that bogie with a burst of .223 slugs, then turned her weapon to a group of black-robes that came charging and squalling at her from a hallway. Beth dropped to one knee and added another full auto to Jersey's. Together, they turned the hallway into a death trap for smelly people, sending blood and other parts of human bodies splattering all over the place.

Ben had dropped an empty drum, refitted a full one, and was busy ruining the day for any number of creepies.

A squad of Gray's Scouts had battled their way through the rear of the huge red sandstone building—which at one time had housed over two million books—and now the Night People who remained alive in the library had but two choices: surrender or die.

They chose the latter.

And did it en masse.

The air filled with the stink of creepies and the sharp smell of gunsmoke as the Rebels closed the jaws of the trap and cleared yet another tiny part of the Big Apple.

Ben stood in the ankle-deep mess and shook his head in disgust and despair at the wanton waste of so many valuable works of the masters. But the cleanup and the inventory would have to come later.

He fitted a full drum into the belly of the Thompson and jacked in a round. "Let's go, people. We've got a lot of work to do."

With Beth and Jersey and Cooper, he stepped outside and breathed deeply of the cold air, clearing his lungs of the stink of the Night People. Together, they stood for a moment, just outside the front door of the library. They could all hear the sounds of fierce fighting as other Rebels struck blows for freedom from fear and cannibalism and ignorance. A crawlie moaned from inside the library. A single shot put an abrupt end to the moaning.

"All those books in there," Jersey said. "Destroyed. It doesn't make any sense. What kind of people do things like that?"

"Ignorant people, Jersey," Ben told her. "Ignorant people are very fearful of knowledge. Books are the light at the end of the dark tunnel of ignorance. People who are ignorant want to keep others the same way. Ignorant people have no power or influence over those who wish to climb out of the pits of stupidity. Ignorant people want only to destroy. Erudite and curious-minded people want to learn more and more. People who stop learning, stagnate. Wherever we go, Jersey, we try to leave it a better place."

"We've got a hell of a job ahead of us in this city, General," Beth said.

Ben smiled at her. "Then I guess we'd better get to it."

Chapter 19

Tina and her Rebels, most of their work done, had little to do except wait and guard the airport. Since their arrival, they had seen nothing of the Night People. The uglies had been at the airport; some of their discarded clothing had been found, and burned. But it looked as though it had been a long time since any of the creepies had visited Teterboro. Which, at first, was a relief. Now Tina and those in her command were getting bored, and a little irritated. Especially since they were monitoring the radio transmission in the city, and knew that Ben had pushed on ahead and was engaged in some heavy fighting around Washington Square.

"There is a reason for General Raines to have us out here," Ham said, during a break in the monitoring. "This airport is a vital link to the city. That's why he beefed us up."

"Yeah, I know," Tina told him, after a long sigh. "But that knowledge doesn't make the waiting any easier to take."

"He sent me and my people along for a reason,"

Doctor Ling spoke. "And that reason is he expects us to take some casualties. I've a hunch he strongly believes this Monte person will try to take this airport and cut off the Rebels' supply route into the city."

"Yeah," Pam said. "Lord knows he sure trucked in enough supplies for us."

They looked up as the still far-off sounds of a cargo plane reached them. "Let's go to work." Tina said.

Emil breathed a sigh of relief as Virginia faded behind them. He had thought for a time they never would get out of that state. Not that he had anything against what used to be known as Virginia; it just took so damn long to clear it.

With Thermopolis's people added to his own force—if that is what Emil's followers could be called with any degree of accuracy—the ragtag-looking bunch now numbered just over two hundred.

And no stranger collection of warriors—and the vehicles they drove—was ever gathered together in recorded history.

Emil, of course, led the column, behind a few guard vehicles. Emil traveled in his black hearse.

The rest of Emil's people rattled and banged along in a collection of vehicles that would send a junk dealer into throes of ecstasy.

Thermy's bunch all drove VW's. Every friggin' one of them either drove or rode in a VW. A Bug or a van. But it was a VW. With flowers painted on them. And peace signs and symbols and other hippie crap that Emil hadn't seen since the 1960's.

Emil wondered if Thermy had himself a pretty good scam going as well.

He decided not.

But that music, man, was fuckin' *awful!* Every VW had a tape player, and together, Thermy's bunch must own a zillion tapes. If it wasn't low down cottonpatch blues, it was some other nasal hideousness with words that made absolutely no sense—the ones Emil could understand, that is.

"No wonder the Russians bombed us." he muttered.

But all in all, Emil had to admit, he liked Thermy and his people. That old 1960's expression fit them very well. What was it? Yeah. They had their shit together. And there was nothing the hippies couldn't fix. No sweat if a car or truck broke down. They could fix it. And they weren't like the hippies Emil remembered from those old days of protest.

These people were clean. They took baths. Not many of the men shaved. But they were clean. Amazing!

And as far as the names went . . . Emil didn't believe any of them. But that was all right. Emil wasn't Emil's real name either. Hadn't been for a long time. Since years before the Great War . . . Emil had been on the run from his third wife when the balloon went up. Bitch had chased him all over three states. Caught up with him once in a supermarket in Kentucky and beat the hell out of him with a ten-pound roll of salami. That was embarrassing. Painful, too.

So it didn't make any difference to Emil about names. Emil was just glad Thermy and his bunch had linked up with them.

If they'd just do something about that music.

* * *

The sounds of battle had faded to an occasional shot; after the fury of the morning it was a welcome calm.

The Rebels had cleared everything around Washington Square, from the Provincetown Playhouse to the E. H. Bobst Library. They had cleared several churches, removing the black-robed stinking blasphemy from the Houses of God and dumping the bodies into the snowy streets; they lay in bloody heaps, awaiting transport to the garbage scows that would take them to a watery grave.

The cold air stank of death.

"There is not a painting left in the Grey Art Gallery, General," West reported. "The main building of the University is completely clear. Would you like to walk over for an inspection?"

The men, accompanied by Ben's ever-present bodyguards, walked through the square, under the arch, past the statue of Garibaldi, and entered the main building. The floor was littered with refuse and rat droppings, but there was no sign of any vandalism of the paintings: there was not one shredded or torn canvas alive with colors. No evidence of broken frames.

"Did they leave anything at all behind?" Ben asked.

"Nothing. Not one painting."

"Somebody, somewhere, certainly has quite an impressive art collection."

"That they do, General."

Outside, the garbage details, masked and gloved against disease, were picking up and tossing into trucks the bodies of Night People. The dull sounds as bodies struck bodies did not carry far in the snowy afternoon.

Ben stepped outside to stand facing Washington Square East. A folded piece of paper, carried by the wind, stuck to his right boot. Ben reached down and removed the wet paper. A brochure of some type, the words faded, but still readable. Some sort of real estate flyer.

Ben carefully opened the folder and shook the water from it.

Seventy-four residential units for sale in the Village, read the flyer. Nine hundred square feet, one bedroom, two hundred and sixty thousand dollars. Call Cindy. Do it today. These units are going fast.

Ben wadded the wet paper into a tight little ball. "Wonder what happened to Cindy?" he muttered, the words lost in the cold wind.

Blister gas had been used in the areas Ben's people had bypassed getting to Washington Square. Screaming in agony, the Night People ran from the buildings, to be shot down by Rebels waiting outside, in full protective gear.

There was nothing glamorous about the action. There is nothing glamorous about war. It was cold, dirty nerve-tearing work. The blister gas had eaten into the flesh of the cannibals, driving many of them mad under the intense pain.

And Ben was in no mood to jack around taking prisoners and giving aid and comfort to any of these filthy, disgusting and savage people.

The Rebels had cordoned off several blocks containing the buildings presumed to be booby-trapped. They would deal with them later.

The chemicals had struck fear into the hearts of the Night People. For they now knew that Ben Raines was no subscriber to any type of so-called rules of war. Just how much fear Ben had struck into the souls of the cannibals soon became evident.

Ike and Cecil and West walked up, joining the group.

Beth suddenly held up a hand, signaling for silence. They stood just inside a building on the corner of Fifth Avenue and 9th Street, across from the Church of the Ascension. Beth smiled grimly and turned to Ben.

"That was Katzman. The Night People have been in touch with him. They want to make a deal."

"Oh?" Ben returned the grim smile. "What sort of deal are they proposing?"

"They will no longer use booby traps if we will stop using the gas."

Ben thought about that. The several blocks that the Rebels presumed booby-trapped had been sealed off and bypassed. The immediate area around them was almost cleared of creepies by use of the blister agent. While the Rebels certainly owed nothing to the Night People, the use of chemicals was repugnant to nearly all of the Rebels.

"And if we don't stop?" Ben felt he already knew the answer to that. Beth confirmed it.

"We will have to kill the women and children they have in captivity before we get to them."

"Nice folks," Ike said.

"Yeah. Just peachy." Ben cut his eyes and nodded to Beth. "All right. But the first time we encounter a booby-trapped building north of West Houston the deal is off. And I want the SoHo and Little Italy districts cleared of explosives. We won't bother them while they clear it, they don't bother us."

Beth relayed the message to Katzman. "He says give him a few minutes. He'll get back to us."

"War certainly produces some strange arrangements between enemies," Dan observed.

"Yes," Ben agreed. "Now if we just knew the locations of the prisoners, we could extricate them and go back to using gas."

"My goodness, General!" Dan looked heavenward, a smile on his lips. "You mean you would go back on your word and resume the use of gas against these poor wretches?"

"Faster than you can dunk a tea bag."

Those gathered around had a good laugh at that. All knew that Ben Raines could be totally and utterly ruthless in dealing with an enemy—especially one as odious as the Night People.

Beth listened to her headphones for a moment. "The creepies accepted the deal, General."

Ben's eyes were hard for a moment. They remained hard as he said, "We scared them with the blister gas. But for them to want to face us nose-to-nose and resume slugging it out . . ." He paused for a few seconds. ". . . That means they've got us so badly outnumbered that they can afford to lose hundreds or even thousands more, knowing they will eventually defeat us, or they're counting heavily on Monte's assistance. Or, a combination of both."

"What's the word on Monte?" West asked.

"They're still in Canada. We bought maybe a week to ten days by blowing the bridge. If they elect to cross at Cornwall, they'll have to spend some time repairing it. Striganov told me that a portion of that bridge had been knocked out several years back. They could cross over about fifty miles on up the road, but I'm betting they won't. That would put them out on a maze of poorly maintained secondary roads. They'd lose a lot of time. I'm betting they'll go on up and cross over just west of Montreal and hook up with Eighty-seven." He pulled out a map and opened it. "Right now, Rebet's people and Dan's Sappers are busting their butts trying to get to this area here." He pointed to the map. "To blow a series of bridges on the New York Thruway. If we can pull that off, that will force Monte over into Vermont, bringing them down to the north of us, rather than to the west of us, and close to Tina's position."

Ben looked down at the map case. "But that entails a lot of ifs, people. Monte is a thug, but he's a smart thug. He's going to see all these bridges blown, and that's going to tingle the short hairs on his neck. If he decides to cut west, bypassing the blown bridges, then he'll eventually link up with Eighty-seven again. And if that happens, we'll be cut off from the airport, and from Tina's bunch."

And from Jerre, Ben silently added.

"You want to split the forces, Ben?" Cecil asked. "I could take my battalion up, and that would put Danjou and Rebet on top of him and me and mine below him."

"I thought of it, Cec. But we're spread thin here

in the city now. Right now we're running the risk of night crawlers infiltrating back across our lines at night." He shook his head. "No. I've got planes ready to go when Monte crosses over. Dan's Sappers will radio us from the bridges, telling us what direction Monte's taking. We'll just have to make a decision when that time comes. And," he added, "hope that it's the right one."

"How about all our people out in America, General?" Beth asked. "You know, the patrols and the Rebels manning the outposts and the ones down in Louisiana?"

Again, Ben shook his head. "No. If we pulled the troops assisting those civilians at the outposts, the warlords and outlaws would attack, trying to reclaim. The same for Joe Williams's troops down at Base Camp One. He's got to guard the ammo-producing factories and food-processing plants and all of that. Hell, Joe's got the thinnest battalion of us all. No. It's up to us." Ben smiled and then laughed, while the others looked at him, wondering what in the hell was going on. "And, of course, we're forgetting a very important ally."

Dan blinked. "Who?"

Ben grinned. "Why . . . Emil is on his way up to lend us a hand, remember?"

BOOK TWO

Let them hate, so long as they fear.
—Lucius Accius

Freedom is a system based on courage.
—Charles Peguy

Chapter 1

On the gray morning that Emil decided it was time to turn east toward New York (if he'd driven much farther he'd have been floating in Lake Erie), he was boosted up onto the hood of his hearse. The hood was slippery with frost and Emil fell off after about fifteen seconds of wild arm-waving and some fancy footwork. His followers thought it was a new dance and burst into applause.

"I think we're about to hear a speech," Rosebud said to Thermopolis.

"I find them entertaining."

She looked at him. "You would."

Emil decided not to chance the hood again. "Gather around, friends!" he yelled. "Come close."

Everybody pushed in and almost smothered Emil. "Get back, damn it!" Emil shrieked. "I can't breathe. That's better. Now listen up. From here on, we're really gonna be in Indian country . . ."

"My old man is an Indian," Wren said, pointing to Whistler.

Two of the faithful lifted Emil up so he could see.

"Oh. Well, sorry." They put him back down. "We're in enemy territory, then. Somebody get me a damn box!" A box was found for Emil to stand on. "Thank you. Friends, our fate is uncertain. But our mission is clear. We go to New York City to aid the great Ben Raines in his fight against the flesh-eating Night People, the scourge of the twenty-first century."

"We know all that, Brother," one of his faithful said.

"Hush up. We go into battle as modern day Joans of Arc . . . ah, Joans and Johns. We carry with us the sword of retribution . . ."

"Can I see that sword, Father Emil?" Brother Sonny said. "Huh? Huh? Can I?"

"Hush *up!* And now, friends, comes decision time. Any who want to leave, any who feel their personal well of courage is dry, had better cut and run now, for once we get near the Big Apple, I suspect we're not going to have time for anything except fighting and staying alive."

"For once he makes sense," Rosebud whispered.

"You having second thoughts about this?" her husband asked.

She shook her head. "No. For all his big army, I think Ben Raines is going to need all the help he can get." She smiled. "Besides, I wouldn't miss the look on his face when he sees this collection of warriors for anything."

Thermopolis smiled with her.

"Thermopolis, you are going to take charge when we get close to the battleground, aren't you? I mean, that little man couldn't lead a charge against a marsh-mallow factory."

"Let's just say that Emil and I will share the command. He really means well, Rosebud."

"I know. Just tell me that when it comes down to the nitty-gritty, you'll make the decisions."

"I suspect that if we do make it into New York City, Ben Raines will call the shots."

"Forward to victory, mighty army of Blomm!" Emil shouted, then fell off the box.

"General Raines?" the runner said. "Radio reports from an outpost in Pennsylvania say that a large force of, ah . . . well, *people* just passed an observation point on Interstate Eighty. About two hundred and fifty strong."

"Children with them?"

"No, sir. At least none were spotted."

"Why did you place such emphasis on 'people'?"

"Well, sir . . ." The runner shook his head. "Katzman said that the Rebels radioing in stated that the column was made up of hippies."

Ben smiled. "Emil's found a commune somewhere. Or they found him would be more like it. Let them come on. Lord knows we can use all the help we can get."

The runner looked very dubious about just what kind of help Emil and a bunch of hippies might bring to them. Ben patted him on the shoulder.

"Relax, son. Back when the world was whole— more or less—I knew a lot of hard-assed combat vets who joined the hippie movement. If they hadn't made up their minds to fight, they wouldn't be coming up here. We'll find a place for them."

The runner left. He still looked dubious.

Ben picked up his Thompson and stepped out of the ground floor of the building he was using as a field CP. The Rebels' advance had slowed to perhaps a third of a block a day—on a good day. Both sides had accepted the method of fighting: nose-to-nose and slug it out without destroying the city; each with their own widely different reasons for wanting to preserve the city.

Ben's people had pushed up to West 12th. Ike had cleared everything from the Hudson River waterfront over to Ben's perimeter and up to West 14th. He was holding there to keep from getting into a bottleneck by pushing too far ahead of the others. Cecil and West had cleared everything from the East River over to Ben's section and up to 14th Street East.

Thanksgiving had passed with no lull in the fighting and no special celebration among the combat troops.

Ben had ordered teams up the parkway along the Hudson River, clearing the parkway up to the George Washington Bridge. A full platoon of Rebels was stationed at and on the bridge to keep it open. Supplies were able to move along the parkway, but it was a dangerous run, always subjected to sniper fire from the creepies, hidden along the way. Tanks always escorted the supply trucks back and forth, and the buildings on the Manhattan side of the parkway began to resemble Berlin in 1945. The cannon fire from the tanks had been devastating.

Ben called for a meeting of his commanders.

"West, I want you and your mercs to take over my section," Ben informed the group. "Keep pushing up Manhattan. Ike, you and Cecil swing your ends around and pick up the slack."

"And you propose to do what?" Ike challenged him.

"I'm taking my battalion straight up the parkway and then cutting over on Dyckman Street and start pushing down."

That was met by a roar of complaints from everybody at the meeting, except Dan. He knew he and his Scouts were going in with Ben. He rather looked forward to the new adventure.

Ben let everybody vent their spleens and then held up his hand for silence. "I've ordered my people to be ready to go at dawn tomorrow. End of discussion."

"God damn it, Ben!" Ike yelled, jumping to his feet. "You get cut off up there and your butt is gonna be between a rock and a hard place!"

"I agree with Ike," West said. "My battalion is the logical one to spearhead north."

"And I agree with West," Cecil glared at Ben. "It is perfectly stupid for you to take a chance like this." He cut his eyes to Dan. "And what about you? Don't you have anything to add to this?"

"Oh, yes." Dan stood up. Looked at Ben. "I shall be ready to go at dawn, General."

Ben had ordered a strict silence about his leaving; most of his own people didn't know where they were going. They just knew they were going to pull out. Absolutely nothing about it had been broadcast.

Ben was up at four, as usual, and rolled out Jersey

and Beth. Cooper, for once, was already up. "Will wonders never cease?" Ben kidded him.

Cooper tried to look hurt; he looked more like a basset hound. "I made coffee."

"All is forgiven." Ben poured a cup and took it outside. He looked up at the sky and said, "Well, crap!"

It was a beautiful night, clear and bright. Ben would have preferred fog and rain. On a morning like this, sound would carry forever, and the sounds of tanks and APC's and Jeeps and trucks all cranking up would immediately bring the creepies into full alert, knowing something big was going down.

But for now, Ben squatted down, next to a building, and sipped his coffee, enjoying the peaceful—or peaceful-appearing—night. It was, without doubt, the loveliest night he had seen since arriving in New York City. The old show tune entered his mind, and he began humming it.

"That dates you, General," West's voice came at him from his left.

"I thought you were a sentry, West."

"I told her to go get a cup of coffee. The girl was cold."

Ben stood up; his bad knee was beginning to ache from the strain of squatting. "Anything happen during the night?"

"Just the usual exchange of gunfire at the usual places. Each side letting the other know they were still there."

"In a way I'm sorry I'm going north."

"Oh? Having a change of heart, General?"

"No. I was just looking forward to prowling through Macy's that's all."

The two soldiers shared a quiet chuckle. West said, "I'll pick you out something nice for your ladylove."

"'Fraid I'm fresh out of those at the moment, West."

"I do know the feeling."

"You and Tina have a fuss?"

West chuckled. "No, Daddy."

Ben laughed aloud and let the subject of Tina drop. "Ever been married?" he asked the mercenary.

West was a long time replying; so long that Ben thought he was going to ignore the question. "Yes. She was South African. One of those cool blondes that only the Afrikaners seem to be able to produce. I was working with security forces at the time. Her family opposed the union, of course—mercenary and socialite—but we plunged ahead. She was killed three months later in an ambush. I found those responsible. They did not die well."

Ben did not pursue the last of West's statement. "I'm sorry, and I mean that. But at least you had that time with her."

The mercenary sighed. "Yes, you're right. And I cherish those moments. And do I still love her? Yes. After fourteen years I love her as much now as I did then."

"I know that feeling."

Ben could feel the man's eyes on him. "It's pure hell, isn't it, Ben?"

Ben knew what he was talking about. Love could be beautiful, or love could be a bitch. "Yes."

"I can put your mind at rest on one issue, Ben. Tina and I enjoy each other's company, but wedding bells are not in our future."

Ben looked at the man. Just before he walked away to join his Rebels, he said, "She could do a hell of a lot worse, West."

The rumble and grumble of the tanks, trucks, and other vehicles filled the air, fracturing the calm of the lovely morning.

The staging area was set well back into friendly lines, and well guarded, so no one worried when Ben walked up and down the row of vehicles, chatting with each driver for a few seconds, smiling and waving at the others.

Both sides of each deuce-and-a-half had been built up higher and reinforced with thick wood and sheets of metal. For the Rebels had a good eleven-mile run through bogie country—subject to fire every foot of the way—and were going to have to hit the ground fighting when they reached their destination. The tanks had a top speed of nearly 50, and they were going to have to hammer down all the way.

"Get set for a wild ride," Ben said, walking up and down the line.

"Be good to get a change of scenery, General!" a woman called.

Ben smiled and waved, walking on. He looked up at a man who'd been part of the Rebels since the outset, so many years back. "Luke, you didn't forget your toilet paper, did you? You're liable to need some before this ride is over."

The veteran of more fire-fights than he could remember laughed and held up a roll of toilet paper.

Ben returned the laugh and walked on, Jersey and Beth with him. "Hey, darlin'!" a man called to Beth. "When are you and me gonna go paint the town red?"

"Never!" Beth fired back. "I'd rather be back on the farm with the cows."

"My heart is broken!" the Rebel laughed.

Ben completed his tour and began walking back up the other side of the column, joking and chatting briefly—never stopping his walking—with the men and women who made up his battalion. They were all races, all religions, and all united, all sharing one goal: the rebuilding of the nation. And many would die long before that dream ever became reality.

"Let's go kick some ass, General!" a Rebel called.

Ben waved at the woman warrior. "On our way, Lizzie. Hang tough."

A rather crude suggestion as to how they could pass the time while getting to the new battle zone was offered to Lizzie from a male Rebel.

The suggestion was received in the same good rough humor it was offered. Lizzie told the man where he could put his M-60.

Ben laughed and held the door open so Beth and Jersey could get into the backseat of the Blazer. Cooper was behind the wheel, the engine idling.

Ben picked up the mike from the radio mounted under the dash. "Lead tanks out. Scouts out. Column out. Let's do it, people! Let's go take another bite out of the Big Apple."

Chapter 2

A flyby had been done of the route just hours before, just before dusk. The parkway was clear up to the George Washington Bridge. But from that point on, the way north was going to be rough: abandoned cars and trucks littered the parkway from the bridge all the way up to the Henry Hudson Bridge, that vital link between Manhattan and Bronx County. Two big Abramses rolled as point, one a tank's length behind the other; it would be their job to shove the rusted hulks of vehicles out of the way, clearing a path for the column.

The column had not been away from the staging area more than a minute before they were in bogie country, and the Night People were instantly aware that something very big was going down.

The Rebels came under fire almost immediately.

Cooper pulled over into the left lane and a Duster clanked up beside the Blazer, in the right lane, shielding the Blazer from hostile fire.

Ben opened his mouth to protest, then closed it. If he ordered the tank away, another would just take its place. And when he had gone through the tanks, deuce-and-a-halfs would fill the gap. Once again, his Rebels had worked out a plan to protect their general.

"We're waiting for you to start bitching, General," Beth spoke from the backseat.

"Would it do any good?"

"No, sir."

All three of them had a laugh at the expression on Ben's face. Ben finally smiled with them. It helped to ease the tension while the hostile fire cracked all around the column.

From the center of the column, Big Thumpers in the beds of trucks started hurling 40mm grenades. With a range of 2400 yards (max effective range of 1650 yards) the 40mm Thumpers thumped the hell out of the buildings that housed the creepies.

Fifty-caliber machine guns (with a range of 2000 yards) began raking enemy-held buildings as the column sped up the parkway at max speed.

"It's going to really get interesting once we're past the bridge," Ben said.

Beth glanced at a map, using a tiny flashlight to see. They still had a long way to go before reaching the bridge. And running this gauntlet was interesting enough for her.

They had just passed West 23rd.

Ben lifted his mike. "Thirtieth Street Terminal is full of creepies," he alerted his people. "And so is the Javits Convention Center. That's where the convoys take the heaviest fire. Heads up."

"How far is that?" Jersey asked Beth.

"We're there."

The creepies opened up with everything they had available to them and kept up the barrage until the column crossed over the Lincoln Tunnel and the parkway changed to the West Side Highway.

"Four trucks disabled, General," Beth told him. "Tires shot out. Orders?"

"Have the people double up. We can't afford the time it would take to change the tires. We've got vehicles running out the kazoo."

"Yes, sir."

"Assign two Dusters as protection and slow the column speed down to thirty."

"Yes, sir."

"I'll take the mike from here, Beth."

Ben lifted his mike. "All right, gunners. We're slowing our speed. Pick your targets and let 'em bang."

The just-graying morning erupted in a roaring of death and destruction from machine guns, mortars, cannon, and 40mm grenades from the Big Thumpers.

Ben could barely hear the words coming out of the speaker. "Trucks off-loaded and rolling, sir. We're coming up on the column's donkey."

"Hammer down, people." Ben ordered. "Let's get out of this area. These folks don't like us at all!"

The column picked up speed and rolled on. Gray and silver were beginning to streak the sky.

"Central Park right over there." Ben said. "A few more blocks and we'll be pretty much clear until we parallel Riverside Drive. Then it'll start picking up again."

"I can use the rest," Beth said dryly.

"How about some coffee?" Ben said, holding up a

big thermos. They all wanted coffee. "Tell you what, Cooper," Ben offered, keeping his face bland as they angled off, taking a detour for a few blocks. "I'll take the wheel and you can sit back and drink your coffee. Come on, just slide over here. There you go."

"Good God, people!" Jersey blurted. "We're goin' fifty miles an hour and you two start playing musical chairs."

"Relax, Jersey," Ben turned his head, grinning at her. "Just sit back and drink your coffee. Everybody got coffee? Good." He picked up his mike. "Get out of the way, truck. I'm coming around."

Ben kicked the Blazer in the butt and stayed in the left lane, passing everything on the road.

"I knew it!" Beth moaned. "I knew there was a catch to it. I just knew it!"

Jersey just cussed.

Cooper was holding his coffee mug with both hands and wondering if the general was going to attempt to pass the lead tanks.

But two more Abrams pulled over, effectively blocking the highway, running in a staggered pattern, two up and two back.

Ben laughed at the move. "Henry Hudson Parkway," he announced. "You kids enjoying the ride?"

"What happens if we gotta go to the bathroom?" Beth asked.

"That depends entirely upon how modest you are and whether or not you have a helmet."

Her reply would have stricken every member of a censor board dead on the spot.

"You ever give him the wheel again, Cooper," Jersey warned, "and I'll shoot you!"

"How the hell do you tell a general he can't drive?" Cooper protested.

"You tell him no!"

Ben just grinned and changed lanes, crowding the ass end of a tank.

"You see, Cooper?" Jersey yelled. "That's why General Ike told you to be his driver. General Ike said he was a madman behind the wheel."

"Madman?" Ben said. "Ike said that about me?"

"And Doctor Chase said he was the worst driver in the entire Rebel Army."

"What!"

"And General Jefferys said he couldn't be trusted. He said Ben Raines will tell you he's going one way and then go the other just to throw off his bodyguards."

Ben couldn't rebut the truth.

"Awright, awready!" Cooper growled.

"Pay no attention to them, Cooper," Ben told him. "They're just jealous because they have to sit in the backseat. Women's lib and all that."

Beth and Jersey groaned.

"Yes, sir." Since Cooper had been just a young boy when the Great War scoured the earth, he didn't have the foggiest what women's lib meant. He guessed it might have something to do with a brassiere.

Ben changed lanes again, trying to figure out how to get through the tank blockade. But the commanders had him in a box and weren't about to let him through.

"Having trouble, sir?" one of them asked politely.

"Not a bit, thank you," Ben radioed his reply.

"Just checking, sir."

"Thank you for your concern."

"You're welcome, sir."

Ben settled back and eased off the tank's donkey—much to the relief of his passengers.

"Columbia University will be coming into range in a couple of minutes, General." The speakers spewed the words. "You want us to shell it?"

"No," Ben radioed. "We don't know if or how many prisoners they're holding in there. Do not shell."

"Ten-four, sir."

"Get set for some more hostile fire, people." Ben told his troops. "We'll be running close to Riverside Drive from here on in. All troops not manning weapons keep your heads down."

His orders were acknowledged up and down the rolling line.

"Tanks, swivel turrets for machine-gun fire. Half-tracks and APC gunners, prepare for returning unfriendly fire."

Those orders were acknowledged.

As Riverside Park ended, just past Grant's Tomb, and the parkway ran in close proximity to Riverside Drive, the bogies began firing on the column. The returning fire from the Rebels was blistering and deadly. Another Rebel truck had tires knocked flat, disabling the vehicle. Once more, the column was forced to slow, several Dusters falling back to protect the troops and equipment as they were off-loaded onto other vehicles. A mass of black-robed creepies made the mistake of climbing onto the parkway. The Duster's 40mm cannons, hurling their "red golf balls," and machine-gun fire turned the crawlers into chunks of chopped meat. In under two minutes, the column was once more rolling at max speed.

"West One Hundred Fifty-fifth Street coming up," Beth announced from the backseat.

"Not far now," Ben said. He lifted his mike. "We've got a traffic maze coming up soon, people. Be very careful that you don't get separated. There'll be creepies on the overpasses, throwing everything they've got at us; Ike said that's SOP for them. Heads up and watch out for firebombs."

"I see cocktails already lighted, General," a tank commander radioed.

"Do not use cannon," Ben ordered. "We've got to keep this place intact. Open up with Fifties as soon as you're in range. Which should be now."

Fifty-caliber and 7.62 machine guns began rattling and yammering and blowing out chunks of death at the bogies gathered on the overpasses and hidden along the roadway. Rebels were standing up in the trucks, giving the Night People ten rounds for every one round the creepies fired.

The besieged column, miraculously, stayed together through the traffic circles and maze of interchanges and heavy bogie fire, with Molotov cocktails bouncing off the vehicles and hostile fire clanking and whining off of metal and concrete, and stayed on Riverside, driving right into unknown territory.

It was full light, and the Rebels in Ben's personal battalion were looking at sights that no outsider had seen since the Great War—at least none that Ben knew of.

They roared past 181st Street, receiving no enemy

fire. When they reached the point where Fort Tryon Park lay to their right, Jersey summed it all up.

"It's eerie. I mean . . . the silence. It's like, well, nobody is out there."

"I'm afraid you may be right in that, Jersey," Ben replied. He picked up the mike. "Column halt. Easy does it, people. Let's don't ass-end each other."

The column slowed, then stopped. To their right, on a hill, looking like a fortified monastery, was the Cloisters.

"Dan?"

"Here, sir."

"Scouts out. Two Abrams point the Scouts. Stay on Riverside and then cut back on Dyckman and rejoin us. Stay in radio contact at all times."

"Yes, sir."

Two IFV's filled with Dan's Scouts, and two Abrams pulled out of the column and moved into the silence. The Infantry Fighting Vehicles, each with a ten-personnel seating capacity, were armed fighting machines: a 25mm cannon, TOW missile launcher, and 7.62 machine gun. In addition, the six Scouts inside could fire ball-mounted 5.56mm port weapons.

Before anyone could object, Ben opened the door and got out of the Blazer, stretching his legs. He was immediately surrounded by a squad of Rebels, Jersey, Beth, and Cooper bailing out of the Blazer right behind him.

"Get Ike on the horn, Beth." Ben hand-rolled a cigarette and lit up. "And don't anybody say anything about my smoking."

No one did.

"And get me a casualty report."

Beth handed him the handset. "General Ike, sir."

"So I'm a madman behind the wheel, huh, fatso?" Ben asked the ex-SEAL, a smile on his lips.

"Did I say that, Ben?" Ike said with a laugh. "No! You know I wouldn't say anything like that about you."

"We made it, Ike. I'm getting a casualty report now. But I think we came through intact. Lost a few trucks, that's about it. It's very quiet up here, Ike. Nothing, and I mean *nothing* is moving."

"You'll recall the flybys we took when we first got here showed very little life up that way, Ben."

They were not using translators. No point. The bogies knew they were here. Only for important communiqués would the translators be used. "I've got Scouts out now, Ike. They should be reporting back in about twenty-thirty minutes; but there have been no shots fired since our arrival."

Cecil came on the horn, listening in from his sector. "Ben. We're meeting a solid line of resistance on all fronts. The creepies have really dug in."

"Switch to translators. Feed through Katzman."

Ben waited until the translators were all in place. The radio transmissions were being scrambled on both ends, then fed to the translators in whatever language: Apache, Sac, Fox, Yiddish.

Ben took it. "We noticed and commented on how slow our advance has been over the past few days. It could well mean that you're getting close to a breeding farm or a feeding farm. Check those first flybys with heat-seekers. We know where the Central

Park survivors are, so we can eliminate them. The printouts might tell you something. Let me know."

"Ten-four, Ben. Good hunting."

Ben rehooked the phone. "Let's take a walk, gang."

Dan appeared at his side. "Where are we going, General?"

"I don't know where you're going. I'm going over there and check out the Cloisters."

Before anyone could stop him, Ben had started walking toward the off-ramp that led into Fort Tryon Park.

"General!" Dan called. Ben turned around. "Would you mind terribly if we rode over into that as yet *unchecked-out-area*? Preferably in this armor-plated and bulletproof-glass Blazer?"

"Just as long as Cooper drives!" Jersey yelled.

"Oh, all right." Ben returned to the Blazer and got in. Dan had taken that time to send a couple of squads of Scouts running into the 62-acre park. He was in a Jeep, leading the way.

"How old is this place, General?" Jersey asked. "And what is it? Is it something religious?"

Ben handed her a tourist guide. "Read that, and you'll know as much about it as I do. I think it's some repository for medieval art."

"What kind of art, sir?" Cooper asked.

"Old."

The Scouts' first reply back was short, and exactly what Ben had been dreading. "Place is a mess. Looks like it was looted and vandalized."

"According to this thing," Jersey said, "it's got several levels."

"Yeah. I think so." Ben pointed to a sign. "Pull

around to the main entrance, Cooper. We'll check it out."

Ben grunted in anger as he walked through the once magnificently appointed main and ground floors. The place looked as though a horde of naughty, malicious-minded, undisciplined children had set upon it with cans of spray paint and machetes. The beautiful tapestries, some dating back to the fourteenth century, had been slashed and torn; rats and field mice now made their homes amid the torn beauty. Once-priceless and irreplaceable statues had deliberately been tumbled to the floor, smashed for no reason. Stained glass panels, some centuries old, were shattered beyond repair. Antique chairs and tables and benches had initials and gang slogans carved into the wood. In the Campin Room, the painted Spanish ceiling had been repainted with cans of spray paint, ugly and obscene slogans defaming the beauty.

Ben muttered an oath that equaled the words on the walls and ceilings and walked on.

Nothing had been spared from the mindless, senseless destruction.

"Why?" Jersey asked.

"Who knows why punks do what they do," Ben told her. "Liberal shrinks used to say it was because the coach wouldn't let them play, or the homecoming queen wouldn't date them, or they had pimples, or some other equally idiotic froth from the mouth."

Ben had seen all that he cared to see. The destruction of such beauty was offensive to him, offensive to anybody with more than an ounce of sensitivity in his soul. And it was depressing.

Ben stepped outside and looked for Dan. The Englishman was sitting on the steps. He turned around at the sound of Ben's boots.

"Barbaric! I could not linger in there a moment longer. The destruction of such beauty is beyond my level of comprehension." He spat on the ground, summing up his contempt for those responsible for wreaking such havoc upon priceless souvenirs of centuries past.

"Come on, Dan." Ben motioned him to his boots. "This is a good time for us to inspect a part of New York we've been ignoring."

Dan rose and looked at him, a puzzled look on his face. "What?"

Ben pointed. "It's right out there, Dan. The 190th Street subway station."

Dan pointed a finger at a group of his Scouts. They took off running for a Hummer and sped off in the direction of the subway station.

"Naturally, you will insist upon inspecting the underground passages personally?" Dan asked, just a touch of hope against hope in his voice.

"Naturally," Ben told him. He looked at Jersey and Beth. "We're looking forward to it, aren't we, ladies."

Jersey blinked and stared at him. "Oh, yes, sir, General!" It would have taken an idiot to miss the sarcasm in her voice.

"I gotta go to the bathroom!" Beth said.

Chapter 3

A foul odor seeped out of the entrance to the subway station. Dan's Scouts had already slipped on their gas masks. A portable generator had been set up and was running. Another masked team was stretching wire for lights. Even lit, the steps down were not in the least inviting-looking.

Beth returned from a visit to the bushes, muttering something about the ever-increasing beauty of cows.

"Cows?" Dan looked at Ben. "It appears that I have missed something."

Ben had to laugh. "It's a long story, Dan. I'll tell you about it sometime." He slipped on his gas mask. "Let's go, people."

A Scout met them just as they were walking down the steps to the subway platform. "What you're gonna see pretty well confirms it, General. The city took a chemical hit."

The Scout led the way down into the now lighted subway and up to the platform, where subway cars were pulled up. Full of skeletons.

"Open the doors," Ben ordered, his voice muffled coming through the mask.

Scouts had to use axes to break down the doors, the hinges long rusted closed.

Ben stepped inside the first death-car. Nearly every skeleton had a camera either on the floor beside the rotting shoes or still draped around the bones of the neck, depending upon the material and quality of the strap. The floor was covered with rat droppings.

With gloved hands, Ben picked up a purse and opened it, taking out a wallet. "Irene Golanski," he read from the driver's license. "From Iowa. Tourists. All of them, or most of them." He replaced the wallet and dropped the purse back beside the bony feet of Irene. Dust popped up from the impact. Ben turned and walked up the car, where Rebels had chopped open the doors.

Each car was the same. A steel and glass and chrome mausoleum for Jim from Mobile, Hazel from Hot Springs, Larry from Dallas.

Hardest for the Rebels to take were the skeletons of the children. Jersey picked up one little plastic purse, started to open it, then shook her head and put the purse back on the floor. "Whoever you are, I'm sorry."

"Why should you be sorry?" a Scout asked her. "It wasn't your fault."

Jersey looked at him. "Jimmy, you'll never be a mother. Well," she smiled, "maybe one kind of a mother."

Dan chuckled and patted Jimmy on the shoulder. "You'll think of something in the form of repartee . . . keep working on it."

The Rebels left the cars. Ben stood on the platform for a moment, looking up the dark tunnel. He removed his mask and sniffed the air a couple of times just as Dan walked up to his side. "That odor is not the stink of the creepies, Dan. That's stagnant water and bat shit."

Dan pulled off his mask and took a whiff, grimacing. "Not quite as bad, but bad enough. Do we press on into the darkness, General?"

Ben shook his head. "No. It's strange, Dan. Amid all that mess at the Cloisters, there was not one sign or smell of the Night People. So . . . let's go find them."

The Rebels began working north, spending all that day in a search-and-destroy mission. They did lots of searching, but found nothing to destroy. Once outside of the Fort Tryon Park area, they did find lots of evidence that the night crawlers had once occupied this area . . . but no creepies.

They swept the area fast, with teams working Staff and Henshaw streets, Payson and Seaman avenues, and up Broadway. They found nothing alive. Not a bird, a dog or cat, or a human being. Nothing.

By the time the teams had finished their sweeps, it was late afternoon. They had worked all the way up to Baker Field, but still had everything from Broadway over to the Harlem River to clear.

Ben called a halt to it. A team had been working clearing a building just east of Inwood Hill Park, on Seaman, for Ben to use as a CP, and several other buildings, along Dyckman, to use as quarters for the Rebels.

The weather was rapidly turning foul, with a light cold rain that was mixed with flakes of snow and pellets of sleet. The Rebels had found a warehouse filled with kerosene stoves and had brought along trucks loaded with them and five-gallon cans of fuel.

"I don't like it," Ben said, over a meal of MRE's.

"The food?" Dan looked up, a twinkle in his eyes.

"The food is bearable. But I can't figure out what kind of meat this is."

"Don't ask."

"It has to be one of Chase's highly nutritional concoctions"

"Correct."

"That old goat is going to starve us all to death in the name of proper nutrition."

"I agree."

"The lack of creepies, Dan. That's what's got me worried. All signs point to them pulling out about a week or ten days ago. But where did they go?"

Dan looked at what was dangling from his fork, sighed, and ate it. "A guess would be to beef up those in Lower Manhattan."

"Maybe. But that is one of the reasons I wanted to split up, Dan. I don't want the entire force trapped in a box. It's going to be damned difficult for Monte and the creepers to trap us all, with Cec and West and Ike ten miles south of us. Unless," Ben held up a finger, "I've badly miscalculated."

"How could you have? You and I figured every angle. What could we have left out?"

"How did the Henry Hudson Bridge look today?"

"Like it hasn't been used in ten years. Car or foot traffic."

"The creepies could have used the subways, though."

"To do what, General?"

"To slip behind our lines. To slip out in any direction; to lie in wait for Monte. To somehow trick us into a trap. I tried to think of everything, Dan. But I have this sinking feeling that I missed something."

"Has Chase concluded his interviewing with those creepie prisoners?"

"Yes. Obviously the only ones privy to that type of high-level information are the Judges. Whomever they are and wherever they might be in the city. Chase told me before we pulled out that the Night People he personally interviewed—if you want to call a drug-induced state an interview—had to be the most degenerate and disgusting people he ever encountered. They told him nothing of substance."

Dan did not have to ask what Chase had done with the crawlers after interviewing them. He knew. He had also been briefed as to Monte's location in the States. They were—or had been as of yesterday—getting close to the bridges that his Scouts had blown. A couple more days and they would either cut east, as the Rebels hoped they would, moving away from Tina's position, or smell a rat and cut west, circling and once more linking up with Interstate 87, putting them in line to hit Tina's small force at the airport.

As if reading Dan's thoughts, Ben said, "It could well turn out to be a series of boxes for all of us, Dan. Monte's people might find themselves trapped between Tina's small force and Danjou and Rebet's people as they drive south. Cecil could find himself trapped if the creepies have—as I suspect—swung around and infiltrated the areas we cleared along the waterfront. And if the creepies have moved up into Bronx County, putting themselves behind us, as I suspect, or are hiding in the subway tunnels—which is a possibility—when they surface, we're cut off. It'll turn into a war with a half a dozen fronts, none of which presenting any enviable situation for anybody."

"Then we very well may end up depending on those survivors around Central Park to break through."

"Yes." A smile played around Ben's mouth. "And Emil Hite and the hippies."

"Dad pulled one of his fast ones and broke away from the main group," Tina told a few Rebels gathered around her, Jerre among them. "That was all the radio traffic we heard yesterday morning." She pointed to a wall map in the airport's radio room. "He took his battalion up here and is sweeping south."

It was before dawn, the day after Ben's wild push to the uppermost northern tip of Manhattan, and the skies were still gloomy and overcast, with occasional freezing rain and flakes of snow. Tina had a hunch that her father would contact her that day, and just after breakfast, that hunch became reality.

"Scramble this and talk through translators, kid," Ben told her.

The arrangements made quickly, Tina nodded at her translator. "Go, Eagle One."

"Heads up, Tina. Go on full alert and maintain it." Ben then brought her up to date on all the certainties and possibilities that might be lurking around the corner of each day's dawning.

"I'm sitting here with less than a hundred and fifty Rebels, Dad. No way I could hold out for very long against several thousand of Monte's troops."

"That's why I've ordered the birds at Base Camp One to start flying day and night, munitions factories to work around the clock, and trucks to start rolling from Base Camp One immediately." He brought her up to date on Emil Hite and the hippies.

There was a long pause from the Teterboro Airport radio room. "Are you joking, Dad?"

Ben laughed. "No. I've got Katzman trying to contact them now to advise them of the situation and if they want to continue, what routes to take."

"Why do I have this feeling that you're going to assign them to me?"

"Don't you need the extra manpower—personpower—whatever?"

"Emil Hite and a bunch of *hippies?* Probably middle-aged hippies at that!"

"Watch your mouth, girl. I'm in the middle-aged category, remember?"

"That's different. You've been fighting all your life. Oh, hell, Dad. If you make contact with them, tell them to come on."

"That's my girl. You take care, baby."

"Jerre is working out fine, Dad."

Ben did not acknowledge the last transmission. He broke off.

"What did Ben have to say about the comment concerning me?" Jerre asked.

"Nothing. He broke off."

"Typical." Jerre walked out of the radio room.

"More than one war going on around this place," Ham commented.

"Yeah. And I think I'd rather be in the middle of the shooting one."

The Rebels under Ben's command began their S&D sweeps. And it was a duplicate of the sweeps of the previous day. They found nothing.

By noon the Rebels had worked their way over to the subway yards, covering everything from West 207th north to West 215th. They found no signs of life, friendly or hostile. Ben stood them down for lunch.

"Fastest sweeps yet, General," Dan commented. "My people are coming up empty."

"Same here. And it just doesn't make any sense to me."

"You're really worried about this lack of bogies, aren't you?"

"Yes, I am, Dan. I just don't know where they've gone or why. We've posted guards at the bridges, and we'll post guards at the University Heights Bridge—when we get to it. But we don't have enough personnel to adequately guard them all. I can't mine them, Dan. I don't want the structures destroyed or damaged. They've got to stand until we turn this country around and get technology on the upswing again."

He paused and tossed his lunch wrappers into a garbage can. There was enough litter in the city; damned if he was going to add to it. He rolled one of the few cigarettes he allowed himself daily and lit up. "Maybe that's what the Night People want, Dan. Maybe they *want* us to destroy the bridges. Or perhaps *they* are going to destroy them and try to trap us over here that way. I don't know. I just don't know."

"Now you've got me worried about it!"

"Well, don't lose any sleep over it, Dan. Come on. Let's go see if we can find some night crawler butt to kick."

Nothing. At four o'clock that afternoon, Ben called a halt to it. His battalion, nearly a thousand men and women, had combed the area and found nothing. The Rebels now controlled—or, as Ben felt, *thought* they did—everything north of Dyckman Street and west of Broadway from the base of Fort Tryon Park.

And that is where Dan found Ben just at dusk: just below Fort Tryon Park, squatting at the entrance to the 190th Street subway station. Surrounded, of course, by Cooper and Beth and Jersey and the squad of Rebels Ike had permanently assigned to him.

Dan squatted down beside him. "What's going on in your mind, General?"

Ben pointed to the subway entrance. "That's where they are, Dan. Down there. They left the cars and the skeletons undisturbed to throw us off. And they are so far back, their stench is covered by the stagnant water and the bat crap. Probably two or three miles back. Waiting."

"For what, General?" But he knew. If Ben was right, they were in deep trouble.

"For us to push further on south. Then, when Monte gets into position, they'll surface and hit us."

"So we blow the subway entrance and seal them in."

"All of them, Dan? There are only about five hundred. You really want to destroy what was, at one time, one of the greatest subway systems in all the world? Who knows, it could be again—someday. And how about the prisoners they might be holding down there? Some for food, yes. But how about the others? God *damn* it!" Ben stood up, the Englishman with him.

Ben took off his beret and ran his fingers through his hair, salt-and-pepper hair. "And if we Claymored the hell out of the places? We'd get the first fifty or sixty of the creepies, and from that point on, they'd push the prisoners out in front of them. And I think under the city is where they're keeping a lot of prisoners, Dan. It would be ideal for beings as odious as the crawlers. So that means chemicals are out."

Dan remained silent, listening to Ben run over the options. But it was rapidly growing dark, and that concerned Dan. Not for himself, but for the general's safety. But he also knew it was not his place to remind the general of the time.

Mouthy Jersey knew no such levels of position— or she didn't pay any attention to them. "It's gettin' dark, General."

Ben looked over at her. "Damn, Jersey. I'm not blind, you know?"

That bounced off Jersey like a rubber ball. "Probably a lot of work on your desk, and you got to call generals Ike and Jefferys."

Ben smiled and shook his head. "Come on, then." As they walked back to Ben's Blazer, he said, "Dan, here in America we had a saying that fits this situation. We're fucked. Do the British have a better term for it?"

Dan thought about that for a few steps. "No, sir. I think fucked pretty well sums it up."

Chapter 4

"So that's the situation, people." Ben had explained his theory to his Rebels, gathered in a huge warehouse along the Harlem River. "And I think the creepies expected me to piece it all together, leaving me with some choices to make. If we stay here, they've really got us in a box. For I think a large force of them have moved up into Spuyten Duyvil and the Kingsbridge area, as well as into the subway tunnels and over into University and Morris Heights. And they didn't use the bridges; they used boats. Dan's Scouts have been out since dawn, and have found where they launched off. I'm going to remind you all, one more time, that just counting the Night People, we're outnumbered fifteen or twenty to one. With Monte's people coming in . . . twenty-five to one. Like that well-known philosopher used to say: Them odds ain't worth a damn!"

The warehouse reverberated with laughter. A woman called out, "What was that philosopher's name, General, Ben Raines?"

Ben joined in the laughter. "Could be." He waited

until the warehouse had settled down. "So we're going to do this the Rebel way, people. I'm not going to order you all into a death trap. I'm going to walk outside and have a cup of what passes for coffee nowadays. You people vote on it. You want to continue clearing out the Big Apple, fine. You want to go home, that's fine, too. Ike and Cecil and West are canvassing their troops now. Take as long as you want. I'll be outside."

Ben walked outside, expecting to be alone. But Beth and Jersey and Cooper walked out with him. They had already voted in their minds. They were staying. Dan and his Scouts walked out right behind them. James Riverson, the big ex-truck driver from Missouri, who had been with Ben since the outset, came next. Ben didn't even have time to get a cup of coffee and roll a cigarette before the Rebels came pouring out of the warehouse. They walked to Jeeps and Hummers and tanks and APC's and trucks.

"We're goin' to work, General," a Rebel Ben knew only as Joe called out, climbing into a Jeep. "You have you a cup of coffee and a smoke. We're gonna start pushing on down south; see if we can find some creep ass to kick. We got a big job ahead of us, you know?"

Ben smiled at the man, then allowed his eyes to roam all up and down the line of Rebels. The lines from King came to him: "I have a dream." Ben looked at the faces of his Rebels. Black and white, Asian, Indian, Spanish . . . they were all represented. The dream worked here, Doctor, Ben thought, and now these men and women are willing to risk their lives to push that dream of peace and equality even further.

And I'm damn proud of them.

Ben saluted his troops as the vehicles rolled past. When the last truck had pulled out, he turned to Beth. "Get Ike and Cecil and West on the horn, please."

The Rebel commanders and the mercenary came on. "What's the word, gentlemen?" Ben asked.

"Unanimous, Ben," Ike took it. "Not one person voted to leave."

"You very carefully explained that this city could well be our tomb?"

"We laid it all out for them, General," West replied.

"Probably made it even more dismal than it really is," Cecil told him. "We're here for the duration, Ben."

"I'm damn proud of you all. I want you to know that."

"Let's go to work." Ike finished it brusquely, but with a very definite catch in his voice.

"Hang tough," Ben told them.

The Rebels found nothing. No Night People, no survivors, nothing. But Ben had felt eyes on him all that morning and well into the afternoon. He said nothing about it; he waited for someone else to experience the same sensation. Beth was the first one to vocalize the eerie feeling.

"We're being watched, General. I don't know where they are, or who it is. But our every move is being observed. I'd bet on it."

"I've felt it all morning, Beth."

"We all have," Beth confirmed it. "Me, Jersey, Cooper, and a lot of the others. And speaking for me, it's a damned weird feeling."

The Rebels had pushed down to Fairview Avenue that cold late-fall day, but not a one of them felt comfortable or secure with it. Because of the near total silence in the city, the sounds of planes coming in from Base Camp One, and their taking off, could be heard if the wind was right. One plane every hour, twenty-four hours a day. Joe had told Ben a huge truck convoy was on the way, carrying ammo, food, medicine, and clothing. Should be arriving in three to four days.

"Come on out and fight, you bastards!" Ben muttered, an edge to his voice.

But the only fighting was far to the south of Ben's position. Ike and Cecil and West were lucky if they cleared a third of a block a day. On more than one day the Rebels and the Night People stood and slugged it out, with no one gaining any ground.

And so far, Ben's people had yet to fire a shot in their push south.

Ben inspected an apartment complex that had been recently declared secure. He started from the roof and walked down. He found the skeletal remains of a man and a woman, sitting in rat-chewed chairs in front of a dusty and long-silent TV set. Ben squatted down on the littered floor and picked up what remained of a *TV Guide*. A daytime talk show had been circled. He noticed with a warrior's dark humor that the topic for that day was gun control.

"Hope you enjoyed the show, folks." Ben muttered, dropping the tattered and yellowed magazine to the floor and standing up. Then felt slightly guilty after saying it. It passed quickly.

He walked across the hall and pushed open the

door, noting that like so many, the Rebels had smashed open the door. A skeleton lay on the floor, a rusting rifle beside the bones. Brass lay among the litter by a window. Ben knelt down and picked up one empty casing. A .30-06. Here was one New Yorker who did not go into that long sleep placidly.

Ben walked to the shattered window and looked down on the street, then back to the bones. Old bones, years old. He theorized that the man gave a number of looters exactly what all looters deserve: a bullet in the head.

Ben found a blanket and covered the warrior's bones. He walked out of the apartment, carefully closing the door behind him.

The apartment building and the old bones therein both depressed and troubled him. Why did the gas kill some almost immediately and let others live? And what had killed the man who chose to fight?

He put those questions out of his mind and stood just inside the doors to the apartment building, in the semi-gloom, knowing he would be hard to spot by anyone outside, and worried his mind about the absence of the enemy. His people were getting deeper and deeper into bogie country—far too deep to leave little pockets of Rebels behind as rear guards. He had too few people as it was; they had to stay together for safety's sake.

What to do?

He stood in the gloom of the foyer, knowing Beth and Jersey and Cooper were just outside, waiting with the squad of bodyguards. His eyes swept the top floors of the buildings across the street. No, they wouldn't be on the top floors. The slithering creepies would be belowground, hiding like rats and snakes. But if that was the case, how were they watching the Rebels? From what vantage point? Had they dug tunnels away from the existing tunnels, coming up under buildings, with hidden passageways?

Maybe.

Ben stepped to the door. "Come on inside, all of you. We're going to reinspect this building. In the basement. Beth, I want a generator set up and lights strung down in the basement."

Dan intercepted the transmission and was at the scene moments after hearing it. "Fresh ideas, General?"

"Could be. Might well be a wild goose hunt, too." He explained.

Dan nodded and turned to a Scout. Before he could give the order, Ben said, "I'll lead it, Dan. You're in command up top."

"Yes, sir."

With the generator humming, the basement filled with light, Ben walked down into the darkness. "Pull everything away from the walls, people. And don't be disappointed if we don't find anything. It might not be in this building, or the next one, but it's the only logical explanation for what's been happening. As soon as we clear a building, they pop out like the blood-sucking leeches they are. Come on, let's go to work."

"You want us to carry this stuff outside, General?"

"No. They'll find out soon enough what we're doing without us giving it away. Just move everything out to the center of the floor, after I inspect the center. But I think they're tunneling in through a wall and hiding the entrance with something solid."

Everything was moved away from the walls. The walls were carefully checked. Nothing. Not even a rat hole.

They moved on to the basement of the next building. Same results. The Rebels tried three more basements before hitting pay dirt. As soon as they pulled several large wooden crates away from the wall, the unmistakable odor of Night People struck them all.

"Bingo!" Ben said. "Get Dan down here."

The Englishman came down the steps quick-time. A grim smile curved his mouth as he smelled the foulness of the creepies and his eyes touched upon the dark hole in the wall. "Tunnel-rat time, General?"

"Yeah. And you're looking at the chief rat. No arguments. Who's going in with me?"

Everybody stepped forward. Including Beth.

"Have you lost your mind, Beth?" Ben asked.

"The boredom of the last few days momentarily clouded reason, General."

"Well, I'll put a little sunshine on it. You stay up here and keep track of the radio business."

Dan had already sent for heavy flashlights and spare batteries from the supply truck. "Pierce, you and Bouten take the point and keep the point. And that is a direct order."

"Yes, sir." The Scouts checked the flashlights and stepped into the foul-smelling darkness. While the Rebels certainly had the technology to produce flashlight batteries, as long as they had millions of rechargeable batteries at their disposal, and the means to recharge them, that technology was on the shelf for a time.

Just before Ben bent down and crawled into the darkness, he turned around to Dan. "Do you know if Katzman ever got ahold of Emil and his warriors?"

"No, sir. I'll have Beth check on that."

"Fine."

"General? Radio contact is going to be bad down there. If you're not out in one half hour, I'm coming in."

"All right, Dan." Ben disappeared into the smelly darkness.

"Father Emil! Father Emil!" the woman shouted, running toward the main camp of Emil and the hippies. "Great General Raines has called us on the radio you got from Colonel Williams. He is welcoming our aid and has given us instructions on how to get to wherever it is he wants us to go."

Emil grabbed the piece of paper, read it quickly, and jumped to his feet, which was a dangerous move for Emil: the hem of his robe seemed to be constantly catching on something—usually his feet.

"Lafayette!" Emil shouted, pointing to the west. Sister Sarah assumed he was talking about General Raines and moved his arm to the east. "We are on our way!" He turned around, caught his feet in the hem of his robe, and fell down in the dust.

"Jesus Christ," Rosebud muttered, eyeballing the antics.

Thermopolis walked to Emil and helped Sister

Sarah get the little man to his feet. "May I read that communiqué, please?"

"Oh. Sure, Thermy."

Thermopolis read the message and paled under his tan. "Did you read all of this, Emil?"

"No. Just the first part."

"General Raines says we may be outnumbered twenty-five to one."

Emil hit the ground again, in a dead faint.

Sister Sarah waved away Thermopolis's help and motioned for some of Emil's flock to come help. Thermopolis walked back to his group.

"We've got to talk, Rosebud."

"I heard; most of us did. I can't speak for the others, but to my way of thinking, if we don't help Ben Raines stop these horrible people now, we'll have to run and keep on running for the rest of our lives. The kids and grandbabies are all right, Thermopolis. They're being well taken care of by the older people back at the village, so we don't have to worry about that."

"Rosebud, all of you, you know that even if by some miracle we help defeat the Night People in New York City, we've only chopped off the tip of the iceberg. We well might be fighting the Night People and under the command of that authoritative bastard Raines for the rest of our lives!" He shuddered at the thought.

"But if we don't hook up with a large enough group to resist," Zelotes pointed out, "we're doomed."

"I don't know which would be worse," Thermopolis said. "Eaten by cannibals or having to listen to Ben Raines's right-wing bullshit for the rest of my days."

"He doesn't force his personal philosophy on

anybody, dear," Rosebud reminded her old man. "He just wants everybody to be educated and to obey the few laws that the Rebels live under. You remember what Jerre told us about him."

"Oh, I know it. He's not as bad as I make him out to be. Well, what's it going to be, friends?"

It was unanimous. They would go on.

"So be it," Thermopolis said.

"Twenty-five to fucking *one!*" Emil shrieked, coming out of his faint, his scream reaching everyone in camp. "Holy shit!"

"Douse the lights," Ben whispered. "Let your eyes grow accustomed to the dark." The flashlights were clicked off. Ben and the Scouts were well away from the opening in the basement. "Now get out of the way." He edged past the point team.

"Colonel Gray said . . ."

"Colonel Gray doesn't give me orders. Just pass the buck back to me if you get any static about it." Ben squatted in the tunnel for a moment, getting his bearings. He had seen at first glance that the tunnels were not new. They were very old. Maybe fifty or a hundred years old. And quite possibly, Ben thought, a lot of unsolved murders in the Big Apple could have been cleared up if these tunnels had been known.

He also had a strong hunch that the Night People had been around for a lot longer than anyone could possibly guess.

He inched forward until coming to a curve in the tunnel. He peeked around it. Not even a tiny finger of light reached him. Touching Bouton on the arm, Ben whispered, "Come with me."

The tunnel both widened and heightened. The men were almost able to stand up erect. Ben inched forward, feeling his way along the wall. Another turn, a sharp one. Far at the end of that stone corridor, Ben could see a small light. He stepped aside and pulled Bouton forward. The Scout saw the light and nodded his head.

"Get the others," Ben whispered. "Remove any loose equipment and tape up for silent approach. And bring me some tape."

The Scout melted into the darkness. Ben waited for what seemed to be an hour. But the luminous hands of his watch told him it was less than three minutes before he heard the slight scrape of boots on stone, the sound not carrying more than a few feet. But even that was enough to give them away.

When Bouton reached his side, Ben whispered, "Pass the word: the next person who drags his feet gets to launder all the dead creepie's robes."

Bouton passed the word.

Ben took the already torn strips of tape and silenced his equipment, then inched forward. He sensed the others behind him, but did not hear them. Low voices reached him; seconds later, the odor and sizzle of cooking meat also reached him. He grimaced, knowing full well what the creepies were eating. There was now enough light in the tunnel for the Rebels to see each other. Ben turned and made an eating gesture to Bouton and the others, then pointed to the end of the corridor.

The Rebels all struggled to keep from gagging.

Ben moved forward, motioning Bouton and Pierce up to him. The corridor was wide enough for three men to walk abreast, while the floor was on a slight but constant slant downward. Ben clicked his Thompson off safety. The others did the same. The voices grew louder.

Ben motioned for the team to halt. He slipped forward, taking a peek into the large stone room. He almost lost what remained of his lunch.

Like sides of beef, naked, very dead human bodies were hung up on meat hooks. Ben could see where, he assumed, the choicest cuts had been carved from the bodies. Strips of meat were cooking over a charcoal fire.

He knelt down and motioned Pierce and Bouton forward and motioned for them to kneel, then waved three more Rebels forward.

Ben lifted his Thompson to his shoulder. One old .45-caliber SMG and five M-16's on full auto ripped the cruel air of the tunnel, sending the ten subhumans sprawling and kicking and squalling and finally, for the good of humankind, dying.

"Jersey, go get Dan. I want him to see this."

"With pleasure, sir."

A moment later, they could all hear the sounds of her upchucking.

No one blamed her a bit.

Chapter 5

Dan, ashen-faced, looked at Ben. "I thought I had seen it all, General. I guess I have. Now."

Ben had sent Scouts forward, up the dark corridor, to see what lay around the next bend. "Get some people to take down the bodies of those . . . unfortunates. Take them topside and bury them properly."

Dan waved a few Scouts forward and pointed to the naked bodies on the meat hooks. "You heard him. Get to it, lads and lassies."

One of the Scouts sent up the tunnel returned. "Steel door just ahead, General. And I mean a big solid sucker. Old. Back when they really made steel, I reckon. It'll take a heavy charge to blow it."

"Not now," Ben told him. "We're going to have our work cut out for us after this, Dan. We've tipped our hand."

Ben walked out of the corridor, into the tunnel, crawled out of the hole in the wall into the basement, and went up the steps to ground level, stepping out into the cold night air. He stood in the darkness for a moment, mulling over the events just past.

All right, so he had uncovered the plans of the Night People. Now what? He had no intention of sending Rebels into the tunnels after the creepies. They would be ready for his people, expecting the Rebels to come after them.

He would not send his troops into a death trap.

But he knew one thing for certain: the areas that had been cleared would now have to be checked again. Not only up here, but also in Lower Manhattan.

Every damned building and basement!

He walked to his Blazer, Beth and Jersey with him, and climbed in. "Back to the CP, Cooper. Let's get some rest. We have to start all over tomorrow morning."

Ben had alerted Ike and Cecil and West of the new developments before he went to bed. He was once more talking to them, through translators, at five o'clock the next morning.

"Damn!" Cecil summed up the feelings of the entire group.

"Back to square one," West said.

What Ike said was totally unprintable.

"There's something else I've been thinking about," Ben radioed. "I think the creepies did this for two reasons: one, to try to put us in a box; and two, because should we discover it, we'd have to retrace our steps, and that would buy them still more time. There is no way for us to inspect every basement of every cleared building before Monte and his people are all over us."

"So what do we do, Ben?" Cec asked.

"I'm going to push on down to the bridge, secure it and make damn sure it stays open. If we're going to be trapped in the Big Apple, I want us to be well-supplied before that happens—if it happens. I want you people to fall back to 14th Street. Block every street, every avenue, every alley, every hole. And look for the sons of bitches to hit you from Brooklyn. I don't think they'll chance the bridges you control; they'll be coming across at night, in boats. Start reclearing everything south of 14th. Plug up the holes with concrete reinforced with anything you can get your hands on: steel grating, heavy compressed metal mesh. We'll start doing the same up here. Pick out a half a dozen or more places to cache supplies. Get your trucks rolling over to Teterboro. Ike, tell your tank commanders to start shelling everything from Broadway to the expressways by the river. Bring it down. Tell them to work the buildings top to bottom. Use Willie Peter and HE. I want those ten miles, from 14th Street north to the bridge, to be nothing more than rubble, unable to be used by the creepies as hidey-holes. If you want to chance it, send Sappers into a section to help bring the buildings down. It's desperation time, people. Let's do it. Good luck."

Ben broke off.

Ike looked at the others. Sighed. "First we're soldiers, now we're combat engineers and tunnel rats. OK, people, let's go."

* * *

Ben listened to an urgent voice breaking the bad news to him.

"Monte smelled a rat, General. He didn't take the bait. They've turned west just north of the blown bridges, looking for a way back to highway. They're gonna roll right up to Tina's position."

"Hang on for a sec." Ben turned to Beth. "Get Rebet and Danjou on the horn." When she nodded her head, signaling that the Canadian and the Russian were ready, Ben took the handset.

"We need your help," Ben laid it on the line, then quickly explained the situation.

"We're at your disposal, General." Rebet told him. "And General Striganov is on his way with another full battalion, including self-propelled artillery and tanks. But due to the condition of the roads, it will be ten days before he arrives. Where do you want us placed, sir?"

"Let's let Monte think you and Danjou have fallen back and gone home." Ben spoke through a Russian-speaking interpreter. "Let him think he's going to be able to just roll right over my people at the airport; then you and Danjou hit him from the rear and force him to fight a double front."

"That is ten-four, General. Are you beefing up the personnel at the airport?"

"Yes. With about three hundred hippies."

A pause from upstate New York. "I beg your pardon, sir. Did you say hippies?"

"That is correct. They should be reaching the airport late tomorrow. I will advise them of our plan. Is that agreeable with you, Colonel?"

The Russian chuckled. "Like politics, General, war does make for some strange bedfellows."

Wait until you see Emil, Ben thought, with dark soldier humor. "Yes, it certainly does, Colonel. Eagle One out."

Ben turned to Beth. "Bump Katzman. See if he can get a fix on Emil's location."

"They were on the New Jersey line last evening, General."

"Hell, they ought to be in walkie-talkie range by now. Get Tina for me."

She spoke briefly and then handed him the mike. "Babe? Use translators on this." Ben waited for a moment, then explained about Danjou and Rebet. "Start radioing Emil and his bunch, Tina. As soon as you get them, speak in double-talk. Emil can sure understand that. Tell them to hold their position and you'll send a patrol out to guide them in. OK, babe?"

"OK, Pop. Will do."

"As soon as we clear down to the bridge, I'll pop over for a visit."

"Looking forward to it. Way-out Scout, out."

Ben had a good laugh at that. Then decided it was a good name for Tina and her bunch. They were way out in the country.

As it turned out, Emil was only about twenty-five miles from the Teterboro airport. Ham took a patrol out to guide them in.

Ham took a good look at the hippies and decided right then and there they were here for a fight, not for a love-in. They were well-armed, and armed with M-16's, AR-15's, and Mini-14's. A few had M-14's. But that was no problem; the Rebels had lots of .308 ammo.

Ham explained to them about Danjou and Rebet.

"Ye gods!" Emil shrieked. "You mean we'll be fighting side by side with savages from the Evil Empire?"

"Relax, Emil," Thermopolis tried to calm him. "From what we've been able to learn by listening to shortwave broadcasts, the Russians are on our side from here on in."

Emil looked very dubious, but shut up about it.

Ham, as ordered by Tina, gave the new people one last shot at turning around. "Once in, folks, for reasons I shouldn't have to explain, there is no turning around. And bear this in mind: Rebels do not surrender—*ever*! You fall back only on orders. Any of you cut and run, another Rebel is going to shoot you. There is a reason for this harshness: two or three people cut and run, they leave a big hole where the enemy can come in and perhaps kill off a lot of other Rebels. Understood?"

The question was met with silence.

"Why can't we leave once we're in?" Emil asked innocently.

"If you're caught and tortured, you could give away troop strength, command leaders, and a lot of other information that might seem trivial to you, but very important to the enemy."

"Don't the sergeants and generals and people like that wear things signifying rank?" Swallow asked.

"No," Ham told her. "And don't ever salute a Rebel officer. That's all that an enemy sniper is looking for." He smiled. "Don't worry. You'll learn very quickly who is in command."

"What happens if one of us wants to have a joint?" Wenceslaus asked.

"For you people, off duty with no alerts on, nothing. What you do with your private time is your business. But a joint or a drink of whiskey better be as far as it goes. And don't offer a joint to a Rebel regular; you'll be picking your teeth up off the ground. Drugs, unless prescribed by a doctor, are taboo. It wasn't always that way. We tried it the other way. It just didn't work out."

"Don't worry." Thermopolis told him. "None of us have any intention of becoming a Rebel regular."

Ham stood up from his squat and smiled. "Yeah. That's the way I got it figured. Probably best all the way around." He walked off.

"I don't quite know how to take that last bit," Santo said.

Thermopolis smiled. "He knows our reasons for coming up here were not totally unselfish. We'll help them, and they'll help us, and then we'll leave, fully resupplied and with a headful of knowledge about tactics and survival. No joints, people. Pack your stashes away and forget about them. We'll play by Ben Raines's rules as long as we're here."

Now the war turned bloody and savage for Ben and his battalion. They backtracked up to 220th Street and began cleaning house—literally.

And Ben gave the orders many Rebels knew were inevitable: "Take some prisoners and find out where the breeding farms and feeding farms are in the city. And I don't give a damn how you extract that information. Just get it."

Ben sent his tanks down to the southern edges of Fort Tryon and Inwood Hill Parks with these orders: "Start leveling the buildings. Clear the expressway at least one full block eastward. HE and WP. Go!"

To Beth: "Bump Katzman. Tell him to contact this Gene Savie. Tell him that Ben Raines said to get his people off their butts and get into this fight or I'll start shelling their goddamn territory at first light tomorrow morning. I am growing very weary of doing for people who won't pitch in and help."

"Yes, sir." After Ben had stalked off a few yards, she turned to Jersey. "The general is getting pissed."

"Highly," Jersey agreed.

"There is nothing wrong with my hearing!" Ben roared.

The women grinned at each other.

Within the hour, smoke from the fires started by the white phosphorus rounds began lifting into the sky. Ben ordered snipers posted along the expressway, armed with .50-caliber sniper rifles, to knock the creepies sprawling as they ran from the buildings being reduced to rubble by the heavy shelling.

"Sir?" Beth caught up with Ben. "Gene Savie on the horn."

Ben took the handset. "Savie?"

"Yes, sir."

"You got anyone there who speaks Yiddish?"

"Yes, sir."

"Get them."

The translators ready, Ben was very brief. "Get off

your butts and get into this fight. You obviously are capable of doing it, so do it."

"Is that an order?"

"You're goddamn right, it is."

Gene Savie was silent for a few seconds. "Very well, General. What would you have us do?"

"How many people in your group?"

"Including children and the elderly, a bit over six hundred."

"How many capable of fighting?"

"Three hundred seventy-five."

There were many questions Ben wanted to ask—including how the man knew exactly how many fighters he had—but realized this was not the time for it. "Can you tell me where the Night People keep their prisoners?"

"I can guess at it, General. But that's about it. I think in sections of the subway system. I also suspect that the Night People have been around a lot longer than anyone previously thought. The Underground People have been fighting them for decades . . . so I'm told."

All that jibed with what Ben suspected. "How have so many of you managed to stay alive for so long?"

Savie's short laugh was totally void of humor. "Actually, our number has been steadily declining. At the outset, there were more than five thousand of us. As to how, the section of the park that we control is very heavily mined. We discovered and cleared several tunnels that run from various apartment buildings over to the park. The Night People just got tired of taking so many casualties trying to infiltrate our territory. They knew—and time has proved them correct—they could take us out one at a time and eventually defeat us. At one time, we controlled all of the park."

"I assume you were going to warn my people of the park being mined?" Ben's tone was decidedly dry.

"Of course we were, General. Are you going to kill my father?"

"I don't even *know* your father, Savie. That is your real name, isn't it?"

"Yes. We have not changed our names."

Ben decided to hell with it; he'd ask as many questions as he liked. Clear the air, so to speak. "You obviously have good shortwave equipment. Why didn't you try to contact us before?"

"The Night People would jam the frequencies. That's one reason. And I told you: my father was afraid you would kill him."

"What did your father do before the war?"

"You never heard of John Savie? He was a writer."

Now Ben was more confused than before. He knew damn well that he did not personally know of anybody named Savie. And he had never heard of a writer by that name. "What the hell did he do, plagiarize some of my work?"

"Hardly, General."

"Fine. Wonderful. Keep me in suspense. I assure you, I can bear it. How much aid can you give me, Gene?"

"How about if we act as spotters for you, General? My people are so few, and spread so damn thin, if I pull any out, it'll leave a hole."

Ben had already put that much together. And in a way, he felt sorry for being so brusque with the man.

The survivors around the park had been living in unbelievable fear for many years. "All right, Gene. That would be a big help. You have any other people with a language background?"

"Oh, yes, General. Many languages spoken here. Our bunch is a real melting pot."

"Good. Always use translators when communicating with us. Gene? Tell your people to hang tough. It's going to be a long and bloody battle, but we'll get out of this mess."

"Thank you, General."

"Eagle One out."

Ben hooked the phone and stood for a moment, his face mirroring his inner thoughts. "John Savie. Used to be a writer. And he's afraid I'm going to kill him. I never heard of a writer named John Savie. And why is he so scared of me? What the hell is going on?"

"The guy didn't have an affair with your wife, did he, General?" Jersey asked.

Ben laughed. "No. I'd sure remember that, Jersey."

"If you knew about it," Beth added.

"There is that to consider," Ben conceded. "But I don't think a woman is the issue." He shrugged his shoulders and checked his battle harness, making sure everything he might need was hooked in place. "Let's go to work, ladies. We've got about a hundred thousand night crawlers to fight."

"I wonder how Lev is doing with the cows?" Beth mused.

Chapter 6

On the second day of the Rebels' newly launched assault on the Night People, one of the captured creepies broke under the exact opposite of friendly persuasion and just before dying confirmed that most of the breeding and feeding farms were under the city, in the subway tubes.

"What do you want to do with the rest of the creepies we captured, General?" Ben was asked.

Dan stepped forward. "I shall see to that matter." When the runner was gone, Dan turned to Ben. "I do hate to bring up what appears to be a very touchy subject, but I feel you should know. Tina has advised me that Jerre knows most of the hippies over at the airport."

"That doesn't surprise me. Probably lived in one of their fucking communes. Play on words intended."

Dan did not press the matter any further. He had never enjoyed handling live rattlesnakes, doing daredevil stunts for fun, or even remotely considered diving headfirst into an empty concrete swimming pool, any of which could be accurately compared to the general's attitude when it came to Jerre.

Or so the man would have one believe. Most Rebels did believe it. Those that knew him knew it was a shield.

"How's it looking down to the bridge, Dan?"

"It's open."

"You're in command here. I'm going over to see Tina."

"Right, sir."

Ben glared at the Englishman. But Dan's face was expressionless. However, his eyes did twinkle a bit.

"Jesus!" Cooper summed it up on the drive down to the bridge. Smoke hung low and heavy over the city; many of the buildings were still smoldering and would be for days. Sappers had gone into the area and planted charges; some buildings had been completely brought down under the massive charges of explosives.

Katzman had been monitoring creepie radio transmissions, and the suddenness and ferocity of Ben's attack had taken them totally by surprise. They had not expected Ben to give the OK to such devastation. The move had thrown them into a panic.

Thermopolis had noticed the Rebels at the airport had suddenly tensed just a bit. He walked over to Tina. "Are you expecting an attack, Tina?"

"That's one way of putting it, Therm. Dad is on his way over."

The hippie leader thought about that for a moment, took off his headband and refolded it, then tied it back around his head. "You fear your father that much?"

Tina looked at him, a puzzled look on her face. Then she got it and laughed. "Oh, no! No, you're reading it wrong." She cut her eyes to Jerre, walking along with Rosebud, chatting.

"Well, I'll just be damned," Thermopolis finally spoke. *"That's* the Ben she used to talk about. She never mentioned any last names. Son of a gun!"

"I'll wager that your wife knew. Ah, your old lady— whatever."

"Oh, we're married. Married before the war. We have grown children, grandchildren."

"You don't look old enough for grandchildren."

"Thank you. As to Rosebud knowing about Jerre and Ben . . . probably."

"Does Jerre love my father, Therm?"

"I would say yes, in a very peculiar way. Much more than platonic, but somewhat less than star-crossed."

"In other words, hopeless."

"For whom?"

"My father."

"There are two people involved here, Tina. One heart can hurt just as badly as the other, albeit both hearts not filled with the same pureness of sentiment."

"Don't misunderstand me, Therm: I like Jerre. Are you a poet, Therm?" She smiled at him.

He shrugged his shoulders. Very heavy shoulders, she noticed. Big arms, thick wrists, big flat-knuckled hands. "I was a musician at one time; I've been a lot of things." His eyes sparkled. "Although never a citizen of the Tri-States."

"You'd be surprised how many free spirits you'd find in the Rebels."

"I'd be surprised if I found *any* free spirits around here!"

She laughed at him. "I think you're in for a shock, my friend."

"General Raines coming in, Tina!" Ham called.

"Come on, Therm. I'll introduce you to my father."

"The moment I've looked forward to with breathless anticipation." Thermopolis's comment was very dry.

But Tina did not take offense at it. Smiling, she asked, "Why do you dislike my father so, Therm?"

"Oh, I really don't dislike him. We could probably have some very lively discussions. Even back before the Great War, I held a dim view of military leaders, and, I suppose, most figures of authority, which included, of course, the cops. Even though," he held up a finger, "I knew they were necessary to a free society. And if that sounds like a contradiction, it is."

"Oh, you and my father are going to have a good time!"

"If we live through all this," Thermopolis amended her comment.

"Have faith, Thermopolis!" Tina slapped him on the shoulder. "Dad. This is Thermopolis. Therm, my father, Ben Raines."

"General." Thermopolis stuck out his hand and Ben took it.

"Good to meet you, Thermopolis. And very good of you and your group to come up to assist us."

"Thank you, General. Emil sends his regrets. He helped off-load a crate—one crate—and injured his back. He's being attended to by some of his flock."

Ben laughed. "That little con artist has quite a

scam going. But I like him. He's goosy as an old maid, but don't sell him short on guts—he can come through when the chips are down. Perhaps out of pure fear, but that's something every Rebel can write volumes about."

Thermopolis studied the living legend called Ben Raines for a few seconds, and found himself—despite himself—liking the man. He was dressed exactly as his Rebels. From the beret to his boots. He wore no insignia, but there was no mistaking who the man was. The aura from him was almost tangible.

"How many of these Night People live in the city, General?" Thermopolis asked.

"We don't know. Twenty thousand, a hundred thousand. Somewhere in the middle of those figures would probably hit it accurately. We've got a small pocket of survivors living around the south end of Central Park. Six hundred or so. About three hundred and seventy-five of them fighters. We also have a group of people—number unknown—who live under the city and have for decades." Thermopolis arched an eyebrow at that. "They'll help us, but I don't know how or when. They seem to be very elusive people. We also have three battalions coming to our aid from out of Canada: two Russian battalions, commanded by General Striganov and Colonel Rebet, and one Canadian battalion commanded by Major Danjou. They'll be coming in behind Monte's people. We don't know how strong a force Monte has; somewhere between two thousand and five thousand. Monte's plans are, we believe, to try to roll over you people here and cut off our supply line. I'm sending over three more platoons to beef you up here."

The last of that was directed at Tina, giving Thermopolis time to think over the situation. When he had first arrived at the airport, he had been, quite literally, stunned by the amount of supplies being flown in; he had never in all his life seen so much war equipment. The first of the trucks were arriving, bringing with them tons and tons of bullets, grenades, artillery shells, gasoline, oil, clothing, bandages and anything and everything needed for an army to function.

Thermopolis then realized that Ben Raines was much more than just a military man. He was a planner and a thinker and a doer. Thermopolis grudgingly conceded that he may have misjudged the man somewhat. "I don't know about platoons and companies and the like, General. What will our strength be here?"

"With your group, and Emil's, approximately six hundred and fifty personnel, backed up by tanks and long-range artillery." He cut his eyes to Tina. "As promised, I'm sending over some eighty-one millimeter mortars and some one-fifty-five SP. Have you picked out FO posts?"

"Yes, sir. The people are in position now and dug in deep and well."

"Very good. As soon as Monte's people come into range, start dropping some goodies in on them."

"Yes, sir."

"I want you to mix your shells, Tina. There are no civilians to worry about, so make it as demoralizing as possible. HE, Willie Peter, Beehive. Monte has only light mortars and his people aren't very good with them, so you won't have to worry about much return. They've relied on brute strength and force for years.

"Now then, in the event you find yourselves cut off, and there is a damn good chance that's going to happen, get the hell out of here and link up with Danjou or Rebet or Striganov. Don't try to rejoin me in the city. And that is a direct order, kid. In two more days, we'll have enough supplies and ammo in the city to last us for a year. If it comes down to it, and it might, we'll fight the slime with axes and clubs and bayonets."

Ben swung his gaze to Thermopolis. He reached into a pocket of his field jacket and pulled out some pictures. "Just in case you or your people think I'm too harsh in saying we are fighting savages, and that I am cruel in that we do not take prisoners, study these carefully." He held out the pictures.

Thermopolis looked at the pictures and very nearly gagged. Ben had ordered shots taken of the naked men and women they'd found hanging on meat hooks in the tunnels. In living color.

"Pass them around," Ben told him. "Let all your people see them. The pictures should settle any doubts."

"Certainly settled my doubts," Thermopolis muttered. He lifted his eyes and stared at Ben. "I have never shot a man trying to surrender, General."

"I have," Ben told him. "Bear this in mind, Mister Thermopolis—or whatever your name is: I am not in the business of attempting the rehabilitation of savages. Slavery and cannibalism are an affront to anyone who possesses any degree of decency. Gene Savie's group around the park once was five thousand strong. The Night People have killed and/or eaten all but six hundred. They have enslaved thousands, fattened them, bred them, and then eaten them and their babies. Monte and his people kidnap civilians and bring them to the Night People, after raping and sodomizing and torturing the unfortunates. It would be a very great insult to the animal kingdom to refer to Monte and his people, and the creepies in the city, as animals. They are far below any species of animal. My goal, *our* goal in the city is simple: we are going to destroy the Night People and their allies. We are going to wipe them from the face of the earth. Now they obviously have children; what are we going to do with them? I don't know. I hate to even think of that. I am not a barbarian, although that is open to debate among some. I have never killed a child. I don't know what we're going to do with them. The very young among the Night People we can take and raise. The others? . . . I just don't know."

All that had been thrown at Thermopolis so fast and hard it took him a few seconds to digest it all. He blinked at Ben. "You're honest about it, at least. But I can tell you right now, I won't kill a child."

"Were you in 'Nam, Thermopolis?"

"No."

"Then you don't know what you'd do. A lot of 'Nam vets had to shoot kids. It was a choice of getting themselves blown all to hell by the bomb the child was carrying, or shooting the child." He stuck out his hand and Thermopolis shook it. "Good to have you with us. Good luck to you all."

He walked away, Tina by his side, accompanied as always by Beth and Jersey. Cooper had stayed with the Blazer. Tapper walked up to his side. "So what do you think about Ben Raines?"

Thermopolis removed his bandana and carefully refolded it, a puzzled look on his face. "Tell you the truth, Tap, I'm afraid I rather like the man."

Tina introduced her father to Rosebud, who was standing with Jerre. Jerre didn't speak to him, and he ignored her. Rosebud picked up on the tension very quickly and split the scene.

"I'll leave you two alone, Dad." Tina told him. "I have some things to do."

"Sure you do."

And then they were alone. Together. Again. As alone as two people can be in a bustling camp, with planes roaring in and out.

"So how are you getting along, Jerre?"

"Fine."

After that short exchange, conversation died. They stood and looked at each other for a moment.

Jerre gave confabulation a kick in the butt and said, "Well, I guess I'll see you around, Ben."

"There'll be a river between us."

"It's always something." She turned to walk away.

Damned if Ben was going to let her get in the last word. "It doesn't have to be!" he spoke sharply.

She whirled around, blues flashing. Before she could speak, Emil came rushing up, every third step his foot catching on the hem of his robe, almost tossing him headfirst onto the ground.

"My dear General Raines! Great and Supreme Commander of all the Forces for Liberty on the face of the Earth. Protector of the old and the young and infirm . . ."

"Emil! . . ."

Thermopolis and some of his bunch had gathered around, smiling.

". . . Savior of the democratic system. Guardian of the rights of all. The great god Blomm has guided my footsteps to this monumental moment in history, when our combined forces shall join to fight and slew . . . slay the nasty worms rotting the core of the Big Apple."

Ben stared at him. "Jesus, Emil!"

"Oh, him, too! Sure."

Jerre was laughing so hard she had to turn her head.

"I have worked out a dance in honor of this moment, Great General Raines."

"Oh, God, Emil!"

"I knew we were forgetting somebody. Right!"

The expression on Ben's face was priceless to the large group of Rebels and hippies gathered around.

"Are you ready, General?" Emil flung his arms wide.

Ben sighed. "I thought you injured your back, Emil."

"Upon sighting the mighty indomitable presence of Ben Raines, my pain was forgotten."

"Right."

"Are you ready, General?"

Ben had to smile. "Give it your best shot, Emil."

Emil did the bebop and rebop and the Twist, and then stopped suddenly, a pained expression on his face.

Sister Beth rushed up to him. "Why did you stop, Brother Emil? It was so lovely! We were all so . . . so moved by it all."

"Yeah? Well, I can't move! I hurt my fuckin' back, Sister. I can't straighten up."

"How can I help, Brother?"

"I think I'm paralyzed!"

"Let me see if I can help." Thermopolis stepped up.

Ben took that time to step out. Lively. Just before he got into his Blazer, he looked back at Jerre. She was looking at him across the tarmac. He almost walked across the expanse to her side.

Then she turned her back to him.

Ben's face hardened. He got into the front seat.

"Where to, General?" Cooper asked, when Beth and Jersey were seated in the back.

"Back across the bridge. It's safer from tiny little arrows over there."

Chapter 7

Ben was dreaming a very jumbled dream. It had Jerre as the central theme, naturally, but as usual, they were fighting. And as usual, they were standing far apart.

Then Ben smelled a very foul odor. He started to look down at his boots, to see if he'd stepped in something, when, even in his dream, he recognized the smell.

He rolled off the bed, his hand closing around the cocked and locked .45 he always kept on a small nightstand by the bed.

The roll and thunder of gunfire and the muzzle flashes from automatic weapons lashed in the room. They were followed by Ben's emptying the .45 into the stinking knots of black-robed figures. Ben's bedding caught on fire and flared up from the hot lead it had soaked up.

His gun empty, Ben hurled the nightstand into the crowd and heard a scream as one corner impacted with flesh and bone. He rolled away, coming up on his knees with his Thompson roaring and bucking and snorting and sending out sparks of fire and hot blunt death from the muzzle.

He was just faintly aware, over the roaring in his own room, and his temporarily impaired hearing, of other shots somewhere else in the building.

Infiltrated!

He was aware of a sticky hot feeling in his side, and of another stickiness running down the side of his head. He'd been hit, but had no way of knowing how bad. The shock of a massive wound would last from two to ten minutes. He made up his mind that while he could still function, he'd best do so.

He tried the lights. They came on. So the generator room had not been hit. Ben threw his bedding to the floor and emptied a pitcher of water on the flames, then jerked on his pants and boots and speed-laced them. He slung his battle harness over his shirt and fitted a fresh drum into the belly of the Thompson.

The sounds of battle were growing louder and wilder and closer. He ran into the outer office. Jersey and Beth were on the floor, gagged and all trussed up like hogs. But alive.

Ben cut the ropes and Jersey came up cussing.

"No time for that now, kid. Get your pants on." He cut Beth free. "The creepies are all over us."

Beth touched Ben's face. Her hand came away bloody. Her eyes took in the spreading bloodstain on his shirt.

"I don't think it's bad. Come on, move, Beth!" He slapped her on her panty-clad bottom and grinned at her.

She blushed.

Ben stepped out into the hall and came face-to-face with a crawler. The Thompson came up before the crawler's AK and Ben blew the ugly face into a thousand bits of blood and brain and bone, slamming the ugly against the hall wall.

Turning to his left, he cleared the hall of black robes just as Jersey and Beth came out and began firing to the right. The screaming of the wounded and the pounding of weapons on full auto drowned out all else.

Their sector at least momentarily clean, Ben glanced at Beth. "Get me a report from somebody. Is this campwide or just here?"

She slipped back for her radio. Ben kept his eyes on one end of the hall, Jersey on the other.

"Just here, General," Beth called.

"Coming around the corner, General!" Dan's voice boomed.

"Come on, Dan."

Dan and his Scouts filled the hallway. He took one look at Ben. "Medic! On the double!"

Dan pointed to a room and several Scouts rushed in, checking it. "Clear, sir!" one called.

Dan literally pushed Ben into the room and into a chair, ripping off his battle harness and shredding his shirt, exposing a long bloody tear along Ben's ribs: painful, but not serious. Taking water from his canteen, Dan washed away the blood from Ben's head just as the medics entered. The Englishman immediately stepped away and allowed the medics room to work.

"It's not serious, sir," one of the medics told Ben after taking a closer look at the wounds. "But you're going to be stiff and sore." He gave Ben two shots and bandaged the wounds.

"Somebody better tell me what happened to security," Ben said. "And what the hell time is it?"

"Three o'clock, sir," Dan told him. "We don't know what happened. Not yet."

"Sir?" Beth came into the room. "Assassination attempts were made on all Rebel commanders simultaneously. General Ike had just last evening changed CP's. The creepies hit the wrong building. General Ike is OK. Colonel West suffered a slight arm wound, and General Jefferys took a round through the shoulder. The situation has been stabilized in all sectors."

"Thank you, Beth. You and Jersey tell me what happened here."

"They were all over us, sir," Jersey said. "They had us gagged and bound before we even knew what happened . . ."

"They came over from the other roof," a Scout explained, walking into the room. "Used planks to cross over four buildings getting here. We found where they came up out of the street, out of a manhole cover. Then used ropes and hooks to climb the building. They killed the sentries with silenced weapons."

Ben thanked him, and the Scout left the room. "I hate to do it," Ben said, looking at Dan. "And it's only a stopgap measure and damned time-consuming, but commencing at first light, have our engineers start welding closed every manhole cover they can find."

"I think it's a good move, General," Dan told him. "When one takes into consideration that we are probably going to be in this city for some months."

"The creepies have us by the short hairs, and they know it," Ben mused, not expecting any reply. "They know damn well that we'll do everything we can to prevent any of their prisoners from being killed by our actions. If it wasn't for the prisoners, I'd pump chemicals underground and flush the maggots out. If it wasn't for the prisoners, we could end this war quickly."

"Perhaps, sir," Jersey vocalized what was on a lot of peoples' minds, including Ben's, "the prisoners would be better off dead."

"I know, Jersey. I've thought the same thing—more than once. But who among you wants to be the one to give the order to kill them along with the crawlers?" Ben met the eyes of everyone in the room. No one replied to his question. "We slug it out." Ben stood up. "That's all we can do."

"Monte is about fifty miles north of Tina's position," Ben was informed. "And moving fast. Katzman has intercepted messages between the Night People and Monte, advising him of the importance of the airport. Monte radioed back that he will attack Teterboro Airport within forty-eight hours."

"He has no choice in the matter," Ben told the gathering in his new office, located just a few blocks from the George Washington Bridge. "Rebet and Danjou are still maintaining radio silence?" He glanced at Beth.

"Yes, sir. And staying one day behind Monte's force as ordered."

"Send them a coded message to close in. I want

them within ten miles of Monte when he begins his attack on the airport. But far enough back to avoid being hit by our artillery."

"Yes, sir."

"Tell Cooper to warm up the Blazer. I want to see Tina one more time before the attack." And Jerre. He pushed her out of his thoughts. She promptly came right back in. Never could tell her a damn thing.

Ben and his party made the short run to the bridge without incident. The savage pounding from his artillery had driven the creepies so far back from the expressway that that area was considered secure, but was still heavily patrolled and watched twenty-four hours a day by the Rebels. The bridge itself was guarded by a full platoon of Rebels at both ends, and the waters beneath it patrolled by gunboats. To relieve the tedium, the platoons were changed regularly. The rains had extinguished most of the heavier fires, but the area along the expressway still smoldered from the killing shelling.

From the bridge to the airport, the loop road was also heavily patrolled. Highway 46, from Terrace Avenue over to Outwater Lane, had been rendered impassable. Highway 17, from the airport down to Highway 3, was heavily mined, a death trap for anyone not knowing the route. If Monte's people tried an end-around, they were going to be in for a very rude and deadly shock.

"I don't see what else we can do," Ben complimented his daughter. "You've thought of everything. How's the new bunch doing?"

"Settling right in, Dad. They've all been advised

that a massive attack is just around the corner. Emil said they came up here to fight, so let's get it on."

Ben walked around the area closest to the tower and terminal, and then, with Tina driving, rode around the airport fence. "The last planes will be coming in late tomorrow afternoon. After that, we're on our own. The last bunch will be bringing in reloading equipment. But I doubt that we'll have to use it."

"Thermopolis was absolutely stunned when he saw the amount of equipment being flown in. I told him that when three thousand automatic weapons are all going at the same time, you burn up a lot of ammo."

"The fence charged yet?"

She shook her head. "We'll do that at the last minute. Dead birds around the fence would be a give-away."

Ben smiled. He had taught her well, and so had Dan. He started chuckling when he saw a battered old sign pointing the way to Redneck Avenue.

Tina pulled over to the side of the airport road. "We all had a good laugh at that, Dad. And just for spite we mined the hell out of it."

Ben got out of the Jeep and stared at Redneck Avenue. He tried hard but could not detect a single mine. "Electrically fired?"

"Some of them. Some of them are trip-wired. We've got some Claymores planted in the weeds just for good luck."

Back in the Jeep, they continued the slow circle of the airport.

They turned north just east of 17 and drove slowly

back to the terminal area. "You have a rabbit hole out of here, don't you, Tina?"

"Oh, yeah, Dad. They who fight and run away, live to fight another day."

He laughed at her. "When they run on orders, that is."

"Right. That was impressed upon the new people very strongly." She was silent for a moment, with only the cold wind whipping around them. "You going to see Jerre before you leave?"

"Why should I?"

"Because whether you believe it or not, Dad, she does care for you."

Ben turned his head away, refusing to reply. But it was not for the reason Tina suspected. "Ike radioed just before we left. They're reclearing their sector, welding manhole covers in place, and so on. During a sweep of the buildings around the World Trade Center they found what was left of Ian. Identified by his dog tags. The creepies captured him and had him for supper."

"Damn! You want me to tell Jerre?"

"No. I'll tell her. It isn't going to make that much difference to her anyway."

"How in the hell can you say something like that, Dad?"

"Because I know her, kid. Come along with me. You'll see."

Jerre took the news without changing expression. "What happened to your face, Ben?"

"I cut myself shaving. I just told you about your boyfriend being eaten by creepies. Don't you even care?"

"And I told you that he wasn't my boyfriend. Of course I care. What do you want me to do, break down and bawl?"

Thermopolis was leaning against a nearby vehicle, watching and listening, an interesting expression on his face.

"I don't know what I want you to do. I just wish to God you had kept your butt in Montana or wherever in the hell you were."

Rosebud joined her husband. "What are they fighting about?"

"Ben just informed her about Ian somebody-or-the-other being eaten by the Night People. He's all bent out of shape because she didn't go into hysterics or faint, or something along those lines."

"That's not her way. Ian was a friend, she told me. She'll cry for him, but in private."

"They're just alike, those two. That dawned on me after meeting the general. Theirs must have been an interesting relationship."

"If your face wasn't hurt, I'd slap you!" Jerre yelled at Ben.

"Hell, don't let that slow you down, Jerre."

She stepped back and hung a good old-fashioned cussing on him.

His reply, another, stronger version of a good old-fashioned cussing, was drowned out by the roaring of an incoming plane.

Jerre called Ben an egotistical bastard!

Ben called her a selfish, self-centered, ungrateful bitch!

Jersey and Beth and Cooper had beat it inside the terminal, out of the cold, for a cup of coffee.

"Ungrateful!" Jerre hollered at him. "I'm here, aren't I? In your army, aren't I? Fighting, aren't I? Where do you get off calling me ungrateful? You . . . you arrogant son of a bitch!"

Tina and Rosebud and Thermopolis had squatted down beside the vehicle.

"Do you suppose this is going to clear the air between them?" Thermopolis inquired.

"Oh, no," Tina told him. "They've been doing this for over ten years."

"Everytime they get together, so Jerre told me," Rosebud added.

"And accomplish absolutely nothing," Thermopolis accurately pegged it.

"Your problem is," Jerre pointed a finger at Ben, "if you don't get your way, you sulk like a child!"

"Sulk! Me? Your problem is if you can't use people, you dump them."

"That's a rotten lie!"

"What in the world is going on?" a familiar voice came from behind Tina.

She turned and rose to her boots, throwing her arms around the very handsome and muscular young man's neck.

"Someone we should know?" Rosebud asked, she and her husband standing up.

Tina smiled. "This, folks, is my brother, Buddy Raines."

Chapter 8

"I never heard anyone speak to Dad in such a manner," Buddy said. He still had a hospital look about him, but was obviously in good shape or the doctors at Base Camp One would have never OK'd his release.

"That, dear brother, is the lady our father has been in love with for about a decade."

"They certainly do have quite an interesting way of exhibiting their mutual affection, I must say. Or is it mutual?"

Tina waggled her hand in a so-so-maybe gesture.

The quartet stood and watched as Ben and Jerre ended their yelling. Jerre stalked off in one direction, and Ben turned to march off in the opposite. His eyes touched and locked in on Buddy.

Buddy walked to him. Father and son shook hands, and then embraced.

"I ought to kick your butt for coming up here, boy," Ben growled at him.

"That might be a very interesting fight, Father," Buddy said with a smile. "After all, you are getting along in years."

Ben ruffled the young man's already unruly mop of hair. Buddy wore his customary bandana around his forehead. The son's eyes lingered on the small bandage on his father's face.

"It's nothing," Ben assured him. "Should you be here, son?"

"I am one hundred percent, Father. The doctors say it should have taken me another three to four weeks to heal. But I was, according to them, in very good physical shape. I have news. Alvaro brought his people in from the west to beef up Colonel Williams at the base, so that freed my company. I brought them with me. They're gathering up equipment now."

"Great, son. That is great news. I, ah, am sorry you had to witness that, ah, exchange between . . ." Ben let it trail off.

The son shrugged. "She's a beautiful woman, Father. Is she worth all the strain?"

Ben laughed at him. "Now, that, son, could be construed as a very chauvinistic remark."

"If the shoe fits, and all that."

Ben studied him. "Well, now. I've got to find a place for you."

"Wherever you say, Father."

"Your company can stay here at the airport to night. You come with me. I'll show you what I can of the Big Apple."

Buddy had been amazed at the skyline of New York City, and dismayed at the havoc wrought on the city by the big guns of the Rebels.

But he had his father's eye for the ladies, and was

quite taken by Beth, even offering to carry her backpack radio for her.

"Leave my damn radio alone!" Beth told him. "That thing's checked out to me."

"I was only going to carry it for you."

"I can carry it, I can carry it!"

Both Jersey and Ben thought it funny. Cooper just drove and kept his comments to himself. Buddy wedged in between Beth and Cooper in the backseat, pretending not to notice the quick glances fired in his direction from Beth.

In Ben's office, Ben brought his son up to date, ending with: "Not the most enviable position to find oneself in, Buddy."

"No, sir, it isn't. The prisoners that Cecil rescued . . . how are they?"

"Still in mild shock. Some are coming around. But very slowly. Doctor Chase tells me that his shrinks say many of these people will never be able to function in any sort of normal fashion."

"So they are going to be wards of the Rebels." Not posed as a question.

"Do we have a choice, son?"

"No. What they have become was not their fault. But hundreds of them, Father?"

"I know, boy. We've already sent many of the rescued back to Base Camp One. They can do menial work while being treated. As we rescue the others, depending upon their mental state at the time, and after treatment, we can send them to the various outposts and hope they fit in. It's a moral responsibility, son. If they were hard-core, vicious criminals, solving the problem would be easy; but these people are innocents, and we are all they have."

"It's always going to be up to us, isn't it, Father?"

"For a long time, son. I'll someday have to hand the reins over to you and Tina." He smiled at the young man. "But don't start making plans just yet. I'm a long way from being over-the-hill." He leaned back in his chair. "I want the doctors up here to check you out. Doctor Allardt, for one. You may have made goo-goo eyes at some of those female doctors back at camp and conned them into releasing you too early."

"*Goo-goo eyes,* Father?"

"After I get a second opinion, and if you are truly one hundred percent, I've got a mission for you and your people. I'll send you down to Staten Island in the morning; that's where Chase's main hospital is located—has been relocated. You'll have to cross over and go down through New Jersey. Since we pulled out of Brooklyn, that area is no longer deemed secure. We'll see what tomorrow's reports state."

"What's the matter, Father?" the son asked, with a twinkle in his eyes. "Don't you trust me?"

Ben chuckled. "From one Raines to another, boy, in a word: No!"

With thirty hours to go until Monte's forces would be in position to attack the airport, Chase called Ben.

"The young man is one hundred percent, Ben. I've marked him fit to return to active duty."

"Thank you, Lamar."

"Don't thank me. Just get him out of here. He's causing all my nurses to get all girlish. I've never seen such swishing and eye-batting and giggling. Jesus Christ, Ben—I want this place to get back to normal."

"And speaking of that place, Lamar . . ."

"I know, I know. Ben, do you think there's a chance you'll be cut off and trapped?"

"Yes," Ben said quickly. "I believe that Ike, Cecil, West and my battalion will be cut off over here in Manhattan—at least for a time. Striganov, Rebet, Danjou, Tina, and Buddy will have to contain Monte and his people and keep them off the island while we deal with the Night People. And speaking of islands, you've got to get off Staten Island. Once Teterboro is overwhelmed, and it will be—I'm not going to lose personnel defending it for very long—we're going to have so many fronts it'll look like a wino's nightmare. You're going to have to split your people up. I've got to have a field hospital up here, one in lower Manhattan, and one to take the people from over in New Jersey. Get cracking on it, Lamar."

"All right. Where do you want me, Ben?"

"Your choice, old friend."

"I'll command the MASH up where you are, Ben. Holly and her people can stay in Lower Manhattan. Doctor Ling can command the MASH over in New Jersey."

"The last load of supplies will be coming into Teterboro this afternoon. After that, it's going to be up to the trucks until we can set up a safe LZ, and that might be a long time coming. So get your old butt up here, Chase. Unless you want me to send a wheelchair down for you."

With that, the conversation became so blue that Beth took off her headphones.

"Don't ever sell Raines short," the man who called himself the Colonel told Monte. "I've known the arrogant jerk for years. He's always planning and scheming and thinking. He'll have an ace up his sleeve. Bet on that."

"I've got him outmanned," Monte brushed the warning aside.

"But he's got us outgunned. Don't ever forget that. Look, Raines stole enough equipment after the Great War to supply ten armies ten times the size of his. Khamsin couldn't defeat him, and look at the people that nut has in his army. Take a lesson from history, Monte. Brute force alone won't defeat Ben Raines."

"I suppose you have a plan?"

"The oldest plan in the world: divide and conquer."

"Spell it out."

"Look, Monte. The Night People have been playing you for the fool." He held up a hand. "Now, just calm down and listen. You're doing all the work, and you're not getting anything for it except some pussy—and you could have that anyway. Hell, man, you could be *King* of New York City. There are dozens of two-bit warlords out in the boondocks who would fall all over themselves to do for you what you've been doing for the Night People. Think about it."

Monte was smart like a fox, in a cunning fashion.

He was dumb as an ox when it came to common sense. "All right. Tell me about this divide and conquer thing."

"I told you that Raines is not a fool. Now, we know he's got a few hundred people at the airport. He wants us to believe that's all he's got around there. That's a bunch of crap, Monte. All of a sudden that bunch of Canadians and Russians behind us just disappeared. Well, I can tell you one thing: they didn't turn around and go home. Raines is pulling something—like sucking us into a trap."

"Get to divide and conquer!"

"We know Raines and Ike and the nigger are in the city. We also know that the Night People are all around them: in Brooklyn, up in Bronx County, under the city. We cut them off from their forces over in New Jersey. Let the Night People and Raines have at each other while we handle those around the airport. All we have to do is come up under the airport—not attack it head-on, like they're probably planning on us doing."

"What the hell's the difference whether we attack it from the top or the bottom?"

"No, no! We don't attack it first-off. All we have to do is blow just one bridge. The George Washington Bridge. And Raines and his people are trapped. They can't go north. They can't go south. They can't go east or west. They can't use the tunnels. They'll be trapped in the city. Once that's done, we can take our time in dealing with those in New Jersey

"I got some boys that was divers, and they're good with explosives. I could go on and send them over east now. Tell them to grab a boat and come down the Hudson at night. Plant their charges on a section and get the hell gone. Yeah, might work at that. Good, Colonel whatever-your-name-is."

"Lance Ashley Lantier, Monte. Originally from Louisiana. And I have hated that goddamned Ben Raines for years!"

"Katzman, General," Beth told Ben. "He's just received word from Rebet that Monte has cut west, angling away from the airport. He's requesting orders."

Ben stood up from his desk and faced a wall map, trying to understand why Monte would do such a thing. He could not see what could possibly be gained by such a move. "Ask Rebet if he'll send a scouting party out to keep an eye on them. Monte is pulling something cute, but damned if I know what it is. Monte's entire force cut west?"

Beth spoke to Katzman, listened, then nodded her head. "Yes, sir. His entire army. Rebet will send scouts out and keep us informed. He'll hold his present position."

Ben walked to a window and looked out. His people had pushed down to within a couple of blocks of the Columbia-Presbyterian Medical Center and were holding, spreading out east and west, securing and blocking off streets and alleys, preparing for a major battle that now appeared would not come.

Or was it coming? Perhaps in a different form and fashion? And that mysterious person traveling with Monte, that person who called himself the

Colonel—who was he? And did he have anything to do with this latest move?

"Tell Tina to take the alert down a level, Beth. No point in the troops staying all tensed up for nothing."

"Yes, sir."

"And get in touch with General Striganov. Ask him if he'll bring his battalion on into the city and join me."

"Yes, sir."

Ben once more walked to the map and studied it for a moment. When Beth had finished her transmissions, he said, "Double the boat patrols under and around the George Washington Bridge. Monte's cutting west just might be a ruse; he could be sending people up or down the Hudson to cripple the bridge."

Jersey sat in a chair across the room, her M-16 across her knees. Cooper was in the hall, flirting with a pretty Rebel from Ike's battalion.

Snowing in the city. Big wet flakes of snow; already the streets were slushy. Ben returned to his desk and picked up the clipboard containing the supply reports. He studied it again, checking off each item in his mind, trying to think of something he might have missed. He could find nothing. Restless, he tossed the clipboard to the desk and rose to his boots, picking up his Thompson.

"Come on, gang. Let's go play in the snow."

Outside, only an occasional shot could be heard, muffled by the growing blanket of white that was covering the city's streets. Ben leaned against what used to be, and what was left of, a magazine vendor's hut.

What the hell was Monte up to? It had to be the bridge; that was the only thing that made any sense.

He looked at Beth. "Tell Katzman to bump Buddy. Tell Buddy to shadow Monte's force. The boy is one of the best headhunters I've ever seen. Tell him to start some terror tactics, get in close and take out any stragglers. I want Monte's people to know they're not jacking around with the faint-of-heart."

"Yes, sir."

Dan rode up in a Jeep and got out. "Something's in the wind, General. The creepies have seemingly vanished. I think a major offensive is not far off."

"I get the same feeling, Dan. What have we failed to do? Can you think of anything at all?"

"Nothing, and I was going over my supply requisitions this morning. As near as I can tell, we're set for a long campaign."

"We better be. I think it's inevitable that we'll lose the bridge. And it's going to come at us all at once. The crawlers will hit us from all sides just as hard as they possibly can. By the way, I asked Georgi to come on over and join us, and I've ordered Buddy to go head-hunting against Monte's people"

The Englishman nodded his approval and brushed a snowflake off his nose. "Wretched weather. But I suppose we're better off dealing with the cold and snow of winter than we would be with the stifling heat in this city during the summer."

"Wounds heal better in the cold, that's for sure." Ben turned just as a rifle cracked. The slug spun him around and dropped him to the snowy sidewalk.

He did not move.

Chapter 9

Jersey located the sniper and shot him right between his eyes as tears filled her own eyes. She turned and almost fainted in shock as Ben rolled over and got to his knees.

Ben shook his head. "That body armor really works, doesn't it?"

Dan helped him to his feet and opened Ben's field jacket. A large red spot was forming, and that would turn into a purple bruise as the day wore on.

"You're just damn lucky he wasn't trying for a head shot," Dan commented.

Ben laughed and winced in pain. "Hell, Dan, with my hard head I'd probably been better off if he had."

A medic took him by the arm. "Let's go check for any broken bones, General."

Ben did not argue. He was not exempt from following his own guidelines.

Ben was checked out and x-rayed at Chase's newly set-up MASH, and was given a lecture by Chase on why he should be more careful. "Even though I know my words are going in one ear and out the other," Chase added.

"Right. OW! Damn, Lamar. Quit poking me. That hurts."

"Oh, don't be such a baby. Put your shirt back on. I'm tired of looking at all the old bullet scars in your hide. You're all right, although you'll be sore for a few days. And, Raines? Try to stay out of trouble, damn it!"

"Hell, there isn't any trouble to get into," Ben bitched. Noon, the day after he was knocked flat on his butt by the sniper's bullet.

Not one shot had been fired—that he was aware of—for at least twenty-four hours. Ben's chest ached, but a couple of aspirin every few hours took care of that. The wound West had sustained during the assassination attempts had not slowed him down. But Cecil had developed an infection, and Holly had plopped him into a hospital bed for a few days.

Ben smiled, knowing that Cecil hated hospitals almost as bad as he did.

Monte and his troops had ceased their seemingly aimless wanderings, and were now bivouacked about forty miles from the Teterboro airport. And that was probably due to Buddy and some of his people slitting more than a dozen throats during the past night. Nothing like waking up and finding all your guards dead.

Buddy had radioed back that Monte had really tightened up on the camp's security. Ben had ordered Buddy back a few miles, told him to keep a few scouts out, and to keep Ben informed.

He had talked with Ike. Nothing was stirring down in Lower Manhattan either. Gene Savie, true to his word, was calling in spotter reports every time movement was noted from their vantage point. Savie's survivors had spotted some Night People scurrying about like black bugs, but could make no sense out of what the creepies were doing.

And neither could Ben.

"Diversion!" Ben said, straightening up in his chair.

"Sir?" Beth looked at him.

"Bump Katzman. Tell him to contact Gene Savie and tell him to stop watching the Night People run around in circles and start sweeping all the other areas around them. Gene's people have been made, and the crawlers are throwing up a smoke screen to conceal what they're really doing."

"Yes, sir."

When she was finished, Ben said, "Come on. Let's get out of this damn office and prowl around some."

They drove to the George Washington Bridge, and Ben chatted briefly with the Rebels on guard, then drove to the center of the bridge and got out. He stood for a time, gazing down at the dark waters of the Hudson, watching his patrol boats constantly checking the area. Which side would Monte's Sappers come down? Where would they place their charges?

He had already made up his mind that the structure was going to go—or at least a section of it, and that's all it would take to cripple the bridge and cut off Ben from his people in New Jersey.

He looked up as several Rebel vehicles came across from the New Jersey side, accompanying the last of the supply trucks. Several of Tina's Scouts were leading the parade, Jerre among them. She stared straight ahead as they passed Ben.

Ben tossed her a sloppy salute and laughed, knowing she was fighting with all her might not to toss him the bird.

When he got back to his office, about an hour later, Chase was sitting there, having a cup of coffee. There was a strange smile on his lips.

"Is the coffee that good?" Ben asked.

"It's the worst I ever drank, so that means you probably made it. I have news."

"Good news or bad?"

"I think it's funny."

Ben poured a cup of coffee and sat down.

"One of the Rebels accompanying the supply trucks had a slight accident about forty-five minutes ago. Had to be hospitalized."

"You think that's funny? I worry about you, Lamar."

"Perhaps I should have said ironic. She'll be with us for a couple of days."

"She?"

"No point in sending her back now. She can't walk. Better off just staying over here. Besides, it was a bad sprain. When I release her she'll have to be assigned a sit-down job. Preferably in an office. Like yours, maybe."

"Fine, Lamar. I could use some extra help."

"Then you don't mind if I assign her here?"

"No."

"Good. Because I've already informed personnel of that decision."

"Naturally. Nobody ever tells me anything."

"Are you going to pout?"

"Lamar I have a lot on my mind. I . . ."

A very dull thudding sound drifted to them.

"Find out what that was, Jersey," Ben asked.

But before the little bodyguard could exit the door, Beth held up a hand, listening to her headset. "They've made their move, General. A part of the New Jersey side of the bridge was just knocked out."

Ben took it calmly. "Sappers probably planted the charges last night." He waited as Beth listened to the reports coming in. When she looked up at him, he asked, "Was anybody hurt?"

"No, sir."

"Well, the lower level was unstable anyway." He sighed. "We all knew it was coming."

"More coming in, sir," Beth announced. She listened for a moment. "Correction, sir. The bridge is intact. They knocked down the approaches." Again, she held up a hand and listened. "Another correction, sir. One approach is down. The rest have suffered structural damage. Our engineers are going over there now."

"That's better," Ben said with a smile. "That's *damn* good news." He stood up. "Let's go look at the damage while we still can."

"I'm going back to the hospital and check on my new patient," Chase said.

"She's going to be assigned to me?"

"Right, Ben."

"Well, when she can hobble around, send her on over. Oh, by the way: what's her name?"

Chase made it to the door before he replied. Over his shoulder, he called, "Jerre Hunter!"

Ben was not in a peachy-creamy mood as he reviewed the damage done to the New Jersey side. He would have sent Jerre back across despite Chase's objections. But to do that, he'd have to send her all the way to Ike's position, transporting her either by boat across to Staten Island or by running the gauntlet through Brooklyn to get to the Verrazano-Narrows Bridge.

"Hell with it," he muttered. "But damned if she'll work in my office." He looked up as an engineer approached him.

"If we had the time, General, we could fix it. But it's going to take some time. Whoever planted those charges knew what they were doing to attain the max structural damage to this side."

"Well, one thing's for sure," Ben said. "We can't use it, but then, neither can *they.*"

"Pardon, General," Beth touched his arm. "Buddy is reporting that Monte's people are on the move. Heading straight for the Teterboro airport."

"Advise Tina to prepare for immediate attack. Tell Rebet and Danjou to stay out of the airport area and to hold what they have. Tina's already worked out a hole for her bunch to use to get out of there."

Dan had joined them on the bridge, and with that remark, he looked at Ben, questions in his eyes. "You're going to pull them out today, General?"

Before he replied to Dan's question, he said to Beth, "And tell Rebet and Danjou to sit very quietly. We'll leave the pinchers wide open. Give Monte's people lots of room. Let's see what they'll do."

With that, Dan began smiling. "Now I see, General."

"If Monte will bite. But this Colonel person seems to know a lot about me. I'll wager that he's the one who had Monte bypass the airport in the first place. I'll also wager that he's the one who planned blowing this bridge. I wish to hell I knew who he was."

"General Ike coming under heavy attack, sir," Beth informed.

"The offensive is on, people. Let's go to work."

Tina's forward observers had been forced to shift positions a half-dozen times during Monte's meanderings. Now, with Monte on the move with a definite goal in mind, the FO's could track the warlord's movements.

The 155's Ben had assigned to Tina's command could lob a shell over fifteen miles with near-pinpoint accuracy. The 81mm mortars had much less range, about 3500 meters.

"We're gonna cream the Interstate system usin' those One-fifty-fives," the most forward of the FO's radioed to Tina.

"Can't be helped. Are they in range?"

"Approximately two more minutes." He called out the coordinates. "And you can walk them in and be right on target."

"You hope," Tina said.

The gunners started counting with thirty seconds to go. They commenced firing one twenty seconds behind the other, to give the FO's time to call in adjustments. The first outgoing HE blew a hole in Interstate 95. The second round took out two vehicles, and the third round of WP hit a truck carrying ammo. The impacting round, combined with the exploding ammo, knocked out a section of the overpass the column was on, forcing them to fall back.

Monte's force had never come under sustained artillery fire before. Even the most battle-hardened men and women cringe before it, especially when every third round is white phosphorus that eats through skin and burns through bone.

"No, god damn it!" Ashley yelled. "Monte! Split your people and press on. Get under the artillery They're firing at twenty-second intervals. That means they've only got three of the big pieces."

"How you figure that?" Monte yelled over the crash and boom and screaming.

"Rate of fire for a self-propelled One-fifty-five is one round a minute. If you let your troops panic now, you'll never get them back together."

Monte stuck a pistol in Ashley's face. "Then you lead, hotshot. We'll follow."

Ashley had toughened considerably over the years. He pushed the pistol away and said, "You and me, Monte. Together, *we* will lead."

"Done. Let's go."

Screaming out orders, finally having to physically confront the men, Monte and Ashley rallied their frightened troops and shoved and pushed and threatened and promised them the moon and stars. They shoved on, driving as fast as they could, just staying ahead of the shelling.

"Cease firing! Cease firing!" another team of FO's radioed. "I've lost them. They're just north of Two-eighty between the Expressway and Twenty-one. Shut it down."

The 155's fell silent.

Monte had split his troops up into five groups, approximately 800 per group. He had never commanded this many troops, usually maintaining a force of about a thousand men. But as his territory grew, he had been forced to take in other warlords and their outlaw followings. Without proper organization, Monte was discovering, commanding this many men could be a pain in the butt.

"Order all your people to lay low in the buildings," Ashley suggested. "Make them come to us."

"Good idea."

Tina radioed her father, telling him Monte's people had disappeared.

"Spotter planes up from the old naval air station, Beth. Tell them to stay high and out of range."

"Yes, sir."

Ben turned to a map. "They're over here in the Belleville, East Orange, Nutley area. The FO's said they'd split up, right? So that means that this Colonel somebody is probably calling the shots. Monte is a thug, not a tactician."

"Spotter planes going up, sir."

Ben looked at the map. "Tell Rebet and Danjou to fall back north of Eighty, into Hackensack. Leave the area between Lodi and Bogota wide open for

Tina. When she's inside, with whatever of Monte's battalions on her heels, she can turn around and Rebet and Danjou can swing around and close the trap."

"Orders for Buddy, sir?"

"None. He knows he's to lone-wolf it and stay loose."

West and Ike had radioed that they were up to their butts in creepie-crawlers, literally coming out of the woodwork. But that they were having no difficulty holding.

"The latest from General Striganov?" Ben asked.

"Still several days out. I believe he had been living in Alberta, General. Is that right?"

"I think so. Several-thousand-mile pull anyway you cut it."

Ben had her check with half a dozen of his posts, stretching west to east along 171st Street. None of them had seen any creepies nor had come under any hostile fire.

"Strange," Ben muttered. "And what were the crawlers doing with that diversion?"

Ben now had six bridges to defend, although he still did not believe the Night People would attempt to storm their way across the bridges. "Check the bridges, Beth."

The Rebels guarding the bridges had seen nothing. Boring.

"Spotter planes are reporting nothing, sir," Beth told him.

"That's what they're waiting for then."

"Sir?"

"Night. Monte probably didn't plan it that way. But

they'll hit Tina tonight, and the creepies will throw it at us tonight. I'd bet a month's pay on it." He smiled at Beth. "If any of us were getting paid, that is. Double the sentries, Beth. Pass the word to arm the electronically fired Claymores." He looked at his watch. It would be dark in less than an hour. "Order all personnel to eat now and return to their posts." He glanced out the window. It was snowing. "Wonderful. It's going to be a crappy night all the way around."

Chapter 10

Dark had just closed its dusky wings over the city. The snow had tapered off into only an occasional burst of whiteness as the temperature dipped below freezing, gradually turning the slush into frozen, dirty-looking piles.

The men and women of the Rebels had draped pieces of dark cloth over their weapons to keep the oil from freezing during the cold waiting period. The Rebels wore face masks for protection against the weather, the interior around the mouth hole lined with silk to prevent the breath from freezing the cloth against the lips.

The Rebels waited in silence, moving only when absolutely necessary. The snowy calmness was very deceiving. In every alley lurked waiting death; behind many doors and windows Rebels crouched with weapons set on full auto. Hidden in the shadows— especially in the dark alleys—were deadly Claymores, ready to be activated electronically; others would spew their killing hail of ball bearings when a trip wire was touched. In the alleys of the city they would be doubly dangerous, for the lethal balls of death would bounce off the brick walls time and time again after the initial blast, whining in fury until they found a target.

The Night People learned just how dangerous the Rebels could be this cold evening in the city. They learned why Ben Raines and his Rebels had earned the reputation of being the most feared force in all of what had once been known as America. They learned their first lesson when a dozen of the black-robed creepies slithered into an alley. One of them tripped a wire that set off an antipersonnel mine. The roaring shattered the deceptive calmness of the night, followed by hideous shrieking from men whose bodies had just been mangled by the ball bearings.

Not one Rebel close by gave away his or her position by opening fire. They were too wise in the ways of combat; this was nothing new to the Rebels. Many had been doing this for more than a decade. Many a Rebel trigger-finger actually had calluses worn on the skin from years of weapons use.

The screaming finally faded away as the snow in the alley soaked up the blood of the night crawlers.

A few miles away, over in New Jersey, Tina and her people were lashing out at Monte's people as the warlord made his first tentative thrusts at the airport. Mortars and heavy machine-gun fire, from .50's and .30's and M-60's, ruptured the cold air and tore into flesh. Dusters, hidden behind recently scooped-up mounds of earth around the airport, cut loose with their 40mm cannon and quad .50's. Big Thumpers thumped out deadly red balls of death.

Monte's people were stopped before they even reached the chain-link fence.

"Fall back, fall back!"

Monte's people did not need to be told more than once.

Ashley gathered the CO's and P'Ls around him. "All right, we took some hits, But we found out what we had to know: a brute force frontal attack won't win it for us. Set your mortars up on flatbed trucks and start lobbing them in. After a half-dozen rounds, change positions so the Rebels can't get a fix on you. Monte, I would suggest you get teams of your best riflemen and have them work in close enough for some sniping. We agreed that this was going to be a long campaign. Tonight proves it. We're just going to have to wear them down and make them back up."

"And then we go in and kill them, right?" a CO asked.

"No," Ashley smashed that thought. "That's what Ben Raines is famous for. When they retreat, we don't follow. That would mean a death trap for us. Raines is famous for trapping people who are foolish enough to follow his so-called retreats. We just keep pushing at them and staying back, avoiding any major confrontations."

Monte stared at Ashley through eyes that the Louisiana man could not read. Finally Monte cleared it up. "You all right, Colonel. You're an educated man. I didn't think much of you at first, but I was wrong. And I admit it. You're now second in command of my army. And you call the shots in this here campaign. She's all yours, Colonel."

* * *

Ben had picked up an M-14 assault rifle and moved two floors up from his office. He kicked out a window and made himself as comfortable as possible. Waiting to begin making whatever black robe he happened to spot as uncomfortable as possible from his vantage point above the street.

He spotted a dark movement in the building across the street from his. Shifting his eyes, he spotted the boards the creepies had used to move from rooftop to rooftop. Still he waited.

Another dark shape joined the one he'd first spotted. "Hand me those night glasses, Jersey."

The shapes leaped into his eyes through the night lenses. A whole room filled with bogies.

"Jersey, Beth. Pick a window but don't kick it out. Step back and fire through it." He handed Jersey the night glasses. "Look at your targets."

Ben lifted the old Thunder Lizard, with a thirty-round clip in its belly and set on full rock and roll. "You ready, ladies?"

"Let's give 'em hell, General," Jersey said.

Ben emptied half the clip, his shoulder taking some punishment from the hard-hitting recoil of the old dinosaur. But those .308's from the M-14, added to Beth and Jersey's .223 slugs, made a great big mess in the room across the street. The creepies were all caught standing up, totally unaware that anyone had spotted them.

"Get on the radio, Beth. Advise our people that the creepies are on the rooftops." He rubbed his shoulder where the M-14 had pounded him just as his eyes caught movement on another roof. Ben lifted the assault rifle and let it bang. The slugs knocked the legs out from under one night crawler and sent him screaming down a dozen floors, to land in a sprawl of smashed bones and a spray of blood that left its mark on a storefront.

Ben slipped home a fresh clip and waited for some more action to materialize.

It was not long in coming.

Creepies began popping up on rooftops, hurling firebombs and grenades.

"How in the hell did they get up there without our spotting them?" Beth called over the rattle of gunfire and booming of grenades.

"They've had a decade to prowl this city, Beth. No telling how many tunnels they've dug just in that time alone. And no telling how many secret passageways they've carved out of hundreds of houses and buildings . . ."

His last words were cut off as a tank clanked up the street and came to a halt far enough back so its main gun could effectively be brought into play. The turret swiveled and the 90mm cannon began spewing out HE rounds, directed at the floor next to the top. The explosions knocked half a dozen creepies off the roof and sent them spinning to the concrete just before part of the roof collapsed under the heavy shelling.

Another main battle tank joined that tank and directed its 105mm cannon at another building, soon producing the same results. That block cleared, the tanks rumbled and clanked on, to wreak more havoc wherever directed.

Ben leaned against a wall and hand-rolled a smoke. "Pass the coffee thermos, Jersey." He licked his smoke closed. "It's going to be a long, cold night."

* * *

At the first graying of the eastern sky, the Night People pulled their stinking cloaks around them and vanished. Many weary Rebels, too tired to move, simply remained at their posts and closed their eyes, catching some sleep behind their guns.

Ben walked down to his office and found the windows shot out, the walls bullet-pocked, and the floor littered with papers. He and Beth and Jersey and Cooper picked up what they could, and stuffed the papers into boxes. Ben retrieved his Thompson and in the other room, quickly field-stripped it and wiped it free of the moisture that had collected after the windows had been shot out.

Ben ate a can of field rations while Beth called in for a casualty report. Three dead and fifteen wounded, two of the wounded in serious condition. The attack from the creepies had been widespread and savage. Rebels guarding the bridges connecting Manhattan with Queens and the Bronx reported heavy infiltration by boat during the night.

Ben surmised that whatever losses the Night People had sustained during the fighting had been made up for threefold by the infiltrators. God alone knew how many Night People they were actually facing.

Ben tossed a sleeping bag on the floor, wearily pulled off his boots, and went to sleep.

He was a man who had always needed no more than a few hours' sleep, so before noon, while the others still slept, Ben quietly bathed and shaved— no after-shave, for many soldiers had been killed because their location was pinpointed by the odor of after-shave or cologne—and dressed in clean BDU's. He stepped out into another cold, dreary, and overcast day.

The city was eerily quiet. The bodies of the slain creepies had been removed from the immediate area and tossed onto the death barges, moored on both the Hudson and the East River.

Ben walked up Fort Washington Avenue for a block before he found where his cooks had set up a mess hall, and stood in line, waiting for breakfast and a very welcome steaming mug of coffee. Doctor Chase waved him over to a makeshift table.

"Out wandering by yourself again, Raines?"

"I didn't have the heart to wake up the others. They were beat."

"You're gonna be *dead* if you don't stop your damned meandering about in a combat zone."

Ben looked at his tray. He could identify the biscuits and gravy and fried potatoes. He did not know what that inert lump might be. It vaguely resembled meat.

"Eat it," Chase told him. "It's good for you."

"Whatever you say, Mother." Ben took a bite, chewed and swallowed, then reached for the hot-sauce bottle. If he got it hot enough the sauce would hide the taste.

Dan joined them. Ben noticed the Englishman had loaded up with fried potatoes, biscuits, and gravy. He had bypassed the meat substitute— a mostly grain concoction from the lab people at Base Camp One.

"Wise choice," Ben complimented him.

"It's worst than squid," Dan said. "I ate that once. I refuse to ever again attempt to ingest any object that insists upon gripping the sides of the plate."

"Have you spoken with Ike or West this morning?" Ben asked.

"Yes. Ike. Cecil is still in the hospital. All fronts were hit hard last night. Ike said that the guards on the bridges in his area reported heavy infiltration last evening. Ike says he figures we're outnumbered about twenty to one just in the city."

"Tina?"

"Monte is being very cautious. They started lobbing in mortar rounds last evening, and snipers are making things rather difficult for the boys and girls at the airport. Monte has changed tactics drastically."

"Then Monte isn't running the show," Ben stated. "He's turned it over to this Colonel person."

"That's the way I see it," Dan agreed. "The troops I've personally spoken with have all resigned themselves to the fact that we're going to be here for a long, long time."

Ben nodded and stood up, walking toward the coffee urns for a refill. He was halfway across the room when a ball of fire erupted at the front of the mess hall. He felt himself literally lifted off his boots and hurled toward the rear of the room. Very faintly, the sounds of debris falling reached him. Through glazed eyes, Ben saw bodies and parts of bodies flying all over the place. Food trays and coffee mugs and chairs and knives and forks and spoons were sent ripping through the air like missiles. The back of Ben's head exploded in pain. Darkness took him winging into an unknown journey.

Chapter 11

Ben opened his eyes, trying to figure out where he was. He knew one thing for sure: he had a hell of a headache.

There were misty shapes all around him. He blinked his eyes a couple of times. The shapes took form. Dan and Doctor Chase.

Chase held up two fingers. "How many do you see, Ben?"

"Two. What the hell happened?"

"Shut up. I'll ask the questions."

The doctor's head was bandaged. "What happened to your head, Lamar?"

"I collided with a wall. You got brained by a brick, we think. Do you feel sick at your stomach?"

"No. Now tell me what happened? How many people did we lose?"

The doctor's face hardened. Ben shifted his eyes to Dan. The man's face scarcely masked his inner fury.

"About fifty, Ben," Chase told him, his voice shaking with anger. "Another fifty or so hospitalized."

"How?" Ben had turned cold with rage.

"Witnesses outside said two men walked over from across the street, carrying duffel bags." Dan said.

"The men were dressed in tiger-stripe BDU's. That's the reason our people didn't think anything about it. Each of them were probably carrying satchel charges. I would imagine about forty or fifty pounds of explosives apiece. It was a suicide run."

"Can the witnesses describe the men?"

Dan shifted his boots uncomfortably, and Ben experienced a numbness in his stomach. "Were they our people, Dan?"

"Plant and Tyler. They'd been with us about six months."

"Find out who recommended them and who they buddied with. Haul them in for questioning. If they're solid Rebels they won't have any objections to the questions. I'd hate to even think we have more of those maggots in our ranks."

"Done, sir." Dan turned. Ben's voice stopped him.

"Dan? Do it quietly. If we do find more Night People among us, I don't want our people to tear them to pieces before we can thoroughly question them."

"And should we find more and after we question them?" Dan asked.

"Shoot them."

"Very good, sir." Dan left the room.

Ben lay back. "So what's the verdict on me, Lamar?"

"Slight concussion. Bump on your head. Very small cut. Didn't even require stitches, darn it. I was looking forward to practicing my needlework on you."

Ben knew the doctor was joking to hide his rage and grief.

"So how long do I have to stay here?"

"Twenty-four hours, Ben. And that's firm. You try to leave and I will personally order security to arrest you and put you in restraints."

And Ben knew Chase would do just that. Ben ran his forces the same way the Navy does on shipboard. The doctor has the last word, even to the point of ordering the captain off the bridge and to his quarters.

"Fine. I'm hungry. I didn't get to finish my breakfast."

"Poor baby! I'll have some soup sent in."

"I'd rather have a sandwich."

"Soup." Chase walked out of the room.

Ben felt the back of his head. A small knot and a little cut. And one whale of a headache. He was restless, not a bit sleepy. He looked for his watch, found it, and checked the time. He'd been out for about thirty or forty minutes. He looked around the room. Not one damn thing to read. His engineers had rewired the lower floor and plugged into a half a dozen portable generators. The light was adequate, if not bright. But Ben knew the OR's would be brilliantly lighted. Chase was a crotchety old poot, but his patients would receive the best he could provide for them, even if he had to scream and curse at Ben to get it. Which he had done more than once.

He looked up at movement in the doorway. Jerre, in a wheelchair, one leg up on the lift. The ankle looked swollen.

Then Ben realized what Chase had meant when he'd called the accident ironic. The first time he'd met Jerre she'd suffered a sprained ankle.

"Seems like you would have outgrown your clumsiness by now," Ben said gruffly.

"Well, Ben," she replied, wheeling into the room and up to his bed, "you said I'd always be about half kid."

That spun Ben back in time, to the short time they'd spent together. Whenever they'd stopped for the evening, and had a drink, Ben would lift his glass and mime Bogart by saying, "Here's lookin' at you, kid." Once, during his prowlings, Ben had found the record "Key Largo;" he wore it out playing it. Never could find another one.

Here's lookin' at you, kid.

I love you, kid.

But Ben would never say the words aloud. And never to her.

"Yeah? Did I say that, Jerre?"

"I seem to recall you saying that. A long time ago."

A nurse stuck her head into the room. "Some coffee, General?"

"That would be nice. And bring Miss Hunter a cup, too, please."

"Thank you, Ben." Jerre waited until the nurse had left before addressing him by his first name.

"You're welcome, Jerre."

"The nurse tells me you're not badly hurt. I'm glad."

"Just a headache. You wouldn't happen to have a couple of aspirin on you, would you?"

"Sorry. Fresh out. Are you supposed to take aspirin when you have a concussion?"

"Beats the hell out of me."

She smiled at him. "I thought you were the man with all the answers."

"You said that, kid, not me."

"You mind company, Ben?"

"Not at all. How's the ankle?"

"Sore. But it's better."

"Chase tells me he assigned you to work in my office when you're able to hobble around."

"Yes. But if you don't want me there just say so."

"I can use the extra help. Of course, I never know from one day to the next where my office is going to be."

A nurse came in with Ben's soup and two mugs of coffee on the tray.

"Where's the salt and pepper?" Ben asked.

"It was added during cooking, General. You know how Doctor Chase feels about sodium." She left Ben and Jerre alone.

"You still use too much salt, Ben," Jerre admonished him.

She'd said that years back.

"Yeah. And I smoke about a half-dozen cigarettes a day, too."

"Well, that's an improvement. You used to smoke about three packs a day."

Ben ate his soup. Vegetable, with no meat. If Chase had his way, theirs would be an almost meat-free existence. And salt-free and tobacco-free.

If Ben could have his way, he'd settle for no more wars. Ever.

Chase would probably get his way long before Ben's dream ever came true.

"Tell me about New York City, Ben."

He put his empty soup bowl on the nightstand. "The way it used to be?"

"Yes."

He smiled. "Used to be exciting, dangerous, cultural, fascinating. Now it's just dangerous." He yawned.

"You're tired, Ben. I should leave and let you get some rest."

"I'm not tired. I'm bored."

"You always were restless."

"True."

A nurse came in and smiled at Jerre. "Let's have a look at that ankle, Jerre." He cut her eyes at Ben. "And you get some rest, General."

"See you, General," Jerre said. And then she was gone, wheeled out by the nurse.

Here's lookin' at you, kid.

Ben was awakened a dozen times during the night by the sounds of hard combat. At six o'clock in the morning he was up and dressed and receiving reports. By ten o'clock Chase kicked him out of the hospital and told him not to come back; he couldn't get any damn work done with Raines around. "You want me to notify your office?"

"No. I've already radioed them," Ben lied, and walked out to the street.

Ben was back in action, armed with his Thompson and a bottle of aspirin.

Only problem was he couldn't find where his office had been relocated.

He finally had to stop a couple of Rebels and ask them. Ben felt like an idiot!

His office had been moved over a couple of blocks, and Ben started walking the distance, enjoying the freedom—he despised hospitals—and glad to be free of the medicinal odor.

A truck passed him, the bed of the vehicle filled with dead creepies. Ben held his breath until the stinking death truck had rolled on. He passed a drugstore, stopped, and turned around, entering the store. It had been looted, naturally, but the looters had taken only the drugs and a few medicines; the rest of the store was amazingly intact. He found a half a dozen books on the top of the rack, only slightly ratchewed, and put them in a paper sack, then moved on past the cosmetics counter to a glass showcase filled with fashion watches. The next counter contained hundreds of lipstick tubes. He walked on toward the rear of the store.

A silent alarm went off in his mind as he looked at a closed door in the rear of the establishment. Something was very wrong. But what? It was just a closed door.

Ben put his sack of paperback books on the counter and stared at the closed door, trying to figure out what had triggered the alarm in his mind. Then it hit him: no cobwebs.

Rebels from the street ran into the store. Ben waved one of them forward and pointed to the crate, which was now leaking blood. "From now on, don't just move the crates and big boxes around. Look in them. That's how some of the creepies are getting past us."

"General!" Dan's voice turned him around. "By the Lord Harry, sir! We've been looking all over for you."

"Well, you found me, Dan." He looked at Jersey, looking at him with a disgusted expression on her face. "What's your problem, short stuff?"

"Tryin' to guard a body that don't wanna be guarded," she bluntly told him.

Ben winked at her.

Dan glared at the squad of Rebels that Ike had sent up. "What's your excuses?"

"He slipped out of the hospital. Told Doctor Chase he'd already notified us."

"Don't yell at them, Dan." Ben walked to the center of the store. "I gave them the slip." He jerked his thumb toward the darkened storeroom. "Take a look in that crate back there. If you can stand the smell. I'll be outside."

Half a minute later, Dan joined him. "More work cut for us, General."

"I reckon. You busy?"

"Waiting for the night."

"Walk over to the office with me. We'll talk along the way."

Dan waved Rebels forward and to flank them. Jersey, Beth and Cooper brought up the rear.

"How about those friends of Plant and Tyler?" Ben asked.

"About a half a dozen of them, when they heard we were looking for them, took to the air. That is when we moved your office. Again. I have issued shoot-to-kill orders on them."

"Good. How many losses from last night?"

"One dead. Five wounded. None of them seriously."

"How many creepies did we knock out?"

"Fifty-two, at latest count."

"Tina?"

"She offered Monte the bait again last night. He didn't take it. Since you were not badly hurt and would be on your feet again today, I did not suggest to her what I have in mind."

"Which is?"

"I fail to see the point of her continually sustaining casualties over that strip of tarmac."

"I agree."

"My suggestion would be for her to bust out and come up behind Monte's people, with Rebet and Danjou on Monte's flanks. If one cannot lead a horse to pasture, there is always the option of herding it."

"Nicely put, Dan. Give her the orders. And tell her to do it now, while Monte's people are least expecting it." Ben smiled. "How is Emil and his bunch performing?"

"Surprisingly well, sir. Both he and his group and Thermopolis and his people have seen the light about dressing in BDU's. The robes and Gypsy outfits have been packed away for the duration. Emil put a general's star on his helmet. He took it off after a sniper dusted his rooty-tooty a couple of times."

Ben chuckled at the visual thought of that. "Beth, run this through Katzman's scramble. Get in touch with Tina and then give me the horn."

Ben took the portable phone. "Tina. Bug out. Right now. Get around behind Monte and see if you and Buddy can push them toward Rebet and Danjou. Shake your booty, girl."

"I will if you'll keep your booty out of trouble, Pops."

"It would be totally undignified for a general to shake his booty." That got him a lot of strange looks from all near him. "Good luck and good hunting, baby."

"Way-out Scout, out."

"I think there was a song about shaking your booty," Ben said. "Do you remember that one, Dan?"

"Heavens, no. The more primitive types of music have never appealed to me." He grimaced. "Shake your *booty?* Was that a dance?"

Ben shook his booty and the street erupted in laughter, while Dan stood looking, shaking his head in amazement.

Chapter 12

"We're under constant observation," Tina told her platoon leaders and Emil and Thermopolis. "So don't give away what we're about to do with a lot of unnecessary packing and moving around. Let one person pack for half a dozen, and we won't load the trucks until the last possible second. Thermopolis, you stagger your VW's between our trucks and tanks; same goes for you, Emil. That'll give you some protection."

Both men nodded their heads.

"Tanks, APC's, and self-propelled artillery will crank up last. We'll take Forty-six out of here, cut south on Liberty and drive right through the middle of the warlord's people down to Highway Three, then cut west and dismount, throw up a line of defense along there. Buddy is waiting for us there. Any questions?"

No questions.

"OK. Nice and easy now, people. Let's do it."

They should have been detected. If Monte's people were professionals, they would have been. But Monte's lookouts were tired, and not accustomed to this type of warfare. They had noticed a little more activity than usual through long lenses, but assumed the Rebels were just switching things around a bit. Had Ashley been alerted, he would have put it together immediately. But he was sleeping, and so was Monte, so they were left undisturbed.

Tina ordered a lot of equipment left behind, but it was nonessential equipment, and could be easily replaced. Since the vehicles were parked in and around the hangars, loading them was no problem.

Thermopolis winced as he cranked up his VW Bug. "Why did I ever let that boy talk me into putting straight pipes on this damn thing?"

Rosebud laughed at him. "We're still not going to be as loud as a tank."

"There is that to consider."

"Hey!" a lookout punched his buddy in the ribs, waking him. "Them fuckers is takin' off!"

His buddy jumped up, looked through binoculars, and cussed. He grabbed for the mike switch just as the tanks and APC's and SP artillery roared into life and lurched ahead, ramming through the fence and cutting onto 46.

Several of Monte's people ran from their holes on the east side of Redneck and ran into a mine field. Bloody hunks of them were tossed into the air following the roaring explosions.

The big main battle tanks pointed the way for the strange convoy, with brightly painted VW Bugs and several stretch limos and one hearse mixed in. With their .50-caliber and 7.62 machine guns clattering and yammering, they cleared the way for the slower self-propelled artillery and mortar carriers.

To avoid being run over, one outlaw jumped onto the long hood of Emil's hearse and held on, his ugly face pressed against the windowshield. "Get off my hearse, you scourge of humanity!" Emil shrieked at him.

The outlaw cursed Emil. Emil leaned out his window and removed the man with one round from a single-action .44. "Redneck," Emil muttered.

Another of Monte's people tried to jerk open the passenger-side door of Thermopolis's VW Bug. Rosebud conked him on the noggin with a ball peen hammer. The deuce-and-a-half behind the Bug ran over the outlaw.

Screaming their fury, Ashley and Monte rallied their people and sent a contingent to cut off the escape route of the Rebels. They ran into Buddy's company lying in wait at the Meadowlands Sports Complex.

Buddy and his company locked horns with the outlaws in close-quarter combat. And for the first time in their evil careers, the warlord's men found themselves facing an adversary who asked no quarter and gave none. Ben Raines's son did not take prisoners unless ordered to do so.

The outlaws were stronger in number, but not as well armed. And for years, the Rebels Buddy commanded had eaten well-balanced meals and received proper medical care; they understood discipline, and were fighting for a cause as a motivating force.

It was a slaughter, with not one outlaw left alive.

Buddy pointed out temporary mortar positions, and his crews quickly set up mortars and heavy machine guns on the east side of the complex and began raking the warlord's men who were advancing toward Paterson.

Others under Monte's and Ashley's command

tried to come down Highway 17 to flank Buddy and his people. They had cleared the road of mines but had not checked alongside the highway. The Claymores began firing as Ham detonated them from his Hummer, spraying the advancing enemy vehicles with flesh-ripping and life-taking ball bearings. Cars and trucks and Jeeps, their drivers dead or badly wounded and confused, piled into one another, creating a monumental mess in the road, and blocking it, giving Tina and her people even more time to complete their bug-out.

The first vehicles in the convoy reached the sports complex and slid to a halt on the Berry River side, Rebels jumping out and setting up machine guns and mortars. Other Rebels raced to the top of the arena and set up their weapons positions there. From that height, they could also act as forward observers to call in range for the mortars and cannon.

Several of Tina's Scouts had jumped out at the radio towers and laid charges. When the C-4 blew, the towers came down, blocking part of the highway interchange, adding more misery to Monte's and Ashley's already maddening and growing frustrations.

A few miles north of the complex, Rebet and Danjou were pulling their troops in closer, stretching them down south from Lodi and Bogota, preparing to close the pinchers if Tina was successful in pushing the warlord's troops into the trap.

But Ashley wasn't buying it. He'd been a student of Ben Raines for years and thought he knew the man better than anyone else alive. He hated Raines, but he also admired him for his cunning.

Ashley found Monte amid the chaos. "Raines is pulling more of his crap, Monte. Don't fall for it.

They're trying to push us north. I'll wager that's where the Canadians are waiting for us. Let's get the hell out of here and regroup over in Passaic."

"You're runnin' the show," Monte reminded him.

A few minutes later, from atop his vantage point at the sports complex, a Rebel radioed, "They ain't taking the bait, Tina. They're pulling out, heading west, toward the river."

"Ten-four. You acknowledge that, Colonel?"

"Ten-four," Colonel Rebet radioed. "I do not understand this game they are playing. This does not at all sound like Monte."

"Monte isn't running the show. We need to meet, Colonel."

The Russian called out map coordinates, reversing them as they had agreed upon.

"That's ten-four, Colonel. I'm rolling." She turned it over to Ham and took fifty Rebels, heading toward the arranged meet with the Russian and the Canadian.

"You are very young and very pretty," Colonel Rebet said with a smile. "And as I have observed, very dangerous. Your father taught you well, Tina."

"Thank you, Colonel." She was introduced to Danjou, and noticed that both men wore wedding bands. "I think, gentlemen, that if Monte were to stand and fight us, we could defeat him."

"But of course," the French Canadian agreed. "That is something Stefan and I have discussed. "With your added battalion we could take them. But it's obvious he has quite different thoughts on the matter. You think this Colonel person is now in command?"

"That's what my father believes, and so do I."

The Russian and Canadian nodded their heads in agreement, Danjou saying, "I believe that we must defeat Monte and get across the river to your father. I believe that this Colonel person is going to play cat and mouse with us, tying us up, so to speak, while General Raines and his forces are slowly chopped up by the Night People." He glanced at the Russian.

Rebet picked it up. "From what we have been able to ascertain, there might be as many as fifty thousand, or more, of the Night People in the city. Your father is facing odds of perhaps thirty to one, or more. We must end this quickly and go to his aid."

"Agreed." Tina met their eyes. "But how?"

"They just may have unknowingly placed themselves in that box we've been trying to put them in." Rebet said with a hard smile. "General Striganov is driving hard, rolling twenty hours, sleeping four. He is now one day away. He crossed the border several days ago, and will come up from the west. You have some artillery, we have some artillery and my general is bringing more. We all have tanks and self-propelled howitzers capable of throwing chemical warheads." Rebet hesitated, his eyes sad. "I suggested this with reservations. General Striganov will agree only if General Raines agrees to it. But while we are waiting for them to make their decision, it would be my suggestion that we erect three sides of the box, leaving the west open."

"I agree," Danjou said.

"All right." Tina sweetened the pot. "I'm for it. But let me ask this: why can't we stand back and toss Willie Peter and HE into Monte's position? I'm just afraid my father is going to nix the use of chemicals."

"Personally I hope he does," Rebet replied.

"As do I." Danjou said. "But that will be up to the generals."

"All right, gentlemen, let's start building that box." Tina agreed to take the south side of Passaic, stretching her people along Highway 3, roughly from Nutley to the Upper Monclair golf links. Danjou would plant charges at the bridge over the Passaic at the junction of 3 and 21 and then stretch his people from that point up to the Passaic Avenue Bridge, and plant more charges there. The bridges would be blown when Striganov and his troops were in position. Rebet would take from Passaic Avenue and loop around to Elmwood Park. Striganov would plug up the last hole.

The men watched Tina as she left. "A very lovely lady," the Russian observed.

"And like her father," Danjou said, "as dangerous as a cobra."

"Hello, you old warrior!" Georgi Striganov's voice boomed over the speaker.

"Georgi!" Ben took the mike. The two once-bitter adversaries greeted each other as brothers. "How's the gout?"

"All cleared up. How's your health?"

"Fit as a fiddle."

"I have spoken with my people, Ben. My opinion is *nyet!*"

"Thank you for that, Georgi. That is mine, as well. We stay with conventional."

"*Da.*"

"Well, you old warhoss, I wish you well and good hunting. I'm looking forward to seeing you soon."

"The same to you, my brother. Farmer Brown out."

"Eagle out," Ben said with a laugh. Since leaving California, the Russian had been working a farm in Canada, living peacefully. He had remarried and was raising a family.

"Farmer Brown?" Rebet looked at Danjou. "He could have taken Bear or Wolf or any of a half a dozen others. Farmer Brown?"

"He is mellowing as he ages," Danjou told his friend. "And when you are not leading troops, Stefan . . . what is your vocation?" That was said with a smile.

The Russian laughed. "I am teaching world history in a high school. You are right, Major: we are all mellowing."

The questions had been nagging at Ben since the Rebels' arrival in New York City: What happened to the people over in New Jersey, over in Brooklyn and Queens, and up in the Bronx? And why had the Night People—*all* of them—congregated in Manhattan? Why would they, why should they, all settle in the city, leaving the outlying areas?

Questions he could not answer. But they bothered him, and Ben did not know why they continually nagged at him.

And he did not understand why he occasionally experienced an uneasy sensation of impending doom.

What had he missed in his planning? There had to have been something; why else would he have these odd feelings?

But if there was something, he could not bring it to the forefront.

Something for granted leaped into his mind. He was taking something for granted.

But what was it? It had to be something of importance. Something vital. But vital to what or whom?

He mulled it around in his mind until he gave himself a headache.

He looked up at a slight scraping sound in the doorway. Jerre stood there on crutches.

Here's lookin' at you, kid.

Ben rubbed his aching temples with his fingertips. "You feel bad, General?"

"Will you knock off the 'General' business, Jerre? We're not exactly strangers."

"Protocol, and all that, General."

Ben opened his mouth to cuss, then realized that would not help or solve a thing. "You've had radio training?"

Jerre nodded.

"Beth!" Ben roared. She stuck her head in the doorway. "Familiarize Miss Hunter with the radio and how we use translators. She can handle that from the office. Take some of the load off you."

"Yes, sir."

"And bring me some aspirin, please."

Jerre smiled at Beth. "I give him headaches."

Beth stared at her through dark brown eyes. "You like cows?"

"I beg your pardon?"

"Nothing. Forget it. Come on."

Out of Ben's hearing, Jerre asked, "Cows, Beth?"

"I love a man very much. Lev. But I don't like cows. Lev raises cows. What is there about General Raines that you don't like?"

Jerre's eyes turned frosty. "I believe you were going to go over the equipment with me?"

"Right. But I think I could learn to put up with the cows."

"Anytime you're through babbling . . ."

"So I tried with Lev. At least I did that. Come on, I won't bring it up again."

Ben caught Jersey making a terrible face and sticking her tongue out at Jerre's back as she and Beth disappeared into the next room. "Let's all try to get along, Jersey," he said softly.

The little bodyguard looked up at him and smiled. "We gonna be stuck with her for the duration, sir?"

"As soon as she's well, she'll be sent back to line duty with Tina."

"So I'll pray for a speedy recovery."

Ben laughed and his headache disappeared. He returned to his desk and the reports. Ike and West and Cec's people were holding their own—even gaining a little ground. A few blocks, but that was something. Cecil was still in the hospital. Striganov would be in position in a few hours.

Everything looked good. But again, that odd sensation of impending doom settled its cloak of darkness around Ben. He did his best to shake it off. They would settle Monte's hash once and for all, and then, as a combined force, start effectively dealing with the Night People.

Ben looked at his watch. It wouldn't be long now.

He leaned back in his chair and waited for Georgi to start raining down destruction on Monte's army.

Chapter 13

"All units report," Georgi gave the orders to his radio operator.

"In position and ready," Tina radioed.

"Ready," Danjou said.

"Ready." Rebet sealed the fate of Monte and his outlaws. Or so they all thought.

"Fire!" The Russian general brought his hand down.

Far back behind the lines, the big guns roared. Closer in, the 81mm mortars and Dusters began spitting out death and mayhem.

"You *bastard!*" Monte cursed Ashley as the shells began dropping in on them. "You put us in the box we've been trying to avoid! I oughta kill you!"

Ashley's reply was lost as a building across the street exploded as a HE round was lobbed in.

Each battalion had been assigned a specific sector of the city on which to concentrate their fire. Some began walking in their rounds from the outside of the perimeter; other gunners began at the center of the city and walked their rounds back.

Not a generally accepted method of shelling, but in this case it produced panic among the troops locked inside the corridors of the shelling.

The incoming mail was mixed: high explosive, Willie Peter, incendiary. The corridor was soon sending up billowing clouds of smoke as the dry interiors of the buildings ignited and went up in flames.

The shelling was relentless, one type of round or the other landing somewhere in the city every eight seconds. From his offices in Manhattan, Ben could watch the smoke and hear the booming as one of the oldest cities in New Jersey, originally named Acquackanonk by the Dutch back in the 1600s, was destroyed, block by block.

The shelling went on, all day, without stopping. At dusk, the hot guns fell silent.

More than four thousand troops, Russian, American, Canadian, with all nationalities mixed in among them, ringed the smoking and ruined city. Gunners lay behind all types of machine guns, ready to repel any who might come charging out of the ruins. Tanks had pulled in close, leveling their cannons.

The night was eerily silent except for the crackle of the fires.

Not one sign of human existence became evident from the smoking ruins.

Tina got Danjou on the horn. "What do you think, Major? Somebody has to be alive in there."

"That would be my thought. Monte had as many personnel as we now have."

"All personnel. This is General Striganov. Stand down to middle alert. Eat and rest in shifts. We'll enter the city in the morning." He turned to his radio operator. "Get me General Raines. Something is very wrong here."

"Georgi. Ben here."

"Ben, unless the gods of war smiled on us, something is dreadfully wrong. There is not one person from the warlord's army staggering out of the city. Not one."

Once again, those nagging doubts entered Ben's mind, accompanied by that sensation of impending doom. "I agree with you, Georgi. I just can't see that bunch of ill-disciplined outlaws wanting to mix it up with you. Not after the pounding they took today. That doesn't make any sense. You going in in the morning?"

"Yes. Carefully. I'll radio you then."

"Ten-four. Eagle out."

"Farmer Brown out."

Ben sat looking at Jerre. "Odd, Jerre. Very odd. People survived the atomic bomb. They survived the Great War. And some of Monte and Ashley's people survived this. But where the hell are they?"

He stood up and walked to the window, the fires from the burning city lit up the skies. "Where in the hell did they go?"

"I want a sector-by-sector body count," Striganov ordered the troops. "Be alert for man-made booby traps and falling walls. Those old buildings took a pounding. Move out."

The Russians, the Rebels, and the Canadians moved into the still-smoldering city cautiously, and began the grisly task of counting the dead. They worked all day to reach the total of six hundred and fifteen dead.

"It's very curious," Tina said, after calling a meeting with Rebet and Danjou, prior to reporting in to Striganov. "We found over fifty bodies that had been shot in the head."

"Same here," both the Russian and the Canadian said.

"And I don't like what I'm making of it," Rebet added.

"And that is . . . ?" Tina asked.

"The outlaws slipped out through a hidey-hole and shot their wounded so they couldn't talk."

"So much for honor among thieves." Rebet spoke the words contemptuously.

"I'm glad I don't have to look my dad in the face when I report this," Tina said.

The Russian grimaced. "Lucky you. But *I* have to face Georgi Striganov."

The Russian general took it calmly. His only sign of irritation came from drumming the fingers of his right hand on a battered desk in the building he was using as his CP. "It's the only thing that makes any sense," he finally spoke. "And your theory is . . . ?" He looked at Rebet.

"I don't have one, sir. It is inconceivable to me that three thousand people could be buried under the rubble."

Georgi nodded and told his radio operator to get Ben on the horn. He then saved Tina the trouble of telling her dad.

"Well, Georgi," Ben said, "there is one way to find out about the bodies."

"Oh?"

"Bring in the earth-moving equipment first thing in the morning."

While Georgi's people—Tina was under his command—began the task of digging through the rubble, Ike got Ben on the horn.

"You notice anything unusual about the fighting last night, Ben?"

"Heavy up here. How about where you are?"

"Same thing. But there was something else. They seemed to be taking more chances, becoming much more aggressive. Did you notice that?"

"Yes. What do you make of it?"

"I don't know, Ben. But something is up for sure, and whatever it is, I got a hunch we ain't gonna like it."

After Ike had signed off, Ben sat behind his desk, deep in thought. He turned in his chair, looking out the window. The day was cold, but the sun was shining—a welcome relief after the days of snow and rain and sleet.

"General Striganov on the horn, Ben," Jerre said.

"Georgi? What'd you find?"

"A couple hundred more bodies, Ben. That pretty well confirms it. They had a hole to run into and they took it."

"Damn!"

"My sentiments also. But what hole would be big enough for over two thousand men?"

Then it came to Ben. That elusive sensation he'd been experiencing stepped out from the murk of his brain into the light. "I'm going to say this once, Georgi. Then you'd better get your people and bug out fast. We've been had. You ask what hole? Tunnels. The Night People have apparently been here for many, many years; long before the war. No telling how many miles, in all directions, they've honeycombed. The war just brought them to the surface, that's all."

The Russian was silent for a few seconds. "The ramifications of that theory—if proven correct—could be . . ."

The horn went dead as the sounds of explosions reached Ben's ears.

"Tina's on the emergency frequency, Ben!" Jerre called. "They're coming under heavy attack from all directions. She says it looks like thousands of the creepies are moving toward them, pushing them south and slightly east."

"Bug out!" Ben ordered. "See if you can get General Striganov."

"Got him!"

Ben took the head set. "Georgi. What's happening?"

"Under heavy attack, Ben. My forward teams say it looks like giant black ants totally covering the earth, coming from the west and the north."

"Cut and run, Georgi. Valor is one thing, saving your butt is another."

"You don't have to repeat that, Ben. Farmer Brown is breaking new ground. Talk to you later."

"Get Ike on the horn, Jerre."

"Go," she told him, seconds later.

"You copied that from New Jersey, Shark?"

"Ten-four. Five'll get you ten they're putting

them in a squeeze. The uglies will have people coming up from the south, Ben. Bet on it."

"No bet. Go to translator, Shark. Beth!" he shouted. "I need you in here."

She took the headset.

"Tell Ike he's got to clear the Holland Tunnel."

She spoke in fast Yiddish. Listened. Smiled. Turned to Ben. "General Ike says up yours, too. But if Great Commander orders, so be it. Wants to know why."

"I'm ordering all our friendlies in New Jersey to swing toward the Bergen Turnpike and head south for Hoboken and the tunnel. That's the only tunnel Ike has in his sector that'll do our people across the river any good."

"General Ike says ten-four and all that happy crap, sir."

"Relay my orders to all friendlies across the river, Beth." That done, Ben said, "Order all our heavy guns to the waterfront, Beth. Tell Gene Savie to have his people start spotting for us; call in the rounds. Tell Georgi to stay on the east side of One-nine. I'm going to be dropping in everything I've got west of it. Tell Georgi to throw up a line of defense around the tunnel. It's going to take Ike some time to clear it. Tell our people to grab their butts and hold on."

"Yes, sir."

Across the river, Thermopolis looked at Rosebud. "Well, dear, you always wanted to see the Big Apple. You're getting your wish."

It was fortunate for Thermopolis that his son had put straight pipes on the VW Bug, for Rosebud's reply would have wilted a field of wildflowers.

Her husband did catch the gist of it, however, and smiled.

Emil had been separated from his hearse when the bug-out began and now found himself crowded into the back of a bob truck with a bunch of Russians. "Never fear," he shouted above the roaring of the engine and the whip of wind. "In the noble words of Churchill: 'We shall not flag or fail. We shall go on to the end . . . we shall defend our island, whatever the cost may be, we shall fight on the beaches, on the landing grounds, we shall fight in the fields and in the streets, we shall fight in the hills; we shall never surrender'!"

The Russians politely applauded.

Tina and her Scouts were leading the wild ride down to the tunnel, her battalion right behind her. Buddy and his company had elected to bring up the rear of the long column, fighting a rear-guard action as the beleaguered troops smashed their way to their only hope for staying alive.

All of the friendly troops in New Jersey heard the shells from the Rebels in Manhattan as they began whistling overhead and landing west of the column.

"Come on!" Ben said to Jersey and Beth. "I'm not sitting in this damn office another minute."

Ben had grabbed his battle harness and Thompson and was out the door before anyone could say a word.

"Hold down the fort," Beth said to Jerre. "And think about those cows."

Jerre shook her head. "Right. Cows."

On the street, Cooper slid the Blazer to a halt, Beth and Jersey jumped in the back, and Ben got in the front. "Where to, General?"

"The bridge." He busied himself with a map. "That's well within the range of our one-fifty-fives. That's about all we can use up here. But Ike can use his One-oh-fives and Eighty-ones from his location. But it's going to be damn close. Beth, tell Ike's gunners to start laying down a field of fire. Keep it all west of One-nine."

"Those Eighty-ones got a max of thirty-six hundred meters," Jersey muttered. "That's gonna be cuttin' it fine."

"I know, Jersey."

"General Ike on the horn," Beth said.

Ben picked up his mike. "Go, Ike."

"Man, the air in this tunnel is *rank*, brother. I got people workin' to hook up portable generators so we can get some of these fans goin'. I'm only going to try to clear one side, Ben—one lane. We're lookin' at a mile and a half of solid black. Cars and trucks abandoned all over the goddamn place. And we got rats down here damn near as big as hogs!"

"Give a time estimate, Ike. Right off the top of your head."

"If our folks on the other side can lend a hand, and we work shifts around the clock . . . forty-eight hours, Ben. We can't use explosives down here; the stalled cars and trucks are gonna have to be winched out of the way. Ben, there is no evidence the creepies have used this tunnel in any way. The air down here is poisonous and possibly explosive. We can't risk a spark until we get the fans workin'."

"Ten-four, Ike."

South of the George Washington Bridge, Ben instructed his gunners. "Work them until the barrels melt, people. We've got to help keep the creepies west of One-nine."

"Yes, sir. Savie's people are right on the mark in calling the shots. They report that the night crawlers have halted their eastward push."

"Very good."

"General?" Beth handed him the mike. There was no point in continuing the use of translators now. The Night People knew what was coming their way. "Tina."

"How goes it, girl?"

"We lost a few on the way, but that was expected. We're setting up our own mortars and heavy stuff now. Buddy and his people have set up just north of the tunnel, along with Thermopolis and Emil's people. I think we can hold until the tunnel is cleared."

"All right, girl. Hang tough. Eagle out." Ben motioned his team back away from the 155's, just going into action. The roaring of the big guns made any type of conversation impossible.

"Order the CP moved down here, Beth. Have a building over on Fort Washington Avenue cleared for me. It's going to be a long forty-eight hours for us. But not nearly as long for us as it will be for our people trapped over there."

Chapter 14

For Ike and his teams under the river, it was slow going clearing the tunnel while above them, the shells whistled across the waters and slammed into New Jersey.

In the tunnel, the men and women were forced to work in gas masks until the engineers could get the ventilation system back in operation. Without any type of maintenance for more than a decade, the twin tubes of the tunnel were showing signs of deterioration. Before any clearing could be started, pumps had to be brought in to suck up the stinking pools of water that had gathered over ten years of leakage.

And the rats sat like big cats above the Rebels, on the catwalks, watching every move, not one bit afraid, their naked snaky tails twitching back and forth. It was a bit unnerving for the workers.

"Ten more years," Ike muttered, the words unheard through his mask, "this place won't be here."

A blast of cold air dried the sweat from the faces of the men and women.

A grimy-faced Rebel walked up to Ike. "We got the

suction pumps working again, General. But we had to divert the outside air to straight in. The expansion boxes under here," he stomped the road bed, "are all screwed up. What we're gonna do, once the suction pulls the bad air out, is set up a series of stations, so to speak, using fire hoses to channel the air around. It still isn't gonna be real pleasant, but it'll beat the hell out of before."

Ike nodded and slapped the man on the back. "Stay with it. Tell me when we can safely cause some sparks in here. We gotta start winching these rust-buckets out of the way."

"Doctor Holly's people said it was OK now. They've tested the air for about three thousand feet in," he waved toward the darkness that yawned westward, "and they haven't found any signs of methane."

Conversation soon became impossible over the squalling and shrieking of metal against concrete as the long-abandoned cars and trucks were pulled out, towed out, or shoved to one side of the tunnel.

A Rebel backed a bob truck up to where Ike was standing in the middle of a lane. "More extension cords, General. But some of them are dry-rotted. Gonna have to be stretched out and taped." He grinned. "Wonder what the record is for the world's longest extension cord."

"All the way under and across the Atlantic Ocean," Ike said. "In a manner of speaking."

"No kidding?" the young man asked. "What'd they use it for?"

"So Mama Leone in Milan could talk to her son in Brooklyn. Come on, let's get back to work."

"Must have been a hell of an expensive phone call," the young man muttered, walking away.

They had cleared a thousand feet of tunnel by nightfall, another five hundred by midnight. The lights were a problem: faulty extension cords were always going out, sparking briefly in the dampness.

And Ike had gotten tired of the rats and assigned a squad to rat patrol . . . armed with pump-up pellet guns.

"First one of you that misses and shoots me in the butt is gonna be in trouble," he warned with his ever-present grin.

At midnight, Ben ordered Ike out and to get some rest.

By dawn, the Rebels had cleared three thousand feet closer to the friendlies trapped in New Jersey.

Over on the New Jersey side, American, Canadian, and Russian were working just as steadily, but much slower, since they could not run into the nearest store and pick up extension cords and sockets and light bulbs. Teams were sent in as far as Bergen Avenue, on a scrounging mission and to set up as many booby traps as they could.

The whistle and crash of the shelling continued all night, but at staggered intervals, and not nearly so heavy. Ben was letting his people in New Jersey handle most of it with mortars and 90mm and 40mm cannon fire. The Rebels' big guns across the river would pick it up again at dawn, when Savie's spotters could see.

"It's going to happen at any moment," Ben

muttered, glancing at his watch just after he had ordered Ike to get some rest.

"What's gonna happen, General?" Jersey asked.

"The creepies are going to pop up and come pouring across the line from Spuyten Duyvil in the north and from University Heights and Morris Heights and High Bridge from the east. That is what I'd forgotten. Passaic brought it back to me. The Night People don't just live underground here in Manhattan. They've been tunneling for years; five or ten or fifteen miles in all directions in New Jersey and over in Brooklyn and up north of us. Maybe even fifty or a hundred years, growing in strength. Beth, use translators on this, and get me our people at the bridges up north."

"Got them, sir."

"Tell them heads up and go on full alert. Advise Ike's people to do the same. Prepare for a mass attack. They're going to be coming up from under us and from all directions. They're going to be coming out of buildings and out of the subways, across the bridges and by water. And I think they're going to hit us with everything they've got—try to shock us, hurt us bad. Hold. Those are my orders. Tell everybody to hold until we get those people out of New Jersey. And tell what Rebels are still over in Brooklyn to bug out and get over here, pronto.

"Tell our Dusters and Big Thumper people and heavy machine gunners to lower down and stack up the bodies until they can't see over them. Everybody on the line, Beth. Tell the cooks and the intel people and the walking wounded to fall out and draw weapons."

"Yes, sir."

"When you've done that, you and Jersey and Cooper get some sleep." Ben tossed a sleeping bag into the back of a deuce-and-a-half and crawled in and closed his eyes. He opened one eye and looked at Jersey. "Wake me up when the action starts."

Then he went to sleep.

They hit at four o'clock in the morning, wave after wave after human wave of stinking, black-robed, screaming Night People. They poured across the Williamsburg Bridge, the Manhattan Bridge, and the Brooklyn Bridge from the east. They came chanting and shouting in a suicide run across the High Bridge, the Alexander Hamilton, the Washington, and the University Heights Bridge. From the north, they came in a dark fury from Spuyten Duyvil.

Jersey grabbed Ben's boot through the sleeping bag and shook it. "They're here, sir. All over the damn place."

"Advise the crews in the tunnels to keep working and the gunners to remain in place. They'll resume shelling across the river at dawn." Ben slipped out of his sleeping bag and picked up his Thompson.

"Yes, sir."

"Get Ike up. Nothing like starting the morning listening to his bitching."

"Yes, sir."

Ben pointed to one of his bodyguards. "See that subway entrance over there, son?"

"Yes, sir."

"I want two M-60's right here. There's gonna be

bogies coming out of that hole in the ground at any moment. Let's be ready for them."

To Beth, it seemed that they were completely surrounded by hostile fire.

"Steady now, Beth," Ben patted her on the shoulder. "We've been in worse spots than this."

She looked at him through serious brown eyes. "When and where, sir?"

Ben laughed. "Good question, Beth."

Night People came out of the subway entrance in a rush, bringing conversation to an end as the immediate night was shattered by automatic weapons fire from the bipodded M-60's.

"Lob some grenades in there," Ben ordered. He did not have to specify what type, since the Rebels almost exclusively used their own version of the Fire-Frag, possibly the deadliest grenade ever manufactured.

The yowls of pain springing from the subway opening offered living, and dying, proof of the Fire-Frag's effectiveness. No more creepies came from that hole.

Ben's presence was a solid one in the midst of what appeared to be mindless chaos. He squatted down beside the deuce-and-a-half and quietly pulled his besieged Rebels together.

"Hold your positions, people," he radioed. "We no longer have an identifiable front. It may seem that you're cut off for a time. Just stay low and hold what you've got. The creepies may be all around you, but so are your friends. Don't shoot at shadows; make damn certain of your targets. Repeat: all Rebels maintain your positions. Hold!" To Beth: "Tell Katzman to keep issuing those orders. Make sure every station understands."

A bullet wanged very close to Ben's head, knocking a hole in the bed of the truck. He lifted his walkie-talkie. "This is Eagle. We have bogies on the rooftops. Let's start clearing them. I need a Duster at Fort Washington and One Hundred and Seventy-third."

A quick little Duster rounded the corner, lifted its twin 40mm guns, and began blasting, the rounds directed just below the rooftops, while the machine gunner added to the death-dealing with .50-caliber slugs.

"Shark to Eagle."

Beth handed Ben the mike. "Go, Shark."

"Our situation is sorta crappy down here, Eagle. We got bogies coming out of holes where there ain't supposed to be holes."

"That's ten-four, Shark. Same here. I have ordered all Rebels to hold their positions. Stand tough, Ike."

"Ten-four, Eagle. Cec is out of the hospital and has resumed command in his sector. Work is continuing well under the water."

"Ten-four. Eagle out." Ben shifted positions, working his way under the truck, Jersey and Beth and Cooper with him. Beth was practically on top of him. Ben grinned at her. "My, isn't this cozy?"

Slugs whined and howled off the street. Beth said, "I have come to the conclusion that cows ain't so bad, after all."

"You'd miss all the excitement, Beth."

"Probably," she admitted glumly.

The actions of the Rebels confused the Night People. They had expected the Rebels to run, to regroup, to attempt the setting up of a defined front from which to fight.

When the Rebels did not run, but chose instead to hold their positions and fight only when directly confronted, the creepies became disorganized. This was not what the Judges had told them would happen.

But theirs was an autocratic society, not a democratic system, albeit a shared dictatorship. The Judges were the law, the first and last word, and all must obey.

The Night People ducked back into their holes just as gray began pushing the blackness into murky light.

Ben slipped out from under the truck. "Get me reports, Beth. Let's see how we fared."

Not bad, he thought, after all stations had reported. A lot better than he had expected, considering all the confusion that had reigned for a time.

"Sir?" Beth said. "Savie's people are reporting the creepies are once more advancing toward the tunnel."

"Tell the gunners to resume shelling. And get me Ike, please."

Ike on the horn, Ben asked, "How's it looking, Shark?"

"Noon tomorrow, Eagle. We ought to punch through at noon. That's the best we can do."

"They'll have to hold. If they want to live, they'll have to hold."

Emil stuck his head into the tunnel, New Jersey side, and shuddered. He hated tunnels, caves, elevators . . . anything that hemmed him in. He stepped inside, on the catwalk. A rat ran across his boots, and he almost invented a new dance before he got himself under control. The crashing and booming of the incoming shells had not let up. He hoped Ben Raines had enough rounds to see them through the tunnels—and through the winter—for it was a lead-pipe cinch they were all going to be trapped over there in the Big Apple.

With creepies all around them.

He beat it back outside and passed Tina Raines talking with the Russian, Striganov. From the expression on their faces, the news wasn't good. Emil hurried on. He didn't want to hear any bad news; he was depressed enough.

"We're almost out of fuel," Striganov said. "I propose we leave the trucks—there are trucks everywhere—and use the fuel for the tanks, SP's, APC's, and mortar carriers."

"I agree. And we've also got to get the badly wounded over. We can't wait any longer."

"Carry them across?"

"That's the only way I see."

"Agreed. You and Young Mister Raines shall lead the teams with the wounded through the tunnel. There is no point in your returning."

"Now, look, General . . . !"

"I give the orders here, Captain. You will do as you are told."

There was steel in the Russian's voice, and Tina knew there would be no back-up in him. "Yes, sir. I'll start gathering up our wounded."

After she had gone, Rebet stepped forward. "A very noble gesture, sir."

Striganov looked at him. "Noble gesture? Bah!

This is war. She happens to be very good at what she does, that's all. Sentiment has nothing to do with it." But his eyes gave away the lie.

Rebet kept a straight face. "Of course, sir. Whatever you say."

"Get the wounded transported down to the tunnel opening immediately, Colonel."

"Yes, sir." He hesitated.

"Something else, Stefan?"

"Yes, sir. I think the . . . strange-looking civilian/ soldiers should go over with Captain Raines."

"Yes. Yes, you're right. See that they are notified, Colonel."

Rebet gone, Georgi motioned for his radio man. "Get me General Raines."

"Translator, sir?"

"No need for that now. The loss of less than a thousand personnel does not make that much difference when one is facing the numbers we face. If Ben's shelling stops, we'll be overrun in a matter of minutes."

"Yes, sir. General Raines, sir."

"Ben! I'm sending our wounded over on the catwalks. I'm also sending the, ah, hippies over with them. Give the devil his due, Ben; they're good fighters. I've ordered Tina and Buddy Raines to lead them through. Tina was not too happy about it when I told her this was not a Return If Possible assignment."

"Typical Raines. Hardheaded."

"You said it, not I."

"I owe you a couple, Georgi."

"Bah! You're worse than Rebet. Always letting sentiment get in your way. You know perfectly well

I would never allow anything like that to muddle a battlefield decision."

"Of course, Georgi. Right. Rough and ready, that's you."

"But of course!"

"Georgi? In case you're worried about the amount of mail we're sending across, don't. I laid in enough stamps to last a long time."

"That is very gratifying to hear. When we get across, I must sign my name on several pieces."

"You do that. See you soon, Farmer Brown."

"Keep flying, Eagle."

Chapter 15

"General?" Beth said. "Savie's spotters say the creepies are backing up. Dropping back in all directions."

"Order all artillery to cease firing."

Up and down the west side of Manhattan the big guns fell silent. Grateful artillery teams slumped to the ground for some much-needed rest. Weary tank crews climbed out to stretch their legs.

"Tell Savie to keep their eyes on the creepies, Beth."

"They are continuing to fall back, sir." She listened for a moment. "Ike has made contact with Tina and Buddy. They're bringing the wounded out now."

"Continue to monitor the creepies' withdrawal. But I think I know what they're up to."

"Sir?"

"They knew what I was talking about when I told Georgi about the amount of mail I had. They knew there was no way I was going to let them get across that field of fire to our people without them losing a lot of troops. So now it's give a little and get a little."

"I understand that they gave some," Beth said. "But what did they get, General?"

"The entire Rebel army, and all the forces of Striganov. Trapped on Manhattan Island. Surrounded by God alone knows how many thousands of creepies, just waiting to invite us to dinner." He grinned at Beth. "How are the cows looking to you now, Beth?"

"They are handsome animals. If you don't walk behind them."

There was not one shot fired from either side for the rest of that day and all night. Ike broke through to the New Jersey side just after dawn and linked up with Striganov, Rebet, and Danjou. Fuel was trucked over so all vehicles could be brought over through the tunnel. Then the tunnel was sealed off on the Manhattan side.

"I have a question," Striganov asked Ike. "What is to prevent us from using some of the ships still docked along the waterfront as a way out?"

Ike shrugged. "Nothing. If we could get the old engines started. I looked some of them over first thing. However, we just haven't had time to do much except fight. But who the hell among us can run one of the big brutes? I can't."

"Another good idea poked in the eye," Striganov said.

"Poked in the eye?" Ike laughed. "Man, you are gettin' Americanized, Georgi."

Laughing, the American and the Russian walked off to find a cup of coffee.

The troops mingled easily with each other. A few

years back, the Russians and the Americans had been locked in deadly combat with each other.

Now they were allies, united against the common enemy. The Rebels and the Russians and the Canadians, some six thousand strong, against perhaps fifty thousand or more of the Night People. But they could still find time to joke and relax.

"Beth, get Ike on the horn. Translator." Ike standing by, Ben said, "Ike, you want to run the risk of a meeting of all commanders?"

"I think we're gonna have to risk it, Ben. And Georgi is nodding his head affirmatively."

The morning had turned out cold and overcast. Snowing in the Big Apple.

"Beth, advise all commanders to leave their XO's in charge and come up one at a time, with heavy guard, fifteen minutes apart. We'll meet at the George Washington Bridge. That includes Buddy and Tina and Thermopolis and Emil."

"Yes, sir."

The first one up was Cecil. The friends shook hands and grinned at each other. "How you feelin', old man?" Ben asked him.

"Shoulder's a little stiff, but getting better. We've got our work cut out for us, haven't we, Ben?"

"I'm afraid so, Cec."

They chatted until the next short column arrived, accompanied by tanks. Striganov. West came next, followed by Tina and Buddy, Thermopolis and Emil. Then Rebet, Danjou, and finally Ike.

A building on Cabrini had been doubly secured and checked from top to basement twice, and the commanders met there.

"Our gunners stacked them up on the bridges last night," Ben opened the meeting. "Everyone held. But it's just a matter of time before they're going to be overrun by sheer numbers. And there are these added worries: if we keep defending the bridges—all of them—the creepies might decide to destroy some of them; and we're going to lose a lot of people defending them. And there is this: for every spooky we killed on the bridges last night, two came over by boat."

"So it was a costly diversion," Rebet said.

"Yes. Proving, again, that the creepies have so many people they don't object to losing some."

"Have you ever thought that we might be doing them a favor, Father?" Buddy asked.

"Would you like to explain that, son?"

"Feeding that many of these . . . savages is surely a monumental task. If the Judges can cut their ranks, and still defeat us, we'd be doing them a favor."

"The boy just may be right," Striganov said. "That's something I hadn't thought of."

"Nor I," Ben admitted. "Damn, I hate to even entertain the thought that we're *helping* these nasties."

"They are nationwide, both in Canada and in America," Danjou said. "And quite possibly worldwide in scope. They're getting too many to feed, so they're culling out the inferiors—so to speak—and becoming more selective. That's just a theory."

"Probably an accurate one," Thermopolis said. "Even living as isolated as my group does, we've heard stories, rumors, and we have found half-eaten bodies, with black robes nearby."

"They've turned on each other," Emil spoke, then

shuddered with the revulsion shared by everyone in the room. "Filthy barbarians!"

"From what I have learned from your people, General Raines," Rebet said, "we will have no defined fronts."

"That is correct," Ben stamped his boot on the floor. "The creepies probably have tunnels right under this very building. There are hundreds of subway openings in this city. Expect them to come out of all of them. We've welded closed a lot of manhole covers. For every one we sealed, there are fifty we didn't; and that's just in the territory we more or less control. They'll be coming at us from all directions."

"Placement of the new people, Ben?" Cecil asked.

"Tina and Buddy, Thermopolis and Emil up here with me. That'll beef me up with about eight hundred people. I'm operating, so far, on the narrow end of the island. As we begin to widen our territory— and we will—pushing north and south, we can shift troops around." He looked at Beth. "Give the orders for those people I named to be escorted up here. Start them immediately."

She went to her radio and gave Katzman a bump.

"When you get your people settled in, hold what you've got. The spookies seem to have gone back to fighting at night. That's fine. When dawn breaks, shift your people around and tell them to *stay put!* We've got supplies cached all around this city. We were fortunate that you people were able to bring most of your equipment over from New Jersey, because this campaign is going to be a long one."

"The prisoners the spookies are holding, Ben?" Ike asked.

"We'll try to rescue them. But I don't think there'll be many left when this war is over. Do I have to spell that out?"

"Good God!" Thermopolis blurted. "You mean . . . while we're fighting to free them, the Night People will be *eating* them?"

"Yes." Ben's reply was soft.

Thermopolis stood up, folding his arms as if he were cold. "I am by nature a peaceful man, General. I wasn't always that way, but as I matured I changed. Which is what growing up is all about, I suppose." He caught the sudden change in Ben's eyes and accurately guessed what it meant. "I may be middle-aged, but I still like rock-and-roll music."

Ben smiled and Thermopolis returned it. "But I have no peaceful, easy feeling toward these Night People . . ."

"To paraphrase the Eagles," Ben said.

Thermopolis cocked his head, looking at Ben. "From a man supposedly wrapped up in the music of Brahms and Chopin and the like, you continue to surprise me, General."

"I like some of almost all types of music, Thermopolis. I just never believed in forcing my music on other people. Is there a point to all this?"

"It's standing before you," Thermopolis said simply. "I came, and I believe we must conquer. Or die attempting it."

"Right on!" Emil said.

* * *

"Enjoying your first day in the Big Apple?" Thermopolis asked Rosebud, after she had made the dangerous run up to Ben's position.

"Oh, yes! I've always enjoyed seeing the still-smoldering ruins of war. And hearing bullets wanging off the sides of the truck was a real kick."

"Place gives me the heebie-jeebies," Zipper said, looking around him. "Where and what are we supposed to defend?"

"This block," Thermopolis told him. "We'll take the second floor facing the street. Emil and his bunch will be behind us, second floor, facing that street." He pointed behind him. "Let's get set up."

"Have you seen Jerre?" Rosebud asked.

"No. But I was told she is working in Ben Raines's office."

"I bet that is certainly a pleasant atmosphere."

"I think they do their best to ignore each other."

"Thermopolis," Rosebud said, "that is ridiculous! How can you work that close and ignore each other?"

"Dear, I don't know. I just came up here to fight a war."

"If I knew where Ben Raines's offices were, I'd go see Jerre."

"Not me. They've been doing this for a decade— or more."

"So?"

"So nothing. Just that I'm staying out of it. It'll be dark in a few hours. Let's get dug in."

Jerre could walk, but not very well, nor for very long without using a cane. She was sitting by the radio in Ben's office, alone, when Tina came in.

The two women hugged each other, and Jerre pointed out the coffee pot to her.

"Feels lonesome in here."

"It is."

Tina poured a cup of coffee and sat down at her father's desk. "So how are you and Dad getting on?"

"We haven't tried to kill each other yet. So I guess that's something." She jerked her head toward New Jersey. "Was it bad over there?"

"We had a few chancy moments. Sure was good to see Uncle Ike's face in that tunnel, though."

"It is good to see you, Tina."

"Well, I wanted to come by. Dad is splitting the family up, so we all won't buy the farm at the same time. I'm going over to the waterfront on the Harlem River. Buddy will be up near Fort Tryon Park." She finished her coffee and stood up. "The other Rebels giving you a hard time, Jerre?"

"Not really. They just kind of ignore me, that's all."

"But you understand why, don't you?"

"Oh, sure!"

Tina glanced out the window. "I better go and get into position."

They hugged and smiled at each other. "Whatever happens between you and Dad, I want you to know that you've earned your place in the Rebels, Jerre."

"Tell you the truth, I just wanted to see if I could make it."

"You made it. See you."

After Tina had left, Jerre walked to the side of the window and looked out, leaning against the wall, being careful not to expose herself to enemy sniper fire. It was raining, a rain mixed with bits of ice and flakes of snow. One flake floated gently against the window and clung there for a few seconds. She felt . . .

She didn't know how she felt. Except that she felt like crying.

So she did.

Problem was, she didn't know whether she was crying for herself, or for Ben.

"You look terrible." Ben told her. "You feel all right?"

"I feel just goddamn wonderful, thank you!"

"Excuse the hell out of me for asking. And get away from that window. You trying to get killed?"

"Would that matter to you?"

"What kind of a stupid question is that? Of course it matters to me. What the hell is wrong with you?"

"Just get out and leave me alone!"

"With pleasure." Ben stalked out of the office. He stopped in the outer room. Beth, Jersey, and Cooper sat looking at him. "What am I doing? That's *my* office!"

Dan and Buddy picked that time to walk in. "What's wrong with your office, General?"

"What? Nothing is wrong with my office. Except I was just told to get out of it."

Buddy blinked. "Who told you to get out of your office, Father?"

"It all comes down to cows," Beth said.

Buddy looked at her. *"Cows?"*

Dan shook his head and stepped into Ben's office, spotting Jerre. "Ahh! Now I understand."

Buddy looked more confused than ever.

Jerre glared at Dan. The Englishman backed out of the office. Quick-time.

"I just came over to say so long, Father," Buddy said. "I didn't know you were in some sort of argument about farming."

"I'm not in any goddamned argument about *farming!*"

"Well, excuse me!" his son fired back. "Ranching, then."

Jerre started laughing. Beth and Jersey tried to smother their giggling, but it was a losing battle. Cooper sat down on the floor and began hoo-hawing. Buddy didn't know what to do, and Dan was having a terrible time keeping a straight face.

Ben began smiling. He walked back into his office and stood for a few seconds, looking at Jerre looking at him. He stepped toward her and put out his hand to touch her. She tensed.

Ben dropped his hand, his face hardening. "Back to square one, I guess."

He turned, picked up his Thompson from off the desk, and started to walk toward the door.

"Ben!"

Her voice turned him around.

"You don't understand. Will you, please, just try to understand?"

"I've been trying for ten years, Jerre. I've been trying to understand your moods and make some sense out of them."

"Damn it, Ben, I was just a kid when the whole world fell apart."

"Is that your excuse for never growing up and facing reality? For constantly running away from people who . . ." He bit those words off. "Kid? Hell, you were nineteen years old when I found you in Virginia. That ain't a kid, darling. When the world blows up in your face, you better grow up fast. Nineteen? So what? I was in Vietnam when I was nineteen. Big damn deal."

"I'm not as tough and hard as you are, Ben!" She screamed the words at him.

Ben laughed in her face. "Baby, you're harder and tougher than I'll ever be. So just get that little-girl-lost look off your face. It isn't working anymore. Not with me."

She threw his words back into his face. "Running away from people who . . . what, Ben? Say it, Ben."

"Why? So you can brag about carving another notch on another poor bastard's heart? No way, kid. See you around."

He walked out of the office without looking back.

"You want me to be here when you get back, Ben?" she shouted at him.

He stopped. "Where else would you go, Jerre? You can't go back on the line—not for a while. Just stay here and keep your head down." He looked at Cooper. "You stay here with her. You've both got cold rations. Enjoy your dinner. I'll be back before dark."

"Do I have to go with you, General?" Beth asked, unexpected ice in her tone.

"No, Beth. You don't." He walked out of the office and slammed the door before either Buddy or Dan could stop him.

Chapter 16

Jersey caught him before he had walked down the flight of stairs to the street. "General?"

Ben kept walking.

"General Raines!" she shouted.

Ben stopped and turned around.

"Don't go out there with your emotions all screwed up, sir. When you get mad, you take chances. Why not just cool down for a minute?"

Footsteps on the landing cut off his reply.

"Listen to her, Father." Buddy spoke from the landing. "Or I will bring you down and sit on you."

A very faint smile touched Ben's lips. "Oh, will you, now?"

"If I have to. Yes, sir."

"Let's go get something to eat, then." Ben turned and caught just a glimpse of dark movement at the base of the stairs. The stink of creepies offended his nostrils. He brought his Thompson up just as he heard the very faint snick of a pin being pulled from a grenade. He fired through the wood partition, giving the spookies hidden there a burst from his

SMG, and at the same time calling out, "Grenade, watch it!"

The words had just left his mouth when the grenade blew. The concussion splintered the wooden partition and blew two bloody night crawlers out into the foyer of the building.

"Full alert!" Ben called. "Buddy, tell Beth to order full alert. The creepies aren't waiting until dark. Go, boy!"

"Coming in, General!" a Rebel called from the outside.

"Come on." The hall filled with Rebels. Ben pointed to the dead spookies. "Drag that crap out of here and toss it in the street. Then dig in. They're hitting us now."

Ben ran back to his offices. "Douse the lights, Jerre. And get ready for a very messy office."

Just as she turned off the battery-powered lights in the room, a burst of automatic fire shattered the windows and knocked chunks of paneling from the walls, sending everybody diving to the floor.

Ben scrambled for the M-14 he kept in the office and smashed out what remained of a bullet-shattered window. The unfriendly fire was coming from the building directly across the street. And there was a lot of it—so much that Ben and those with him in the office were forced to keep their heads down until one of Dan's Scouts had raced up to the floor above them and fired a rocket into the pack of creepies.

The room across the street exploded in flames, the blast tossing one burning body out into the street.

"Now!" Ben shouted, rising to his knees and leveling the M-14 as the others in the office followed suit.

The room reverberated with the sounds of automatic weapons set on full rock and roll.

Thermopolis and his people beat back one screaming attack, the bodies of dead and dying and badly wounded night crawlers piled in the street in front of their position offering stinking, bloody testimony that the band of twenty-first-century hippies came to the Big Apple to make war, not peace.

In the block behind them, Emil crouched behind an M-60 and let the spookies invent new dances as they jerked and tumbled into death. "I didn't think anything could be worse than Hiram Rockingham and his damn rednecks," Emil muttered. "I guess anybody can make a mistake."

A night crawler came charging into the room, fell over an ammo box, and went crashing into Emil.

The M-60 hung up and lead started flying in all directions—fortunately for Emil, all of it going outside the room and into the street.

"Ye gods!" Emil hollered, taking a deep breath and instantly regretting it. He kicked the spook in the face with a boot, setting him up for Sister Lynn. She cleaved the black-hooded head with a camp axe.

Emil tore the belt from the M-60 and managed to right the weapon back on its bipod and refeed the weapon. The street filled with creepies, and Emil went back to work, wondering if anything would ever be the same after this war was won?

Tina and her team had been caught at the bus terminal facing 179th Street and had been forced up to the roof, fighting as they went. It was going to be a very long and very cold few hours for Tina and her team.

One Duster was knocked dead in the street by a satchel charge thrown under a tread. The tank couldn't move, but its 40mm cannon could still hammer out a lot of misery until a second Duster arrived at the scene, giving the crippled tank's crew time to dismount and scramble for cover, fighting as they went.

Creepies were popping out of manholes and racing up and out of subway entrances; they surfaced out of hidey-holes carved through basement walls and hidden stairwells.

A rifle grenade slammed into the room next to Ben's office, the concussion knocking Jerre, who was crouched next to the wall, into Ben.

"About the only way I can get close to you," Ben muttered, hauling her to her boots.

Jerre's reply was short, somewhat profane, and very much to the point.

The room that took the rifle grenade burst into flames.

"Let's get out of here!" Ben yelled, turning to duck-walk toward the door.

Jerre remained by the window, firing across the bloody street.

Ben grabbed her by the seat of her tiger-stripe britches and pulled her toward the door.

"Turn loose of me!" she screamed at him.

"All right," Ben said, then slung her spinning and sliding toward the door.

If her previous comments had been somewhat profane, these were decidedly vulgar.

Ben laughed at her and shoved her out the door.

In the hallway, Buddy and Beth and Cooper and

Jersey were mixing it up with a corridor filled with creepies. Dan pulled the pin on a grenade, popped the spoon and lobbed the Fire-Frag into the direction of the spooks.

When the deadly grenade blew, Ben tossed a smoke grenade into the moaning mass and shoved Jerre down the hall.

They crouched in a bunch in the foyer, waiting for a break in the action to run for the building next door.

"Now!" Dan called, and charged out the smashed front door, running to the sidewalk and ducking to his right.

With all of them safely out of the burning building and on the floor of what had once been a clothing store, Ben said, "Hold your fire. Let's see what's happening. Beth, get on the horn."

"Translator, sir?"

"What's the point?"

But the radio was out of it. It had taken several hits and was useless. Beth shoved it away from her. A naked mannequin fell on top of her, and she yelped and kicked it into Jersey, almost scaring Jersey half to death until she realized what she was fighting.

Through the gloom, Ben watched the antics of the two and chuckled. "That reminds me of a joke."

"I think you told it to me about ten years ago," Jerre said. "It wasn't funny then."

"Did I ever tell you what the all-female flight crew renamed the cockpit?"

Jersey sat up. "What?"

Jerre groaned and shook her head. "You just had to ask."

Ben told her.

Before Jersey could come back at him, a large burst of gunfire tore through the already splintered windows, showering those inside with broken glass.

"Behind us!" Jerre yelled, lifting her M-16 and holding the trigger back. She knocked several black robes spinning. Ben's M-16 lay on the floor beside him. He lifted the old Thompson and let it chug and cough.

While .223's and .45's cleared the rear of the store, the others directed their fire toward the street and the alley facing it.

It was that time of day where sight can be tricky: that time between daylight and dark where there appears to be a dirty translucency preventing full vision from penetrating.

Ben looked at Buddy and cut his eyes to the rear of the store. "Finish them."

Buddy pulled a long-bladed knife from a sheath and slipped through the gloom, adding the finishing touches to some of the sourness of the Big Apple.

Jerre rolled to one side and tried her walkie-talkie. She handed the radio to Ben. "B Company, sir."

"How's it looking where you are, Brad?"

"Quiet at the moment, sir. They hit us hard there for several minutes, though."

"I do know the feeling. Any word from the others in this sector?"

"Ramos reported taking some casualties. Andersen is one hundred percent. Tony is still pinned down on Overlook."

"Have you heard from Tina?"

"Negative, sir. Sorry."

"OK. Hold what you've got. Eagle out."

"You want me to get a radio, Father?" Buddy asked, returning from the rear of the store, wiping the blood from his knife on his field trousers.

"No. Dan, you have any idea where the rest of your people might be, or the squad from Ike's group?"

"No, sir. They were waiting just across the street when you opened fire on the creepies. I suspect they're in that building right there." He pointed.

"Give them a bump on your radio, Jerre."

"Eagle One to Bodyguard."

"Bodyguard."

"What is your twenty, Bodyguard?"

"Half block south of your position, Eagle One, second floor. The Scouts are covering the rear of the building."

She relayed that to Ben. He nodded. "Tell them we're going up top. We ought to be able to reach Tina from up there."

"I'll take it," Buddy said, and headed for the stairs in the rear of the store.

"Dan, Cooper—go. Beth and Jersey—go. Jerre, follow them. I'll take the drag."

The ammunition they had left in the offices blew as the fire reached it, and that touched off more unfriendly fire from across the street, but it was all directed toward the blazing floor of the offices.

They encountered no unfriendlies on the way to the roof.

Up top, Ben whispered, "Buddy, see if you can find a way over to the next building—north."

His son grinned at him in the cold night air.

"I didn't think you wanted to return to your offices to warm up, Father."

"Move, boy!" But it was said with a smile.

He was back in a moment. "Easy hop over to the next building."

Ben gave him a jaundiced look. "What is an easy hop to you, son, bearing in mind that we're eight stories up and I never have bounced worth a damn?"

"Oh, about six feet."

"Find some boards," Ben told him.

"Yes, sir."

"Tina, sir," Jerre said.

"I'm getting tired of this 'sir' and 'general' crap, Jerre."

Jerre held out the radio. "Tina, sir."

Mumbling under his breath, Ben took the radio. "How's it looking, Tina?"

"We're trapped on the roof of the old bus terminal, Dad. But we're holding our own. It appears to have slacked up some."

"Same here. OK, baby—hang in. Eagle out." He looked around for Buddy. The young man had hopped over to the other building and was securing cable wire he had found. Cooper was standing by to lay a door across the wires.

"I suppose," Beth said dryly, "you are expecting us to crawl across that thing?"

"The fire is spreading to this building, Beth. Unless you have some marshmallows you'd like to toast, I suggest you make ready to vacate the rooftop."

"I thought it was getting warm."

"You thought right. Now move, before the creepies see us up here."

Cooper went across, followed by Beth, Jerre, and Jersey. Jersey was muttering prayers under her breath. Dan waved Ben forward. "After you, General."

"You're so considerate."

"Thank you."

Jus as Dan stepped onto the door, the alley filled with night crawlers.

Ben leaned over and held the trigger back on his Thompson, fighting to keep the powerful weapon from rising as he filled the alley with .45-caliber death. The heavy slugs bounced and whined and howled around the closely spaced buildings, the ricochets doubly dangerous because they had flattened out and were jagged, ripping and tearing great holes in the dirty flesh of the night crawlers.

Dan scampered across, and Buddy pulled the door over just as the roof of the burning office building collapsed and fire leaped out into the night, sending flames and sparks surging upward, licking at the dark and misty sky.

"One more rooftop, gang," Ben said. "Let's get clear of those flames."

The cracking and popping of dry wood igniting and the spit and hiss of flames filled the night as the small group of Rebels cleared another rooftop and suddenly came face-to-face with a band of uglies, charging upward out of the top floor of the building.

Ben smashed the stock of the Thompson into the snarling face of a creepy. Buddy grabbed the bloody-faced spook by his dark robe and spun him, hurling him over the side. His screaming was cut off abruptly as he splattered on the street below.

Dan stuck the muzzle of his M-16 into the belly of

an ugly and gave him a lasting case of indigestion. Cooper dropped to one knee and leveled his M-16, holding the trigger back, the slugs clearing his immediate perimeter.

Jerre and Beth and Jersey were directing their fire toward the open door leading to the rooftop. Black-robed bodies were rapidly piling up, blocking the entranceway.

Ben lobbed a grenade over the growing pile of bodies; all could hear it bounce down the stairs, the sound coupled with the yelling of those uglies still remaining on the stairs.

The mini-Claymore blew, crimson slashing the walls of the entrance.

Ben and Buddy, Dan and Cooper began tossing the bodies of the night crawlers off the roof, to the street below. They did not check to see if any were still alive. They were not the Red Cross.

The Night People began slipping back into their holes and tunnels, slithering deep under the city, to gather in stinking groups. Many had doubt in their eyes, although they did not vocalize that uncertainty. They did not have to. They had never before encountered such a ruthless adversary; they had relied on the time-proven fact that those who lived aboveground were by nature a compassionate, caring people, given to indecision and always showing tolerance and leniency toward the enemy.

Then along came Ben Raines and his Rebels and blew that theory right out of the water.

Nobody had explained to them that the philosophy of the Rebels was very simple, very basic: The Rebels went in to win. They had zero tolerance for lawlessness. They were clearing a land to once more make it a law-abiding, productive society, and they would roll right over anyone or anything that stood in their way.

Upper Manhattan fell silent, void of gunfire; the hostility had scurried like rats to their hovels below the city.

Ben looked over the lip of the roof. "It's over for this night. Let's go get some coffee."

Chapter 17

The previous night's reports came in, and they looked good to Ben. The Rebels had five dead, a dozen wounded, with only two of the wounded serious.

The holding action of the Rebels was confusing to the Night People. It seemed to the creepies that the Rebels were not trying to gain more ground, just hold on to what they had, and the uglies were taking terrible casualties fighting in this manner. They did not know how to bring defeat to Ben Raines and his Rebels.

The stench of the underground world had finally forced Ashley and Monte and their people to the surface. After their pounding in New Jersey, the outlaws had crossed over into Manhattan using a railroad tunnel. They were now bivouacked around the Central Park area.

"If I could find Raines," Monte said, "I'd make a deal with him."

Ashley looked at the warlord, disgust in his eyes. "I told you, Monte: you don't make deals with Ben

Raines. If he ever gets his hands on any of us, he'll either shoot us or hang us."

"Well, that's stupid!"

"You don't know how he ran the old Tri-States. Ben Raines's philosophy reads like this: if you don't have criminals, you won't have any crime; so he gives you one chance. If you blow that, hang it up, or he's going to hang you up. I went into the Tri-States as a tourist. One time. I can truthfully say it was the damndest experience I ever had. Everybody respected everybody else's rights, or the offending party got the hell out. Scared me half to death. The outside press couldn't deal with it either. Two or three of them got the crap kicked out of them until they learned that in the Tri-States, if you print something about somebody, you damn well better be able to prove that it's the truth, or somebody's going to come looking for you with a gun.

"Nobody locked their doors or took the keys out of the cars or trucks. One reporter got it in his head to climb over a fenced-in area; the gates were locked. Man stepped out of his house, walked up to the reporter, and hit him right in the mouth with the butt of a rifle. Knocked that reporter's teeth out."

Monte was astonished. He stuttered for a moment. "You can't do stuff like that! That's against the law. Criminals got rights, too, man!"

"I can't get through to you, Monte. Rebels don't think like other people. And Ben Raines is not going to make any deals with outlaws or warlords. For us, this city is do or die. That's the name of the game."

"Ben Raines has gotta go," Monte said. "Can't nobody live in a society like Ben Raines wants."

"A lot of people did, Monte. And made it work. The old system, back before the war, was breaking down . . ."

Monte grinned. "Damn sure was!"

". . . Ben Raines and his people set up a new system—a curious mixture of compassion and hardness. It was unique, had never before been attempted. And slowly but surely, he's setting it up again."

"Over my dead body!"

"Yes," Ashley said dryly. "That is his plan."

Ben had spoken with all his commanders. They all agreed that the holding plan was confusing the creepies; but to a person, they wondered for how long. And what would the creepies come up with to counter it? And when?

Then Ben said the words that chilled them all. "They'll probably force us to come into the subways and tunnels after them."

Rebet was the first to speak over the radio hookup that linked all commanders by translators. "That is not something I would look forward to doing."

"Nor do I," Ben admitted. "But if I were in their shoes, that's what I would do."

Ike looked out the window of his CP in lower Manhattan. "I think we're going to get some rest this evening, Ben."

"How do you figure, Ike?"

"The way it's snowing outside, those black-robed creeps would stand out like black candles on white icing."

"I have a suspicion they'll change into white robes, Ike. Don't put anything past these bastards."

The temperature stayed right at the thirty-degree mark, and the snow came down in thick wet flakes. Soon the entire city was blanketed in white, and the snow showed no signs of letting up anytime soon.

Ben gave the orders by translator: "Dig in and brace yourselves to get hit hard. I've got a hunch they're going to throw everything they've got at us tonight. Double your ammo on hand and lay in extra rations. Everybody draw a pocket stove and plenty of fuel tabs for hot coffee or tea. Layer your clothing and be sure you have extra socks. Hang tough, people."

Ben felt eyes on him and turned. Jerre was looking at him.

"Are we going to have another night like last night, Ben?"

"Worse."

"My God, Ben, how many of these . . . creatures are we fighting? It seems like we killed hundreds last night."

"Less than two hundred was the final tally. Our team racked up more points than any other. How many, Jerre? I don't know. A conservative guess would be thirty, forty thousand. It's probably double that."

"Or more."

"Or more."

She stepped forward and stuck out her hand. "Let's be friends, Ben. Bury the hatchet."

He took her hand. "We'll bury the hatchet, Jerre. But don't expect me to be your friend. The waters between us run too deep. Friendship is something I won't settle for."

She dropped her hand. "Perhaps that's all there is, Ben."

"Then so be it. How's your ankle?"

"Getting better. Why?"

"Because just as soon as Chase says you're ready for the line, I'm transferring you back to Tina's command."

Hurt came into her eyes. "I suppose I understand."

"Neither one of us can help the way we feel, Jerre. Call it a cruel trick of fate. That's as good as anything, I guess."

They stood gazing into each other's eyes for a moment. Jerre blinked first.

"Take your position downstairs, Jerre."

"Yes, sir—*Dad!*"

Ben's smile was very thin.

When she had left the room, her back very straight, Ben checked his M-14 and his Thompson. Cooper had carried the ammo boxes downstairs. Ben slipped into his field jacket and buckled his battle harness on. He reclipped his grenades and slung the M-14, hand-carrying his Thompson. He glanced out the window. About an hour's daylight left and the snow was coming down just as hard as when it began.

Ben had a very bad feeling about this approaching night.

He cut off the battery-powered lights and walked downstairs to what had once been a neighborhood grocery store. He looked out the open space where the window had once been, checking his perimeter for that night's upcoming fight. Clear.

Cooper lay behind an M-60, already in position. Ammo boxes were stacked beside him. Jersey lay beside him, all bundled up against the cold. Ben slipped on his face protector. The others already had theirs on.

"Eat now," Ben ordered. "Whether you're hungry or not. The cold will sap you before you know it. You might not get another chance to eat for hours."

He leaned his M-14 against the wall and sat down on a box, opening a packet of cold rations. Off to his left, a portable stove had been fired up, heating coffee. There was almost no wind, and that would help combat the cold. Ben guessed the temperature right at 30 degrees.

After eating, he put on a headset and listened to what radio chatter there was. Changing frequencies, he monitored the troops down south. Everyone appeared to be in place and ready.

Ben poured a cup of the chicory-laced coffee and leaned against the wall, keeping well back from the open front of the building. Dressed as they were, in dark battle dress, until his people opened fire, they were as difficult to detect as the night people would be—providing the creepies did dress in white to blend in with the snow—for Ben had ordered no lights and no smoking, and until the attack began, as little moving around and talking as possible, for movement will give away a position as quickly as conversation.

Just as dusk began to settle quietly over the city, Jersey softly whispered, "In the alley about ten o'clock. They're dressed in white, just like you said, General."

Cooper swung the M-60.

"Hold your fire," Ben whispered. "Let's see what they're up to."

"Creepies to our left, about three o'clock," Jerre whispered.

Ben cut his eyes. He could detect no movement, but he could see a hump in the gathering snow that had not been there before. He lifted his walkie-talkie. "Dan, put a rocket into that alley a couple of points to the right of our position. As soon as he fires, Jerre, put some rounds in that hump in the snow."

The whooshing sound of a rocket launcher being triggered was immediately followed by a wall of flame erupting from the alley. Several uglies were blown out of the alley and one staggered out, his white robe blazing.

Jerre put a three-round burst into the hump in the snow. The hump lifted upward, the snow staining red, then fell back to the street and did not move.

Another rocket was fired into the alley, the 81mm rocket finishing any night crawlers who might have survived the initial blast.

Ben had knelt down, presenting a low profile, but still able to see what was going on.

From the building across the street, a creepie returned the rocket fire, the rocket smacking into the floor just above Ben's position, momentarily blinding those on the ground level with dust and smoke.

But Cooper had already spotted the location of the ugly and began spraying the area with M-60 fire.

Ben cursed. They had just cleared that building hours earlier. The night crawlers had more hidey-holes than a field full of rabbits.

His eyes detected movement, and Ben hit the floor

just as automatic weapons fire sprayed their location from a window on the second floor across the street. Beth, Jersey, and Jerre all fired at the muzzle flashes. An AK fell to the snow-covered sidewalk.

"Clear that floor, Dan," Ben spoke into the cup of his walkie-talkie.

Big Thumpers and rocket launchers began pounding the second floor. Flames soon consumed the floor, licking up the dry walls and dancing out of the shattered windows. Creepies began running out of the ground level, to be chopped down by Rebel fire.

No more enemy fire came toward Ben's position. The burning building threw waves of heat at the cold Rebels across the street. "Something good came out of it," Ben muttered.

"Dan reporting no dead or wounded among his people," Beth said.

"Tell him we're OK here."

The old building went up quickly, the flames soon spreading to another building, but not moving across the alley to torch that structure.

Darkness touched the city as the snow kept up its steady fall.

Nothing that the Rebels could detect made itself visible on the city's streets during the long hours of early evening. Was the short attack all that was coming at them this night?

Ben doubted it; that nagging feeling he'd experienced about the night being a bad one was still with him.

"General," Beth broke into his thoughts. Ben cut his eyes to her. "The creepies are making the prisoners, naked men and women and children, march in front of them as they advance toward Ike and Cecil's positions."

"Here, too," Jerre's voice was tense.

Ben turned, then followed her pointing finger up the street. There was just enough light for him to make out the pale white bodies of the prisoners, shuffling and crying and shivering in the cold as they advanced toward Ben's position.

Ben lifted his walkie-talkie. "See them, Dan?"

"I see them, and I can see where they have prisoners all mixed up among their ranks."

"Buddy is calling in the same reports, General," Beth told him.

Thermopolis radioed in by walkie-talkie. Same thing was taking place in his sector. Emil's report came right on the heels of Thermopolis. Emil's report differed only in that the man used a great deal of profanity in tracing the ancestry of the night crawlers.

Ben was conscious of eyes searching his face; everyone in the store was looking at him.

"Put your eyes back on your perimeter, people," he ordered.

"They're getting close to all positions, General," Beth said. "Commanders need orders, sir—now!"

"Order everyone into gas masks. Everyone start lobbing in tear gas and smoke grenades. Now!"

The cold snowy air soon became filled with smoke and tear gas.

Ben laid down his Thompson. "Order them out, Beth. Pistols and knives for close combat. Go!"

Ben was out in the street before the echo of his words had faded.

Chapter 18

The charge of the Rebels, some armed with pistols and knives, others with pistols and camp axes, took the uglies by surprise. And that one or two seconds that they hesitated cost them dearly. For wars are not won by hesitation; the bones of hundreds of thousands who hesitated lie decaying in the ground, offering mute proof.

The Rebels, screaming like Odin's Vikings and Valkyries, hit the Night People in a rush. While some busied themselves herding the confused and shivering prisoners into the relative warmth of buildings, the other Rebels were bloodying their blades in the bellies and chests and heads of the nearly blinded creepies.

The Rebels chopped the Night People into the snow, now crimson and trampled and littered with the dead and the dying.

When Ben sensed that valor was overriding discretion, and that as many of the innocents as possible had been saved, he yelled for his people to fall back and pour in the lead.

Within seconds, the rattle of automatic weapons

fire shook the snow-covered and bloody streets of the city. Some innocents died. And Ben would have to live with that knowledge. But for every one who died, Ben and his Rebels pulled ten to safety.

Thermopolis had never killed a man close up, never looked into the dying eyes, fading as the soul winged away. It was not something he enjoyed. But he did begin to understand something that had always eluded him: there really was a high in combat. A rush unlike anything he had ever experienced.

And he also knew that he would never again be the same person. The siren's call of the maidens who waited for the slain warriors to walk through any of the 540 doors of the palace of Odin had reached his ears. And he knew that at least part of him would always be so, until the day of Ragnarok, when he would march into his final battle.

Probably beside Ben Raines, he thought. He didn't know whether to be irritated or pleased.

Emil had fought like an alley cat, leaping and slashing and yelling and spitting and talking in tongues. That in itself was enough to startle anyone.

And far below Ben's Rebels, West and Ike and Cecil and their troops were exacting a heavy toll on the creepies, and rescuing a large number of badly frightened and confused prisoners.

The Night People would make no more attacks during that snowy time of darkness. They had lost several thousand people, thanks to Ben Raines's unpredictability. The creepies who had managed to break free of the charge of the Rebels slipped under the city. No more for them, not this night.

Ben looked down into the still-savage face of a dead creep. He felt no compassion, no pity. Nothing but contempt for any human being who would allow himself to sink as low as the Night People.

"Compared to you," he muttered, "Khamsin's a pussycat." He turned away and found Beth. "Stand the people down to a low alert. Get me reports from all units and start a count of the rescued. I want each one of them questioned. Sooner or later we're going to have to go down into the bowels of this city. And we're going to need every scrap of information we can get."

A creepie came out of the snow, bloody but still alive. He had a knife in his dirty hand. A shot rang out; a hole was punched into the ugly's head. Ben turned. Jerre was standing a few feet from him, the muzzle of her M-16 still smoking.

"Thank you, Jerre."

"You're certainly welcome, Ben." She turned and walked into a bullet-pocked building, leaving Ben standing amid the bodies on the bloody snow.

"Always gets the last word," Ben muttered. "Never fails."

For the first time in several days, most of the Rebels got a good night's sleep, awakening to a very cold, sunny, and almost blindingly white dawn.

Ben ate a welcome hot meal and then went over to Chase's hospital, located in the old Jewish Memorial Hospital across from Fort Tryon Park on Broadway. His son met him there.

"That was a very daring move last night, Father. It took everybody by surprise."

"Have you spoken with Doctor Chase this morning?" Ben sidestepped the compliment.

"Yes. The newly freed prisoners are poor, pathetic creatures indeed. Most of this group are Canadians; been here about a year. Those who would respond to the questioning at all have confirmed that the empire of the Night People stretches around the world. That would confirm your theory as to why Khamsin left South America. But those here in the city are getting desperate. The move last night was an act of desperation. They're running out of food."

Chase walked out of the hospital. He had on so many layers of clothing he looked like a small bear. And could roar like one. "Raines!" he bellowed. "My arthritis is killing me. I am not going to stand out here in the cold like an iceberg and talk with you. So will you kindly bring your butt inside?" He pointed at Jerre. "And I want to take a look at that ankle of yours, too." He chuckled. "Nice ankle, I might add."

He walked back into the warmth of the hospital, Buddy and Ben and the others following. Cooper stayed with the Blazer.

"Old goat," Ben said, smiling. But he did not feel like smiling, not after receiving an urgent communiqué from Katzman just before leaving his CP. The message had numbed him for a moment.

While Jerre went with a medic to have her ankle looked at—she was no longer limping—Ben and Buddy went into Chase's office and poured coffee.

Chase took note of the expression on Ben's face.

"You look like a thundercloud, Ben. What's the matter with you—you coming down with something?"

"Later, Lamar. Bring me up to date on the prisoners."

"Physically, most of them will probably make it. Mentally, they're a disaster area. Some of them even worse than that first bunch Cecil found over in Brooklyn. Buddy's probably briefed you."

Ben nodded his head. "The creepies are really running out of . . . food?" He grimaced at the last.

"Oh, they've got enough prisoners to sustain them through the winter and possibly the spring. I've been able to piece that much together from talking with the doctors treating them. They're basket cases, Ben. We can probably bring the kids back . . . in time. Perhaps some of the adults. Maybe. But most of the adults? . . ." He shook his head.

Ben rose, refilled his coffee cup and paced the office. He looked at Chase. "What do you intend to do with them, Lamar?"

"I intend to treat them, Raines." His reply was very frosty.

"Hell, I know *that*, you old buzzard. Where do you plan on housing them? We don't have a safe zone anywhere in the city. This hospital could be overrun at any time."

"Then you're going to have to make this a safe zone, Ben."

"What am I, Lamar, a miracle worker?"

"Relax, Ben. Sit down. I don't mean to pressure you. Seeing these poor people's got me edgy, that's all. I think we're going to have to talk about the use of chemicals again, Ben. We're going to have to weigh the law of diminishing returns."

"And you think I haven't been doing that?"

Buddy sat quietly, saying nothing.

"Ben, I know you have. I understand that a lot of things have been weighing heavily on your mind. And now something else had been added. You're worried. Sometimes I can read you like a good book, old friend. So come on, spit it out."

With a sigh, Ben said, "Katzman's decoding people have been working for several days breaking down several coded messages received from South Carolina. It seems that Khamsin has worked out a deal with the Night People. Khamsin and his army will be in the New York City area in about ten days."

After the shock of that had settled in, Ben looked at Buddy. "There's more, son."

"I thought there might be. Let me guess. My mother has also joined forces to try and defeat the man she hates: Ben Raines."

"You got it, boy."

Chase drummed his fingers on the desktop. "A-hundred-to-one odds, Ben?"

"At least. Probably more than that. But," Ben held up a finger, "after last night, I think the creepies are going to stay in their holes and wait for reinforcements to get here. We gave them a drubbing last night. Several thousand dead. I would imagine these so-called Judges are in a state of shock. Buddy, tell Beth to bump Katzman through translators. I want a meeting of commanders, up here, right now."

* * *

They were all professional soldiers; they took the news without changing expression. To a person, their minds were already working on the problem. They had no other choice. They knew, of course, that they could bust out; it would be tough, but they could do it.

But that would not solve the problem. It would still be on their backs. And the horror would continue to grow until it consumed them all.

That must not be allowed to happen.

"Khamsin has long-range artillery?" Danjou asked.

"Oh, yes." Ben replied.

"But I don't think his plan is to destroy the city," Cecil said. "That would be counterproductive . . . in more ways than one."

West spoke. "I agree."

Thermopolis and Emil stood near the back of the room, saying nothing, listening to the exchange. Both were changed men since their arrival. Although it wouldn't take much for Emil to revert. Something he planned to do if this war ever ended.

"The city is going to get very crowded, very soon," Striganov said. "We might even have to light up Times Square." He smiled. "I'd like to see it once before I die."

"I don't know about lighting up the city," Ben said. "But we very well may have to empty every fuel storage tank in New England, flood the subway with gas, and then blow up the city!"

Ben had given the orders: "West, you'll take a convoy filled with weapons and ammo and grenades, four tanks to accompany you, and break through to

Central Park. Savie's people have got to be ready to fight for their lives. If you want to stay up there with them . . . that's up to you."

"It might be best if I did, General. We could at least get better field reports back to you with my men doing the scouting."

"Whatever you think, West. Take whatever supplies you'll need for a sustained operation."

The mercenary shook hands all the way around, paused in the door to salute Ben, and then left the room.

Ben looked at Striganov and smiled. The Russian picked up on it and grinned. "I'd love to join you, Ben! I hereby place myself and my battalion under your command."

"Give the orders, Beth. Get Georgi's battalion on the move."

The Russian general moved around the table to stand beside Ben.

"Rebet," Ben said, "your two battalions will link up with Cecil."

Rebet popped to attention. "Yes, sir!"

"Cecil, you'll take everything east of Broadway over to the river."

"Right, Ben."

"Major Danjou, link your battalion with Ike's people."

The Canadian likewise popped to attention. "Yes, sir!"

"Ike, you take everything west of Broadway to the waterfront."

"Gotcha, Ben."

"Thermopolis, Emil, you'll stay up here with General Striganov and me."

The hippie and the scam operator nodded their heads.

"Tina, I'm having Jerre reassigned back to your command. Effective immediately. Chase gave her a clean bill of health today."

"Yes, sir."

"Buddy." He looked at his son. "You and your company are now under Dan's command." He handed the muscular young man a thick sheaf of rolled-up paper. "Study these very carefully, son. These are the blueprints of the subway system. I want to know what's down there—and you'll find out for me."

"Yes, sir, Father."

"Now comes the hard part, gentlemen. I already know where West stands. I need to know your feelings on the matter." Ben walked to the coffee pot and poured a cup, then carefully hand-rolled a cigarette, licked it tight and lit up. He smiled grimly. "Surgeon General Koop would be unhappy with me, I know."

Ben sipped his strong coffee and let his eyes touch each person in the room before speaking. "I also know Doctor Chase's feelings on this. He said he was too busy healing people to stand around with a bunch of rank-happy gunslingers making war talk."

They all smiled at that. On more than one occasion, Chase had picked up a rifle and confronted whatever enemy the Rebels were facing at that particular moment . . . and held his own. Of course, he bitched the entire time; but everyone was used to that.

The men and women in the room waited, eyes on Ben.

"We have to weigh options, people. And we have to do it slowly and painfully. We've got, hell, ten maybe twelve thousand people coming at us from South Carolina. Maybe a thousand or more from the Ninth Order. We're already facing unbelievable odds as it is." He rubbed his eyes and sighed. "The more lucid of the rescued prisoners are firm on one point: that being, they would rather die than live the way they are forced to live. I am not going to make this decision alone, gang. I am not going to force any Rebel to kill innocents against their will. This is something that you all will have to take up with your people. I'll expect your answer within forty-eight hours."

"And during that forty-eight hours you want me to give you a preliminary on the subways and the tunnels," Buddy said, not posing it as a question.

"That's correct, son."

"Will we use chemicals, Dad?" Tina asked.

"God knows, Tina, I don't want to subject these poor wretches to any more misery than fate has already dealt them. This is a decision that every head of every army that was ever assembled under the flag of freedom has dreaded, but a decision that most had to make at one time or another. Yes, Tina, if it comes down to it, we'll use chemicals. We can't be defeated, people. That can't even be considered. We are the only thing in the North American continent standing against lawlessness, anarchy, and barbarism. We have to weigh options. We have no choice in the matter. We have to survive. This is not our last fight. I wish it was. But as it stands, we're going to have about ten days to defeat one enemy, and then turn right around, and face another.

"I want all of you to go to the hospital complex and take a good hard look at the rescued prisoners. If they'll talk to you, talk with them. And that is not a request, that is a direct order. Then go canvass your troops. We'll try tear gas first, to see if we can get deep enough to flush them with that. If that fails, then we'll use . . . poisonous gas."

Everyone in the room grimaced at that, and at the thought of the hard decisions they had to make.

"Forty-eight hours, people. That's it. Get cracking."

Chapter 19

Dan handpicked Buddy's team, and the tunnel rats spent the rest of that day poring over the plans of the subway system.

Buddy had already made up his mind about the use of chemicals.

The Rebels shifted their personnel and locations, stretching out, reforming, resupplying, and resting during this lull in the fighting.

And talking about the options.

It had turned bitterly cold in the Big Apple; most of the snow remained on the streets. The bodies of the dead creepies had been removed and taken to the barges. They lay in grotesque frozen death, awaiting transport to a watery grave.

Jerre had packed up her gear and was awaiting transport to Tina's position. Ben had been deliberately avoiding his CP that day, not wanting any type of goodbyes.

He was across the street from his CP, standing alone, his usual entourage a respectful distance away, when the Jeep pulled up to take Jerre to her new unit.

Their eyes met over the trampled snow of the street. Neither one made any effort to speak or wave. Jerre tossed her gear into the Jeep and got in. A few seconds later, she was out of sight.

Buddy and Dan watched from the other side of the street. "Both of them caught up in the grips of the first deadly sin," Dan observed.

Buddy put a name to it. "Pride. And one of them very much in love."

Dan smiled. "Ever been in love, Buddy?"

"Ah . . . no. Infatuated, yes. But love, no."

"It will be interesting to watch when you are smitten, young man. For you and your father are very much alike."

Neither of them heard Ben mutter, long after the Jeep carrying Jerre had rounded the corner, "Here's lookin' at you, kid. Take care."

Ben walked across the street to join his son and Dan. "How are you and the blueprints coming along, son?"

"Just fine. I'm looking forward to going underground, Father."

Ben glanced at him. The young man really meant it. He looked at Dan. "His team all picked, Dan?"

"Yes, sir. They're drawing equipment now. They'll be going in this afternoon."

Ben stuck out his hand, and Buddy took it. "Luck to you, boy."

"Thank you, Father."

"Try to link up with those friendlies living down there if you can. Doing that might help keep you and your team alive."

"I plan to, Father."

Ben looked at his son for a long moment, nodded,

and then walked off, toward the CP. Beth and Jersey and Cooper and Ben's bodyguards followed.

"You're taking chemicals with you?" Dan asked.

"We are," Buddy confirmed it. "Tear gas and smoke only. This time," he added.

"Verify the outside grates up here that lead to the subways have not been blocked off. We don't want the gas blowing right back at us."

"Yes, sir."

"I'll see you at the jump-off point, then."

"Right, sir."

Colonel West and his mercenaries had traveled to the survivors' location around Central Park without encountering a single creepie.

Gene Savie met the men in Columbus Circle. Gene and his people could not hide their joyful smiles at seeing West and his mercs.

"My God!" Gene said. "I cannot put into words how good it is to see you people."

"General Raines briefed you?"

"Yes. How many of these terrorists are coming?"

"Khamsin's people? Probably a full division. Perhaps a thousand of those nuts that make up the Ninth Order. Do you know the story behind this Sister Voleta?"

"Colonel, we've been cut off up here for years. We really don't know what's been happening, for sure, outside the city."

"Back when the world was whole, more or less, Ben Raines had a very brief affair—a one-night stand— with a woman in Tennessee. That brief encounter produced a son. Buddy. Buddy is as fine a young man as I have ever seen. His mother, unfortunately, is a nut. She hates General Raines. Her name is Sister Voleta."

"Good God! Does the son know his mother is coming up here?"

"Oh, yes. Come on, let's get these supplies off-loaded. We've got to set up defensive positions and make ready for the night. They haven't been attacking the last couple of nights. But I have a gut hunch all that is about to change."

Back at his CP, Ben was going over the final preparations for all-out war. "Beth, have Katzman get in touch with all our outposts in the way of Khamsin's march. Tell them to observe the route and keep us posted. But do not—repeat: *do not*—attempt to engage the enemy. No roadblocks, no bridges blown, nothing. It would be like a gnat attacking an elephant and all it would accomplish is getting a lot of our people dead."

He waited until his orders had been relayed to communications central.

"Get me all commanders, including West and Savie on scramble, Beth." Radio link established, Ben took the mike. "West is in position; he encountered no resistance on his way up. He says he believes Savie's people are ready to finish it—one way or the other.

"I have tunnel rats about to enter the burrows. If they have to—if all else fails—they're carrying enough C-4 to start doing a lot of damage. Khamsin is approximately eight days away and pushing hard. I want reloading sites to start working around the clock. Pull in all tanks, APC's, and mortar carriers and go over them; if any part is showing the slightest bit of wear, replace it. From here on in, we'll be fighting from the defensive—I don't have to tell any of you what that means. Have you canvassed your people on the use of chemicals?"

They had, and gave Ben their answer.

"Ike, you still have those flamethrowers you found at that old military depot?"

"Ten-four, Ben."

"Get them out and juice them up. I want every company to have a couple of them and lots of fuel."

"I'll get right on it."

"There isn't much else to say, people. So I'll just say good luck to you."

Buddy and his team of tunnel rats entered half a dozen subway stations and five hundred feet into each one, and found the same thing at all of them: the creepies had constructed steel-reinforced barricades, track to ceiling, side to side, with steel doors that would take a lot of explosives to even dent them.

They saw no uglies during any of the forays into the dankness of the underground world, nor could they make contact with any of the friendly people who inhabited the subterranean world.

When Buddy reported back to his father, Ben leaned back in his chair and thought about the news. "Did you feel they were watching you, son?"

"Yes, sir. I think to fight any type of war in those subways would be a sure death trap for us all."

"You're probably right. Suggestions?"

"Or opinions?"

"Certainly."

"There is no way for us to rescue the prisoners being held underground. No . . . humane way to bring them out of there alive."

"That narrows the options, doesn't it, son?"

"Yes, sir."

"Thank you, Buddy. Get some rest."

The young man left the office. Ben turned in his chair and looked at the city, cloaked in winter. Harry Truman's words returned: The Buck Stops Here.

He almost called for Beth, almost gave the orders that he did not want to give.

Jersey stuck her head into the room. "General Ike's people just got here with the flamethrowers, sir."

"Thank you, Jersey. Tell Colonel Gray to take care of the unloading and the distribution, please."

"Yes, sir." She looked at him. "You feel all right, sir?"

"I'm all right, Jersey. Just have some hard decisions to make, that's all."

"You can't use tear gas, sir."

"Oh?" Ben leaned back in his chair and smiled. "And why is that, Jersey?"

"Because it's got to be done quickly, sir. And I wouldn't use mustard, either."

"What would you use and why, Jersey?" He pointed to a chair. "Come in and sit down. The flamethrowers can wait. Tell me what's on your mind."

"Me and a bunch of the others been talking, sir." She took a chair in front of Ben's desk: an old door placed on concrete blocks. "We can't go in and get them out; you said so yourself. And the creepies are going to eat those people if we don't end this war right now. If I knew I was gonna be strung up on a meat hook and eaten, I'd be praying for someone to kill me."

"There are kids down there, Jersey," Ben reminded her. He cut his eyes as Dan stepped into the doorway, to stand listening.

"I don't think so, General. I don't. I think becoming a creepy is a learned thing. I don't think there are any kids down under the city. Either creepy kids or prisoners. Not anymore. I think they would like for us to believe that. But I think they've been moved out of Manhattan. But even if they haven't, General . . . I been doing some reading from some books we've found. Didn't kids die when the atomic bomb was dropped in Japan? Didn't kids die during all the bombings of the Second World War? Haven't kids died in all wars? I love kids, General. I love kids and puppy dogs and little kittens; but I also love freedom, and freedom don't come cheap."

Dan stood in the door, smiling.

"You see, General," Jersey kept it going, "the way I see it, we got maybe a couple of million kids out there." She jerked her thumb toward the west. "A couple of hundred kids down there—maybe. And it's a big maybe. I've said my piece, for what it's worth." She stood up. "I'll go see about them flamethrowers."

Dan stepped in after Jersey had left. "I thought you might like to know this, General: Katzman, unknown to us, had his people plant bugs all over the areas controlled by us. Super Snoopers, he called them. He also directed shotgun mikes into the subways. He's picked up a lot of useless chatter over the past three days. But not one child's whimper. Not one baby's cry. Sir, do you want me to give the orders to use the gas?"

"No. No, Dan, I don't. Because I'm not going to pump the subways full of Mustard or Sarin or Soman or cyanide or Mycotoxin or any V-series. I can't do it. About ten minutes ago, I thought I could. I almost gave the orders. I don't know what I'm going to do, how I'm going to handle it. But it won't be with germ warfare or poisonous gas. Maybe tear gas. I'll make up my mind about it by morning."

Dan sighed. "Tell you the truth, General, I'm glad to hear that."

Ben stood up. "Let's go have a look at those old flamethrowers."

As they walked out of the building, Dan said, "I did something last night I have not done in many a year, General."

"Oh?"

"I got down on my knees and prayed for some heavenly guidance about this poisonous gas business."

Ben looked at him and smiled very faintly. "Well, Dan, I guess He heard one of us."

Chapter 20

No attack came. The Night People apparently were content to let the Rebels have free rein in the city while waiting for the arrival of Khamsin and the Ninth Order.

The Rebels made the most of their strangely un-restricted time in the city. They spread out all over New York City, setting up mini-bastions of defense, finding hidey-holes that led from one building to the other, caching supplies and ammo, working fast, preparing for the defensive fight they all knew they would be forced to wage. The reloading of empty brass went on around the clock.

The Rebels had captured several thousand of the enemy's weapons—mostly AK's—and thanks to Rebel ingenuity, they were turned into twin-mount machine guns: a little hard to handle but capable of spitting out a lot of lead.

And Ben finally met John Savie, the man who was afraid Ben was going to kill him.

Ben stood, looking at the small, frail, white-haired

man, fear very evident in his eyes. Ben held out his hand and the man shrank back in fear.

"Mister Savie, you have nothing to fear from me. I've never met you; don't know you. I don't understand your fear."

John Savie did not answer. He seemed too frightened to speak. Ben looked around the apartment and knew where all the priceless paintings and other works of art had gone. The apartment, and the apartments of all the survivors, were filled with hundreds of paintings from the masters, busts and vases and rare books.

Kay Savie, Gene's wife, brought them coffee, and Ben sat down on a leather couch. Kay sat down and said, "John was a book reviewer, General Raines."

Ben blinked. If that statement was meant to explain it all, it went right past him. "Is that supposed to mean something to me?"

No one replied.

Ben sipped his coffee, really very good coffee, then started smiling. He placed the delicate china cup into the saucer and started laughing. "Did you review one of my books, John?"

"Yes," the old man said, his voice no more than a whisper.

"And you didn't like it?"

"No. I wrote that it was too violent. That it glorified war. That people would be putting their money to better use by giving it to a street person."

Ben shrugged. "John, I never read reviews. I told my agent not to send them to me. Because I am, was, of the belief that anyone who would read or not read a book, or see a play or a movie, based solely n the opinion of one person probably isn't too bright to start with. There is an old saying about the guilty fleeing before they are pursued. Well, you can stop fleeing. I never heard of you, Mister Savie." Ben leaned over and patted the old man on the shoulder. "And that probably hurts you even more than if I'd hit you."

Ben leaned back and rolled a cigarette. He really didn't want one, but had noticed there were no ashtrays in the room.

"We don't smoke in this apartment," John said primly.

Ben fired up and puffed. He finished his coffee and then dropped the butt into the cup. He stood up and looked at the survivors. Kay was looking at the coffee cup as if Ben had stuck a big cow turd into it. "Nice meeting you folks. I think."

He walked out of the apartment and down to the street. West was leaning against his Blazer, a smile on his lips.

"Nice folks, aren't they, Ben?"

"Oh, just delightful. I get the impression they're glad to see us but will be much happier when we've fought their battles for them and get gone."

"Isn't that the way it always is for soldiers?"

"So true, friend. So true."

Special teams of Rebels worked long hours in the subways. Ben knew the night crawlers probably had thousands of holes they could pop in and out of, but he was going to make damn sure that 465 of those holes were closed.

His Rebels welded the steel doors closed, putting a bead around them that would take a bulldoze to break loose.

The Rebels studied maps of the city, committing as much of the city's streets to memory as possible. Doing so might save their lives, and they knew it.

West sent a patrol over to the Columbia University complex and upon their return radioed an urgent request for Ben to come down.

West met him on the north side of the complex. "Empty, Ben. They've deserted it. Pulled out. But good God, that place stinks like nothing I have ever smelled in my life. I think we are alone aboveground."

Ben stamped his boot on the street. "I'm not even sure they're down there at this moment."

"I wondered why you were holding back with the tear gas."

"No point in wasting it. Is this place clear?"

"Some of it. I wouldn't advise going in there."

"Don't worry. I can smell it from here."

Beth touched his arm. "General? Katzman reports that Khamsin is about twenty-four hours away from the city."

"Thank you, Beth. Order all personnel into position." He looked at West. "We've done all that we can do to make ready."

"Yes," the mercenary replied. "Now it's all up to God and guns."

On the last day of their lull in battle, Ben toured the island of Manhattan, touching as many battle stations as possible.

"Ike." He shook the man's hand. "You all set to rock and roll?"

Ike grinned at him. "This old fat man's ready to boogie-woogie, Ben."

Ben laughed and slapped him on the back, moving on Danjou's perimeter.

"*Bonne chance, mon général!*" The French Canadian said, shaking Ben's hand.

Ben drove over to Cecil's area and had a cup of coffee with his old friend.

"It's eerie, Ben. I get the feeling that we're alone in this city."

"I know. But Katzman's mikes are picking up a lot of scurrying sounds belowground. Scraping of metal against concrete and so forth. Unless the rats are building a city down there, the creepies are back."

"When do we start pumping the gas in, Ben? Everything is in position and ready."

"At dawn tomorrow we start flushing them. That will put Khamsin just outside the city but not yet in place to strike us. The creepies know we've been gearing up for a defensive action. I've been deliberately letting a few noncoded radio messages through saying we have decided against the use of chemicals. Hopefully, the uglies have taken the bait."

Cecil smiled and stuck out his hand. Ben shook it. There was nothing left to say.

Ben met with Rebet. "The gas is ready to go, General."

"Dawn tomorrow, Stefan."

The Russian looked startled, then he smiled. "You deliberately let us all think it was noon today." He chuckled.

"You ought to know by now I'm not to be trusted

The men shared a laugh and Ben moved on.

Ben drove up the east side and met with Tina.

"You think this is the war to end all wars, Dad?

"Well, history states that was said back in 1917 ar again in 1941. So I doubt it, girl. Get some rest ar roll your people out, very quietly, at oh-four-hundre tomorrow. That's when we start pumping the gas in

She kissed his cheek. "Luck to you, Pop." The she smiled strangely.

"Hang in, baby."

He drove up to his own sector, meeting wit Buddy, Dan, Striganov, and Thermopolis and Em

He explained his plans and Georgi chuckled. had a hunch you were dropping false clues, Be Think the creepies took the hook?"

"It looks that way. All we can do is hope."

He shook hands all the way around and the went over to Chase's field hospital.

The first person he saw reminded him of som body. She turned around.

"What the hell are you doing here, Jerre?"

She held up her left hand. There was a tiny ban age on her little finger. "I cut my hand. Tin reassigned me back to Chase." She smiled ver sweetly at him and batted her blues.

Ben shook his head and walked out of the ho pital. "I'm cursed. That has to be it."

Jerre followed him. "Aren't you glad to see m Ben?"

"Yes, Jerre. I'm glad to see you."

"I knew you would be. Perhaps Chase will assig

ne to working in your office during my time of
great discomfort?"

"I can hardy wait."

He walked to his Blazer. "Move over, Cooper. I'm
driving."

"Oh, God!" Beth said.

"You give up that wheel, Cooper," Jersey warned,
"and I'll shoot you!"

"Well, hell!" Ben said, but he was smiling. "I'll walk!"

It was only two short blocks to his CP. As he walked,
he looked toward the east. Khamsin was very near. The
creepies were under his boots. "Come on, you sons of
bitches. Tomorrow is going to be a good day to die!"